# CHINESE CHECKMATE

## A TALE OF BOATS, GIRLS, OLD FRIENDS AND POWERFUL INTERNATIONAL ENEMIES.

### BOOK 8 IN THE FIREBIRD SERIES

## IAN DOLBY

# DISCLAIMER:

This is a work of fiction. While names, characters, businesses, events and incidents are the products of the author's warped imagination, places and locales are as correct as possible, but are used in an entirely fictitious manner. Some characters are a composite of several personalities the author has encountered in his travels across Australia as such richness of true-life character could not be ignored. However, any resemblance to actual persons, living or dead, or actual events is unintended, accidental and purely coincidental.

The opinions expressed by the various characters in this story are deemed appropriate for their role and should not be assumed to be those of the author. I ride bikes and embrace the right to freedom of the open road on two wheels for everybody.

Published in Australia by Silverbird Publishing

First published in Australia 2025

This edition published 2025

Copyright © Ian Dolby 2025

Cover design, typesetting: WorkingType (www.workingtype.com.au)

The right of Ian Dolby to be identified as the Author of the Work has been asserted in accordance with the Copyright, Designs and Patents Act 1988.



Dolby, Ian

*Chinese Checkmate — Book 8 of the Firebird Series*

ISBN: 9781763676602

pp388

# CONTENTS

# PROLOGUE... BEIJING

Within an unmarked building located in the forbidding Ministry of National Defence compound in western Beijing, the seven most powerful men in China sat around a beautifully carved and inlaid wood table in a luxurious conference room. Naturally enough, red was by far the predominant colour of the wall drapes and other luxurious furnishings. Two of the men looked relaxed, secure in their positions of power, while the other five glowered at each other across the table, planning how best to undermine the credibility of one of the others, to hopefully make their own positions more secure. Together, they comprised the Central Military Commission, the body in charge of all military matters, which in turn controlled the various arms of the services. As with most of the upper level Chinese governing bodies, the Commission Chairman was the all-powerful and self-declared, permanent President of China. He was also the General Secretary of the Chinese Communist Party.

Although this meeting was routine, the junior member, whose portfolio included overseeing foreign expansion and base acquisition, had indicated that he had an important subject to present to the meeting. Graciously, the President allowed him to speak first, although he was barely into his presentation when he was forcefully interrupted by an older man opposite.

'Copper? What ridiculous nonsense is this! Why would we want to spend billions of yuan to re-open someone else's copper mine which has become overgrown by the jungle after decades of disuse following a civil war? We are already the third largest producer of copper in the world!'

The junior member fumed internally at the insult, but submissively bowed his head slightly to his elder, in acknowledgement of the truth of the statement.

'True words, my wise comrade. However, allow me to explain the reasoning behind my seemingly pointless plan.'

Without waiting for any response, he hurried on. 'The world is aware that in regard to the Panguna mine, it was the combined greed of the Papua New Guinea government and the Australian-owned mining company Bougainville Copper, which alienated the area's population in the first place. This greed meant that nearly 80% of the profits from this most prolific mine were taken by the arrogant Australians and nearly 20% went to the corrupt, financially-incompetent PNG government. Notably, neither Bougainville Copper nor the PNG government, contributed anything to improve the standard of living on the island. This left less than 2% of the profits to be returned to the Bougainville people and the tribal land-owners.

To make matters worse, the miners made no attempt to control or clean up the massive amounts of pollution which the mining operations created, and that became another major cause of discontent to both the local landowners and all villagers downstream.

In time, these injustices caused the angry land-owners to form a rebel group which seized control of the mine, such action in turn leading to a civil war which ultimately caused the death of 15,000 people and caused mine production to cease. The long-term effects of these events were to plunge the country into even greater poverty than it was before.

The provincial capital, Arawa, formerly a thriving town, was almost destroyed in the war. Since then, the locals have been forced to revert to subsistence-level farming. I hasten to add that the situation within the entire country has only slightly improved to this day.'

Before he could draw a breath, he was challenged again by the older man across the table, who growled, 'We know all this – as we also know that since 1989, many recovery plans have been proposed, but agreement has never been able to be reached by the various parties concerned. We also know that despite the passing of thirty-two years since the mine ceased producing, the rebels still guard the mine and only allow selected journalists to visit under strictly controlled conditions. They are very suspicious of all outsiders. Therefore, I do not understand why you persist in reiterating this ancient, irrelevant information.'

While continuing to fume beneath his smiling mask, the younger man nodded agreement. 'Concisely put, comrade, but my proposal to have China offer to intercede in a cold civil war and re-open a copper mine is only the start of my plan.'

While internally shaking under the intense scrutiny from across the table, he took the lack of retort from neither his adversary nor the President as encouragement to proceed, adopting a different approach with his presentation.

'Allow me to pose the following questions for your consideration. What if we were to be the ones who presented a plan to successfully resolve the civil strife impasse, as well as enabling the mine to be re-opened? This plan would offer to fund the clean-up of the mine site and restoration of the polluted rivers, supply all the hardware and supplies necessary to recommence mining and ore production, supply skilled managers and technicians, and by necessity, to greatly expand the Kieta Harbour facilities to cope with the huge increase in shipping activity.

This offer would give our nation a great amount of bargaining power with what has become the Autonomous Region of Bougainville, as well as with the local land-owners. Most importantly for us, the Bougainvillians could hardly refuse our offer to greatly improve the harbour facilities. They are a quasi-independent state after all, although still loosely attached in a very untidy fashion to Papua New Guinea. Fortunately, the meddling and greedy Australians are no longer involved. Additionally, if we were to guarantee a generous return of profits to the landowners as well as a substantial return to the impoverished Bougainville government, we can state with conviction that the plan would settle the dispute, stabilise the region and generate the income which the landowners and country desperately need.'

He paused in his narrative to sip water to ease his dry throat, slightly unnerved by the silence in the room, but pleased that no further challenges were fired at him... yet.

'In return for our efforts to broker the deal with the rebel land-owners, plus the offer of all the necessary money and resources to re-activate the mine, we would be in an excellent position to provide the necessary protection of the port facilities. We would point out that to achieve this level of protection, we would need to have unlimited access for our military ships to the re-developed Kieta Harbour, one of the finest deep-water ports in the entire South Pacific region. With this port under our total control, the ships of our Peoples Liberation Army Navy would have access to a port which has immense strategic significance. It is right beside the Solomon Islands, relatively close to many other South Sea Island nations, including Papua-New Guinea, Australia and the annoyingly-strategic American base of Guam.'

First there was a deep silence, followed by a round of intelligent questioning, before the Chairman rapped on the table and declared, 'That is enough for now! After listening to your comments and questions, I have decided the idea shows considerable merit and would like our Comrade to develop a more detailed proposal, including a projected income and expenditure report, for presentation at our meeting next week.'

It was some time before the junior member was able to gather his files with shaking hands and rise from the table.

Sweating heavily, and with a racing pulse, I surfaced from the depths of a thankfully rare, but terrifying dream in which I was trapped underwater, my foot held painfully in the wicked, curved-fanged grasp of a huge moray eel who was slowly, but relentlessly pulling me closer to its rocky den. (Why do I always get trapped underwater in these rotten dreams? It's either a bloody moray eel with a body as thick as my leg, or a giant clam!)

When the sleeping underwater nightmare was thankfully replaced by a less-dramatic, above-water, but sweaty wakefulness, I found the moray eel had morphed into my big cat, Jasper, who was tugging gently on my exposed foot with his own sharp teeth, one of his favourite ways to wake me when danger of some sort threatens. Being a cross-bred version of an Indonesian jungle cat, he had always been big, but over the last eighteen months, a delayed growth-spurt, had expanded his 25-kilo mass into more like 35 kilos of mostly muscle.

'Okay, okay, fur-ball. Stop already, I'm awake.' I muttered softly, sliding gently out of bed and groping for my shorts.

Sandy, the beautiful love of my life, mumbled something incoherent, rolled over and went back to sleep.

Led by my impatient black guard-cat, I padded quietly up the steps to the saloon, where I kept below the window-line until I worked out what had stirred my overgrown pussy into protective action. As if fully aware of my uncertainty, he gave a soft growl which I've learned meant there was human danger, rather than something else endangering the boat.

The sliding doors to the cockpit were partway open for ventilation, with just a mozzie screen across the opening, and this allowed me to hear soft murmurs from the right-hand stern area, followed by a gentle bump as might be produced by a dinghy nosing against the padded edge of the boarding platform.

I'd anchored my 83-foot catamaran, *Firebird*, in the shallow Myora inlet in Moreton Bay, a short distance north from the township of Dunwich on North Stradbroke Island. Aboard were two cats, big Jasper and little Krazy, my lovely lady Sandy, a Queensland Police Inspector, and our two very dear friends and permanent crew, Alex a giant South-African ex-mercenary, and Bree, a petite lady who was the light of his life. Bree also looked after all the business and financial aspects of running the boat, as well as cooking for us to the standard of a Michelin-starred chef.

Our presence at Myora was simply because we just felt like a weekend away from our usual mooring at the Southport Yacht Club, and was something we frequently did. As Sandy was the only one who actually had a real job, the timing of these trips was governed by her work schedule, although being an Inspector and having an indulgent boss, gave her a lot of latitude. The Myora anchorage was one of my preferred spots as it was rarely crowded, had clean, clear water and offered good fishing in the deeper Rouse Channel close by. In this case there were just two smaller power-boats anchored a short distance away, with only a single, white anchor light showing from each.

The general isolation of the anchorage probably accounted for the un-welcome presence of two dark shapes creeping slowly up the stern steps toward the closed safety-railing gate. A surge of adrenaline pumped up my heart-rate and respiration, as the faint loom of light from the distant township silhouetted our uninvited guests. My hope that they were just your basic, opportunistic burglars trying to nick the outboard off our dinghy, was dashed when I saw the glint of what appeared to be a large knife in the hand of the much larger lead figure.

'Bugger!' I muttered under my breath, 'why can't these clowns respect people's privacy?' I then reached down to the switch panel set into the rear bulkhead beside the sliding door, flipped up a switch guard, and moved the protected three-way switch to the centre position. Moments later, as the first tall, shadowy figure reached to open the safety-rail gate, there was a brief, but brilliant blue flash accompanied by a loud, crackling sound. That was followed by a brief cry of pain and fright and the drumming sound of bare feet, as the figure appeared to be dancing an Irish jig, while holding onto the not-so-safe safety rail for support. After a few moments of happy dancing, there was another, smaller blue flash as the figure tore free of the rail and promptly collapsed in an untidy heap on the deck. I flicked the switch off, and patted Jasper on the rump.

'Go, boy. Hold, but don't kill!'

There was a blur of vengeful darkness as 35 kilos of black-furred muscle brushed the mozzie-screen aside, shot across the cockpit, floated effortlessly over the gate, then with unerring aim, fell upon the second, smaller figure who was frozen with indecision just one step down from the top. Several loud thumps resulted as the figure, with Jasper firmly attached, disappeared from sight, followed by a groan which was overlaid by Jasper's savage snarl, suggesting the second intruder could be considered safely under control.

I turned on the dim blue cockpit courtesy lights mounted at foot level, which revealed the smelly pile of dark clothing on the other side of the now-safe, safety-rail gate, encased the inert form of a large man in less-than-optimal condition. The electrified rail system I'd installed had two settings, the lower of which was usually enough to merely stun an unwary intruder. The other switch position guaranteed there would never be any repeat offences, but on occasion, this created disposal problems.

After kicking the smelly big lump in the ribs to check for genuine unconsciousness, I stepped over him, collecting his large, razor-sharp knife on the way, before stepping down to the swim platform, where I found Jasper astride a smaller person, his jaws clamped lightly around its throat. In between Jasper's muffled snarls, a series of terrified whimpers rose from the figure, as I took a quick look around, and spotted another large knife half-hidden under the black-clad leg of the other intruder.

'Release him please boy, but stay close.'

I was careful not to relax as Jasper immediately released his grip and stood back, but replaced the snarls with a deep rumbling growl which was no less menacing.

I kicked the person in the side, not trying to be gentle despite my bare feet.

'Okay, sunshine, on your feet. But don't even think about bailing out by going swimming. Jasper loves the water.'

With a knife in each hand, I retreated slowly back up the steps, rolled the unconscious intruder aside with one foot, and edged through the gate. I kept a very close eye on the slight figure now shuffling nervously past Jasper who remained in a threatening, rumbling half-crouch.

'That's the way,' I encouraged cheerfully, 'keep moving... no, no, don't worry about checking your mate, he'll be out of action for a while. Step forward so I can get a decent look at you. Behave yourself, and there's a slight chance you might even survive the night.'

By now there'd been enough noise to wake Alex and Bree who had the other stern cabin, and they were joined by Sandy, who'd also wandered out to see what the fuss was about. With a brighter cockpit light on, we saw that our walking intruder was actually a girl, somewhere in her twenties and decidedly unattractive with a mass of dirty, tangled hair half-concealing her grubby face. Small trickles of blood down each side of her neck, and a pungent aroma from the spreading patch of wetness around her crotch, were the only signs of Jasper's attention.

While I contemplated this miserable specimen of humanity, Alex straightened out her mate and checked for more weapons, but the knife was all he had. They were both dressed in dark clothing, with bare feet.

'Harry. You'd better look at this,' Alex called from the boarding platform where he'd gone to inspect their transport. It was a rather battered, outboard-powered open fibreglass boat, about 6-metres long, and contained an interesting collection of two small outboard motors, fuel tanks, oars, small anchors, fire extinguishers and a pile of other items including plastic rubbish bags full of clothing, purses and wallets.

'Looks like they were trying to score some five-fingered discounts,' the huge man growled in his deep voice, 'I hope they haven't hurt those other boaties.'

'We'd better go check,' I said, 'just in case they did.'

Leaving Sandy, Bree and Jasper to guard the terrified captive, Alex and I took the robber's boat and headed for the nearest of the two power boats, neither of which showed any signs of life.

Swinging up to the stern, we called out and banged on side of the hull until, to my great relief, there were some muffled thumps from inside, but still no one appeared. We climbed aboard and found the occupants, a middle-aged man and woman, laying in their bunks, securely tied up with gaffer tape and gagged. Bruises and a cut lip on the man were the only injuries, so after releasing them and promising to return, we left them to recover while we headed for the remaining boat.

There we found a similar scene, this time with two adults and two teen-aged girls tied up and gagged the same way. They told the same story of being woken at knife-point, restrained, then their boat ransacked. After telling both families to stay calm as we already had the intruders captured and police organised, we returned to *Firebird*. There, we found the male intruder was showing increased signs of life, although in my experience, he wouldn't be walking, talking or thinking too well for a while. Thankfully, Bree had made welcome mugs of tea and coffee. Our female captive wasn't offered a drink, but instead was bound hand and foot and tethered to a cockpit cleat with her newest best enemy, Jasper, keeping close company.

After Alex and I brought the others up to date, Sandy asked the big question, 'Okay big dog. What do we do with them? Bearing in mind that this time, other people are already involved.'

She raised her eyebrows in a pointed gesture which I couldn't ignore, so I sighed resignedly, 'Yeah, yeah, I know. I guess we can't just shoot them and push the bodies over the side for the sharks to dispose of?'

Sandy shook her head, and smiled indulgently. 'No dear. No way. Not this time. That'd be a really bad idea.'

Another wave of pungent urine smell from the female captive suggested that she also agreed it was a bad idea.

Alex spoke up, 'I know this might be a really radical thought, Harry, but how about we call the local coppers and turn the whole thing over to them. Sandy can even do the official arresting bit, and we can let the people in the other two boats press charges.'

I grinned at Alex's sarcasm, something he'd been getting really good at lately. Must have been talking to Sandy too much.

'Gee, Alex. That really is a radical suggestion, but under the circumstances, I guess we'd better handle it that way.'

Smiles broke out all around, except for the miserable bound and gagged figure in the corner of the cockpit.

Therefore, Sandy dragged out her badge, formally identified herself and made her arresting statement to make the arrest official. Then as part of my unwinding process, I had enormous fun waking the Dunwich senior constable from a deep sleep. When he suggested that the situation could be better investigated during office hours, I passed the phone over and let Sandy pull rank and give him an earful at the same time.

When he finally turned up in his official half-cabin runabout, we were able to hand over the two intruders, their weapons, the boat load of stolen items, then left him to spend the rest of the night taking statements from the two crews who'd suffered being tied up and robbed. With all the evidence of their crimes either in the robber's boat or on the other two boats, there wasn't much investigating for anyone to do, but we were still tied up with interviews with detectives from the mainland for most of the next day.

It turned out the pair had been indulging in this caper for a couple of years, and their rented house in Dunwich looked more like a marine chandlery, literally packed to the rafters with items pinched from many boats. There were a few awkward questions about the origin of the male intruder's injuries, but I covered that by saying that I must have given him such a fright when I turned the lights on and yelled at him, that he had a seizure. However, Sandy's presence and rank fortunately stopped too much discussion in that direction. Jasper, of course, remained out of sight, his place taken, as usual, by his tiny, adoring female companion, the equally black-furred Krazy cat, so any talk from the girl about a huge black cat who had almost ripped her throat out, was ignored by the detectives as delusional fantasy.

Once the local police and the mainland detectives had finished and left us alone, we were swamped with gratitude by the two families. To avoid too many invites to eat and drink in celebration of their escape from the clutches of the bad guys, we decided to leave the pretty anchorage and return back to base. Returning Sandy to work was a good excuse to bail out early.

A couple of weeks later, on a sunny Friday afternoon, I was sprawled back in a comfortable chair aboard *Seeker*, the 100-foot, super-fast, sleek Italian sport cruiser owned by our dear friends, Corrine and Dave. The collection of empty beer bottles which littered the table bore testament to the depth of verbal crap we were presently tossing back and forth, while waiting for Sandy to knock off work and join us. That was when my phone rang.

Thinking it was her, I was about to make a smart-arsed answer, until I saw it was a Melbourne number.

'This is Harry.'

*'Hi Harry, this is Georgia Wesley. I'm one of the vets who visited you on Lord Howe Island to study Jasper. You might remember us better as the 'little old lady professors."*

'Oh, yeah. Gidday Georgia, how could I forget stepping on my dick as hard as that! Thanks for reminding me. And your mate was a real hard-arse, as I remember. But how are you?'

*'Ah... yeah. I'm really well and the hard-arse was, and still is, my associate, Beth Tremaine.'*

As usual, alcohol clouded my judgement and loosened my tongue. 'Yeah, that's right. Beth. How could I forget. What a ball-buster! But what can I do for you?'

*'Look, Harry. We wanted to ask a big favour of you, but this doesn't seem to be starting out very well.'*

I laughed. 'It would seem so! Although I thought things were going great until you mentioned Beth's name. Jasper's welfare has always been my highest priority, but your dopey mate seemed to want to disregard all my rules about working with him. I'm afraid I didn't take very kindly to that.'

*'Yeah, we sort of noticed that! But perhaps if I could explain our*

*situation, you might consider helping us.'*

I took another mouthful of beer and cheerfully said, 'Sure, Georgia. It's always a pleasure to talk to you, so I'll listen.'

*'Thank you. You might remember when we first met, that Beth and I were doing research on animal-human interaction.'*

'Yep. I remember that's what caused most of the problems when your argumentative mate wanted to pull blood and do biopsies on my cat!'

*'Yeah. Got that, thanks for the reminder – again. But I'd really like to move on, if you'll give me a break.'*

'Oh... yeah. Okay. Sorry about that. Bit of a sore point, so to speak. Go ahead.'

*'Thanks. To keep the story short, Beth and I are working on getting our PhDs, based on the same subject.'*

With several beers down my hatch, I cheerfully butted in. 'I didn't think two people could base their thesis on exactly the same subject?'

*'Yeah, that's usually the case, but we've been allowed to split the main body of our research into animal/human interaction, and animal/other non-human species interaction. I have the human aspect, while Beth has the non-human one.*

*What has us and our mentors excited, is that Jasper seems to have the ability to interact and communicate amazingly well with both humans and other species. Based on the limited data we collected last time, along with those amazing videos of him with that giant crocodile, Jasper has become the focus of our research since he's the only animal we've heard of who can do this.'*

'Yeah, well. I know he's a clever pussy, but what about those tame gorillas in America who can talk in sign language?'

*'We've looked at all the data on Koko, and as good as she was, it seemed that she mainly replied to actual signed questions, and only to a limited extent to human speech. And while she was able to have an empathetic relationship with other species like kittens, there was no evidence she could actually communicate with them. Therefore, it seems*

*that Jasper is still unique in what he can do, having abilities far above what Koko could do.'*

'Okay. That's very interesting, but how about you cut to the bottom line. On the understanding, of course, that regardless of PhDs, ABCs or any other fancy-bloody-letter combos, I still won't let anybody take blood, do a biopsy, or perform any other invasive tests on him. With that in mind, what are you asking?'

I heard her draw a deep breath, and my usual depraved and fertile imagination immediately produced an image of what that was doing to her shirt. Presuming of course, she was still built as nicely as what I'd seen when I first met her on Lord Howe Island.

'*We've scored a decent grant for this research, but in order to proceed further, we need to spend time with Jasper. Therefore, we'd like to visit you again. Like for at least a week, or even more if we don't wear out our welcome too quickly. The only physical tests we would like to do will be totally non-invasive, consisting of just a normal veterinary physical examination. The main thing is, we just need time to be around him to record and take notes of how he interacts with you, other species if that's possible, and even with us if he accepts us well enough in the time available.*

*We can more than pay our way, so we won't be a financial burden. What do you think?'*

I ran possible problems through my mind, not the least of which was the likely effect of Beth's abrasive personality on the laid-back, harmonious relationship the crew of *Firebird* currently enjoyed. I balanced that against the fact that Georgia should be a moderating influence on her hot-headed, impulsive and loud-mouthed partner. Of course, I could always tell my big pussy to cut loose if he sighted anyone approaching with a syringe. Resolving to do just that, I reluctantly said, 'Okay. You can come, but strictly under the conditions as discussed. You can inform Beth that I'll be telling Jasper he's free to take whatever action he wants to defend himself, should either of you try to approach him with a syringe, a knife or any other pointed object!'

'*Agreed, thanks Harry, although I've already said we wouldn't do anything like that. But what if Jasper misinterprets something we do? I've heard enough stories about how he treats people he doesn't like.*'

I gave an evil chuckle. 'Easy answer. Don't do anything he might misinterpret! Look, Georgia, I've heard you say that you'll behave and I trust you, but I haven't heard Beth make the same promise. So having Jasper watching both of you for any sign of misbehaving with medical equipment, should be excellent incentive for Beth to keep strictly to my terms for your visit.

And speaking of which, to avoid too much coming and going, it will be better for Jasper, your research, and less disruptive to the crew if you both stay aboard. You'll have your own cabin with ensuite, and your room and full board will cost $1,000 per head per week. I suggest that two weeks should be long enough to gather the extra data you need, but if that's not enough, we can discuss it. Finally, I reserve the right to terminate this verbal agreement at any time if I decide your research is upsetting Jasper or disrupting the harmonious atmosphere on the boat.'

I gave a slightly evil, booze-enhanced chuckle. 'Always bearing in mind that upsetting Jasper will very effectively terminate your research in a most unpleasant way. I hope that is understood and acceptable?'

Even in the face of my dire warnings and restrictions, she sounded remarkably upbeat when she replied, '*Oh, yes! No problem at all. Thank you Harry. That's more than I expected after our last visit. I'll make sure things go smoothly.*'

'Okay. When do you want to start?'

'*Umm... we are rather keen to get going as soon as possible, so this being Friday, we can be packed and there on Sunday if that fits your plans.*'

Now that I'd mentally committed to the visit, I felt more relaxed and said, 'Sure. That'll be fine. We aren't planning on going anywhere for now. If you text or email your flight number and arrival time, I can pick you up at the airport.'

*'Oh, I wouldn't put you out like that,' she replied, almost gushing with relief, 'we'll get a taxi. I think you said you were located at the Southport Yacht Club? Are you still there?'*

I mentally shrugged, 'Yeah, we are. The cabbie will know where to go. Call when you get here and I'll come ashore to pick you up.'

*'Brilliant! Thanks again Harry. This is absolutely fucking fantastic. See you Sunday. Bye.'*

I passed all this onto Corrine and Dave, who were highly amused by the prospect of refereeing my coming clash with the argumentative and abrasive Beth, and immediately started making bets with each other as to how many minutes or hours it would be before I threw her overboard, and whether or not there would be an anchor attached to her leg.

I'd just finished re-hashing the conversation, when my lovely lady, Sandy arrived from work and once she had a frosty beer in hand, I had to tell the story all over again. Like Corrine and Dave, Sandy was highly amused by the situation I'd let myself in for, but told me to 'lighten up' and try just being nice for a change.

I tried putting on my best cranky face, but that caused more hilarity, so I just shrugged and accepted another beer instead.


It was just after 11:00 Sunday morning, when Georgia called to announce that they were on the Yacht Club jetty. I duly made myself decent by pulling on my cleanest dirty T-shirt over my favourite paint-stained shorts, then headed ashore in the dinghy.

It'd been a couple of years since I'd first met the two female professors at Lord Howe Island, where I made a right goose of myself by asking the airport staff if two old dears had arrived on the daily flight from Sydney, and were looking for a lift into town. My excuse at the time was that anyone who rated the 'Professor' title must be old and somewhat decrepit. I'd been gobsmacked at the time to see that Georgia was a good ten years younger than me, was tall, blonde and very pretty, while Beth, of similar age, was equally-tall, but had flaming red hair and was equally attractive. Both ladies were also built very nicely – not unlike Sandy in that respect. In fact, very close in most dimensions as best I could tell.

Today, they didn't look much different, although Beth held back to let Georgia start the greetings. I copped a big hug and a kiss on the cheek from her, but a much more sedate handshake from Beth, although she was gracious enough to crack a smile and thank me for allowing them to visit.

All morning I'd been telling myself, as Sandy had, frequently and often, to be nice and accept the ladies as they were.

'Time enough for aggro later, dearest, if it seems really necessary,' she had cautioned, so I was on my best behaviour. At least for the moment.

Thankfully, the girls had managed to travel light, with only a large backpack each and a couple of waterproof Pelikan cases. Once aboard, they knew Sandy, Bree and Alex from Lord Howe, but hadn't seen the new *Firebird* before, and were amazed at the size, the all-over Ferrari-red colour, and the huge increase in internal space. Bree had put them in the relatively spacious twin-bunk cabin located forward in the left hull ahead of the laundry/workshop. It had its own ensuite and even a small workstation with mains-power and internet connections.

Jasper remained out of sight until the ladies got themselves settled in, then came out when they reappeared. He'd already recognised them both by their voices, as well as by peeking from his favourite perch on top of the cockpit roof when they'd arrived. I was intrigued to see that he greeted Georgia like an old friend by nuzzling her crotch and shaking hands, but he was very reserved with Beth, to the point of not shaking hands. At least he didn't growl at her, which perhaps was an improvement in relations, but I cursed myself for not explaining the situation to him before they arrived.

Although Georgia was delighted by her welcome, I don't think she fully appreciated the complex level of animal/human interaction which had just taken place. While Beth looked a bit miffed, I hastened to rectify the situation by squatting down beside my beautiful, lethal and often-mystical cat, while making sure our visitors heard me.

'I'm sorry I didn't tell you sooner, boy, but Beth and Georgia are going to stay with us for a couple of weeks. They want to get to know you better, so I'd like you to play nice and help them as much as possible. But they aren't allowed to stab or cut you with anything sharp, or hurt you in any way. If they do try to do anything like that, you are allowed to do whatever you want in return.'

Jasper looked at me, huffed gently and bared his fangs in his version of a pussy grin, but which looked extremely menacing to the un-initiated, or perhaps to those with a guilty conscience.

Accordingly, Beth and Georgia looked quite horrified as I flashed them a grin. 'There you are ladies. Ground rules established, discussed and agreed to by the cat. Jasper will co-operate fully, as long as you both behave.'

'But you virtually told him he could attack us if he didn't like what we were doing!' Beth ground out, her eyes blazing. 'We're paying you for co-operation – not to have to defend ourselves from potentially lethal attacks!'

Despite feeling a surge of rage at the stupidity of excessively-educated, supposedly intelligent persons, I kept my expression neutral and looked up at her from my squatting position. 'Once again, Beth, you didn't listen, did you? If you had, you would have heard that I asked Jasper to co-operate with both of you and play nice, and he agreed. That is unless you try to betray our trust by attempting to take blood or any other fluids or bits from him. You're welcome to as much of his pee and poop as you want, once it's deposited on his toilet mat, but as I've already said to Georgia, do not try to stick him or spray him with anything. In fact, I'd strongly suggest that you don't even approach him with anything sharper than a pen! I've neither the time nor the inclination to watch you 24/7, but now that Jasper knows the rules, he's more than capable of looking after himself.'

When Beth, clenched fists parked aggressively on her hips, still glared at me while she obviously struggled to come up with a suitably stinging reply, I shrugged. 'It's entirely up to you. Stick to the terms of the agreement Georgia and I made before you even left home, and all will be well. If you've planned on acting outside those terms in some way, you just wasted an airline ticket because as far as I'm concerned, you can go get your gear right now and leave.'

I stopped to take a deep breath, mentally cursing as once again, this rotten, pig-headed woman had managed to make me angry. Sandy recognised the signs and before I lashed out again, laid a calming hand on my shoulder, then addressed Beth in her very best Police Inspector voice. I was terribly impressed – it was almost better than my 'pissed-off Major' one.

'Regrettably Beth, once again you've managed to make Harry and me angry by your stupid refusal to just smile nicely and say thank you very much for the stunning opportunity you've been handed. What you don't seem to appreciate is that although we've tried hard to keep Jasper's abilities a secret, too many people already know about him. Therefore, his reputation has reached the stage where we get several requests every week from researchers, military persons and assorted weirdos who want to come and take blood and biopsy samples from him, but you two are the only ones we've ever allowed to have such open access to him. As I'm sure Harry has already explained, our main concern has always been to make sure that Jasper wasn't just hauled off to a lab where he'd be treated like a test rat, until some idiot decides that carving up his brain might reveal more of what makes him special. It beats the fuck outta me why you cannot understand that we have set some very simple and easy to follow rules, just to protect Jasper. But even though Georgia happily agreed to those terms with Harry before you even left home, here you are arguing with us straight away. Quite amazingly stupid for someone who dares to use the title of Professor!

Therefore, I completely agree with Harry and think the best thing for our collective sanity, is for you to go get your gear right now and get the hell off our boat! I'll even call another taxi for you, but you might have to find your own way ashore! Those watertight Pelikan cases will make good floats.'

A stunned silence greeted the end of that superbly-worded statement, until Beth, whose frown threatened to turn her whole pretty face into a permanent mass of wrinkles, started to open her mouth to retort. That was when her colleague turned and in one smooth movement, delivered a very un-professorial, very hard, open-handed slap to her face which snapped Beth's head sideways, and sat her down hard on the deck, fair on her admittedly shapely arse.

'Don't you dare say another word, you silly, stupid bitch, unless it's to apologise unreservedly to Harry, Sandy, Alex, Bree, and me as well. I've worked my arse off for the last couple of years trying to get this PhD, and now, right on the verge of scoring a huge amount of world-leading, exclusive data, you've fucked things up yet again by being a pig-headed fuck-wit. Even if you do make an apology, we're still getting kicked off the boat and will have lost for all time the opportunity for some ground-breaking research, but at least you can do the right thing by admitting how stupid you've been.'

She glared at her companion for a few seconds in silence, and although I was about to suggest another slap might be a good idea, I actually kept my mouth shut for once.

Georgia resumed, 'I'm going to leave you here to hopefully do that, while I go below and collect my gear. At least we hadn't unpacked.'

With the whole left side of her face an unattractive bright red, Beth looked stunned as her friend and co-researcher stormed through the saloon and went below.

Sandy stood glaring at Beth, while I smiled gently, waiting to see what she'd do.

What she did was to gingerly touch the side of her face, painfully work her jaw a few times, then awkwardly drag herself off the deck, wincing with the pain of a badly bruised bum, before stammering her way through an apology.

'Look. I truly am sorry for my rudeness. I don't know what I was thinking to say what I did which provoked this argument. All I can say is that perhaps I was way too anxious to get as much data as possible from this time with Jasper. He really is an amazing animal and I'm convinced that he's utterly unique. We haven't heard of any other animal who even comes close to having his set of cognitive abilities, so research on him is incredibly important to us, and to veterinary science in general. I guess I just let my desire for data overcome common-sense. I also didn't realise that you hadn't let anybody else study him.'

She took a deep breath, which immediately drew my attention and eyes, while it dulled my anger just a tad.

'Look. I know things have gone way too far for me to make amends, but maybe you'd consider letting Georgia stay. I promise I'll leave without any further fuss, just as soon as I can grab my gear, if you wouldn't mind running me ashore.'

Just then, Georgia appeared with her backpack and a Pelikan case, which she sat down by top of the stern steps, before grumping at Beth.

'I'm ready, so if you care to grab your stuff, I'll try to sweet-talk Harry into running us ashore... otherwise we're going to get very wet.'


She parked her bum on the Pelikan case and stared unseeingly at the deck, as Beth went below. Sandy looked at me wordlessly, with a neutral expression, so I looked at Bree and Alex who weren't any help, before looking back at Sandy, who made the classic Italian hand and shoulder gesture that said, *'Well. What now?'*

I cleared my throat and looked at Georgia who still looked very cranky.

'Okay, Georgia. Here's the go. Beth has apologised, but we remain unconvinced that she really intends to stick with the program. She seems to have a serious problem with anybody telling her what she can't do. She has, however, suggested that we allow you to stay on condition that she goes. So, the question is, can you do the necessary research by yourself to cover the needs of both of you?'

Georgia looked surprised, then happier that we might allow at least her to stay.

'Not that easy,' she said, 'but I'll gladly do what I can if that's the offer on the table. You won't be getting any arguments from me about anything, that's for sure. I'll happily pay the full fee and sleep in the dinghy, if necessary.'

I looked to Sandy for guidance, but she just gave a brief nod and seemed to send a mental message which confirmed my feelings, so I turned back to Georgia.

'Alright. Thanks for being honest, so here's the new deal. Against my better judgement, you can stay as agreed for as long as necessary, and Beth can stay for two days on probation to see if her attitude improves. We'll review things on Tuesday evening and make a final decision. Do you accept that?'

Her body actually slumped with relief, and tears glistened in her eyes.

'Oh, yes, Harry. Thank you very much. I'll try very hard to sort the silly bitch out, but if things aren't any better by Tuesday, I'll pull the pin for both of us and we'll leave you in peace.'

I nodded. 'Okay. We'll say no more for now, and leave it up to you and Beth to see if things improve.'

I scored another really hard hug for my trouble, which was rather pleasant even under the current fraught circumstances. Or maybe because of those circumstances. Who knows? Sandy thought it was amusing, although I think she probably just wanted a hug as well.

Georgia promptly picked up her bags and headed back below before someone changed their mind.

Our guests were very quiet for the rest of that day, staying well out of my private space, but next morning, Monday, their mood seemed to have lightened considerably. Which was just as well since we'd always been a happy crew on *Firebird*, so having festering tension in such a relatively confined environment was very unwelcome. Sandy had gone to work, so late morning, I managed to get Georgia by herself and asked what she'd done to improve Beth's attitude.

She grinned. 'I guess I spelled out a few home truths. Like how she's allowed herself to become fixated on the need to take blood and tissue samples from Jasper when it wasn't going to make the slightest bit of difference to our line of research. We're here to analyse his behaviour, not his blood or general physiology since we don't need to know why he does what he does, just what he can do! She's let this obsession blind her to the wonderful opportunity you'd presented us with. There was a lot more hard talking before we went to sleep, then this morning she apologised to me, and said she felt much more relaxed about the situation. I don't know what she worked out, or how she did it, but so far it seems to be working.'

'I'm very glad to hear that, and it's a good point about what's not necessary for your work. I'd wondered about it myself.'

She nodded. 'That's the main thing I tried to get through to her She somehow had it in her mind that the answer to what Jasper does was in his physiology. By what she said, and the way she worded it, I have a suspicion that one of her fruit-loop work-mates with a different agenda planted that idea. They'd be the ones you really need to keep away from Jasper. Anyway, now she seems to have sorted her thinking out, maybe we can get on with our real job of finding out what the big pussy can do.'

'Good work,' I beamed, 'but purely out of interest, what is your plan of action?'

'For my work, which is interactions with humans, I just need to watch and video Jasper in his normal environment with humans around. Particularly in regard to how he reacts to you and the others he knows and trusts – those who interact and speak to him on a daily basis. We would also like to get him used to us being around and document how he interacts with us as known persons, but still effectively strangers. That's all my area of research, but Beth's part depends on Jasper's interaction with other animal species, which I can see will be more difficult as there are obviously very few opportunities around here. I don't think Seaworld would be willing to let Jasper go play with the dolphins and seals for a day.'

She grinned, 'Unfortunately, your beautiful little Krazy cat doesn't count. But I don't suppose you have any plans to go visit somewhere else for a few days or so where there might be a chance of encounters with another species?'

I mulled over her words and request for a while, before cautiously replying.

'Hmmm... maybe. I mean, we can certainly visit Moreton Bay, which is close-by, or even head up to the Great Sandy Strait and Hervey Bay which would offer a few more chances to meet up with other creatures, both in the open ocean and in sheltered waters. That's easy. However, for some time we've been putting off a visit to Vanuatu for business reasons, and although we've not decided when, our business manager Bree, would prefer it happened sooner rather than later.'

Georgia's hazel eyes lit up with excitement.

'Bloody hell, Harry. Vanuatu! That's a bit extreme! I wasn't thinking of going that far. Just up or down the coast a way might have been enough, but going to Vanuatu would be a brilliant chance to come across other species.'

I couldn't help grinning at her infectious enthusiasm.

'Settle down. I only said it was a possibility. Sort of 'two birds with one stone' type of thing. I'll talk it over with Sandy, Bree and Alex and let you know, but if we did, it might extend your stay a little, as the trip will be at least three days each way, depending on conditions, plus at least a couple of days at Port Vila so the ladies can buy more clothes. Although why they need more, I'm buggered if I know – they wear little enough normally.'

Georgia giggled, then said. 'Time isn't a problem for us. We're on a research work-break for now, with no teaching assignments for a while, so we can be flexible. I just didn't want to impose too much on your hospitality.'

'That's alright. Paying guests are allowed to extend their stay. Apart from Sandy, it's not as though we were doing anything else right now.'

She looked at me oddly, and I saw her shift mental gears.

'If I might ask, just what is it that you do normally? I mean, I know Sandy's with the Queensland Police, but what do you, Bree and Alex do? You all seem to be a bit too young and wired to be retired.'

I blandly returned her questioning look for a few moments, before replying. 'Let's just say that on occasions, our... rather unusual set-up and situation allows us to become useful to certain Government departments. Those occasional jobs stop things getting boring and allows the occasional decent earn to fall into our laps. That, in return, keeps the roof over our heads and plenty of booze in the fridge.'

After she'd pointedly looked around the huge expanse of very expensive, gleaming red gel-coated carbon-fibre we called home, she gave me a carefully considered look. 'Okay. I'd better not ask more, but it would appear to this simple vet that your 'occasional jobs for the Government', might be a lot more lucrative than you care to mention. And a lot more dangerous, if that limp and the fresh scar on the side of your head you didn't have last time is any indication.'

I reserved comment at that and settled for a Mona Lisa-type smile. At least it made her chuckle.

'I think you can be a very bad and dangerous man, Harry Stevens, but at least you seem to be on the side of the angels, so for now I'm happy with that.'

With that, and humming the theme from 'Jaws', she wandered off to catch up with Beth, with iPad in hand, was patiently stalking Jasper around the boat, much to his amusement as she didn't realise he was playing with her, by randomly and pointlessly wandering all over the place.

Tuesday passed without incident and Beth really did seem to be a greatly changed person. She actually smiled and laughed at the antics of Jasper and Krazy in one of their many play sessions together, and joined in with intelligent, non-confrontational conversation with everyone, even me. On Wednesday morning after breakfast, Georgia took me aside and predictably asked, 'You didn't say anything last night, so may I ask what your decision is on letting us stay or not?'

I gave her a suitably bland look. 'Based on how Beth has been behaving, I'm prepared to say you both can stay, on condition that she remains happy and social. Also, after discussing the trip idea with Sandy, Bree and Alex, I've decided we'll head for Vanuatu, departing Saturday morning. Sandy needs the rest of the week at work to sort out or off-load a few on-going problems, and Bree wants to rearrange the pantry, then restock it with more food and booze.'

Her expressive shoulders slumped with relief again, and she gave me another of those very hard hugs... you know – one of those full-body-contact ones from a nicely-rounded female that feels really, really nice. Well, it did to me, anyway.

'Oh, thank you, Harry. That's brilliant. If we get lucky, Beth might be able to get the extra data she needs, although having copies of all your videos will still do a great job if that's all we'll have.'

I laughed. 'I can't guarantee another giant croc encounter. That was probably a twice-in-a-lifetime deal.'

'Understood. But anything we can witness ourselves will be

fantastic. First-hand reporting is always the best.'

She hustled off to the foredeck where Beth was with Jasper, who was now quite happy to sit with her and tolerate being scratched while she talked softly to him. Shortly, the lady herself came aft.

'Thank you for what you're doing for us, Harry. I'm very happy now we might have a chance to see Jasper interact with something else, but I know you can't guarantee anything. I just wanted you to know how much I appreciate everyone's efforts and that I'll keep doing whatever I can to help.'

I nodded. 'That's fine, Beth. I'm glad to be able to provide the opportunity. As I told Georgia, we have a small matter of business to attend to in Port Vila, so there's no need to stay very long. It's a good thing you have your passports.'

'We never leave home without them when we travel for work,' she commented, cracking a rare and lovely smile which was so much nicer than the semi-permanent frown we'd become used to seeing.

'By the way,' she added, 'has Jasper grown since we last saw him? He seems a lot bigger than I remembered.'

'Yeah. He is. He was the same size and weight for what seemed like a long time, then had a sudden growth spurt for no apparent reason. That's what packed on a lot of extra weight and size. His weight is up to around 35 kilos, so hopefully, that'll be end of it. He eats like a horse as it is.'

I was going to talk more, seeing as she was in a relaxed mood, but my mobile rang, so I excused myself.

Thinking it must be Sandy, I was about to make one of my usual smart-arse comments, but then noticed the blocked number.

'Yo!'

*'Harry, dear man. How the hell are you?'*

'Charlie, you lovely lady! We're all terrific. How are things down there in the bullshit capital of Australia?'

*'Only knee deep at the moment, although surprisingly, the level isn't rising, so something must be going right for once. Anyway, I just called with an update on the latest doings of your band of wayward waifs.'*

'Oh, good. I haven't heard anything about them for a while, so presumed all was well. I hope that's still the case?'

'Yep. All going very well. In fact, they've adjusted so well that quite a few have taken over positions to help run the place. That has allowed Mrs James to take in more private, paying customers. The resort is close to being self-supporting now, and if this keeps up, the place will soon start making a profit. The Boss is very pleased, both with the way things are going, and how it's diverted attention from the Army camp.'

'Very glad to hear all that Charlie. They're a special bunch of kids. And how are Andy and Lara?'

'They're well, but the Boss is very tired. This session of Parliament has been a real meat-grinder, so he's looking forward to a break when the place shuts down for a few weeks. I don't suppose you feel like three visitors for a while?'

I laughed. 'Of course, dear girl, we'd be delighted. Whenever it suits you. What did you have in mind?'

'Oh, that's so good to hear, Harry. Really, just to get away from people and politics for a while on your lovely boat will be just what he desperately needs. He really loves that thing. We don't have to go anywhere special, and all your marvellous comms gear still works as well as usual, I presume?'

'Yep. No worries about that, Charlie. You and Andy can stay in touch with Tinsel-Town all you need. However, I have to say that we do have a pair of veterinary professors from Melbourne Uni staying with us, doing a study on why Jasper's such a smart-arse. There's no problem with space of course, and it's no hassle for us, so long as it won't be a problem for you and Andy. I presume you'll need to do the usual security check?'

'That's interesting. Yes, I'll run their names past Spook Central if you have them, please.'

'They are Beth Tremaine and Georgia Wesley. Both associate professors at Melbourne Uni doing research for their PhDs. So, when would you like to turn up?'

'Got that. So, as Parliament breaks up on Friday, we can start the *bail-out process Friday arvo if that's okay with you. We may have to do the usual amount of artful dodging to cover tracks, but we can be there Friday evening. I'll let you know once we're airborne. It'll just be the Boss, Lara and myself, if that's okay?'*

'Delighted to oblige, but bring your passports. I've got a bit of a cunning plan.'

*'I get nervous when you start talking about cunning plans Harry, but I'll go with the flow on this one. I'll just tell the Boss it's a surprise cruise.'*

'Perfect! Let me know if you need any help staying under the public radar getting here.'

*'I'll do that, thanks. I'll call again Friday. Cheers, lovely man.'*

'Bye, Charlie.'


Bree and Alex were laughing at me as I terminated the call.

'Getting the Boss again, by the sounds of that,' Alex said.

'Yep. Looks like Friday night. Just Andy, Lara and Charlie for a couple of weeks.'

'Excellent. And no trouble with the ladies?'

'Charlie's having them checked, but I can't see there would be any problems. And we'll still go to Vanuatu. That'll get rid of the cash and be a fun run. It should work out fine for our Jasper investigators as well. At least we won't have to disguise Andy over there apart from dress him down and slap a hat on his head!'

They had a good laugh at that. On the two previous occasions when Andy had been on a trip with us, he'd proved to be a very congenial and competent crewmember who loved sailing and thoroughly enjoyed a bit of a party, but when we went ashore, Bree had to disguise him a little.

After lunch, I went ashore to visit Dave and Corrine on their 100-foot Italian phallic symbol, *Seeker,* where I told them about having Andy, Lara and Charlie join us.

'Did you guys want to join in?' I asked, since they knew and liked Andy and his lovely lady Lara, as well as Sandy and I did. 'There are still a couple of spare beds.'

They looked at each other, then Corrine shook her head, before uttering some terribly prophetic words. 'Nah. That's okay, thanks Harry. You've got plenty of crew, so we might sit this one out. It's not as though you're heading into trouble and need us to bail your arse out again.'

'Anyway, Dave's been threatening to take me on a romantic holiday to the snow country, so this might be a good opportunity. What about that, snookums?'

'Snookums? Romantic? You've got to be kidding, you rotten woman! Arrrgh! Go wash your mouth out.'

'Arsehole!'

'Bitchface!'

Corrine smiled sweetly. 'There. That's settled. It looks like we're going to play in the snow for a week, thanks Harry. Presuming there will be some this early in the year. I'll go make the bookings while Dave's still in a state of shock. We'll leave on Sunday if I can get in somewhere at short notice.'

I chuckled, 'Wave some cash around. That usually works for me.'

That prompted me to call Sandy before she left work so she could tell Bob Casey, her Superintendent, that she had once again been nominated to head up the Prime Ministerial guard detail for a week or two. That escalated her holiday up to a work detail, and kept Bob happy as he loved that Sandy was involved with the PM, even if he couldn't tell everyone about it. After our less than relaxing trip to Moreton Bay recently, she was delighted with the thought of spending some laid-back, quality time with Andy, Lara and Charlie who all fitted in seamlessly with the *Firebird* crew.

I had a few more beers with Dave and Corrine, until Sandy arrived, then let her drive the dinghy out to *Firebird*. She sort-of insisted on driving anyway, after she saw the height of the heap of empties on *Seeker's* cockpit table. Once on board, she went to change, while I got her favourite LillyPilly Winery Sav Blanc for her and a beer for myself. Alex, Bree, Georgia and Beth already had drinks in hand, so

I told our two guests that we'd be having good friends Andy, Lara and Charlie as additional guests for our cruise to Vanuatu.

'This should be great, they're fun people,' said Sandy, waving her glass of wine in a grand gesture, spilling some on Krazy cat in the process. 'Oops. Sorry, pussy. Don't worry. Jasper will lick you clean. He likes Sav Blanc.'

In hindsight, it was probably due to the distraction of cleaning up a wine-soaked, and thoroughly disgusted small black cat, that I think I may have forgotten to mention to Georgia and Beth exactly who Andy, Lara and Charlie were, although I did say they were close friends, and had cruised with us before. Too bad. They'd adjust.

Over the next two days, and in-between following Jasper around with an iPad and video camera, Beth and Georgia helped Bree check all the stocks of food and booze, then went with her to help buy what was needed. Sandy had already placed her order for several cartons of the LillyPilly Sauvinion Blanc which was only available from one outlet on the Gold Coast. While that was happening, Alex and I went over *Firebird* from bow to stern and masthead to dagger-boards, checking everything. We didn't find any problems, but nevertheless lubricated everything that moved, re-painted some things which didn't and weren't supposed to, tested every system, and end-for-ended several of the sail-control lines. The electric drive power systems needed very little maintenance, but were checked anyway.

Buying everything on the grocery and booze list, plus all the extras which seem to fall accidentally into the trolleys, getting it all aboard and stowed to Bree's satisfaction, took a full day, but at the end of all the re-stowing, we were prepared for anything.

Charlie called again to confirm that our two guests had been officially checked out and approved as suitably benign company for the Boss. She also confirmed they'd be arriving at Gold Coast airport on Friday evening and would appreciate a low-profile pickup from the general aviation parking area at 19:00, and that security was alerted to let me in through the gate opposite Kirribilli Street.

32

Once again, seven of the most powerful men in China, who comprised the Central Military Commission, sat around a table in the same luxurious conference room in the Ministry of National Defence compound in western Beijing. As was his preference, the Chairman called for reports from each department head in turn, going counter-clockwise around the table. While most reports were routine and only served to keep everyone informed about what other projects were happening and their current status, the delegate in charge of overseeing Expansion and Base Acquisition looked nervous – again. At the last meeting, his novel, but hideously expensive idea to acquire a new military base had been soundly decried by the powerful, hard-faced older man sitting opposite. Oddly enough, at that time, his plan had received the guarded, but positive support of the Commission Chairman who, unknown to the others, had continued to encourage the younger man to develop his ideas since the last meeting.

At the first mention of the word 'copper', the older man snorted loudly and rudely, then drew a deep breath as preparation for another scathing put-down, but was instantly forestalled by the slight lifting of the Chairman's finger.

'Do continue, Comrade,' The Chairman murmured into the sudden silence, 'and be so kind as to inform our commission members of the developments to your harbour acquisition plan since our last meeting.'

The Junior Member swallowed and bobbed his head in gratitude to the top seat of the table, before glancing quickly around the now-curious faces of his colleagues, all of whom were surprised and wary of this unusual open support by the Chairman. It had taken only moments and a finger-lift from the Chairman, for the Junior member to gain a huge amount of 'face'.

'Thank you, Comrade Chairman. With the invaluable and generous assistance of our Comrade Defence Minister, the first stages of the plan to acquire a major deep-water port at Kieta on Bougainville Island has been put into motion. In the first stage, we have requested our diplomatic service to ask the Autonomous Region of Bougainville Government to allow one of our warships, the Type 071 amphibious transport dock, the *Changbaishan*, to make a good-will visit to the island. They will naturally expect that our ship will anchor near Buka Town, the capital in the north. However, the *Changbaishan* will proceed straight to Kieta Harbour, where if necessary, his captain will claim storm damage as the reason for using the different port-of-call.

The ship had planned to visit Fiji with an engineering battalion plus construction equipment and materials to assist with cyclone-damage repair, but if this plan is approved, it can be diverted, and could be at Kieta Harbour within four days. Coinciding with the arrival of the *Changbaishan* in Kieta harbour, we would dispatch a small diplomatic group by air direct to Buka Town to confer with the President directly in an effort to provide a suitable distraction for the main activities taking place in Kieta Harbour.'

As he paused to take a sip of water from the glass at his elbow, his previously hostile opponent opposite asked in a surprisingly gentle tone, 'The Type 71 can carry six to eight hundred marines. How is he loaded on this occasion?'

The junior member kept a carefully neutral face as he replied, 'In line with the declared purpose of this visit, there are only fifty troops plus the engineering battalion aboard, but this is considered to be more than sufficient for our real purpose. We expect that intimidation will be our best weapon in this situation, but we have planned to bring in further reinforcements should it become necessary.'

Mindful of the brooding, all-powerful presence at the head of the table, the gruff senior member maintained a neutral face, nodded politely, then leant back, allowing the younger man to continue.

'The purpose of the diplomatic visit to Buka Town is to open face-to-face discussions with the local Government regarding the investment by China in re-opening the Panguna copper and gold mine, in return for port rights for our military vessels and a suitable share in the profits from the re-opened mine.'

Another member leant forward and interrupted, 'Pardon my interruption, comrade, but as I understand the situation, despite the island calling itself the Autonomous Region of Bougainville, the Papua New Guinea government still retains a strong voice in how internal affairs are handled. Surely they are not going to stand back and allow these talks to proceed without intervention? And even those meddling fools, the Australians, could involve themselves again.'

'While all that is true and possible, Comrade, it is hoped that with our diplomatic crew initiating direct talks in the capital, along with the presence of our large and imposing amphibious assault ship in Kieta Harbour, talks will quickly proceed to an advanced stage without attracting outside attention until it is too late, and an agreement has been reached. I also forgot to mention there is already a trained negotiating crew aboard the *Changbaishan*, whose task it would be to make direct contact with the local rebel leaders to commence immediate discussions regarding an appropriate and generous level of compensation for the Panguna mine's local landowners, and to determine their requirements for land rehabilitation prior to mining resuming. They are, after all, the key people in any of these discussions. If we can get their early agreement to our proposals, we believe that our other aims will be achieved much more easily.'

Despite the presence of the Chairman at the head of the table, the older man opposite leant forward to make a gentle protest.

'Comrade. You are to be congratulated on your plan to gain an important strategic deep-water port in this region, but I cannot help but ask what the considerable cost of this enterprise might be. Even if, as you pointed out last time, we could ultimately recoup those massive costs from our share in the profits, these returns will be many years in the making, is this not so?'

The youngest member took a deep breath as he allowed his gaze to drift around the faces of his comrades.

'Comrades, indeed this would be a huge and expensive undertaking, given the difficulty of the mine re-opening and the re-building of the port facilities, both of which are currently very run-down! However, the other part of my plan removes nearly all the cost of the proposed operation.'

Like all good showmen, he paused to take another small sip of water from the glass in front of him, while he allowed curiosity and tension to build.

'The other part of my plan is simply that apart from the cost of upgrading the port facilities, we will not actually get around to spending any money on the re-opening of the mine.'

He didn't have to make a showy pause, as the table erupted in startled mutters. Surprising himself with his temerity, he held one hand up in a call for silence.

'I speak true! The crux of my plan is that talk truly can be cheap, so it is hoped our Diplomatic Service teams can extend their talks sufficiently with the President, the rebels and land-owners until the refurbishment of the port facilities are at least well under way. At that stage, there will occur a regretful, but irreconcilable breakdown in relations with all parties involved, despite on-going efforts by our tireless diplomatic teams to repair the damage. Therefore, all we will have to actually spend will be what is needed to elevate the port and its facilities to the standard required by our People's Liberation Army Navy. Even while the port facilities are being built, we will slowly stock the harbour with enough of our ships so as to make a such a show of force that even the loud-mouthed Americans will be reluctant to try to remove.'

'But if there is to be an irreconcilable breakdown of talks, the regional government will surely demand that we immediately leave their country,' pointed out the defence minister.

The junior member nodded his head, 'This is so, Comrade. But if the breakdown in negotiations were made to appear to be the result of minor, but active skirmishes between the factions, then we will immediately offer the protection of our marines who happen to be ready and waiting. This assistance will be loudly proclaimed to be offered to calm the situation and prevent another outbreak of civil war. I have every confidence that our operatives in the Ministry of State Security will be able to massage the situation in such a manner as to achieve the desired result. By the time the apparent threat of civil war has passed, and the minor skirmishes have been suitably 'suppressed', we will be so well entrenched that even the regional government will hesitate to try to evict us. And all for just the cost of building up the port facilities.'

There was silence for a few moments as the Ministers considered the audacity of the plan, then the old man opposite the Minister for Expansion and Base acquisition allowed a smile to crack his usual scowling visage, as he commenced applauding the junior member.

When all present had joined in, the Chairman waited until the room quietened, before calling for a vote. With his obvious backing of the project, there were no objections and the project was approved to continue as discussed.

# CHAPTER 5

At 17:00 on Friday afternoon, the gates of the Lodge, the Canberra home of Australia's Prime Minister, opened to allow the Prime Ministerial white BMW 760 Li, closely followed, as usual by the security detail in their BMW X5 SUV, to exit the property. Any watchers would have noted that the two-vehicle convoy sedately followed the motorway to the west, which then curved south until eventually it picked up the Monaro Highway leading to Cooma, the gateway to the Snowy Mountains wilderness area as well as the beautiful south coast region of New South Wales.

An earlier routine press release from the Prime Minister's department had briefly and blandly stated that the Prime Minister would be leaving Canberra to enjoy several weeks of rest at a remote retreat with personal friends, following a challenging period of Parliamentary sitting.

Three vehicles trailed along well behind the two BMWs, swapping position often enough to attempt to prevent the appearance of an obvious tail. Their efforts were partly thwarted when, just south of Cooma, the two BMWs turned into the long, gate-protected driveway of an isolated and very private, rural property, where it was impossible to follow. They were well satisfied, nevertheless, that their quarry was bottled-up in a position where the only access driveway could be kept under discreet surveillance.

Back in Canberra, just fifteen minutes after the official two-vehicle convoy had departed the Lodge, a nondescript, aged and rather dirty dark-blue Toyota Camry belonging to one of the kitchen staff, with just two persons aboard, also exited the gateway and turned left, but then took the first turn right off the highway, before heading deep into the quiet, leafy suburb of Deakin. There were no followers this time, as the plain sedan twisted and turned through the curving streets, before nosing into the driveway of a modest, single-story house, with tall, bare-limbed trees marking the property border.

A tall, slim woman stood waiting outside the front door, two soft bags at her feet, and an easy smile on her lovely face as she spotted the front seat passenger.

'Hello my sweet lady,' Andy Friar greeted his lady-friend, Lara Bishop, after hopping out of the car to hug her tightly and share a lingering kiss. 'Let's get you aboard and our little show on the road.'

'Lovely. I've been so looking forward to this,' Lara responded, as Andy tossed her bags in the boot and Lara slipped into the back seat.

'Hi Charlie,' she said to the female driver who wore a baseball cap pulled firmly down over her forehead.

'Hi ya, Lara,' Charlie replied, grinning, as she expertly reversed out of the driveway, retracing their path back to the main road, then headed for the airport.

'No tails Boss,' Charlie reported as she completed a somewhat circuitous route through the city centre and several small, adjacent suburbs, before heading to Fairbairn, the Royal Australian Air Force base on the eastern side of Canberra International Airport.

By prior arrangement, there was a total lack of saluting or any other form of formality as they were passed through several military checkpoints, and their car was cleared to drive up to the edge of the main tarmac where two Boeing 737s, and a much smaller Dassault Falcon 7X tri-jet, all part of the RAAF VIP fleet, were parked. Unlike the 737s, this particular Falcon bore no military markings or insignia on its glossy white paint, apart from its civil VH registration. Turning the car over to a lone uniformed female Flight Sergeant, the three collected their bags from the boot and without escort, walked toward the Falcon, with its distinctive three tail-mounted engines and downward-sloping tailplanes.

The three figures were all clad in jeans and dull-coloured parkas, zippered up against the biting south-west wind. They could have been anybody, and in a city which was primarily devoted to government business, were totally un-remarkable. The all-female Air Force crew greeted them inside the cabin, the two pilots immediately returning to the cockpit, while a Flight Sergeant stowed their bags and let them choose where to sit.

'The flight time to the Gold Coast is just one hour, sir,' the pretty Flight Sergeant informed Andy with a genuine smile, 'so can I get you any drinks?'

'Yes please. A beer for me would be great, and a chardonnay for Lara and Charlie if I'm not mistaken, thanks Flight.'

Smiles from the two ladies approved his choice.

## GOLD COAST

According to Charlie's cryptic instructions, and with 19:00 fast approaching, I wheeled our old, weather-beaten Falcon sedan into a short access road between two hangars in the General Aviation section of Gold Coast Airport, before being stopped by a substantial sliding gate. From out of the gloom on my right side, a man in a security guard uniform materialised silently by my window, scaring the crap out of me.

'Commander Stevens?' he asked politely after I'd settled my heart-rate and manually cranked down the window.

'Ah... yeah. That's me,' I confirmed, scratching around for my ACP ID card.

He carefully inspected the card and compared it to my face with the aid of a small LED torch, before handing it back.

'Thank you sir. When I open the gate, please pull forward to the edge of the tarmac, turn off your engine and lights, then wait in the car for your passengers. On departure, the gate will open automatically as you approach it. Have a good evening.'

Without further ado he stepped back, quickly fading into the soft evening gloom as the gate opened. I drove forward and parked as ordered, looking out over the quiet General Aviation tarmac in front, with the soft murmur of highway traffic and the sound of surf behind me providing a soothing background. Beyond the open area in front of the hangars, a variety of small to medium-sized private aeroplanes were parked to my right front, while to my left, a smaller row of helicopters sat, their rotor blades drooping forlornly. Directly ahead across the tarmac, was a large gap in the parking line-up.

At this early evening hour, the airport was still in full operation with arrivals and departures every ten minutes or so, although the GA area was quiet and appeared deserted. That meant the soothing surf sounds were routinely over-ridden by rather high noise levels, to the extent that I had a very fleeting moment of sympathy for local residents, although that's as long as my sympathy lasted, since the airport was in place long before any of the current crop of residents moved in to take advantage of cheaper house and land prices. That made their complaints about noise and pollution quite hypocritical. Their choice... suck it up and live with it or move out!

While philosophically mulling over the vagaries of human nature, I failed to notice an aircraft peel off the main taxiway and turn into the GA area. That was until a quartet of brilliant white taxi lights painfully stabbed my eyeballs as it turned to taxi toward the open area across from where I was parked. I briefly saw the now-familiar shape of a plain-vanilla Falcon tri-jet, and as it turned through 180° to park nose toward me, the lights were cut and the engines spun down to a muted idling whine. That is if one could be excused for calling a $54 million executive jet, plain-vanilla!

As if synchronised to the engines reducing to idle, the forward door opened and a set of airstairs did their complicated, multi-articulated unfolding trick, before a figure in Air Force blues trotted down to stand expectantly at the bottom. Three more figures followed, each carrying two small bags, although the shorter, stocky one had a briefcase as well tucked under one arm. As the trio headed my way, the Air Force person re-entered the cabin, retracted the stairs and closed the door. Moments later, the engines spooled up and the sleek jet eased out of the parking bay, heading for the taxiway.

By then, and with strong, hot gusts of the Falcon's whiffy kerosene exhaust washing strongly over us, I was greeting my dear friends, Andy Friar, the current PM of Australia, Lara Bishop, his fiancée, and Charlie Langley, Andy's PPS and the loyal, real power behind the throne.

'Great to see you again, Harry', Andy enthused, giving me a man-hug and beaming widely.

'You too Andy, and Lara and Charlie.' I scored a hug and kiss from both ladies, extra close from Charlie as usual, then slung their bags in the boot and retraced my path back to the north-bound highway. Twenty minutes later, we were unloading in the carpark of the Southport Yacht Club, the lighting sufficiently dim that Andy didn't need to disguise himself more than just wearing a base-ball cap, even given the ebb and flow of cheery, boozy, Friday-night Yacht Club patrons.

As we nosed up to *Firebird's* starboard boarding platform, Sandy was waiting ready to take the bow line and help unload. She scored hugs and kisses from all three visitors, before they reached the cockpit and they did the same with Bree and Alex, whom they'd come to know so well on our Indonesian operation as well as our encounters with the Japanese on the west coast of Tasmania. Jasper and Krazy remembered Andy and Lara, and it was Jasper who greeted them with his solemn paw shake and an affectionate nuzzling. Hovering in the background were Georgia and Beth, looking very confused and anxious.

However, I don't think they were mentally prepared to find the affable and ruggedly handsome form of Australia's Prime Minister, stepping forward to shake their hands.

'Hi Georgia, hi Beth. I'm Andy Friar. I can't wait to hear about your work with Jasper. I hope that cheeky pussy has been behaving himself.'

Georgia rallied nicely as she said, 'Pleasure to meet you too, sir, and we'll be pleased to go over our research any time you're free.'

He laughed. 'Andy, please, ladies. This is our holiday and I'll be free all the time. Well, most of it, anyway, I hope,' he added with a cheeky glance at Lara, who had the grace to blush.

Georgia and Beth still looked a bit gobsmacked, and didn't know what to else to say, until Lara pushed him good-naturedly aside.

'Don't mind him, ladies. He means well, but does take some getting used to. Sort of like a good wine, he's an acquired taste. Anyway, I'm Lara, this is Charlie and we're just here as Harry's guests for a holiday. Please ignore who he is. Charlie and I do – it helps bring him back to earth for a while.'

Beth found her voice and hesitantly said, 'Ahhh.... hi Andy, hi Lara and hi Charlie. Lovely to meet you all, although Harry seems to have a lot to answer for. Like a lapse in memory about telling us who his extra guests were going to be.'

She looked around and asked, 'But aren't you supposed to travel with a bunch of security dudes protecting you?'

Andy chuckled again, 'Sometimes, yes. But here I've got an ex-SAS Major, a Queensland Police Inspector, a giant ex-mercenary South African defence expert, Bree who is very handy with a gun, and a potentially ferocious cat with numerous kills to his credit. I think I'm quite well covered, don't you? Anyway, that's what I've told my head of Security, even though she's not totally happy with the arrangement.'

They all laughed and while I tried to look both humble and contrite, it didn't work. As I went to organise welcoming drinks, I did notice that Beth and Georgia had noted the reminder that despite his normally benign just-a-big-pussy-cat behaviour, Jasper had a very dark and unforgivingly violent side when it came to defending those he considered part of his extended family.

Sandy took Lara and showed her their cabin, the centre midships in the left hull, even though they'd stayed there once before on our way back from Tasmania to Sydney. Bree showed Charlie to her cabin, the centre midships twin-bunk in the right hull, just ahead of Sandy's and my bathroom.

Over drinks, there was a lot of catching up to do, with Andy and Lara obviously very interested in the finer details of our last operation when we rescued such a large group of mostly female young adults from a sex-slavery racket. That in-depth discussion opened Georgia and Beth's eyes wide as they sat silently soaking up every word, and I could almost hear the questions being formed as the reason for my latest limp and head crease was revealed. Finally, repeated yawns announced closing time as discussions were put on hold, and everyone split for bed.

Next morning, Alex and I were up before sunrise to ready *Firebird* for sea. The rigid-hulled, inflatable dinghy was snugged up tight under the day bed which projected aft of the cockpit between the hulls, and double lashed with webbing straps, while everything else which could come loose in a heavy sea was stowed away or tightly secured. Then while Alex quietly dropped the mooring buoy chain, I switched on the electric drive motors, and in near-total silence and gloriously calm conditions, we departed. By the time we crossed the Southport Seaway, the sun was just clearing the eastern horizon. We immediately set course to the north-east, heading across the lower portion of the Coral Sea, before passing just to the south of the broad, shallow expanse of the South Bellona Reefs, sitting in splendid isolation in the middle of open ocean. This in turn led to threading a passage through the string of atolls stretching north from the northern tip of New Caledonia.

As the hazards of South Bellona Reefs were just over two days away, and the challenge of navigating through New Caledonia's reefs the best part of a day beyond that, there was no hard stuff for us to worry about hitting for a while. Naturally, that wasn't counting the usual array of cargo ships, many of which had the unfortunate habit of belting around the world's oceans at 20+ knots on full autopilot, and because they seemed to believe that 'might is right', they seldom bothered to keep much of a lookout for smaller boats.

Having shut down the motors, I'd just raised all sails to pick up the first few puffs of the forecast south-east breeze, when Andy wandered out to the cockpit. He had a mug of tea in hand, and was yawning and scratching various parts of his anatomy in the time-honoured manner of all males, since whenever it was that our ancestors discovered it was the second-best way to start the day.

'Morning,' he greeted, before looking around the horizon. The Gold Coast was just a dark blue line on the western horizon, with the occasional wink of reflected sun from the highest of a high-rise tower window. He gave a grin and said, 'I'm guessing we're not heading for Moreton Bay or anywhere north of there?'

I flashed him a welcoming grin. 'Nope. The girls wanted to go international shopping again, and as we have a bit of business to conduct in Port Vila, Vanuatu seemed like a good destination.'

'That sounds interesting. It's been ages since I was there. Lovely people. What's the travel time?'

'About three days if the winds co-operate. We'll pass north of New Caledonia in just under three days, then it's about one more day to Port Vila. The weather should be mostly good, although there's a low starting to form south-east of Vanuatu. It's not supposed to turn into anything nasty, but we'll keep an eye on it. Otherwise, it'll be sunny, low seas and good sailing.'

'Brilliant. In that case, I might just take the wheel if you don't mind. I've missed driving this red rocket.'

I waved my hand. 'Go for it, Andy. Just note the course, then turn George off with that switch on the lower right of the panel and it's all yours.'

Moments later, with George the autopilot put to sleep, he was happily in charge, holding a course to the north-east with a big grin on his face as the breeze continued to build and our speed slowly rose toward 20 knots. Then one by one, the ladies drifted out, and someone thankfully started generating lovely cooking smells in the galley.

Georgia was immediately comfortable with Andy, chatting brightly and making him laugh, but Beth stayed stiff and faintly formal, although we figured she'd work it out sooner or later. Familiar with how our communications system worked, Charlie fired up the Internet and Sat-coms for her regular series of checks on the health of the nation, but as she didn't come out to consult our driver, Alex and I decided she had Australia's affairs well under control. As usual.

For most of our seasoned crew, life quickly settled into the at-sea cruising mode. Georgia and Beth loved the speed and easy-riding qualities of *Firebird's* hull design under these ideal conditions, and when the day warmed up, they took time out from bugging Jasper and happily joined Lara, Charlie, Sandy and Bree on the foredeck to soak up some sun and watch the water flashing past just below the trampoline netting, while Sandy made sure they all slapped on plenty of sunscreen. As usual, we were joined by pods of dolphins at various times, with Jasper and Krazy joining the girls to watch their agile friends with avid interest.

Our researchers kept hoping Jasper would do something mystical with the dolphins, but apart from mewling at them a few times, nothing developed as the sleek grey creatures kept on doing what they loved best – riding the bow pressure waves and rolling on their sides to eyeball their human friends.

I spent some time checking the weather charts to keep a close watch on the low-pressure system and saw that it was, unfortunately, showing all the signs of developing into a something, as the isobars closed into the familiar and dreaded tight circular pattern. The forecasts reflected much of what I could see, and predicted that it would continue to drop its central pressure and further tighten up the isobars, which meant the wind around the system was continuing to build. By early afternoon, it had moved to just south-west of Port Vila, and continued moving away from the island nation toward the west-south-west. If it stayed on that course, and we continued on ours, it would remain well south of us. In its early, developing stages, the low had given Port Vila a drenching rain with some strong winds, but caused no damage. Currently, the weather at the capital was clearing quickly as the growing system trundled away from our destination.

Back in the cockpit, I brought Andy and Alex up to date.

'Please excuse me having a sense of deja-vu,' Alex chuckled, 'but this is just like the last time we made this run, when we managed to stay on the north side of the low.'

I agreed, remembering the exhilarating fast sailing we had in the old *Firebird*, with a strong, quartering wind, and told Andy about the experience.

'It'd be nice if that happened again,' he said, boyish excitement in his voice, obviously relishing the thought of sailing the new boat even faster than our present speed.

I nodded, 'With the old boat it was great sailing, but even in this bigger and faster *Firebird*, I wouldn't like to get caught on the southern side of any system like that. This one seems to be deepening very quickly, so there'll be some bad winds if it does head our way.'

Alex thought a moment, then added his considered opinion.

'If we aren't in too much of a hurry, why don't we just divert further north to stay well clear? Given its rapid development, I feel a bit uneasy.'

'Your feelings are correct,' I replied, 'but there are a few other considerations. Firstly, diverting north isn't an option for now as there's a bunch of shallow reefs just north of our track, so we can't safely head that way until tomorrow morning at the earliest. Secondly, we could turn around, but if the system heads north, we might get caught ahead of it which could be unpleasant as we'd cop headwinds. There's an extensive shallow area stretching north of New Caledonia which I'd planned to duck through if the weather remained good, although even in a minor blow, that'll be the quickest way to clear the area. On the bright side, as long as the system keeps tracking roughly west, we should hardly feel any effects at all apart from a bit more breeze.'

Alex agreed with that summary for now, so with the weather-dodging issue on hold, we settled in to the far more pleasant task of watching the ladies up front, three of whom, as was customary, had already removed all their clothes.

They were a contrast in body types, with Sandy being tall, broad-shouldered, narrow-waisted and well-built – Lara was also tall, but slender with a neat, tidy body, Charlie was short and pleasantly rounded. Bree was still wearing a bikini as always, but it was small enough to be token covering only, while Georgia and Beth, although very similar in build to Sandy, remained fairly modestly covered by normal-size bikinis.

'Georgia and Beth are interesting characters,' Andy said after we'd been perving for a while with the girls obligingly shifting position to help hold his attention.

'I agree,' I jumped in quickly, 'although I'm not sure it was their character you were finding interesting just now.'

'Actually, Harry,' he chuckled, 'you're correct. But I was going to say that I wish I had professors who looked like that when I went through Uni.'

'You should have been here when we had thirty-seven of the lovely young things running around. We found that even though they all came from abusive backgrounds, once they were freed, they behaved much the same as the ladies are now. That is, they were happy to take all their gear off, even though Alex, Dave and I were strangers.'

Andy looked at me. 'That really is interesting! I would've thought that having come from abusive backgrounds and just been rescued from sex-slavery, stripping down in front of strange men would be the last thing they'd want to do.'

'Yeah, that's what we thought too. But after several days of chatting and getting to know them, Sandy worked out that once they accepted that they were free to do whatever they wanted, they were happy to keep doing what they had been all along. The difference was that now it was their choice, didn't have to follow someone else's orders, and no one was going to abuse or take advantage of them.'

Andy nodded. 'Good call. The psychologists at that retreat must be having a great time generating enough material for a couple of books. Although I do wonder how long it will be before any of them can have a proper caring and intimate relationship. If ever.'

I smiled, 'Funny you mention that. But I heard that a few of the girls at the retreat have already overcome that little hurdle and hooked up with workers they fancied.'

Andy laughed. 'That's a quaint way of putting things, Harry. Not like you at all. But I'm glad to hear that not all of them may have lasting psychological damage.'

'Amen to that, Andy.'

Around 16:00, Bree came aft and laughingly told us that the fore-deck crew had insisted they were in dire need of a bucket of Pina Colada. We had a stainless-steel wine cooler bucket, mysteriously acquired on a drunken night out somewhere, which had proved perfect for the cocktail hour. Occasionally, the call was for something different like a Margarita brew, but Pina Colada remained the staple. Before long, she was carefully heading back for'rard, the bucket of behaviour-modifying sustenance in one hand, and a sling bag of plastic mugs around her neck.

Alex offered to help, but was told that we menfolk were banned from the party as we had to keep doing important boat stuff and couldn't be trusted around naked ladies and booze. They weren't exactly the words she used, but the meaning was the same, and they became very funny to watch as the level in the bucket went down and their general pissiness level went up.

I did notice that the breeze, which had been steady out of the south-east all day, was becoming stronger and had veered about 20° further south, so when Alex suggested rolling a few turns in the big gennaker, I agreed, as the bows were starting to dig deeper into the backs of the higher waves under pressure of the huge sail. The sea state, although sneaking up a bit, wasn't really a problem as we were cutting across the backs of the waves at an angle, and any spray was blown off to leeward away from the foredeck party.

The sail area reduction eased pressure on the bows, but made little difference to our speed, so that Andy continued having a ball on the wheel, especially as the boat speed often surged well over twenty knots with the assistance of a larger wave.

As the sun dipped toward the western horizon, we were treated to a glorious display of colours, orange through to red, filtered through a filmy haze of high cirrus ice cloud. The female-only foredeck party finally decided to move aft to the cockpit and put on some clothes as the air temperature started dropping. They were in a very giggly mood, including Bree, our chief chef, so Alex and I decided to give her the night off, and told her that we'd fire-up the BBQ for the evening meal.

It was an uneventful night for the watch on deck, as I generally reduced sail at night to prevent being caught by unexpected squalls which could sneak up unseen in the gloom. The only exception to this rule was if we were trying to outrun a storm system and needed the extra speed, something we weren't doing just yet. I'd taken the first watch to midnight, and after a good sleep from then on, woke to a clear sky over a gentle ocean, although there was a long, ominous swell. If not for the swell, there would have been no hint of the weather situation which was unfolding to the south-east, since the breeze had gone back to a light southerly, as it had been for most of the night.

After the daily topside inspection of all ropes and fittings, I checked our position on the chart plotter, verified it against the two independent GPS systems, then transferred that position to the backup paper chart. The next job was to take a look at the latest weather charts and forecast.

Our indicated position was just twenty-five miles south of the South Bellona Reefs, a quartet of shallow coral hazards at the southern end of an equally shallow and infamous area comprising the South and NW Bellona Reefs, Booby Reef and Bampton Reef. This put us in the middle of a bizarre undersea landscape of sea-mounts, shoals and undersea canyons, between which the water depths plummeted to seven thousand feet and more. Passing close to a major reef system like this was perfectly safe in good conditions, but would be insanity in bad weather. Today, I was comfortable as our position was verified by three separate GPS receivers. Unfortunately, my feeling of comfort didn't last, being replaced by one of deep unease once I'd scanned the weather charts.

During the night, the minor low which had huffed and puffed around Port Vila, before tracking safely south-west away from Vanuatu, had decided it wanted to play at being a big boy. Although still small in area, it had dropped its central pressure a lot, which raised the wind speed considerably, and the system as a whole had sped up. Also, in defiance of how tropical lows are supposed to behave, rather than curving south, then east to go and annoy the Fijians yet again, it had made a sharp right turn to the west and was heading for the southern tip of New Caledonia. That also meant it was heading straight for our current position, but as I had no intentions of remaining stationary, there still wasn't any immediate problem.

Optimistically, the forecast suggested that it should revert to normal behaviour before long, and curve toward the south away from the French island and *Firebird*. In the absence of further information, I reverted to my usual action plan of, hope for the best, but plan for the worst.

Andy was back on the wheel, even in the currently light conditions, so I found Alex and we joined him for a chat. I explained the charts and forecasts, adding my misgivings about the forecast.

'So, if this thing keeps heading west, and might become a problem,' Andy asked, 'why don't we just turn around?'

I gave him a rueful look, 'Yesterday, if we'd known what we do now, that might have almost been an option, although on its present heading, it still would have ended up chasing and catching us. But now, it's movements are so unpredictable, our best chance to stay well clear of the rotten thing is to keep heading as we are to the north-east and maintain best speed. That way, we keep the best sailing wind and can clear the area in the shortest time. If it develops further and speeds up, we absolutely don't want to be directly in front of it. Small, tight cyclones like this have been known to move at 45 to 50 knots. The other problem with turning around is that we'd face head winds as the system moves west since we're on its north side. We can't run north from here because of the reefs, but in another hundred miles or so, there will be an alley of good water where we could run north, although we'd be hemmed in between the reefs to the west, and the reef areas north of New Caledonia. However, having said all that, I still reckon we're heading the right direction for the situation, so long as we continue to make good speed.'

Alex leaned over and checked the chart.

'I wouldn't be comfortable trying to head north in restricted waters in case we have a gear malfunction, so I agree with your thoughts, Harry,' he observed

I nodded and addressed Andy again. 'With a guaranteed good breeze, we can be crossing the shoal area north of New Caledonia in about ten or fifteen hours, and as we would be heading roughly in the opposite direction to the system, we'll be clear of its main influence fairly quickly.'

Alex agreed, and Andy, an experienced Sydney-Hobart race entrant, nodded understanding, his eyes gleaming with barely suppressed excitement.

Accordingly, we set the huge and lightweight Code 0 sail to make the most of the light breeze while we waited for it to build.

As we weren't changing our course, I just mentioned to the girls that there was some bad weather developing to the south, and we might cop a bit of breeze if the system strayed our way. As the local conditions were still perfect, they weren't bothered by my words and happily made breakfast, then fussed around tidying up inside before returning to the foredeck to watch the water slide past and the dolphins at play under the bows.

# CHAPTER 6

An hour later, we were unfortunately still ghosting along at six knots or less under a very light breeze which only occasionally filled the huge Code 0, when there was an excited call from the trampoline sun party.

'Harry! Come take a look. There seems to be two big sharks up ahead,' called Beth excitedly, 'we can see their fins.'

I left the cockpit and went forward to the bow, immediately spotting two tall fins, black-edged with pale grey centres, cutting slowly through the small wind ripples on the gently heaving ocean. They stayed about six metres or so apart, and managed to rise and fall in perfect synchronisation, something which was very un-shark-like behaviour. After a few moments of watching the almost hypnotic movement of the tall fins, the penny mentally dropped for me and I chuckled.

'Okay smart-arse,' said Sandy, as she and Beth stood beside me right up in the port bow, 'what are they?'

'They aren't sharks. If you look carefully, you can see there's a slight disturbance and a faint shadowing in the water between the fins?' I asked Beth.

'Yeah, now you point it out I can. What other things are causing that?'

'It's a singular, not plural. You're looking at a giant manta-ray, *Mobula birostris*. They can span more than seven metres across wing-tip to wing-tip and weigh close to one and a half tonnes. Those 'shark-fins' are just the tips of its pectoral fins or wings as it flaps slowly. Along with dolphins and whale-sharks, they are the gentlest and most human-friendly creatures in the ocean.'

At six knots, we were slowly closing up behind the giant ray, still gently flapping its huge wings and appearing utterly unconcerned by our presence, as it cruised along in search of a school of krill and other tiny sea-creatures which made up its entire diet. I hastened aft and had Andy free the gennaker and jib sheets, then hit the buttons to furl them. By the time I had returned to the fore deck, Jasper was hanging over the left bow, mewling loudly as our speed dropped to match the manta ray who was still just flapping quietly along, by now almost under the bows and nearly close enough to touch.

Luckily, Beth always kept a video camera ready in case of any note-worthy Jasper behaviour, and had taken up station on the right bow. The manta maintained position for another minute, then slowly rolled slightly on its left side to allow one huge eye to break the surface and stare up at Jasper and the crowd of chattering humans hanging over the bows peering down.

It held that position for several minutes, apparently checking everyone out, before rolling back level, then peeled off left to lazily circle the boat. I called to Andy to free the mainsail sheet so that we lost all drive and drifted to a stop. I also had him raise the dagger boards, in case the manta decided to swim directly under us.

As I quickly rummaged for snorkelling gear in a cockpit locker, Jasper, still mewling loudly, tracked the manta as it continued to slowly circle us. Just before I dropped into the water, Georgia tossed me a waterproof 4K Go-Pro camera.

'It's already recording,' she called, an excited grin on her face, 'so get what you can, please. This is brilliant!'

The water was warm, crystal-clear and dominated by the huge shadow of *Firebird* above me with the giant manta gently flapping slow circles just a couple of metres below.

When it saw me appear, it broke off the circle and angled in toward me, brushing the broad expanse of its black and grey-mottled back against the tips of my flippers, and I was again inspected very closely by one huge eye which, like a whale or dolphin, displayed an amazing depth of awareness and intelligence. As it lazily turned to come in under me again, two splashes above me revealed first Beth, then Georgia joining me. The ladies didn't have weight belts on, so remained quietly on the surface just watching.

Then, in a cloud of bubbles, a familiar black form appeared between them, as my beautiful, but sometimes really dopey black cat jumped in to join the party.

He normally only goes swimming when I do, although he often enjoys having a play in the water with a group of humans he likes. This time however, I saw a cloud of bubbles erupt from his mouth, and a really weird, strangled, watery 'merowl' sounded.

Amazingly, the manta broke off its second approach to me and headed for Jasper, so I kept the camera pointing in the right direction and followed.

The huge fish slowed and floated gently up underneath Jasper as Beth and Georgia frantically swam out of the way. As soon as Jasper's four paddling paws touched its broad back, the manta rose a little further, then slowly moved away to circle the boat again. Its back was just breaking the surface, with Jasper standing up like a performer at Sea-World, his mouth open in his version of a big cheesy grin. The manta made two slow circles of the boat before depositing Jasper back at the stern where he'd picked him up. It then performed some loops, rolls and somersaults, displaying an incredible degree of agility for such a large creature, before heading slowly off toward the south, ending what had been a most unusual and rather magical encounter.

Beth and Georgia were almost falling out of their bikini tops with excitement, acting more like young kids than seasoned researchers.

'That was stunning, Harry!' Beth exclaimed. 'I've never seen or experienced anything like that before. Oh, please, please tell me that you caught it all on camera?'

As I'd been recording the antics of both ladies in close-up since leaving the water, I grinned and passed the Go-Pro to her, still in record mode. 'All there,' I said.

Sandy stepped forward and held up the compact video camera which Georgia had used earlier.

'And I caught all the above water action with this. It looked so amazing to see Jasper being carted around on the manta's back. It was being so careful with him, too. Quite incredible. Not quite in the same league as the giant croc encounter, but I reckon it's right up near the top of the list of Jasper's weird encounters.'

After they'd rinsed themselves with fresh water, Beth and Georgia could hardly wait to make a quick review of the videos. As I rinsed and removed the salt from Jasper's thick fur, I could hear their excited comments and gathered that everything had been successfully immortalised in glorious 4K-definition and digital colour.

While they hastened to transfer the precious video to their laptops and flash drive back-ups, and Andy got us underway again, my attention re-focussed on the reality of preparing to dodge a major storm.

Our aim was still to make as much distance to the north-east as possible, which meant keeping the big Code 0 up longer than I normally would. Soon after the manta departed, the breeze finally decided to kick in properly, and steadily increased through the day.

Naturally, Andy didn't mind in the slightest and only surrendered the wheel to Alex or me when he needed a pee break, something he did over the stern to save time.

I kept a regular check on the development of the low, and by late morning, was able to tell everyone that it was now officially classified as a Category 2 cyclone and was expected to escalate to a higher number within hours. The other disturbing bit of news was that once again in defiance of what cyclones were supposed to do, the little beast had picked up speed alarmingly and was now tracking west-north-west at thirty knots. While this speed apparently set some sort of record for cyclones in the area, what really bothered me was that it was angling a lot more in our direction, and was due to make landfall on New Caledonia by midday.

I was hopeful that the impact with the island would knock the stuffing out of the storm.

As cyclones and hurricanes gain their power by the massive amount of water vapour rising off warm tropical water, conversely, they usually lose their power as soon as they cross land. Cut off from that endless supply of moisture and heat energy, normally the system quickly degenerates into a comparatively benign rain depression.

However, the high speed of advance of this unholy terror, meant that it took just one hour to blast straight across the narrow French island colony, hardly losing any power in the process. It was then back over warm water, picking up water-vapour and heat as fuel, so that like a frustrated and petulant child who has got its own way, it was delightedly winding itself up even more.

Although we were still some 250 nautical miles away from the storm centre, and tracking nearly at right-angles to its course, that distance was rapidly decreasing due to the speed of the system, so we were already feeling its effects. As the morning rolled on, the breeze picked up further and veered more into the south-west, which was a great help, as it meant we were running with the wind coming over our right rear quarter and the increasing swell and wind waves were also from that direction. It made for exhilarating sailing, although we had to reduce the area of the heavier and smaller gennaker a few times to stop the bows burying too much. It was the sail which had replaced the light Code Zero which was only suitable for light winds. The other good thing was that boat speed remained consistently in the high twenty knot range, and drew a whoop of excitement from Andy each time the speed read-out briefly flickered past 30 knots as we surfed down the gentle face of one of the larger swells.

As the afternoon faded rather noisily into evening, the wind was blowing harder, the swell waves were higher, and all hatches and portholes were fastened tightly shut. The sun had long since disappeared, hiding behind the banks of thick, dark clouds which rolled over us. In turn, they slowly lowered and peppered the decks with squalls of huge, fat raindrops and occasional small hail. By now, the gennaker was tightly furled and a safety sleeve had been pulled up its length to prevent an unscheduled deployment.

I normally would have lowered the whole rolled-up sausage of the sail to reduce windage, but as we were going to have the wind mostly behind us, I judged that leaving it tightly furled and sleeved wasn't going to cause a problem.

The mainsail was also down to 30% of its area, yet boat speed was still in the mid-twenties, mainly due to surfing. Normally the prudent action would be to stop and either lie nearly stationary to the parachute sea-anchor, or continue running slowly before wind and waves, with the long and hard-to-retrieve Jordan drogue train deployed on a bridle over the sterns. However, I still believed that our safest action was to maintain speed so as to get past the shoal area ahead as quickly as possible and thereby put the bulk of New Caledonia between ourselves and the cyclone, should it decide to continue to behave unpredictably.

Therefore, slowing or stopping was off the agenda, so it was a case of securing all loose objects, finally reducing sail to just the inner stay-sail, before threading the needle of the reef-free gap.

Once we had passed through this potential danger zone, we had just one atoll to by-pass before it was a clear run to Port Vila. It would also mean we'd be well out of the cyclone's path. As the pass was only 35 nautical miles across, we could cross it in about ninety minutes at our present speed.

The shoal crossing turned out to be a fairly wild ride as the relatively shallow water increased the wave height to the extent that we took several breaking white tops over our sterns. What is it about storms at sea at night? No matter how many I've been through, they always seem much worse at night. Perhaps it's not being able to see, but the wind automatically sounds louder, takes on a more menacing tone and the waves seem to double their height the moment twilight fades from the western sky. There's also the pulse-racing experience when a breaking wave-top suddenly leaps up out of the gloom astern, to smother the transoms in tonnes of foaming water which fills the cockpit so the boat drags its bum until the drains do their job. The darkness also makes the bass droning of the hollow carbon mast take on an especially mournful tone which has the uncanny ability to turn the most hopeful thoughts to those of impending disaster. These bass tones were the mad orchestral counter-point to the high-pitched shrieking of the wind in the carbon-fibre rigging.

Under such conditions, I have trouble sitting still and tend to prowl about the boat checking for any early signs of a problem, and it was on one such pass through the saloon that I found Beth scrunched up into a shivering ball on the lounge. I popped down beside her and spoke with my lips almost touching her ear. I wasn't trying to be amorous – she simply wouldn't hear me otherwise.

'Are you frightened?'

She nodded vigorously, not lifting her head from her knees, so I wrapped my arm around her and gave her a tight squeeze.

'It's okay to be scared when scary things are happening. That's normal. The important thing is that you're up here facing the scary stuff, rather than hiding in a locker down below. That takes guts.'

She slowly turned her head to look at me, her eyes looking wet and wild in the dim red night-lighting.

'But everything is so incredibly violent and noisy,' she whimpered, 'just a few hours ago, we were sailing quite peacefully – now all hell seems to have broken loose!'

I chuckled and squeezed her again, quite liking the feel of her firm, toned body.

'It always seems worse at night,' I offered, 'but the reality is that the waves actually aren't very big at all and the wind is only up at gale-force levels. We had much worse than this for days on end during our delivery trip from South Africa, when we went to visit Heard Island.

That seemed to divert her attention from the screaming demons outside and her own internal ones. 'Isn't Heard Island down near Antarctica? What on earth were you doing down there?'

'Well... it's a long story, but when we took delivery of this boat from the builders in South Africa, we had to get it to Australia, and sailing it home was the best and most fun option. The constant west winds are in the higher latitudes, so while we were down there, I thought it might be a great opportunity to see Australia's most southern possession, so we went a little further south – actually, a lot further south. It was very rough, very windy and freezing cold, but the scenery was fantastic, plus just being there at all was amazing. We got caught up in some man-made problems while we were there, but that's another story and is all over now. It's a fascinating part of the world which very few people get to see, so I'm glad we did.'

I was glad to see the haunted look had receded from her eyes as she focused on me and mulled over my brief story. Recovery was helped along by Jasper jumping up on the lounge beside her and plonking his head in her lap looking for a scratch or three.

We awkwardly chatted as best we could for another few minutes, before I gently withdrew my arm and prepared to stand to resume my wandering inspection of things. Before I did, Beth reached out and hugged me, planting a long, soft kiss on my lips, making me ponder on the vagaries of female mind sets. Not that I was complaining about this latest change of heart.

'Thanks, Harry. I'll be alright now with Jasper for company.'

Around forty minutes later, it seemed like the waves suddenly settled down a lot and a quick look at the water-depth sounder on the chart table instrument cluster showed the depth plummeting. In a matter of seconds, it had gone from tens of feet to many thousands of feet, a slightly disturbing thought if one was cursed with an over-active imagination. I joined Alex in the cockpit, and he confirmed the wave height and wind strength had diminished considerably. As our direct track from this crossing point to Port Vila would take us straight through another atoll, I'd already worked out a minor course deviation which would see us bypass the treacherous shoals.

It was therefore without further drama, at 07:00 on the humid, overcast morning of the fourth day after leaving the Gold Coast, that I made VHF radio contact with the always jovial Port Vila harbourmaster who directed us to a mooring reasonably close to shore and asked that I bring the boat's documentation and crew passports ashore to be processed. With that done, we were free to do as we wanted. Andy was aware that we had private business to attend to, and tactfully suggested that he, Lara, Charlie, Georgia and Beth would go wander the town while we took care of that little task.

To maintain some sense of decorum, I ferried them ashore first, then we loaded the dinghy with two large suitcases filled with cash, comprising the seized proceeds from our last operation when we busted up a sex-slavery ring.

With Jasper and little Krazy left behind to guard the boat, our dinghy was riding low in the water as Sandy, Bree, Alex and I quietly puttered ashore to a hotel jetty where we paid a small fee to tie up and safely leave the dinghy. The bank was super helpful as usual, and supplied a discrete van and escort to collect us and our heavy cargo. It's surprising how much $7M worth of pretty printed plastic weighs!

The counting process was very efficient, secure and relatively fast. As usual, the ladies feeding the note-counting machines were securely locked in a well-guarded room, although we were able to observe the process through bullet-proof glass. Our business manager, Bree, had all the details printed out for the disposition of the funds, and with the final total on a slip of paper, a polite and efficient manager rapidly followed her instructions. Within two hours, we were back on the street, our general account reimbursed after paying a small fortune for the rehabilitation costs of the bunch of rescued young adults we'd placed in an abandoned resort complex in the bush behind the Gold Coast. Said resort was now under the discrete and very indirect control of the Australian government.

Along with feeling more comfortable having the money off the boat, there was the good feeling of having completed a worthy task by saving so many lost souls from their dreadful fate at the hands of many truly evil, perverted men and women. It was in this happy mood that we joined our guests at a pub in the main street where an open-sided beer garden fronted the narrow main street. We joined in with a mixed bunch of happy, semi-pissed locals and visitors who were drinking wine and beer and scoffing down luscious-looking hamburgers.

When in Rome and all that crap – so we did the same.

Finally, with full bellies and a rosy glow in everyone's cheeks, Andy burped in a very un-Prime Ministerish manner and asked, 'What's the go now, Harry?'

I grinned at Sandy, 'If I'm correct, having just looked around town, the ladies want to go hit the markets along the shore-side park for some clothes shopping. If we're smart, we three males might just stay here and make sure the beer doesn't go off.'

Sandy bestowed an indulgent smile on me and gathered up the other ladies. 'We'll see you at the jetty in one hour,' she declared firmly. 'A no-show means no nookie for you tonight, boy-o!'

'Ouch!' I exclaimed indignantly. 'That's a bit rough!'

'Take it or leave it,' she fired back. 'Besides, any longer than that and you three won't even be able to find the jetty, let alone something infinitely smaller!'

With a grin hovering on her lips, she wheeled away, so we did the right thing and ordered another round of the very excellent local on-tap beer.

With the threat of sexual deprivation hopefully averted, we needed to make two dinghy trips to get everyone back aboard without too many problems. Sandy, of course, refused to allow any males near the outboard controls, stating that we were 'incapable of straight speech, let alone straight steering.' We suffered that insult in silence, as the gleam in Andy's eye meant that as soon as we were dropped off and she returned for the ladies, Andy made a beeline for the cockpit booze box and cracked open three long-necks so we could toast the ladies when they were safely deposited on the stern platform, numerous shopping bags in hand. The pussies were very happy to see everyone back, so I suggested that since the cats needed to get off the boat for a forbidden run ashore, we should spend the rest of the hot and humid afternoon cooling off in the gin-clear water. There was an isolated sandy beach just inside the northern arm of the harbour which we'd visited on previous trips and was perfect for illicit pussy exercise and crew booze-ups.

I had vague memories of becoming rather pissed over there on at least one previous occasion.

Strangely, the ladies all thought that to be a splendid idea and once they'd changed into bikinis, we made the few hundred metres transfer to our new favourite beach. Under the quarantine laws, I wasn't supposed to let the cats off the boat, but the little beach we aimed for was suitably remote from the rest of the town for them not to be a problem, and they loved to play and run in the soft sand. To Georgia's amusement and professional interest, I told Jasper to stay close and not run off too far, which he did and made sure Krazy didn't wander into the nearby jungle. Alex had thoughtfully packed an esky with a good supply of beer, wine and vodka coolers, a drink to which our two professors seemed to have become very partial.

So much so, that after chugging down several each, they became quite pissy. Andy, Alex and I were lying back in the warm, shallow water, sucking on long-necks, when Beth, who had somehow misplaced her bikini top and looked much better for the omission, splashed up, dropped to her knees between us, hiccupped, burped and announced, 'You're not such a bad sort of bloke sometimes, Harry Stevens. I thought you were a promptious... ah, pranpious, ah fuck it... stuck-up prick, when we first met, but I quite fancy you now. What'd you think about that, baby-cakes?'

I blinked in surprise and before my befuddled brain could think of a good comeback, she swung her attention to Andy.

'And for a PM, you're a pretty good sort too, Mr Prior. I never did see one up close before, but I reckon you're okay. Bugger what anybody else thinks!'

With that she planted a sloppy kiss fair on Andy's lips, before losing her balance and flopping back across my lap.

'Oops! Someone just beached the shift! Or maybe I'm just a little bit pissed. 'Scuse me. I'll just have to perch here for a few minutes or I'll fall on my arse again.'

She clumsily swung one leg across so she was straddling my lap, nearly clipping my chin on the way.

'Oops again. Sorry about that. I tink... think I'm a bit discon... ahh, fuck-it again, something-ated, but this feels better.' Having her lovely firm boobs jiggling in my face, as well as where she was squatting, caused the expected reaction my body usually has to a semi-naked female, and I saw out of the corner of my eye that both Sandy and Lara had seen her antics and were having a major, uncontrollable fit of the giggles. Aware that my lovely lady occasionally fancied fooling around with a girl for a change, I knew she wasn't going to be offended by Beth's drunken antics.

Andy and Alex were also trying unsuccessfully to stifle a laugh as I tried to shift position to ease the growth in my shorts.

Beth finally seemed to feel what was growing rapidly beneath her, and looking down exclaimed with remarkable clarity, 'Goodness me, Harry. Do you always keep a spare bottle of beer in your shorts, or are you just glad to feel me?'

'Well, Beth. I suppose it could be a bottle of beer, but in this case, I'm happy to say I'm very glad to feel you.'

'Aren't you nice,' she replied seriously, while unconsciously shifting about in a very disturbing manner, 'and I am too, I have to admit, but as pleasant as it is, I probably shouldn't carry on like this. Sandy might get upset.'

As usual, not thinking before I put my mouth into gear, I blurted out, 'Oh, she definitely won't mind. Probably the opposite.'

I was immediately aware that I'd stepped in it again, when Beth gave a contented little smile, murmured, 'Oh, goody,' then with a final disturbing wriggle, lurched clumsily to her feet and splashed away to where Georgia promptly pulled her down onto the beach before she toppled over again.

Andy was still chuckling at my discomfort. 'What the hell's going on with her? Isn't that the girl who hates you?'

'Yeah, that's the one,' I growled at him, 'although I'm buggered if I know what's got into her. Probably too many vodkas.'

He gave a wry grin, 'I reckon it's more a case of what hasn't got into her. You'd better watch that one, mate and good luck with it. I never could figure them out either and reckon it's safest not to even try!'


It wasn't long after that little interlude, that Sandy started rounding everyone up for the return to the boat. Walking up to Andy and me, she asked sweetly, 'Will you be okay to stand up, my darling, or shall I fetch a cold spoon?'

That set Andy off again, so I stood and proved that I was half-way decent again.

'Good boy,' she purred, 'nicely done.'

I wasn't sure what she meant by that, so I rounded up the kitties, brushed most of the sand out of Krazy's fur which was thankfully dry, then washed the sand out of Jasper's who was wet anyway. They'd had a lovely time romping on the sandy beach and playing with the whole crew.

However, between the sun, heat, humidity and booze, we were all rather wrecked, so it was a quiet and early night for everyone. I half-expected Beth to follow-up on her drunken revelations on the beach with something interesting, but she and Georgia retired early as well and stayed there until morning.

The next day, Beth made little reference to her behaviour the previous afternoon, but she certainly was far more friendly toward me than she had been. I did notice she and Sandy having several amicable chats, so as usual, I guessed I'd eventually find out what was being cooked up.

That night as Sandy and I climbed into bed, I got in early by asking her what was the go with Beth.

'I've got to say that it's all a bit confusing to a simple male like me. Up until yesterday, she either hated me with a passion, or at best has been barely civil. Then she gets pissed, kisses Andy, says she fancies me, and squats on my crotch for a while. You saw what that did to me!'

Sandy giggled, which made her lovely bare boobs jiggle just like Beth's had yesterday. It had the same effect and was equally distracting.

'Well,' she replied carefully, 'today we had a few chats and it seems she's had a very unusual upbringing. Her parents were high-level academics and were very driven to succeed in their respective fields of law and medicine. Therefore, Beth, who's an only child, was left alone a great deal and pushed hard to study, instead of going out and socialising.'

Without really thinking before putting my mouth into gear, I let the intolerant side of my psyche out for a bit of a run. 'Oh, no. Don't tell me that she's got this giant chip on her shoulder because she's had an emotionally deprived childhood by being denied parental love and affection? That's such a cliché! Don't forget we just saved a bunch of genuinely deprived and abused kids from a very nasty fate. They were far worse off than Miss Socially Deprived, and once rescued, seemed to rally very well without any lingering neurosis. I find it hard to equate Beth's privileged upbringing with that of those unfortunate kids.'

Patiently, Sandy drew a deep breath, waited to make sure I'd noticed the effect it had on her chest, then patted my leg.

'Settle down, precious. Just because her parents were wealthy, doesn't mean Beth had an easy or even remotely normal childhood. In their own way, her parents were almost as abusive as those of some of our rescued kids. In her case, because of the pressure to study so much, she hasn't really learned how to relate to others in a social atmosphere. Amongst her peers in academia, she's up there with the best of them, but when it comes to personal interactions, she's a child.'

'I hope she doesn't claim to be a virgin or that she was raped by her uncle when she was 14, and has never gotten over it?'

'No. None of the above. But she is socially inept, and has had very little sexual experience, and what she has had was set-up with someone who was equally nerdy and socially dysfunctional, so the encounter was very mechanical and contrived, with zero emotion involved. She said that afterwards, she failed to see what all the fuss was about.'

I admit that I struggled to understand her peculiar situation, and the look on my face must have said so.

'I know it's hard to understand, but that's the way it is. The reality is that when she first met you, she was actually quite smitten, but didn't have a clue how to show her feelings. Therefore, as a fallback, all she could think to talk about was her work. And being so focused on getting what she wanted, and not knowing how or when to listen, all she achieved was to stir you up. Once the battle lines were drawn, she couldn't work out how to find a way out of the hole she kept digging deeper every time she opened her mouth.

So relations with you naturally went downhill from there. She was far more frustrated and upset with herself than with you, but didn't know how to resolve that either.'

I still felt puzzled and kept trying to get my head around her attitude. 'But on this trip, after that first day, she's been a lot better. Not naturally happy-friendly like Georgia, but at least pleasant to talk to about her work.'

'Georgia has helped her as much as she can, but that's the whole point! Beth is permanently stuck in her work persona and doesn't know how to step out of it since she hasn't created a social persona yet. She can't relax and interact with others in a purely social mode, because she's never done it. Georgia said she's always like this at Uni. Totally work-focused and comes across as cold to everyone. She's called the 'Virgin Ice Queen' because nobody has ever seen her with a boy or girlfriend, or even to go on a date.'

'So, what's changed?' I asked, still trying to work out how people with weird social problems think.

'It seems that it took this odd combination of circumstances – the boat, Vanuatu, the manta-ray, meeting Andy, plus several vodka coolers, to make her drop her guard. She was as surprised as we were by the result, since she never drinks alcohol back home, but she did admit that she enjoyed the afternoon.'

I held up my hands in surrender. 'Okay. I accept all you've said, even though I can't really work it out, but where does it go from here?'

Sandy gave me one of her lovely smiles. 'Just leave it to me, dearest. Sometime in the next day or two, I might have some special girl-to-girl time with her to see if we can lower that guard some more. You don't have to be involved if you don't want to, but I'd like you to at least be pleasant and supportive of whatever happens.'

As usual when one of Sandy's schemes in being put into play, I'm never sure what my role is supposed to be, but that was enough arcane female psychology for one evening, so I turned the light out and showed my lovely, sexy lady how pleasant and supportive

I really could be when I put my mind to it. An hour later, she indicated that I'd achieved that goal very nicely.

With no further business to conduct, we stayed in Port Vila for just two more days, relaxing and playing at being casual tourists, including another visit to our little beach.

Back on the boat that afternoon, Andy asked about our plans.

I shrugged, 'Head for home tomorrow, I guess, unless you had something else in mind you'd like to do?'

'Yeah, there is actually, if you don't mind. You know I like diving?'

I nodded, remembering how keen he had been during our Indonesian adventure to leap overboard strapped to a tank of compressed essential life-support. 'We're certainly in the right place for that,' I commented enthusiastically. 'Vanuatu is world-renowned for water clarity, its coral reefs and wrecks.'

'Yeah, I know that. But where I'd really like to dive is someplace that few, if any others have been before. If that makes sense?'

I nodded again. 'Yeah. I can understand what you mean. My mate up north on Bokissa Island has some of the best diving in the world literally at his doorstep, including a famous wreck, but it's very busy since lots of divers from all over the world go there. Did you have any place in mind?'

'I was thinking maybe one of those atolls which seem to be dotted around the place might be just the shot. If we can find one that's safe to get into and isn't inhabited.'

I thought a few moments, then pulled out a chart. 'That narrows the choice down a lot. There's the Bellona Reefs west of the north tip of New Caledonia, which we passed on the way out, but they're mostly just shallow, open reefs with no dry land at all, so if strong winds brewed up, there are no decent anchorages. The atolls north of New Caledonia would be better as there are at least some specks of dry land, but they're controlled by the French and I've heard they don't like casual visitors. Apparently it can take months to get a permit.'

I ran my finger further north up the chart, then said, 'Here's a possibility. It's a bit further away, but how about these atolls west of Rennell Island which is south-west of the Solomon Islands? The atolls are nearly fully enclosed by shallow barrier reefs and have what looks like reasonably deep passes allowing access inside. This northern-most one, imaginatively called North Reef, looks interesting. There are passes on both the north-west and north-east sides.'

Andy peered where I was pointing, then shrugged. 'Looks good to me if that's okay with you. How long will it take to get there?'

I spread the dividers between here and there, laid the points along the vertical latitude markings. 'It's about 580 nautical miles, so we could be there in two or three days depending on the winds, so it's somewhere different to go. I rather like investigating new, uninhabited places.'

He gave me a big grin. 'That'll be great, thanks Harry. I really appreciate it.'

'No problem, Andy. It'll be fun and I'm sure the girls won't mind so long as they have plenty of Pina Colada mix available.'

I announced the new plan to the crew, who were also keen to see somewhere new. Since we didn't know how long we'd be hunting for a decent dive-site, Bree wanted to go ashore to stock up on some more food and booze, and I needed to let the harbourmaster know about our departure next morning.

While Andy and I took care of business, Bree, Alex and Sandy went shopping. As if by magic, Sandy found us an hour later in our favourite pub on the esplanade. They'd already ferried the groceries out to the boat and it only remained for her to prise Andy and me away from the pub, the live music and its usual happy collection of pissed patrons.

'I can't leave you two alone for a moment,' Sandy grumped good-naturedly as we headed across the road to the hotel jetty.

'Just being convivial, my dear lady,' I breezed. 'Besides, we only had two beers. It is sailing day after all.'

'Convivial, my arse,' she laughed as we climbed aboard.

'Well, yes now you mention it, it is rather a nice arse,' I said, as I patted her left cheek. 'Don't you think so, Andy?'

'Absolutely, my friend,' he observed, bending down to peer closely at Sandy's close-fitting shorts, 'I couldn't agree more.'

Sandy giggled, 'Actually, Andy, I reckon you've definitely had more than two beers, since that's not actually my bum you're inspecting so closely. It's around behind me, but never mind. You've seen it all before and no doubt will see it again. What's got into you two? I'd better warn Lara.'

Back aboard, I found that Alex had begun making ready for our departure, and as the breeze was light, we motored away from our mooring while the ladies were still stowing supplies under Bree's supervision. Once clear of the harbour mouth, we hoisted all sails in the gentle easterly breeze, and at a sedate six to seven knots, accompanied by a soft gurgling of water from the sterns, we laid course to the north-north-west, direct for North Reef atoll.

Sandy and Lara were topping up the large cockpit booze cooler, which I'd converted from a huge plastic, insulated icebox by attaching an electric compressor to one end and fitting coils of copper cooling tubing to the inside. As they stacked the beer, wine and vodka coolers, I heard Sandy say quietly to Lara, 'You'd better watch out for Andy today. He and Harry were acting very amorous after their trip ashore. Must be something in the beer.'

Lara laughed delightedly, 'Oh, that's excellent. Andy's still very tense and hasn't properly relaxed yet, so maybe now he's starting to. I'm really glad Charlie hasn't had to bother him with any official crap so far.'

It was one of those days where the breeze stayed light and for once, the normally crushing tropical humidity had blown away, allowing the breeze to keep everyone cool. The whole crew seemed to be in a light-hearted, almost excited mood, about leaving civilisation for a while and heading for a remote atoll in an uninhabited area.

While we idled comfortably along, and the rest of the supplies were being stowed, Beth and Georgia took the opportunity to set up a test for Jasper which they'd spent some time devising. Georgia was careful to explain to me what they wanted to do.

'It might seem like a very basic test, compared to the things you've told me Jasper has already done, but in terms of human/animal interaction, it's quite complex as it introduces a number of diverse elements. As far as we know, no animal has ever managed to pass this type of test with a score of more than 50%. Naturally, we need to document and record all the details and remove any factors which might be seen to skew the results. Therefore, we'd like no one else to speak or gesture to Jasper while the test is running, please Harry.'

We solemnly agreed and the whole crew gathered in the cockpit to watch and be out of the way. Georgia asked me to get Jasper to sit in the cockpit facing astern so he couldn't see what she was doing in the saloon.

She went inside and on the lounge, laid out three clean, folded face washers, a folded white T-shirt, a pair of thongs, two pair of jeans and a rolled-up leather belt. The face washers were the same size, but were coloured red, yellow and dark blue. One pair of jeans was blue, the other black, while the belt was black. She placed a similar belt, brown in colour, on the chart table over the other side of the saloon, with one end hanging over the edge.

Beth had the video camera with an oversized microphone stuck on top, and videoed the setup first, before Georgia came out to the cockpit, squatted down in front of Jasper, and asked him in a clear, calm voice, 'Can you bring me the red face washer from the lounge in the saloon, please Jasper?'

My lovely big cat looked at her, then looked at me, as if asking if this was okay.

Mindful of Georgia's request to avoid any possible assistance or bias, I just nodded to him.

He looked back at Georgia, huffed quietly, then padded into the saloon, where he selected the red cloth without hesitation, returned to the cockpit and carefully laid it at her feet, before sitting back in anticipation.

'Thank you Jasper,' she said politely, even though I could see that both girls were starting to fizz with excitement. 'Could you bring out the black jeans from the same place, please?'

He didn't bother asking me this time, just huffed again, went inside again, and gathered the black jeans in his mouth, before returning and laying them at Georgia's feet beside the red cloth.

'Thank you Jasper,' she said again, and scratched the top of his head.

'And finally, would you bring out the brown belt, please Jasper?'

My big, black cat patiently huffed again, went inside and looked on the lounge. He ignored the black belt, looked around the saloon, then spotted the brown belt on the chart table. He then returned with the brown belt, its buckle clinking as it dragged on the deck and placed it on the jeans.

Before she stopped recording, Beth panned around to show that no one was in the saloon who could give signals, and the audio track proved that no other commands or prompts had been given.

They just stood and grinned madly at each other and Jasper for a few moments, until I asked politely, 'Was everything okay?'

Still grinning wildly, Georgia drew a deep breath, 'Oh, Harry. That was more than just okay. That was mind-blowing. Like, it'll be the pivotal piece of my dissertation. No one has been ever able to prove beyond doubt, that an animal can understand complex human speech by carrying out a series of tasks requiring an understanding of colours and what the different objects were. And especially since Jasper has had no specific training in any of this. I'm a virtual stranger making the request, and the test provided a choice of articles, colours and locations to choose from. He didn't even hesitate. He knew what the colours were, what a face washer was, and what jeans were. The bit with the belt was the real kicker though. He knew the black one wasn't the correct one and looked around for the brown one. That showed a depth of reasoning and deduction that has never been demonstrated before. I can't say absolutely that Jasper is unique in having this ability, but we've not seen or heard of anyone who has been able to show that an animal can convert a complex, spoken request into such accurate, selective action. Absolutely fuckin' incredible!'

'Yeah, Harry. That was amazing,' offered Beth. 'Almost better than us seeing his interaction with the manta-ray.'

A sudden random, out-of-left-field thought struck me, sending a chill through my whole body. *'What if someone lets on about the remarkable healing properties of Jasper's saliva? Beth would be desperate to take saliva and blood samples and perform biopsies.'*

Therefore, I sidled up to Sandy and quietly asked her to spread the word amongst those who already knew, that they must keep quiet about Jasper's extra little talent.

After an early lunch of Bree's gourmet sandwiches, Sandy, Lara, Charlie and Bree went to the foredeck armed with towels and sunblock lotions, although Beth and Georgia remained absorbed with their video and writing up notes of the morning's test for a while.

Finally, they also left their notepads and video, and joined the foredeck party. With the weather forecast calling for calm seas and skies for at least a few days, we three guys relaxed as well and enjoyed the sight of our six lovely ladies decorating the foredeck in various stages of undress. Sandy, Lara and Charlie were naked as usual, Bree kept all her bikini on, as was her habit, while Beth and Georgia took their tops off.

Andy, Alex and I had a great time comparing the attributes of each, finally concluding that there were no winners — they were all lovely.

A while later, some dolphins appeared and stirred the female crew into action, but once again, none stayed to chat to Jasper, so the ladies soon resumed their places. Lara came aft after a while, murmuring something about wanting to pee, so Andy excused himself off the wheel and followed her below, murmuring something about, 'what a good idea', except they were gone for a good twenty minutes or so before re-appearing. Lara was grinning and looked a bit flushed as she made her way forward again, while Andy just looked... contented. After she re-joined the group, the sound of giggling drifted aft from the girls and soon Bree was sent to make a bucket of cocktail brew. I helped carry the bucket and mugs for her and appreciated a closer inspection of the array of delightful female flesh spread around. Naturally, I copped a round of rude remarks, but all in good fun. I did note that Charlie, who had always been a nicely-rounded lady, had lost some weight, but was still very pleasantly curvy. Beth and Georgia had a similar build and proportions and were quite like Sandy, while Lara was long and lanky and Bree was shorter and had smaller boobs.

After this comparison scrutiny of our lovely ladies, and before my body had time to misbehave too much, I beat a hasty retreat back to the cockpit, but not before I enquired of Sandy, 'Anything I can get for you, my darling?'

'No, thanks,' she replied, 'nothing I need for the moment, anyway.'

I beat a hasty retreat with their laughter ringing in my ears.

# CHAPTER 8

The beautiful day ended as it had started, with everybody happy, although as the girls were a bit wobbly again, Andy and I cooked a mixed grill on the cockpit BBQ. After the girls cleaned up after dinner, I made a batch of NQ teas, and for those who hadn't had the pleasure, I explained it was just black tea seasoned with a very healthy dollop of dark rum liqueur. Beth and Georgia took to them like a fish to water, and I had to caution them about the delayed after-effect. Alex and Bree retired early as Alex had the midnight watch along with Charlie. I let George the autopilot take care of the steering, while we all sat around the cockpit table discussing where we'd been and where we were going.

I became engrossed in a discussion with a rather pissy Georgia about her work, and failed to notice Sandy and Beth slip away. Georgia had volunteered to sit up on watch with me, so we continued our discussion as one by two, the others drifted off to bed.

Georgia finally looked around, surprised to find we were alone. 'Where'd they all go?'

'To bed, I guess, leaving just thee and me in charge on the sea.'

She looked around at the placid seascape, barely ruffled by the light breeze which had hardly changed all day, a rare event in the tropics. I'd furled the huge Code 0 at dusk, just in case of sneaky nocturnal squalls, but that was highly unlikely under these conditions.

'I know I'm supposed to be on watch with you, but I need a pee rather badly. Will you be alright by yourself for a few minutes?'

I looked around and chuckled, 'Yep. No problem. Go for it.'

'Thanks.'

She scampered below, returning in just a few minutes.

'That feels much better. Those NQ teas are rather potent.'

I grinned, 'I did warn you.'

'Yes, you did. Oh, I almost forgot. Beth isn't in our cabin, or the saloon and I can't see her on deck. Did you see where she went?'

Sandy's words of the other day suddenly flashed through my head and I had a little grin to myself.

'I'm just guessing that if you went to the right-side aft companionway in the saloon, went quietly down the steps and slid the curtain aside, your question might be answered.'

The moonlight showed a puzzled frown on her pretty face, as she went and did what I said, but she wore a different expression when she came back.

'She's in bed with Sandy!' was her slightly shocked statement.

I nodded. 'Yep. I thought she might be. Sandy's very good at applying healing therapy to tormented souls. You could say she has the right touch, if you'll excuse the play on words.'

That one went through to the keeper, as Georgia looked puzzled, her mind churning to process unaccustomed data. 'I wouldn't have said Beth was tormented or anything like that. Where did that one come from?'

'After the swim party on the beach at Port Vila when she started acting rather... amorous, she confided in Sandy about her early, very sheltered life devoid of social interaction.'

'Oh, wow! She really did open up. But shouldn't you be upset, annoyed or something?'

I chuckled, 'No. Why should I be?'

'Because Sandy's your fiancée, and you sleep with her. Doesn't it bother you that Beth's down there with her? I mean, it's very obvious what they've been doing, and probably still are, for that matter. I didn't stay long enough to see. They're pretty much wrapped around each other.'

I smiled at her. 'Sandy told me Beth also revealed that she had a very conflicted upbringing and still has serious problems relating socially to others. I'm sure you would've seen that.'

Georgia nodded, 'Yeah, I have. She's never talked about her past, and because I didn't want to push, I never really knew what the problem was. It didn't seem to affect her work in any way, so I didn't worry about it. How did Sandy manage to find out all this secret stuff?'

'Sandy is very good at finding out what people really think, feel and want, and even better at helping them resolve their mental conflicts. Along the way, she occasionally takes a fancy to a kindred female soul, so if the attraction is mutual, some of that conflict resolution takes place in bed. Perhaps it's my background and I'm just weird anyway, but I found it makes her far more appealing, not less and I trust Sandy completely. Therefore, I'm happy to go along with whatever she's comfortable with. In this case, it would seem that she and Beth are getting along very well, since Beth is still there. But the real question is, do you have a problem with what you've just learned about Beth, Sandy and myself?'

She sat in silence for a few minutes, a thoughtful look showing in the pale moonlight. 'I guess I'd never really thought about alternate sexual relationships before. I've always been busy with my career, and haven't had time to get too deep into the social scene. I'm probably not much different to Beth in that regard. I mean, I really enjoy sex with the right guy in the right environment, and I've had a couple of boyfriends over the years, but they were only ever a casual thing and nothing serious. I've never wanted to join the one-night-stand circuit, so my answer is no, I guess I don't really have a problem with it. What Beth does with her private life is her own concern. Even though we're close friends, as well as work colleagues, I've become used to her not having a social life.'

She paused to giggle. 'I must admit that it's a bit mind-bending to see my friend, the virgin ice queen, getting close and very personal with you and Andy on the beach, then going to bed with your fiancée.'

I laughed at her summation, and was pleased that she seemed more comfortable with Beth's situation, although a small frown creased her forehead again.

'Sorry to keep banging on about this, but don't you feel your relationship is threatened when Sandy fancies a female? Like, what's going to happen when we get relieved in an hour's time? Do you get to sleep on the saloon couch for the rest of the night?'

I laughed, my mind running briefly over the few previous occasions when this had happened. 'Hell, no. I don't feel threatened, because I love Sandy and she loves me, for some reason. Neither of us get jealous if we show affection for someone else, or vice-versa. Tonight, when we get relieved, I'll just go below and get into bed. If Beth is still there it doesn't matter, ... there's plenty of room, so I'll go to sleep. This has happened occasionally before and we all found it a lot of fun because no one took it seriously. I can guarantee you that only those with the right attitude ever get invited in the first place.'

Georgia looked a bit stunned by that revelation. 'So, Sandy doesn't get upset if another woman shows interest in you?'

'No. She didn't the other day when Beth started all this by squatting on my lap and wriggling around which really diverted my blood supply! Sandy and Lara watched it all happen and thought it was hilarious.'

'Oh.' She thought some more, and I blamed the NQ teas for this heavy dose of feminine introspection.

'Well, for example, what would she do if she came out now and found us kissing and cuddling?'

I chuckled again. 'Probably laugh and tell us to go find a room!'

'Really?'

'Yep. Guaranteed.'

'And what if we did go below together?'

'Apart from her going back to bed, nothing would happen from her side, that's for sure. I know that I wouldn't behave like the gentleman I was once supposed to be. You're a very lovely and sexy lady.'

'Hmmm. Thank you. But I was being serious. This is an aspect of relationships which I've not considered before.'

I smiled gently. 'That's fine. But I was being just as serious. You must have noticed by now what's already been happening on this boat. When mature, open-minded people relax properly in a safe, isolated environment, relaxed moral standards tend to follow on from there. As an excellent example, before you came on this trip, how often have you sat with a group of other females who were very recent acquaintances, some of them naked, with your own top off, being perved on by three males you also hardly know. One of whom, I should add, is the Prime Minister of Australia.'

She looked totally flustered.

'I... I've certainly never been in that situation before, and the thought of doing so would never have crossed my mind. But now you mention it, on that first day when we left the Gold Coast, it just seemed natural, and felt really good to be sitting there, topless in the sun with the water streaming past just below us. I was a bit uncomfortable for a few minutes when Sandy, Lara and Charlie took their pants off as well, but after that, it all seemed perfectly normal. Quite liberating really, when I think of it. And to be really honest, once I'd relaxed, I felt like taking my pants off as well, but I wasn't brave enough. Does that make me depraved?'

'Absolutely not! Look at the large number of people who are naturists. They take their whole families on holiday at resorts where everyone is naked, and with very few exceptions, they are the most well-balanced, normally-behaved people you could hope to meet. Their kids never seem to develop sexual hang-ups, nor turn into sexual predators as they get older.'

I paused a moment, considering. 'In this particular environment, I blame it on just being on the water. Real boating people who embrace the lifestyle, tend to leave most, if not all their social hang-ups back ashore, as they don't feel obliged to live up to anyone else's standards or prove anything to anybody. Initially, Beth didn't know how to do it, but it would appear she's been converted, or at least is well on the way to being so.'

Georgia nodded, almost to herself, then smiled. 'You've given me a lot to think about, Harry. I think I need to examine my own perceptions more closely. But I'd really like to talk more about it, if that's alright.'

'Of course, dear lady. Anytime. We can even resume on watch tomorrow night if you can wait that long. At this speed, we won't be at the atoll until the day after.'

'Great. I look forward to that.'

I nodded, pleased that she seemed to have accepted the truth of what I'd been saying and said, 'Look. Why don't you head for bed? Alex and Charlie will be up here shortly and I'll be fine by myself for the last fifteen minutes of the watch.'

'Are you sure? I don't mind staying.'

'No problem. Go start examining perceptions and I'll see you in the morning.'

She gave me a tight smile, then stood, stepped up close and gave me a full body hug which was very pleasant and more than a little bit stimulating. She definitely had her girly bits in all the right places. She also planted a long, lingering kiss on my lips, which stirred my pot even more, and I saw that she felt it.

'I'd better go, I think,' she said huskily, standing back, 'before I do something I might really like.'

With that, she turned and went below, leaving me with a set of mixed emotions and the usual rush of blood to my nether regions, so my evening pee over the stern before the watch change was slightly awkward.


Right on midnight, Alex and Charlie showed up to take over, and I updated them on conditions – benign and unchanged as they were, and said I'd see them in the morning.

'Sleep well, Harry,' Charlie called with a twinkle in her eye, and I remembered she was in the cabin just forward of our bathroom.

I checked the radar and the forward-looking sonar, as well as the chart-plotter for our current position, found that they were all talking to and agreeing with each other, so all was well and I could head to our cabin. There I discovered Sandy and Beth fast asleep, mostly uncovered by the light sheet. As they both happened to be lying on their backs at that time, the similarities in their build were obvious and very pleasant to look at, but I reluctantly put those thoughts aside, shed my clothes and slipped into bed.

As I'd told Georgia, there was plenty of room and despite the assortment of thoughts, racing around my head, most of which were lustful, I soon drifted off to sleep.

I half-woke a couple of times with movement in the bed, and made the assumption that Beth must have bailed out and gone back to her cabin when she discovered me on her other side, but when I woke fully just before dawn, as is my habit, I reached out to cuddle Sandy and found a warm body which felt a lot like Sandy, but some things weren't quite the same.

Nevertheless, warm, naked ladies are still warm and naked, and are meant to be cuddled, so as I fitted myself up against her warm, curvy backside and cupped a firm breast in one hand, I heard a soft gasp which definitely wasn't from Sandy. Then I heard the gentle snoring on the far side of the bed from the real Sandy, which meant the warm body I was snuggled intimately up against really was Beth. Interestingly, she didn't try to escape, but she did quietly hiss, 'What are you doing?'

Frankly, I thought it was fairly obvious to anyone what I was doing, but maybe life in the higher levels of academia doesn't automatically prepare one for some of the more basic realities and pleasures of life.

'Just thought I'd get to know you a bit better,' I murmured in her ear, 'you are, after all, in my bed without any clothes on. Then of course, the other day on the beach you did say you fancied me, so maybe I'm just taking you up on your offer.'

'I'm not sure it was actually an offer,' she replied softly, and still not trying to squirm away, 'more like a fleeting thought expressed in a moment of alcoholic weakness.'

'Oh... very good, well, whatever you did say it, even if it was a momentary lapse of reason,' I said, with what I thought was perfect logic, as well as revealing my level of music appreciation.

She didn't reply, and still hadn't said 'no', so taking her silence and lack of further negativity as encouragement, I suggested mildly, 'Seeing as we are still here, perhaps if you'd like to just move this knee up a bit... yes, like that, but just a little bit more should do... perfect!'

'I'm really not sure about this,' Beth murmured as I made a few more minor adjustments, some to my position and some to portions of her anatomy. 'What are you doing now... that's... that's not... oh my goodness! That's very...'

'Yes, exactly. Couldn't have expressed it better myself! Now if you'd care to keep your comments reasonably quiet and perhaps not bounce around too much, you mightn't wake Sandy.'

'I'm hardly bouncing around,' was her reply, sounding as though she had her teeth clamped together, 'although when you're doing... doing that to ... oh, hell! You might have warned me... oh that's very... fulfilling, is maybe the word I think I was looking for?'

'That's what happens when you're such an attractive, sexy lady,' I replied cheerfully, then encouragingly added, 'and I must say that for someone who didn't know what I was doing a few moments ago, you've caught on very quickly.'

She didn't reply for a few moments, then murmured, 'I'm not really doing anything – you seem to be doing all the work. Although so far, you've exceeding all my very limited expectations and... oh, goodness me... especially that!'

From that point, things proceeded as intended, as well as extremely nicely, to the extent that it was quite a while later when Sandy woke, yawned, stretched and looked over at Beth. 'Oh, goody. You're playing nice. Be good to her, Harry.'

'Yes dear, I am trying.'

'You certainly are that at times, but do make a special effort this time to be a good boy.'

Beth gave a strangled giggle, then composed herself. 'I'm so sorry Sandy. I woke up – Harry was there, and this sort-of just seemed to happen. He's still... oh, that's... please Harry, I'm trying to ...oh god... talk to Sandy.'

It was Sandy's turn to giggle. 'Yeah, ease up a moment, Harry, and let the girl have her say. Although it's perfectly alright, dear girl. Nothing to say, really.'

Beth tried to say a few other things, but continued to have trouble doing so, so finally stopped trying and concentrated on more important things after Sandy rolled away on her side and seemed to doze off.

My efforts to be nice to Beth paid off big time, and it was a while later when she suggested it might be a good idea for her to wander off to the bathroom. After I let her out my side of the bed, and she left, Sandy said softly. 'Good boy. You were gentle. She's still very fragile and not used to our ways yet.'

I chuckled. 'I'm sure you'll sort that out, my dear.'

'Yes, I think so. She's actually very nice when she drops the ice queen persona.'

'I agree. Couldn't feel a cold bit anywhere!'

After cleaning herself up, Beth decided to dress and go back to her cabin. When I finally went up top, I saw the weather conditions were unchanged, and Bree and Georgia were starting breakfast.

'Perfect timing as usual,' Bree welcomed me.

'I do try,' I grinned back, 'especially when it smells so good.'

I turned to Georgia and innocently asked, 'Is Beth sleeping in this morning?'

She giggled, 'I don't think she's doing much sleeping. She came in a while ago, had a shower and said she was going to lie down to think a few things through. You wouldn't have contributed anything toward that, would you?'

I grinned, 'I'll blame Sandy. All I'll say is that she was in excellent condition when she left.'

Georgia gave me one of those weird female looks, as she shoved a steaming hot plate of sausages, beans, tomato and bacon in my hands.

Before tucking into my all-time favourite breakfast, I made a quick check on our position and worked out that if we maintained the present rate of progress, we would reach North Reef sometime during the next night. As deliberately approaching a mostly submerged reef complex in the middle of nowhere and at night is really dumb, then at some point well short of the reef we'd need to slow down or stop for a while so we could arrive when the sun was high enough for best visibility.

With breakfast served, Beth appeared, looking a bit sheepish, but greeted everybody quite normally. Sandy and I were given a conspiratorial squeeze on our shoulders which I chose to mean that she had come to terms with what had happened, had enjoyed herself and had no regrets. Or maybe I was reading too much into a friendly shoulder squeeze.

While they ate, I told everyone of our altered timetable and that we'd sail as usual through the day, but at nightfall, we'd heave-to for the night to hold position, rather than deploying the huge parachute sea-anchor, which was a life-saver in bad conditions, but a total bastard of a thing to get back aboard. Getting a circus tent out of the water would be a similar exercise in bloody hard work, but probably easier than the para-anchor.

The breeze did get up throughout the day, but still not enough to get us to North Reef with the sun high enough for safety, so I decided to leave the big gennaker furled to reduce speed. This let us enjoy the easy, swooping motion of sailing partly downwind. Everyone was still in a semi-party mood which meant that the girls decorated the foredeck again, and after lunch, requested the obligatory bucket of happy juice. The rest of that day and evening was a virtual repeat of yesterday, which meant a bunch of happy, pissed possums finally wobbled off to bed, save for Georgia and myself who took the watch again.

'So, how did last night really work out?' she asked as we settled in to monitor the odd sensation of the boat in heaved-to condition, with the inner stay-sail pulled across to the wrong or upwind side of the foredeck, and the main adjusted to keep us balanced while making about one knot upwind at 45° to the light easterly breeze. That meant we were heading slightly away from the atoll group. However, as we were still some fifty miles from hard stuff in any direction, there was nothing to run into, especially at one knot.

'It all seemed pretty good to me,' I answered frankly. 'I mean, she was asleep when I went to bed, although I felt some movement during the night, and thought she'd left. But when I discovered she was still there, she didn't run screaming in terror when I cuddled up to her in the pre-dawn hours, and I know she enjoyed herself immensely with both experiences. However, I can appreciate that she might be feeling a bit conflicted because she was exposed to a whole bunch of new happenings, all in one night, but judging by the way she's been today, I think she's sorted it all out pretty well. What do you think?'

'Well, yeah. You're right. She seems… sort of excited and happy, which is very unusual for Beth, which is why I asked. She's normally 100% serious and totally focused on work. I haven't been below yet to see if she went to her bed or with Sandy. Did you see where she went?'

'No, I didn't, but go check your cabin. She'll only be in one of two places.'

'Good idea.'

She was back within a minute, reporting that Beth was in her bed, asleep. She was about to sit down, when she muttered softly to herself.

'Everything alright?' I enquired.

She gave a wry grin in the dimness of the moonlight. 'Yeah. I was just cursing myself for not having a pee while I was down there. I don't want to disturb Beth.'

I shrugged. 'Have one off the stern. That's what I usually do. Saves on a toilet flush. Just be sure to hang on really well, even though the boat is hardly moving.'

She briefly gave me a strange look, then stood, saying, 'Okay. I will.'

As we were in the middle of the ocean, and purely for safety reasons, I kept a close watch on her, but she seemed to do what was necessary without being put off by that, and re-joined me without comment.


After Georgia had sat a while, she said, 'After our discussion last night, I said I might have some more questions about your relationship with Sandy, but I think that between what you said last night, what I saw today with Beth and Sandy, and what you've just told me seems to have already answered them. As in, there is no problem.'

'That sums it up very neatly, and so long as you feel comfortable with the situation, that's good,' I replied, sounding casual, but trying the suss out her meaning.

She nodded, almost to herself, 'Yes. I really think I am, thank you.'

# CHAPTER 9

Two Chinese gentlemen impassively regarded Mathias Tari, the President of the Autonomous Region of Bougainville, as he stood behind his plain desk, displaying his level of agitation by a deep frown on his face, and occasionally restlessly pacing back and forth like a caged lion.

'Really, gentlemen. This is just too much, too quickly. You arrive on my doorstep without prior notice, and without regard for the fact that our country is in a state of particularly delicate political balance. While your country's offer to fund the re-opening of the Panguna mine is both surprising and exceedingly generous, you would seem to have pre-empted any of our considerations by parking a monstrous naval vessel in Kieta Harbour, without any sort of official approval.'

The tall, slender chief envoy, Dr. Chen Min, bowed his head in acknowledgment of the rebuke. 'Indeed, Mr President. We understand that it might seem as though we have acted with undue and unseemly haste. However, we felt that the presence of our vessel, which has mainly engineering personnel aboard, might assist you in a demonstration of our intent to the local inhabitants in your most troubled province. We only wish to show the level of sincerity and commitment of the Chinese Government has toward this huge, expensive and very exciting enterprise, which will surely bring a new wave of prosperity to your beleaguered country.'

His colleague, the short and much better nourished Mr Huang Yong, nodded enthusiastically, but remained silent.

'Yes, yes. Pretty words. But you still don't seem to understand, gentlemen,' Mathias stated. 'We don't need to have any sort of demonstration made to the Kieta locals. Not by you, nor by anybody else. I am merely the democratically elected President of the Autonomous Region of Bougainville – not some self-appointed-for-life dictator who can make arbitrary decisions of this magnitude with the flick of a finger. I have earned the trust and confidence of the fractious regional leaders, and the voting people by being fair, non-partisan and always doing what is truly best for our country. I must respect their well-being by taking the proper avenue of consultation before even discussing such a project.'

His unwelcome visitors remained silently impassive, forcing Mathias to continue.

'This means that I will have to consult with my Council of Ministers and together we will consider the ramifications of allowing this huge undertaking to commence. All of the ramifications!' He emphasised, before pausing to deliver another glare at his visitors, who allowed the words to float past them while maintaining suitably urbane expressions.

'Additionally, we must consider whether the port access and usage concessions you demand will be ultimately in the best interests of our region and all its people. I must warn you, our people do not respond well to pressure from foreign countries. Especially the leaders of the Panguna Mine province. They still kill unwelcome visitors, you should know.'

Dr. Chen coughed politely and ignored all that. 'Surely you cannot have any doubts that removing the pollution and re-opening the mine will bring great benefits to your country and its people?' he asked, ingenuously, his otherwise clear brow creased in a delicate frown.

Impatiently, Mathias shook his head. 'Of course not, if that were the only consideration. But your extremely brief presentation and its associated demands have made it very clear to me that it isn't!'

Having had to deal with the many different and difficult regional factions in his troubled land, Mathias truly was known and respected for his impartial dealing with such things, but not for his diplomacy. Even so, he took a deep breath before getting to what he perceived as the crux of the proposal.

'My greatest concern, gentlemen, is what will be the real cost to our country of your astonishing offer to reopen the mine. You are effectively asking that we turn Kieta Harbour over to the Chinese Government to do with as you see fit, and that sounds like it will be filled with Navy ships.'

This time, Dr Chen developed a full-scale frown at this dreadful breach of rushed diplomacy. No one ever spoke of the true agenda so soon into negotiations, if at all, and certainly not in such bald terms! This level of astute thinking was as unexpected as it was unwelcome!

Then he made another of several mistakes already committed that morning. 'Surely, Mr President, you cannot be suggesting that we make this offer purely to gain control of your harbour? That idea would be absurd in the extreme, and quite insulting! You must understand that this proposed restoration project will be incredibly expensive for our nation, and we offer to do so only in order to play our part in assisting our less fortunate neighbours on the world stage.'

Mathias countered with a humourless laugh, 'I'm afraid that's become a rather trite phrase in my opinion, my dear Dr Chen, and one which has been used by your country rather too often! But to claim that we are neighbours is a very long stretch of anyone's imagination, with Beijing being more than six thousand kilometres from here. Your country's aspirations toward expansion of your number of colonies is too well known in these parts for me to accept your statements at face value.'

Chen developed a serious tic below his right eye, as he perceived the discussion wasn't quite going to plan.

'Well, ah… naturally, in making such a generous offer, we look to recoup some of the expense of the enterprise through a share of the eventual profits from the mine. Therefore, being granted use of the suitably upgraded port facilities, which we will be paying for I might add, is an integral part of that process. The advance presence of a small number of military personnel at Kieta Harbour should be viewed by you and your countrymen as China simply providing a measure of security for the region while the consultation and re-construction process is in progress.'

Frostily, Mathias drew himself up to his considerable height. 'Once again Dr Chen, it would appear that you and your government are making gross assumptions before we have even had time to consider your poorly detailed proposals! Should we decide that Bougainville needs additional security for any purpose, we will use our own people. You don't seem to be aware that the people in the Kieta region have been providing their own security most effectively for decades. Ask the employers of all the foreign spies who have disappeared attempting to infiltrate and subvert the regional leaders.

Furthermore, be assured that we would not choose to use the armed troops from a nation with a most unfortunate record of pushing its uninvited ambitions onto smaller nations who are not properly equipped to push back! And speaking of the 'consultation and re-construction process', I am informed that the actions of your unwelcome warship crew in Kieta harbour, which are proceeding as we speak, appear to have moved this process from the consultation phase to the re-construction phase in the all-time record period of less than one day! Do you really expect that my ministers and I are so stupid as to take this proposal at face value, when your uninvited and armed troops are already on our soil, and your engineers are hard at work dismantling our port facilities?' He barked another humourless laugh. 'No, my dear sirs. I fear this is barely even a token offer of assistance and much more like an attempted military take-over!'

Dr Chen struggled to refrain from allowing the deep dismay he felt, show on his face. It seemed impossible that his precious proposal process had become so totally, rapidly and possibly irrevocably derailed. Rulers of such backward third-world nations as this one, weren't supposed to be able to think so rationally.

Fully aware that he'd made a devastating, near-fatal riposte, Mathias looked at his two visitors in silence for a few moments. 'Nevertheless gentlemen, despite your blatant lies and the fact that your country has effectively just made an un-announced armed invasion of Bougainville, I shall pretend for the moment that your offer could possibly have some merit. You have made your sales pitch, pathetic as it is, so there is nothing more to discuss at this time until I have had the opportunity to present your version of utter insanity to my full Council of Ministers. That won't happen for many days, most likely, so may I ask how do I contact you when we have an answer?'

Dr. Chen gave a weak smile. 'We shall remain close at hand and at your service by staying here in Buka Town until you have completed discussions with your Council. Should you or your ministers require further information at any stage of your discussions, we remain at your service day or night. We have already chosen modest waterfront accommodations for that purpose.'

A fleeting grin passed over Mathias's face at that small piece of information, as he provided yet another diplomatic insult, by watching his visitors find their own way out.

## FIREBIRD

Next morning, we hoisted sails again shortly after dawn, with the sun making its usual dramatic appearance by dragging its golden, glowing bulk from the clutches of a gently heaving sea. The light allowed us to see what our electronics had already revealed – there was nothing around, above or far below us but water. As we moved slowly toward our target atolls, I spent some time at the nav station re-examining the chart very closely, before consulting with Andy and Alex.

'We've been heading toward North Reef, the smaller of the three reef systems lying west of Rennell Island, but as none of them have any permanently dry land, I'm now inclined to head for the middle one. It has what looks like two deep water passes on the southeast side, which look to be safer to access than the shallow pass on North Reef. About three miles up from the north pass, there's a broad shallow area of coral on the inside of the reef barrier, which should provide a decent anchorage, good swell protection if the wind gets up, and plenty of diving in a variety of depths while remaining inside the shelter of the lagoon.'

Andy looked closely at where I indicated. 'Yep. Looks good to me. I'm not that keen to try a dive outside of the reef, anyway. Not out here by ourselves. It looks more than deep enough on the inside.'

I grinned with relief, 'I'm glad to hear that. The seaward depth contour line that runs almost up against the passes on the middle atoll is marked as 3280 feet, so the drop-off is virtually vertical for one kilometre!'

Andy looked thoughtful and nodded as he let that one pass without comment, so I went on, 'Even though Alex has volunteered to be your safety buddy, I heard that Lara wants to go as well.'

'Yeah. She got her open-water certificate down the south coast a couple of months back ,and has enough time logged to be safe within the lagoon. Don't worry, we won't get too adventurous.'

He looked at Alex. 'Having you along as well will be very welcome. Thanks Alex.'

The huge ex-mercenary grinned and nodded. 'My pleasure, Andy. I'll enjoy it. It should be interesting.'

When we arrived at the north pass on Middle Reef, as we came to call it, we found that it was heaps deep enough and around 350 metres wide, but as the submerged atoll was 42 kilometres long by 15 kilometres wide, there was a colossal volume of water trying to get in and out of the lagoon with each tide change. There was a wide, but very shallow opening on the north-west side as well, but when we arrived, it became obvious why the two narrow passes on the south-east side were so deep. The tide run was around ten knots or so, pouring out through the narrow opening like a horizontal water-fall. Some quick calculations with the tide tables showed that this should be the last hour of the ebb tide, so I decided to hang around clear of the torrent until it settled down.

It was a weird feeling to be holding position in almost calm water using the motors, with a ten to twelve knot torrent just metres away beside us. The narrow demarcation zone between calm and raging, was marked by an undulating line of foam and a series of small, but savage whirlpools. Some of them were two metres across and new ones kept forming, making loud sucking sounds until they made like a series of black holes in space before consuming themselves. Watching those, as well as making sure we didn't get drawn sideways into the stream was good entertainment, so the time passed quickly. When the stream slowed to about three knots, I powered up and nosed into the pass. The turbulence generated by the uneven bottom was still powerful enough to jerk *Firebird's* mass side to side, but we were able to ease through the nearly one-kilometre length of the passage without problem. The lagoon end of the pass was guarded by a large, shallow coral mass, like a giant bommie, but there was plenty of space to safely slip past either side of it.

I felt a great sense of relief when we were far enough inside the pass to break free from the grip of the current, and entered the vast, calm body of the lagoon. I also felt very glad I hadn't attempted to run the pass in darkness. That would have been insanity!

Once inside, the size of the lagoon was mind-blowing. Even the reef on the western shore ahead of us was way out of sight over the horizon, and the northern limits of the atoll would take an hour and a half at 15 knots to reach! As we made our way north to our proposed anchorage about three miles north of the pass, I was curious to see what the depth was like away from the inner reef edge, and was surprised find the sounder showing 50 to 100 feet. While it was a lot better than the more than 3,000 feet just metres outside the pass, this depth was unusual as most atolls are very shallow in the centre due to the weathering of the coral fringing reef as the core of the original island subsides. Despite the lagoon being deeper than expected, the forward-looking sonar gave ample warning of the numerous shallow coral bommies poking up dangerously close to the surface. This was just one of many occasions I gave thanks to the inventors of this marvellous piece of nautical electronics.

With no dry land visible, and just the endless white line of surf breaking on the outer edge of the barely-exposed reef, I found I was having trouble getting my head around the scale of things inside this lagoon. When we arrived at our chosen anchorage, the broad, shallow section I'd spotted on the charts, was more than 700 metres of relatively shallow water over a white, pulverised coral bottom. Toward the inner reef edge, the blinding expanse of coral sand terminated abruptly against a sheer wall of coral which reared up, just barely breaking the surface, and this marked the back of the fringing reef which itself was still more than 700 metres wide at that point.

Being low tide and seen at relatively close quarters, the outer expanse of reef was showing all its horrifying glory – an endless line of brown, ship-breaking coral. Even with a low swell, there was constant surf on the outer edge, but no waves penetrated the barrier. Naturally, at high tide, the reef would be well underwater, which would allow smaller waves to cross to the interior, but as we weren't going to stay more than a few days and the forecast was for relatively quiet weather, we could put up with a bit of high-tide rock and rolling.

Anchoring over the coral-sand bottom in 20 feet of gin-clear water provided better holding than I'd expected, and that helped me relax from the high-tension state I'd worked myself up to. Sandy noticed and came over, asking quietly, 'You look tense, dearest one. Is every-thing alright? Do you need de-stressing?'

I flashed her a quick smile, 'Yeah, always. But I'm better now that the hook has a good grip on the bottom. I didn't realise the inside of this lagoon was so full of dangers. It's the first time I've entered a submerged atoll, so we'll have to be very careful leaving.'

'Oh,' she said, looking surprised, 'I thought everything went very smoothly.'

'Yeah, it did. But this place isn't like that tiny atoll back home where we parked when we were being chased by that boatload of bikies. There's no dry land to act as a wave break for starters, so it wouldn't be a good place to park in a storm.'

'But we won't be staying that long, will we?'

I shook my head, 'No, you're right. Two or three days should take care of Andy's need to scratch his remote-diving-time itch. He's welcome to it, although between dives when they're resting, I might jump over with the hookah gear and scrub the bottom while we're here.'

Although I had equipped *Firebird* with all the necessary gear for scuba operations, like a collection of tanks, regulators and a decent compressor to re-charge the tanks, I wasn't all that keen to dive myself. I'd do it when necessary to check the anchor, scrub the bottom, or untangle a rope which had fouled a prop, but diving for fun didn't float my personal boat. The hookah gear was for shallow use only and looked after most of the needs of boat maintenance.

The other surreal feature of the lagoon was the incredible clarity of the water. I'd thought that Port Vila harbour water was clear, but where we floated it was 20 feet deep and with the surface barely ruffled by the breeze, the bottom looked to be within touching distance. From the bows, I could see every link in the anchor chain, sharp and clear, right out to where the oversize Rocna anchor had buried itself almost out of sight. I could also see the bottom didn't have the smooth, fine texture which normal sand has, and showed a coarse, pebbly texture with larger pieces of broken coral scattered about. As there was no feed or cover for the smaller fish, I only saw the occasional larger fish swimming lazily past, on its way to the teeming feeding grounds of the inner reef wall ahead of where the anchor lay.

Past our sterns, the water depth increased rapidly, the edge of which was where I'd had Alex drop the stern anchor as we eased into position close to the inner reef wall. The idea of deploying it was to maintain our position, regardless of wind and tide flow, thereby remaining clear of the hungry coral wall lurking ahead of us.

While coral reefs can, and usually do display every colour of the rainbow when viewed close-up underwater through a diving mask, from the deck of a boat they show as an unpleasant and faintly sinister brown shade which makes the hairs on the back of any skipper's neck bristle.

'Bloody marvellous, Harry,' Andy exclaimed excitedly, coming aft and looking around. 'This will be perfect. Alex and I can get Lara settled in by working along the edge of the wall ahead of us, then we can see what's down below off the sterns. We might start getting suited up, if that's okay?'

'Of course,' was my reply. 'We'll keep an armed shark watch while you remain close by, then I'll break out the hookah gear for a bottom scrub-down when you come back.'

'Good on you, mate.'

While our three intrepid divers got ready, I went to a couple of the concealed lockers I'd had built to hide the various weapons we'd acquired by devious means, while carrying out operations mostly on behalf of my employers, the Australian Commonwealth Police.

For shark watch, which is the most frequent reason we had weapons on deck, I prefer a long-barrel, 12g pump-action shotgun loaded with rifled slugs, and our only fully-automatic gun, a captured Mini-Uzi which used 9mm pistol ammunition. The shotgun was the most effective, having the longest range and good water penetration by the heavy, slow slug, but the little Uzi made a lot of fuss and was the best for close-range deterrence. Its only drawback was that in full-on, automatic rock 'n roll mode, it was a ridiculous waste of ammunition, firing at a rate of 950 rounds per minute. Therefore, the standard twenty-round magazine only lasted a little over one second on full auto.

I'd just finished checking over the guns and loading them, when Sandy appeared and said, 'Why don't you get your hookah gear ready and do the bottom? Bree and I will do shark watch.'

That seemed like a great idea, since both ladies were highly competent with the guns.

'Lovely, thank you dearest. Offer gratefully accepted.'

The shark patrol collected their weapons and in the case of the Mini-Uzi, two more magazines, then went to the bows, accompanied by Charlie, Georgia, Jasper and Krazy. As I dug out the hookah shallow-water breathing apparatus, Andy, Lara and Alex splashed into the water at the stern. With them out of the way, I carefully checked the hookah hoses, masks and compressor, finding all was well. I was organising the scrubbers, when Beth came out of the saloon to see what was happening, and was full of questions about the shallow-water gear. When I explained what it did and what I was going to do, she offered to help.

'Have you done any diving before?' I asked.

'Very little scuba,' she admitted, 'I'm just a snorkel-sucker. But I love being underwater.'

Since being less than two metres underwater isn't much different from snorkelling, I happily accepted her help and had a brief chat about how to use the gear, along with the standard warning about not holding one's breath while ascending from even such shallow depths. She was quite excited to be involved, so I set her up with fins, a weight belt, the second air-hose and comms line, and attached the scrubbing brush cord onto her wrist with a velcro band.

A recent upgrade I'd made to the system was full-face masks with a waterproof speaker and microphone for hands-free, two-way communications. Distractingly, Beth removed her bikini top before jumping in, although I didn't complain. We headed for the bows, and could still see Andy, Lara and Alex in the distance, working their way slowly along the reef wall.

We each had a suction cup in one hand to maintain position, otherwise, we'd just float away as soon as we tried to scrub the hull. The slime wasn't as thick as I feared and came off easily. For safety, I had Beth work close to me, and we finished one hull in about thirty minutes or so. As there was little tide flow, the removed slime tended to hang around us in a green cloud, which quickly attracted a large school of tiny silver fish with a bright, multi-coloured stripe down each side, gulping down the tasty tendrils, thoughtfully provided by the strange intruders to their realm. In turn, they caught the attention of several larger fish a stage or two higher up the food chain, until we were soon in the middle of a battle for fishy survival.

Beth was laughing at the antics of the brightly-coloured horde, until a couple of small reef sharks, each barely a metre long, made a series of strafing runs through the pack.

'It's okay,' I soothed as she skittishly backed away from the sleek, grey missiles, 'they won't bother us at all. They're just trying to grab a free feed.'

Despite the warm water, we still became chilled as we weren't wearing wetsuits, so I called a warmup break once one hull was finished. The dive crew returned for a break as we were getting ready to get wet again, and were raving about the corals, the great visibility and the super-friendly fish life.

'I had what looked like a two-metre grouper kissing my face mask,' laughed Andy, 'it was quite surreal. He was totally unafraid of us and just hung around to see what we were doing. They're so friendly, it'd be a crime to spear any, so we didn't.'

Beth and I left them chattering on excitedly to the others, and returned to work. Our crowd of fishy onlookers soon gathered again and made Beth laugh again as they brushed against and nibbled at her bare skin trying to get all the bits of slime they could.

Finally, the job was complete and we wearily left the water. The hot, fresh-water shower on the starboard stern platform was very welcome, as was seeing Beth remove her bikini bottoms to rinse them out. I was severely tempted to take advantage of the situation, but fought down the urge by telling myself to be content with just making a detailed inspection which she didn't seem to mind at all.

With gear rinsed and laid out to dry, we joined the others on watch on the foredeck. I was pleased to see that Beth hadn't got around to putting her pants back on, which I took to mean she had adjusted to life aboard and was in her newly-created 'happy place'. She might have been influenced just a little by the fact that Sandy and Charlie were also naked. Seeing Sandy standing naked while competently cradling the Remington shotgun as she scanned the water for grey-brown shadows, was something I found incredibly erotic and tempted me once again to do something about it, but I somehow found the strength to resist. Just. Pity about my erection, something Charlie found hilarious!

My lustful thoughts and bulging shorts must have communicated themselves to my lady, for she turned her head, gave a wicked grin as she eyed me up and down, then mouthed the word, *'Soon'*.

I was also pleased to see Jasper was a lot more comfortable around Beth and now treated her much the same as any of us.

Shortly after, Andy, Lara and Alex returned safely from their second dive without the need for the protection squad to make any loud bangs, still delighted with conditions and the fish life. Two long dives per day were enough for casual divers, and even being so elated, they looked tired as they replaced some energy with a late lunch.

With lunch stuff cleared away, most of the crew took to the foredeck to laze away the afternoon, while I unashamedly took my lady to our cabin and became seriously intimate with her. The erotic sights of the morning proved to be most stimulating, so the afternoon was well advanced before we emerged to join the others.

That evening was a happy time without too much booze, with our three divers planning the next day's activity, before most went to bed early. Given the remoteness of our location, as well as the close proximity of a ship-busting reef, I still thought it wise to keep a watch, although I was surprised when Beth volunteered to join me instead of Georgia. The dive crew needed a good night's sleep, so Sandy and Charlie would take over from us at midnight.

The evening breeze remained steady and although the

softly-booming surf on the outer reef edge was nearly one kilometre away, it still sounded uncomfortably close. I'd set various position-shifting alarms on the dual GPS units, so we had nothing to do, but be there just in case. We had already noticed that with the high tide, a much smaller version of the swell waves made it over the now-submerged reef to disturb our smooth anchorage, although the movement was more soothing than uncomfortable.

Nevertheless, it did look weird to be anchored, while able to peer out across the moonlit water to see just a low line of surf in what appeared to be the middle of the ocean.

Beth was still quite excited by her bottom-scrubbing experience, the fish-feeding frenzy and the baby sharks, and chattered happily on. She wound down after a while and wanted to snuggle close, which started off another line of conversation.

'You were very naughty the other night,' she said, her voice muffled by being tucked against my shoulder. 'I was still in very pleasant shock from Sandy's attentions, when you thrust yourself upon me.'

I gave a chuckle, 'To be pedantic, I think I was actually in you rather than on, but really, I was just behaving the way I would anytime I found a lovely, naked lady beside me in bed. Anyway, you didn't say 'No' or try to run away even though you had plenty of chances to do that, and if you'd have said 'No'... then that would've been it.'

'Yeah. I guess so. But it was just such a surprise. I mean, I'm not very experienced with sex. Been too busy with work, I suppose.' She gave a giggle. 'It was very nice, though. No complaints.'

'I'm glad. I thought it was very good as well,' I reassured her.

She lifted her head to look at me. 'Really? I was alright?'

I looked back. 'Definitely better than alright and if you can let yourself relax, you'll probably enjoy it even more.'

'Oh. Yeah... maybe. I guess I was a bit tense.' Then she hit me on the chest. 'But I had a good reason to be, mister you! Being assaulted by that... that... thing in a very unusual and unexpected position was enough to make anyone tense.'

My chuckle earned me another punch before she grew quiet and burrowed closer in against my side.

Her voice was muffled again when she said wistfully, 'I don't suppose I'll get the chance to do it again.'

I was a bit slow to work out what she said, but when I did, I said, 'Why ever not? You're going to be on this boat for another week at least, and I sure Sandy will be happy to give you another one of her counselling sessions.'

'Oh. Really? That would be nice. But what about you? Are you going to want me again?'

My reply was to start to unbutton her top, which didn't take long as there were only two buttons holding the thing together. Taking my rather blatant hint, she managed to dispose of her pants almost as quickly, before we adjourned to the spaciousness and softness of the daybed, where she discovered that the delightful experience we'd shared two nights ago could be repeated. Several times. As a way to pass an otherwise boring watch, it had a great deal to recommend it.

We were cleaned up and fairly decent by the time our relief arrived and Beth even had the kettle boiling for them. I passed the watch information onto Sandy, patted her affectionally on the bum and headed below.

Morning produced another beautiful sunrise into a cloudless sky, with no overnight dramas to report, and was accompanied by the lovely smell of a hot breakfast cooking. There was no rush to do anything as the diving would be much better with the sun high, so everyone made a slow, lazy start to the day.

That was until Charlie made her usual morning check of the health of the nation via satellite, so she could make up Andy's daily report, something he received whether on holiday or at work.

The girls were cleaning up in the galley, letting Andy, Alex and I behave like lounge lizards in the cockpit, sipping teas and coffees, while playing with the cats. The first hint of trouble was when Charlie came out to the cockpit moving faster than usual, a concerned frown on her normally happy face.

'Boss. We might have a bit of a hot potato,' she announced bluntly, sitting down across from him, a sheaf of paper in hand.

Andy flashed her his usual trademark grin, waved at the glorious day around us and remarked, 'Absolutely no dramas allowed, my dear. I just made an executive decision – nothing is permitted to spoil a day like this!'

Charlie with her business face on was an unstoppable force, as she slid a sheet of paper across the table.

'Maybe, but how about you eyeball this for a start.'

Alex and I started to get up to allow Australia's future to be discussed in private, but Andy waved us down, so we waited politely as he scanned the document, his brow taking on frown lines the more he read.

'Bugger!' he said, looking up. 'Basically, what we have here is an oblique, second-hand call for help from the President of the Autonomous Region of Bougainville to the Prime Minister of

Papua New Guinea, who has promptly hand-balled it onto us. Something which could turn into a real hot potato!'

Noting with a grin that he had our undivided attention, he went on.

'It would seem the Chinese are up to their usual trick of trying to expand into the south-west Pacific region, conning a third world nation into giving them rights to their best harbour by offering development assistance. In this case, they've gone a few steps beyond what they usually do, by offering to underwrite the horrific cost associated with the re-opening of the Panguna copper and gold mine on Bougainville, including settling all the internal district squabbles. All they say they want in return for bringing prosperity to this badly impoverished nation, is a percentage of the return from the mine and full usage rights to Kieta Harbour. It's apparently one of the best deep-water harbours in the southern hemisphere, albeit severely lacking in decent, useful infrastructure.'

He paused to scan our faces, but no one spoke so he continued.

'To back their claim of trying to help a remote and backward neighbour, they've flown a diplomatic negotiating team into Buka Town, then improved their position by parking one of their Type 071 amphibious assault ships in Kieta Harbour. They'll probably claim squatter's rights if someone doesn't convince them move its fat arse fairly soon. Mathias Tari says he had no advance warning of the diplomatic team's arrival, nor that of the assault ship. He's apparently more than a little pissed-off about the whole deal, reckons it's all a big con but is unable to do anything about it except scream for help!'

Andy drew a deep breath. 'Having these buggers lay claim to most of the South China Sea has been bad enough, but strategically, this can be considered almost on our front doorstep.'

Charlie looked up from scanning some other pages of information. 'Just remember, Boss, that Australia isn't officially involved in Bougainville any more. In fact, we were responsible for much of the original cock-up with the Panguna mine.'

'Yeah, yeah. I remember. But there must be something we can do to keep these thieving mongrels out of the area.'

Charlie looked doubtful. 'This is me looking very, very doubtful, Boss. Officially, we have to be seen to be doing absolutely nothing. At best, we can let the Chinese ambassador know via the Embassy kitchen door that we're very unhappy, but that'd be the limit of our protest at this stage. Any form of action, strong or otherwise, assuming you can come up with an idea, would have to be very much on the quiet – super low profile – no official involvement, and all that crap. That's my considered opinion.'

Andy nodded soberly. 'Understood Charlie, and appreciated as usual. However, while appearing to do nothing, we might just make a few enquiries, starting with a call to my good mate, Jimmy Mori.'

Charlie grinned, 'I thought you might. I've looked up his number, so I'll just get him on the bat-phone.'

'Would you like some privacy?' I offered. 'These are, after all, major affairs of state.'

He waved Alex and me down again. 'Hell no. I value the opinions of you two blokes far more than that arse-licking bunch of so-called advisors back in Tinsel-Town. Besides, as well as being the PM of Papua New Guinea, Jimmy and I went through uni together. He's a bloody good bloke. Doesn't mind a few rums, either, with the right people.'

He gave a sly grin, 'And it just occurred to me that this red chariot we're on, might be an excellent way to remain low profile if I do decide to give this situation a discrete nudge in the right direction by taking an innocent look at the situation.'

I reflected that it was just as well Charlie was in the saloon fetching the SatPhone and didn't hear that last remark.

Charlie returned with the device in hand. 'Mr Mori's on-line, Boss.'

'Gidday Jimmy. How's things?'

... 'Yeah mate. I just received your message. I don't like the sound of it any more than you do.'

... 'Yeah, got it. Anything official from Mathias?'

... 'Unofficial only. Okay. That's fair enough under the circumstances. What do you want us to do, given that we can't really be seen to be doing anything official at all?'

... 'Help him what? Ha, ha. Good one. I didn't think such a God-fearing bloke like Mathias would talk like that. He must be really upset.'

... 'Yeah, yeah. I'm thinking. Give me a moment, old mate....... Look, how about this. Just to turn up the heat a bit, so to speak, you call Mathias back and ask him to issue a back-dated invitation to the Australian Government for a Royal Australian Navy ship to make a good-will visit to Bougainville. Better date it about two months back to make it look all proper and above board, eh? Then I'll see what I can find floating around the neighbourhood at very short notice. Will that do for the moment?'

... 'Good.... No, definitely don't call the office, I'm not there. You can get me on this number any time, 24/7.'

... 'Yeah. It's a long story, but funnily enough, and for your ears only, I'm almost in Mathias' neighbourhood myself. I'm on a holiday cruise on a private yacht and we're not that far away.'

... 'No, really. It truly is a coincidence.'

... 'Aww, c'mon, mate. Don't be like that, Jimmy. Honestly, I didn't know anything until I just read your message. Anyway, don't worry about that now. I'll get back to you as soon as I get word on the closest grey boat I can get to head for Buka Town. Just get Mathias to send that back-dated paperwork through ASAP.'

... 'Yeah, no worries. And to you too, mate. Talk soon. Bye.'


Andy disconnected and placed the phone carefully down, sitting back with a predatory gleam in his eye. After a couple of minutes of thought, he addressed Charlie.

'Get hold of Alan Stallman, please Charlie, while I ask Harry for a favour.'

While he'd been talking to the PNG Pri-Mincer, I'd guessed what he was thinking and headed for the chart collection for the small-scale chart of the south-west Pacific area. Returning to the cockpit, I spread it out.

'The answer is 'of course we can' if you were going to ask if we can head in that direction.'

I made some rough measurements on the vertical latitude scale. 'It's about 500 nautical miles, and should take us between thirty-six and forty hours to get to Kieta Harbour. Shall we head that way now?'

Andy thought some more. 'Yeah, please, mate. It can't hurt to at least be heading in that direction. We can always turn around and head for home if the situation settles down again.'

I grinned happily... the thought of maybe getting into some interesting action was very appealing.

'Done.'

Alex stretched and lazily stood. 'I'll look after getting us moving, Harry. You stay with Andy for now in case he needs some advice or information.'

'Great. Thanks Alex.'

In remarkably short order, the big South African had the stern anchor winched in, then started on the bow anchor. We hadn't used the dinghy, so it was still snugged up securely under the overhanging day bed. Therefore, as soon as the bow anchor was reeled in and locked in place, Alex backed us away from the shallows and headed down the lagoon toward the pass. Just before the connection to Admiral Alan Stallman, the Navy Fleet Commander, Australia went through, I had time to check the tides and was relieved to find that we were just past peak high tide, which meant we would have the tidal flow helping us out of the lagoon, although it promised to be a wild and rapid ride.

..... 'I'm very well thanks Alan. And you, Kelly and Hilary?'

..... 'Excellent.'

..... 'Yeah, there is. I've just heard that the Chinese are playing their favourite game of, 'let's create a new naval base in someone else's country,' again, only this time it's in Bougainville.'

..... 'Yeah, I thought it's getting a bit close, and to pre-empt any objections by Bougainville, they've already parked one of their Type 071 amphibious transport ships in Kieta harbour and have a two-man diplomatic team on the ground in Buka Town. They're pissing in the pockets of the Regional Council President, and although he's telling them to pack their ship and diplomats and nick off, the Chinese aren't listening. Therefore, President Mathias Tari is yelling for help, but diplomatically we have to tread very lightly. However, for starters, I've suggested that he sends a back-dated request to Foreign Affairs and Trade, asking for a Navy ship to make a good-will visit to Buka-Town.'

..... 'Exactly, that's what I thought! That's why you're the Admiral paid the big bucks, and I'm just the PM. So, Alan... who've you got that's closest and is flexible enough to cope with a job like this without tripping over his dick too often?'

..... 'Yeah. I can hang on, it's Harry's phone bill after all.'

..... 'Yep, that Harry. Who else? We're having a bit of a holiday on board, and Harry decided on a surprise cruise for us.'

..... 'Oddly enough, we're just west of Rennell Island which is about 500 nautical south of Kieta Harbour.'

..... 'Nah. Purely coincidental. Geeze, Alan. You lot really are suspicious! I just had this conversation with Jimmy Mori in Port Moresby. Anyway, Harry needed to go to Vanuatu for some reason, then I wanted to do some remote-area diving. That's how we ended up in these atolls. Now my perfect diving trip has been buggered up by the bloody Chinese.'

..... 'No offence, but I dunno what the Navy would do without Hilary. She's a great girl. Listen. How about I put Harry on the phone and you can tell him what you've got. He's just been appointed my official in-situ military advisor. Stand by.'

Andy chuckled at the look on my face as he handed the handset over.

'What? You are my preferred military advisor when I can get you to stay still long enough to give me advice. Better than most of those self-serving political hacks back home who haven't got a clue and think Defence is what keeps their chooks in. Anyway, see if you can sort out something with Alan.'

With a feeling that I was stepping into quicksand with my hands tied behind my back, I took the phone, but took the precaution of putting it on speaker-phone first.

'Gidday Alan. I've got you on speaker. Good to hear you and Hilary are still on the ball.'

*'Great to hear from you, too, Harry. Once again, you seem to be in the wrong place at the right time, or maybe that should be vice versa.'*

'Yeah mate. As Andy just said – purely coincidental, I can assure you. We were already here diving when we got the news. Even Charlie had no warning until an hour ago. But getting down to business, while I've only just heard of this plan to send a grey boat on a sight-seeing junket, I agree it's the only thing which might slow the Chinese down a bit if we can get someone there quickly. Who's closest?'

Hilary's voice came on the line. *'Good morning Harry. Nice to be working with you again…. Dad, we've got Ballarat underway as we speak with Jim Sanders driving, and she's heading east across the Top End, currently halfway across the Gulf. She's a frigate, Harry.'*

'Thanks Hilary. I remember briefly speaking to Jim when we were heading back up from Heard Island. He sounded like a good skipper, and a frigate would be very nice. Is there anything else closer?'

She gave a small chuckle. *'Oddly enough, there is. We have our one and only off-shore patrol boat, Arafura, with Paul Davy driving. She's in Cooktown at the moment, impressing the locals, before heading to Darwin for a crew change.'*

'Ah. Now you're talking! Paul's an excellent operator when faced with unusual situations and the *Arafura* is big enough and has enough muscle without appearing too over the top. The Chinese might make the mistake of underestimating her abilities. Paul would be my pick and I reckon he's a fair bit closer than Jim. The timeline would seem to be pressing if we're going to try to stall this quasi-invasion.'

Alan and Hilary chuckled together, before Alan replied. *'Yeah. We thought you'd go for him. Okay, if they're my orders, I'll have Hilary send the tasking through to Arafura immediately.'*

Andy gave me a thumbs-up as he leant forward closer to the phone.

'Thanks Alan, copied all that. You can take that as being official and I'll have Charlie send the request to your office immediately. Please give Paul this number. We'd like to hear from him as soon as he's underway and has an ETA.'

*'Will do Andy, we'll talk soon. And Harry, if you're still there, please don't break my new boat! Or yours for that matter.'*

I laughed. 'I'll try hard not to, Alan. Cheers.'

Charlie grabbed the phone off the table and headed back inside to take care of business.

Andy leant back, grinning at me. 'See. It's not hard at all being my de-facto Defence Minister when you know what you're doing.'

I shook my head. 'I'm winging this one Andy, and still trying to get my head around the situation, but it seems to be the right move to start to counter the Chinese. Someone has to stand up to these buggers, but an Offshore Patrol Boat seems like a pawn compared to the Chinese queen in the form of that Type 071 amphibious assault ship.'

He nodded sombrely. 'Yeah. You're right there. She's a big bugger and can carry a lot of troops. Let's hope they don't have a full load.'

Commander Paul Davey, the tall, handsome skipper of the *Arafura*, strolled slowly along the wharf, idly inspecting the hull of his pride and joy. The 80-metre length of grey-painted steel was in pretty good nick, he thought. The paint was barely marked by rust stains and he knew the Bosun had scheduled a work party for that morning to tidy up the few patches showing before the off-duty watch was released to go ashore and sample the delights of Cooktown. The past two days had been a welcome respite from the boring routine of patrol, despite the various weapons and emergency drills. His tanned, fine-chiselled face wore a gentle smile as he contemplated the remaining few days of the patrol back to Darwin, then the hand-over to the relief crew before a welcome dose of leave.

That gentle smile slipped a little as he spotted a young female seaman trotting down the gangway and hustling toward him. As a good skipper should, he strode back to meet her, returned her snappy salute, before accepting the envelope. As he removed a folded sheet of paper, he smiled at the young woman.

'What problem has caused this unseemly rush, Seaman Jones? Are we running low on the rib-eye steaks again?'

'Ah... no sir. It's an eyes-only, secure email direct from Fleet Command.'

He grinned at her nervous look. 'Relax, Jones. I'm sure no one else would read a secure, Skipper eyes-only dispatch.'

'Ah... No, sir. Thank you sir.'

Paul read the email, which was headed with all the authenticating codes and phrases necessary to prove that it was indeed a tasking order direct from Rear Admiral Stallman, the Navy Fleet Commander. After all that stuff, the message said:

*'Depart your current location soonest possible, once fully-fuelled and*

*fully re-stocked with everything necessary for an extended deployment. Proceed at best possible cruising speed to Buka Town, Buka Island, Bougainville, on an official diplomatic courtesy visit. Back-dated paperwork authenticating your visit to follow. As there are additional complicating sub-elements to this visit, mission-critical information should be obtained soonest by calling the SatPhone number shown below. These orders have come from the highest authority and the possibility of hostile action should be taken into planning consideration.*

*Good sailing and good luck. Stallman.'*

'Fuck me!' he muttered not so quietly to himself, 'what the hell are we sailing into this time!'

'Ah... pardon me, sir?' enquired the young seaman, not sure what she'd just heard her Skipper mutter.

Paul shook his head. 'Sorry, Jones. Big change of plans again, so Darwin will have to wait. I hope your boyfriend isn't going to be too upset. Let's get back aboard and get this show moving.'

'Aye, sir. And... ah... no boyfriend to worry about for me, sir.'

Paul grinned at her, a spark of excitement lighting up his eyes, even though his mind was fizzing with the thousands of things which needed doing.

'It's just as well you won't have to make up an excuse for someone in that case, although for your ears only, it sounds like we'll be too busy to notice.'

As they hurried back to the gangway, Jones grinned back, thrilled to be confided in by her Captain. 'Aye, sir. No loose lips here.'

Paul couldn't help but grin at the junior seaman. "Thanks, Jones. Let's rock and roll!'

Feeling the fizz of excitement herself, Jones quickly preceded her Skipper back aboard.

From the bridge, Paul issued a string of orders which stirred the crew into frenzied action, all aimed at making the boat ready for departure in the shortest possible time. The Catering Officer was quickly on the phone to say that additional provisions were necessary, as stocks had been deliberately run down in anticipation of the change-over of crews in Darwin. Therefore, several provisioning parties were being assembled to go raid all the local butchers and supermarkets.

As the boat hummed with pre-departure activity, Paul asked his XO, Lieutenant Clare Stahall, to follow him below to his cabin for a briefing. The attractive and highly competent former gunnery officer on the old patrol boat, HMAS *Glenelg*, was as puzzled as the rest of the crew about the change of plans, until Paul handed her the email orders.

'Bloody hell, Skipper,' she said, after reading it a second time, 'what the hell's going on now? Being sent into international waters is a big step up for us, even though we're classed as an Offshore Patrol Boat. This sounds more like a job for a frigate, especially if hostile action is possible. And what's this bit about calling a SatPhone number to get more info. It's hardly normal Navy procedure to be told to 'phone a friend' for order clarification!'

Paul nodded, a frown creasing his face, 'My thoughts exactly, Clare. I'm inclined to call Admiral Stallman's office to get additional authentication for this.'

Clare nodded, 'Yep. That's what I'd do. This is all too weird.'

Within a few minutes, with a measure of efficiency born of long practice, Paul had managed to penetrate several layers of secretaries, and was connected to the inner sanctum.

*'Good morning, Commander. This is Hilary Stallman. I've been expecting your call.'*

'Good morning, Hilary. Sorry to bother you, but despite the authentication codes on this tasking order, I felt the need to verify the instructions concerning the SatPhone contact for additional instructions. The tasking order itself is fine, of course, and we should be ready to depart within thirty minutes or so.'

Hilary gave her characteristic husky chuckle, *'No need for apologies, Commander. I can put you through to the Admiral if you want, but since I drafted the order, I can tell you that the SatPhone contact order is correct, and everything will be explained at that time.*

*I might add that due to the developing situation, any additional orders you might receive from that contact can be taken as being from the highest authority, and no further verification through this office is necessary.'*

'Oh. Very unusual, but if you say so, that's good enough for me, so there's no need to bother the Admiral. We'll report our movements as usual once underway. Thank you Hilary.'

She chuckled again, *'Thank you, Commander. We're certain you will handle this very unusual and challenging mission successfully.'*

With that ominous sign-off hanging in the air, Paul terminated the call and from the look on her face, saw Clare was even more concerned than before.

'Bloody hell, Skipper. This is even more weird! What the hell's going on?'

At that moment, the intercom from the bridge squealed and the voice of the officer of the watch announced the return of the provisioning parties.

*'Provisions are being brought aboard, sir, and Engineering reports the fresh-water and fuel tanks will be topped in ten minutes.'*

'Thank you, Lieutenant. We'll be right up,' was Paul's reply, before he said to Clare, 'I agree, but let's get underway first, then as soon as we're clear of the coast, we'll call this mysterious number and find out what's really going on.'

## BACK ON *FIREBIRD*

As expected, our exit from the lagoon was a fast and lumpy ride, with the one-kilometre-long channel through the reef now a boiling, heaving torrent which constantly tried to spear us sideways into the carbon-fibre-unfriendly coral walls flashing past at deadly speeds. With the motors at full-power to give best rudder control, the walls of coral flashed past at around 25 knots, which made for a couple of terrifying minutes of wrestling with the wheel, before we were spat out into the tranquil open ocean, the depth sounder immediately plunging from fifty feet to over three thousand feet in less than two seconds.

I felt like I'd just run a mini-marathon, with sweat soaking my favourite old T-shirt.

'Good job, Harry,' Andy commented, 'although in hindsight, it might have been less exciting to have waited for slack tide.'

I chuckled with relief, as I turned the wheel over to Alex. 'Can't argue with that, old mate. If we come here again, and aren't in a hurry to go check the Chinese, that's exactly what we'll do.'

The breeze was still light, although the forecast suggested that now the stable high-pressure system responsible for the run of calm weather was moving on, it would soon build up to normal trade-wind strength. Accordingly, Alex hoisted all sail and set a course which initially was to the north to clear the atolls, but then would curve to the north-west on track for Bougainville. There would be a lot of islands to dodge as we got closer, but for now, there was just a great deal of open gently-heaving ocean as we entered the unfamiliar southern limits of the Solomon Sea.

While the ladies, their sunblock and bare flesh adjourned to the foredeck again, Andy and I remained at the cockpit table so Alex was included in the discussion.

Andy led with, 'What's our first step, Mr Defence Advisor?' he asked with a cheeky grin.

Fortunately, I'd been giving this a lot of thought while we were extracting ourselves from the atoll, so was able to reply without too much hesitation.

'That depends on whether you think the greatest threat is the assault ship or the negotiating team.'

Andy must have also been considering this point, for he fired back, 'I would have said the ship was the main problem. I know Mathias won't give in to extortion. Do you agree?'

'Yes, although without knowing him, I agree. Talk is cheap, so if Mathias does play tough and *Arafura* gets there fairly quickly to provide psychological support and some international scrutiny, I don't think too much can come of that in the short term. But that bloody assault ship is a real problem. She's the ultimate squatter and to legally remain in port, all her captain has to do is claim he has damage of some sort and cannot safely put to sea. International Maritime law will side with him unless an inspection team proves otherwise. That could take way too long to organise, and further delays would be easy for the Chinese to manufacture.'

Andy mulled my words over for a minute. 'Yeah, got that. Good point. So, how do we persuade a 25,000-tonne helicopter carrier/assault ship to piss off without resorting to official muscle? Tell me you've come up with one of your cunning plans. Please?'

I gave him a bit of a grin. 'I do have the makings of a plan, but it depends on whether Paul will go along with it. It might involve a bit of live action.'

Andy shrugged, 'Mathias didn't invite these buggers to lob on his doorstep, and we certainly don't want them setting up shop in our backyard either. So long as you can hide any hint of active Australian government involvement, then feel free to do whatever you can.'

With that level of encouragement, I gave them an outline of my plan, but I needed to hear from Paul ASAP, as his part in the operation was critical.

Fortunately, for the state of my nerves, the SatPhone rang soon after, and Andy indicated that I should take the call, so once again I put it on speaker.

'Yo!'

There was silence from the other end, and we could almost feel the puzzled thoughts running through at least two heads at the other end.

*'This is Commander Paul Davey of the Royal Australian Navy. Who am I speaking to?'*

I grinned at Andy and put my finger to my lips.

'About bloody time you called, sport. The Navy must be really getting slack.' I said, 'Gidday Paul, it's Harry.'

*'Harry? Harry Stevens?'*

'Yeah, of course. Who else were you expecting?'

*'Bloody hell. I was expecting some senior naval person. I must have dialled the wrong number. Sorry mate, but I'm going to have to hang up and try again. I'll catch up with you another time.'*

'Ah... Just before you go, Paul, I believe you're just leaving Cooktown, en-route to Buka Town, Bougainville, on a diplomatic courtesy visit. Would that be correct?'

There was another period of silence.

*'Ahhh... yeah? Maybe?... How do you know that?'*

I gave a chuckle, 'Sorry mate. Just yanking your chain. Can't help myself sometimes. Must be a personality disorder. Anyway, I was talking to Alan Stallman about two hours ago when we cooked up this scheme. There's rather a lot we have to discuss, but before we get into that, there's a bloke here you need to hear from.'

*'Listen Harry. If it was anybody else but you, I would've hung up already, but you'd better start making sense quickly or that's what I'll do. I'm under orders.'*

'Okay, okay. Cool it. I know all about your orders, sport, since I was the one who suggested them, so keep your knickers on for a moment. I'll put him on.'

I pushed the phone across to Andy who leant forward to speak clearly into it.

'Hi Paul. This is Andy Friar. I'm with Harry on his catamaran *Firebird*, where we'd been enjoying a holiday cruise before a spot of trouble kicked-off all this fuss. Do you recognise my voice?'

*'Indeed I do, and good morning to you, sir. But if you don't mind my asking, what's the name of Harry's dog?'*

Andy chuckled, 'Good one, Paul. Harry doesn't have a dog. Jasper is a West Indonesian jungle cat, is black, large and has an impressive record of defending Harry and his tribe of happy misfits, including me. He's also currently sitting on a cockpit cushion beside me.'

It was Paul's turn to chuckle, '*Good one back at you, sir. I do recognise your voice and that eloquent description of Jasper and the Firebird crew is correct. What can I do for you?*'

'We've just been advised of an international situation which has occurred in Bougainville, and we're in the process of working out how best to defuse it without Australia appearing to be directly involved which wouldn't be proper. The request to have an Australian warship make a courtesy visit to Bougainville has come from President Mathias Tari at our suggestion, and that request has been back-dated a couple of months for reasons which will become clear shortly.

I've appointed Harry as my official Defence Advisor for the moment, as there cannot be any suggestion being leaked from Canberra that Australia is doing anything, or has any official involvement in this business. That's why I can't run this past the movers and shakers back home. Parliament House leaks worse than a sieve.

For that reason, I'd be grateful if you would listen to Harry as he explains the situation and your role in it. Whatever he says, regardless of what it is, has my full support, although for obvious reasons, I can't put anything in writing. Given that Admiral Stallman will be copied in on all operational info, will those unusual operating conditions be acceptable?'

'*Yessir. That will be fine. Over the last few years I've become almost used to being involved in Harry's wild schemes.*'

'Thank you, Commander, for your support and discretion. It's greatly appreciated. I'll pass you back to Harry.'

'I'm back, Paul. I presume you have Clare there with you?'

'*Hi Harry, I'm here and listening with great interest.*'

'Lovely. Now, this is the situation.'

I gave them a briefing on what we knew at that time, then said, 'To enable a rough plan I'm cooking up, there's some stuff I need from you. I don't suppose you still carry some of those lovely MK47 grenade launchers, do you?'

*'Yes, we do. They're still a standard item on most Navy ships. We have two, and I'm guessing you want one. Is that correct?'*

'Gee, I must be getting transparent in my old age, or maybe you know me too well. Yes, please Paul, but I need to get my hands on it before you get to Buka Town, as we won't be going there and can't be seen to have any direct contact with you once we get to Kieta. Your task is to stay at Buka Town to keep the psychological pressure and hopefully international scrutiny on the Chinese diplomatic team, and support Mathias Tari. Also, unless we call for help, you can't go swanning around having fishing trips, although having your crew be seen as much as possible in Buka Town will be good for local morale, and bad for Chinese attempts at diplomacy.'

*'I'll have to check with the Admiral on all this, but I suppose he'll say to give you whatever you want.'*

'Yeah. I'm afraid he will, but if you feel the need to, please do speak with him.'

*'Okay, Clare's doing that now, so assuming he says yes, how do we get it and the crew to you?'*

I chuckled. 'I knew you'd insist on sending a crew, but that's good because I'll need the very best you have. The job I have in mind for that thing will require the best accuracy from a moving platform. But as for getting it to us, I suggest we have a mid-ocean RV.'

*'Yes, that'll work, but it depends on where you are, sport, and how fast you can pedal that plastic tub along.'*

'Cheeky bugger! However, with the benefit of prior knowledge, I see on the chart there is a place in the Solomon Sea called Muyua Island.'

..... *'Yep, found that.'*

'Okay. Off the southern tip of Muyua Island, is a very small island called Nubara Island.'

.... *'Found.'*

'I suggest we meet three miles due south of Nubara Island. RV co-ordinates will be S 09°-16.812', E 153°-6.410'.'

'*Got that.*'

'The sea state is forecast to be just 2 to 3 which shouldn't be a problem for the transfer. We'll need plenty of rounds for the MK47, and if you can spare them, two or three crates of .50 cal. rounds as well, please.'

'*Shit, Harry! This is becoming really serious shit! You can't start a shooting war with the Chinese! Not as a private individual and certainly not as a retired Australian Army Major. That's insane! And that Type 071 amphibious transport carries a decent array of defensive weapons, including three Close-In Weapon Systems plus missiles. You'll be blown out of the water in seconds if you try to take on that big bitch!*'

'Yep. I've allowed for that consideration, but my plan still holds up if a few things go our way, to make sure Australia won't be dropped in the doggy doo-doo. Anyway, back to business. I worked out that if you can maintain 18 knots, and we average 15 knots, we'll meet at the RV in about 35 hours. Does that suit?'

There was a significant pause from the other end, then Paul sighed theatrically, '*Yeah, yeah. Okay. That adds up and Clare reports that the Admiral approves giving you anything you ask for, without reservations, although he did ask that I try very hard not to get any holes in my new boat or its crew in the process. Can you bear that in mind while you're planning how to head-butt a large chunk of the Chinese Navy? Please, Harry?*'

I chuckled at the mournful tone of his voice. 'C'mon Paul, lighten up, old mate – when have I ever failed you? This is going to be fun. Way better than messing around with boring old terrorists or rogue fishermen. Anyway, if you have any more questions or concerns, call at any time. Otherwise, we'll see you south of Nubara Island. Cheers, mate.'

I disconnected and grinned at Andy. 'There. That went well. Paul has the shits with me again for dropping him in the poo, but he always does a good job.'

Andy nodded, 'Thanks, Harry. That was well done, but I'd really like to hear how you intend to tackle a 25,000-ton chunk of the Chinese Navy with a grenade launcher and that .50 cal. machine gun you aren't supposed to have.'

## ARAFURA

With a sigh, Paul disconnected from his good, but incredibly frustrating friend.

'How the fuck does he keep doing this?' he grumped to Clare, 'He just happens to have the PM aboard for a holiday cruise, just when the Chinese decide to make a move on Bougainville trying to grab the best harbour within a thousand miles. And Harry just happens to be within striking distance? Then the PM keeps his head down, diplomatically-speaking, and hand-balls the whole fuckin' thing over to Harry, who is apparently planning to start a shooting war with a major Chinese Navy ship!'

Clare nodded, then offered, 'Well said, but at least we won't be anywhere near any potentially violent stuff, Skipper. We'll be tucked up safe alongside the main wharf in Buka Town, looking suitably threatening to the big, bad two-man Chinese negotiating team.'

Paul nodded, 'Yes. Let's be thankful for that. But we'll still have two crew members with Harry, and I'm certain they'll be directly in harm's way even if things don't go pear-shaped. Speaking of crew members, are you thinking of Boone and Smith? They are still a unit, I presume?'

Clare grinned. 'Yep. Professionally and un-officially romantically, they seem to get along remarkably well, and are still the best we have with the MK47. They also know Harry and his methods very well, especially after that extended trip through Indonesia. There's still some odd stuff that happened on that operation they won't talk about and I can't even find out from their mess-mates.'

Paul was full of sighs this morning, and let go another one as he reached for the bridge phone again, 'Okay. We'd better tell them first, then I'll give the crew a briefing on some of this crap.'

Within minutes of his call, there was a soft knock at his door, and two Petty Officers entered. Terry Boone was tall, blonde and still looked like the professional surfer he used to be, while Gillian Smith was almost as tall, equally blonde and probably even more athletic, looking lean and polished against Boone's scruffiness. They both tried very hard to keep an impassive look on their faces, while their Skipper and XO shuffled around to make room for them in the cramped cabin. Despite the increased size of the Offshore Patrol Boat, cabin space for officers remained compact at best, so the two Petty Officers ended up perched on the edge of the Skipper's bunk. Paul closed the cabin door, before he grinned at the looks on their solemn faces.

'I've been told to lighten up once this morning by a good friend, so you two can do the same. You're not in trouble, although I can guarantee you're heading deep into it.'

That comment provoked frowns, so Paul hastened to explain. 'Long story, but here's the short version. We left Cooktown in a hurry because we've been ordered to proceed to Buka Town on Bougainville for a courtesy visit. There is some considerable urgency about this, as it seems the Chinese have come up with a crazy plan to foot the bill to clean-up and re-open the Panguna copper and gold mine. In return for this, they want exclusive access rights to develop Kieta Harbour for their commercial and naval ships.'

Both Petty Officers looked puzzled, but nodded.

'Naturally, having what will quickly become a major Chinese naval base on our doorstep, would be a bad thing for Australia, and much worse for the Bougainvillians. Unfortunately, we, that is Australia, cannot officially get involved at this stage. Therefore, our PM has decided to play what will hopefully be seen as a very background role, by asking the Bougainville Government to send a back-dated request for a courtesy visit by an Australian warship. Since there is a Chinese negotiating team already on the ground in Buka Town, we're heading there to show tacit support for the Bougainville Government, as well as what can be seen as international scrutiny, while negotiations are proceeding, although officially, should anyone ask, we're purely on a pre-invited courtesy visit.'

As well known for his competence as for his very direct nature, Terry Boone asked, 'That's understood and makes some sort of sense, Skipper, but how does that bunch of political crap involve the two of us? I mean, it sounds like the boat's been sent to do what we've just been doing in Cooktown, but in another country.'

Paul nodded, 'Yep, that's exactly the case, Boone. But there's one snag. At the same time as their small team of negotiators flew into Buka Town, the Chinese, without getting permission or giving any warning, parked one of their 25,000-tonne amphibious assault carriers, the *Changbaishan*, in Kieta Harbour with an unknown number of personnel aboard. She is capable of carrying 600 to 800 troops, four large transport helicopters and four 150-tonne, heavily-armed air-cushion landing craft which can do 80 knots. However, we have no information at this time as to what their actual offensive capability is, and it is definitely not the role of this boat to directly confront the *Changbaishan* and find out the hard way, as she is quite heavily armed in addition to the stuff already mentioned.'

Boone and Smith nodded, and Terry said, 'If I may say so, sir, that's more than a bit cheeky of them, but...' Paul held his hand up.

'Yes, I know. You still want to know what this has to do with you two. The answer is plenty, because in about 35 hours, we're going to rendezvous with a private yacht south of an island in the Solomon Sea, where you and PO Smith are going to transfer aboard. You'll also be taking an MK47 grenade launcher, a lot of ammunition for it and a heap of .50 cal. machine gun rounds. While officially remaining on *Arafura's* crew muster, you will be on temporarily detached duty, under the direct command of Commander Harry Stevens who you unfortunately know all too well from past operations.'

The two Petty Officers had pleased, but puzzled looks on their faces at that news, so Terry said, 'Of course we know Commander Stevens very well, and it'll be a pleasure to work with him again. So, may I presume that our job is to look after the MK47 and do everything requested by the Commander?'

Paul nodded. 'Yes. You and the MK47 are under his control, with no requirement to clear any of his orders back through me, as he has the blessing of the highest authority. That is your role as I understand it at this time, and the rest is apparently up to him. I don't mind telling you that the XO and I have literally only just found out all this stuff and I'm not very happy about my two best POs being seconded off my boat, even if I also know the Commander very well. I must add, perhaps un-necessarily, that this detachment is strictly a volunteer assignment only and nothing will show on your record should either of you decline.'

'I volunteer,' both said simultaneously, causing Paul to say to Clare with a wry grin, 'please note XO, that both POs have volunteered without reservation, for this potentially dangerous assignment.'

'Duly noted, Skipper.'

Paul clapped his hands, signalling the end of the briefing, 'Okay. That's it, so back to work. I'll be telling the crew shortly what's going on, but you might like to check out the MK47, set aside at least a couple of hundred HE and some armour-piercing rounds, and three crates of .50 cal ammo. Take personal kit for at least two or three weeks, as no one has any idea how long this operation will last. Add a couple of flak vests if we have some without Navy markings on them. And one last point. No uniforms or service ID of any description to leave this boat. Casual civvy clothes and civvy passports only. You're going on a five-star holiday cruise with what I think you'll find is a very interesting set of characters. You already know how to fit in with that bunch of degenerates!' The last was said with a fond grin.

Trying unsuccessfully not to grin back, both POs said, 'Aye

Skipper. 'Thank you, sir,' before leaving the cabin. Moments later, Paul and Clare smiled to hear a pair of muffled but enthusiastic, 'Yes! Fuckin' fantastic!' comments echo down the passageway.

'I must be getting old, Clare,' Paul commented in a rare moment of philosophical introspection, 'but they sound way too keen to be going to tweak the Chinese dragon's tail.'

# CHAPTER 12

Since the unannounced arrival of the Chinese delegation, their ridiculous proposal and the appearance of their monstrous warship in Kieta Harbour, Mathias Tari had been trying to round up his fourteen Cabinet Ministers. As one of his staffers tasked with the job put it, 'it's worse than trying to herd a mob of cats!'

However, after several days, the near-impossible had been achieved, with all Ministers in the one room, although getting a consensus on the situation was proving much more difficult.

The strong incentive of the mine re-opening was causing several short-sighted members to accept the proposal at face value, and discount or overlook the threat of a permanent Chinese presence in Kieta, along with the strong possibility that they would have little or no say in how the port was used.

Two days of argument ensued behind closed doors, with a stenographer the only non-Minister present, before Mathias, frustrated beyond reason, announced loudly and unusually forcefully, 'Ladies and Gentlemen. These useless arguments must end! Despite what their documents say, and because I have spoken at length to the Chinese delegation, I am of the firm opinion that from the outset, it is the Chinese intention to renege on their mine re-opening promise at the earliest opportunity. I also believe that if left to proceed unchecked, they will upgrade the port to the requirements of their military, and that's where the spending will stop! The rest are elaborate, but empty promises designed to allow them unlimited access to our deep-water port which is the best in the region.'

He anticipated the noisy storm of criticism which followed, which served to further convince him that most of his colleagues were suitably dazzled by the prospect of peace in the troubled southern province and a vast in-pouring of wealth to the near-empty Government coffers. Before things got to the stage of raised fists, he silenced the room again.

'I continue to push this unwelcome consideration, because I have received a number of reports from highly reliable persons at Kieta Harbour, that the Chinese have already commenced work on the harbour facilities. They have transported many hundreds of engineering persons and workers on their huge warship, including heavy earth-moving machinery, cranes, trucks, plus cement, steel and wood materials. They have commenced this work without discussion or permission of any description, while we, the country's leaders, are successfully distracted by their so-called diplomatic delegation, mouthing sweet-sounding words and making promises which I am convinced they have no intention of keeping. To further support my allegations, my spies also report that contrary to what they have already promised, there has not been any attempt by the Chinese to contact the leaders of the local landowners, or to determine what is required to rehabilitate the mine and surrounding area. I assert therefore, that this is proof they are only interested in the port and the upgrade of its facilities for their own use. This talk of spending vast amounts of money to 'help our less fortunate neighbours' is just that. Cheap, useless talk! I don't need to remind you how cheap talk is!'

The resulting discussion raged on again, but finally a strong majority emerged which was at last in favour of determining ways to evict their un-welcome squatters.

'But how can we do anything about such a powerful nation and their large ship?' mournfully asked one Minister, who saw the dream of a prosperous nation drifting out the windows on the cooling evening breeze. 'We have no military forces, only local police. They are no match for even that single warship.'

Mathias stood with both hands raised until silence again prevailed. 'At this time, I do not know exactly what can be done to rid our land of this scourge,' he stated, 'but I want you to know this.

We have friends. They are genuine, powerful friends who want to help us without making any demands in return. If you give me your total support, I give you the promise that I will consult with these friends and come up with a solution. Do not lose hope, my friends and colleagues. We have been doing a good job of slowly resolving our difficulties by ourselves in our own way, and while this offer by the Chinese appears that it is all too good to be true, I am convinced there will be a way to turn this situation to our advantage. I ask that we now leave further discussion until we meet again here in three days. I hope to have better news by then. Thank you.'

Taking the lack of immediate protest as assent, Mathias hastily closed the meeting.

## FIREBIRD

I spent the rest of the day and most of the next doing a lot of thinking, consulting charts, doodling thoughts on notepads and consulting Wikipedia via the internet. I also prevailed upon Andy to establish direct contact with Mathias Tari. The first such call was both interesting and useful.

'Good afternoon Mr Tari, this is Andy Friar. I trust you are keeping well under these trying circumstances?'

*'Good afternoon to you too, Mr Friar. It's a pleasure to hear your voice, and I thank you for the very timely suggestion for me to issue an invitation for one of your splendid warships to make a courtesy visit. I trust that plans for that event are still proceeding?'*

'Indeed, Mr Tari. There is no problem with that and I am advised that our newest vessel, an Offshore Patrol Boat named *Arafura*, should arrive in the morning of the day after tomorrow. Will that be timely enough?'

A deep, rich chuckle sounded from the SatPhone's speaker. *'Extremely timely, Mr Friar. Your idea to back-date the invitation prevents our Chinese visitors from accusing your country of meddling* in international politics, although I'm sure they will try to do so anyway, but it will help make their posturing an empty gesture.'

'Yes. It is unfortunately necessary to appear to be impartial at times, but you can be assured of our assistance in less obvious ways, which is why I wanted to talk directly to you. But before I pass you over to my senior military advisor, Commander Stevens, I ask that you call me Andy, if you would.'

*'That'll be my pleasure, Andy. And of course, I am Mathias. But you say you have your senior military advisor with you, this Commander Stevens. That is very convenient as our mutual friend, Jimmy Mori, tells me you are not actually in Australia at this time?'*

'That's correct, Mathias. But it might be best for deniability if I did not reveal my exact location at the moment. Nevertheless, be assured that I am in a position where I can closely monitor all that is happening.'

*'That is reassuring, Andy. So, while I can get rid of the pseudo-diplomatic team very easily, I must now speak with your Commander Stevens to see what I must do to rid my country of this ugly, grey parasite in my lovely harbour.'*

As had become usual, Andy pushed the phone across the cockpit table to me, where I regarded it about a fondly as I would an angry taipan. But finally, I picked it up.

'Good afternoon, sir. This is Commander Stevens.'

*'Hello to you, Commander. I must say that I will be very grateful for any advice you have to offer which might speed a resolution to this matter. Andy seems to hold you in high regard.'*

'Indeed, sir. I am very fortunate to have been able to be of assistance to Mr Friar on several occasions in the recent past. As I hope to be able to do the same for you in this matter, there are some things I need you to do for me to help that process.'

*'I shall do whatever is within my power, Commander, you have only to ask.'*

'Thank you, sir. That will make my task much easier. Now, if you have a notepad handy, this is what I'd like you to do.'

Twenty minutes later, I disconnected the call, with a slightly puzzled, but grateful President promising to do all I'd asked, not to tell anyone, and to personally email the required information to me as soon as possible.

'Nice job, Harry. I must confess that I'm not totally sure I understand what you plan to do, but I guess we'll see what shakes out.'

'That's about it, Andy. It's a bit like a chess game – a lot depends on how others are going to react as we move pieces into place, so we have to stay flexible with the planning.'

By early evening the following day, we were still some hours away from the RV, but roughly on time. I brought the ladies up to date on the latest doings, and while Bree, Sandy and Charlie were used to my cunningly convoluted plans, Georgia and Beth were either dismayed or over-awed, by our apparently casual attitude toward involvement in international politics. It made them particularly uneasy that one of the nations concerned was the fearsome Red Dragon itself. They responded by distracting themselves from all thoughts of affairs of State, by setting up yet another game with Jasper and Krazy which, I was assured, would contribute to their Jasper research, while keeping both pussies amused.

As darkness fell, we were still under full sail, running west before a steady south-east breeze, and under a total cloud cover. The moon wouldn't appear until the wee small hours, which gave me the cheeky idea to have some fun with the Navy. The girls were more interested in having some post-dinner NQ teas, so they left we three males to plot and scheme, while they took their potent brews into the saloon to join in the games with the pussies.

Andy and Alex looked at me expectantly, so I explained. 'This has absolutely nothing to do with the operation. It's just a way to have a bit of fun with Paul, and maybe a bit of a training exercise as well. As we know where he's going to be, and where he's coming from, I thought we might try to ambush the *Arafura*. I first thought it was being a bit unfair, but I half suspect that Paul might be going to try something similar as an exercise for his troops, so hopefully he won't think that we'd be so devious as to do the same.'

'I thought you said he knows you very well?' Andy asked with a sly grin.

'Good point, O Great Leader, but maybe not well enough. Look upon this as our humble efforts toward helping the Navy stay sharp.'

I showed them the chart we'd been using all day. 'As I remember, the *Arafura* has its radar antenna atop the bridge, with the thick comms mast directly behind it, which should create a small blind-spot, or at least a fuzzy area directly astern. I was thinking that if a very low-radar-signature boat, somewhat like ourselves, were to approach from that position under sail alone, that boat would be very difficult to pick up on radar or passive sonar, and with the night being totally dark, we might even escape visual detection as well.'

Two broad grins answered my statement, so Alex duly altered course to make a broad, sweeping curve to the south, then tried to intercept what I thought would be *Arafura's* track when entering the Solomon Sea.

'I expect they'll be ahead of us by now, so if Paul stuck to 18 knots, which is his normal cruising speed, once we complete this wide turn, we should be some eight to ten miles astern, so we need to crank up our speed by using our motors as well as all sail. Having electric motors, we should stay under his sonar threshold as well.'

'Won't they pick up our radar emissions?' Andy asked very sensibly.

'Absolutely,' I replied, 'which is why I've already turned it off.'

'Okay. But how do we find them since it's so dark?'

I grinned, 'Technology, dear sir. We have something they don't, in the form of a stabilised digital masthead camera with 45X zoom, auto-track, and both infra-red and daylight colour modes. The camera is mounted 35.5 metres above the water which might give us an early advantage, since their radar antenna is a lot lower.'

Andy nodded appreciatively, 'That is indeed a worthy cunning plan, Harry. I dips me lid to you, sir.'

I grinned in appreciation at the ancient Aussie complement, then transferred the camera IR display onto one of the cockpit screens. We saw nothing for fifteen minutes or so, but then a few small flecks of red showed up well to the right side of the otherwise green-black screen, slowly coalescing into a growing red patch surrounded by a minor rainbow of other colours, which represented different heat levels.

'Gotcha!' I exclaimed triumphantly, making a series of small course alterations. Minutes later, the red patch was expanding further, until, as we adjusted course to follow, it lay directly ahead.

## ARAFURA BRIDGE

'XO,' Paul enquired.

'Sir?'

'For training purposes, we'll make this RV under stealth mode, or the best we can achieve under the circumstances.'

'Ahhh. Excellent, sir. In that case, I suggest we reduce speed to 12 knots, fire-up the turbine and shut down the diesels, sir. Much lower noise signature with the water-jet. It tends to sound like rain on the sea surface, and will improve the sonar reception.'

Paul nodded appreciatively. 'Good thinking, XO. Make it so.'

'Aye, sir. Talker. Without warning horns, broadcast darken ship. All above-deck lights extinguished and all portholes closed and covered. No un-necessary personnel movement or noise. Start the turbine and shut-down the diesels the moment it's online. Set revolutions for new speed of 12 knots. Radar to single-sweep mode at thirty-second intervals, concentrating on the forward starboard sector.'

The talker repeated the instructions for confirmation, then passed them onto the appropriate sections.

*Arafura* swept on, as quiet as a now turbine-powered boat at 12 knots could be with just a soft whistle from the exhaust, and a gentle whoosh of displaced water from the stern. The lack of any navigation lights was a clear violation of international maritime law, although Paul justified that by the training value which would be provided when he spotted *Firebird* from a long way off on radar. He chuckled to think of the surprise Harry would get when they suddenly turned on the ship's searchlight at a safe, but still close distance.

Twenty minutes later, as they were approaching the RV position, the quiet bridge atmosphere was disturbed by a soft chime. 'Bridge-radar.'

'Bridge.'

'Speaker please, Talker.' ordered Paul.

'We have a ghosting contact bearing approximately 180° relative, but it's really vague – not solid. It jumps around and only shows every second or third scan.'

'When did it first appear?'

'Just a couple of minutes ago, sir.'

'Your best guess? Is it a genuine target and what's the range?'

'It's nothing like anything I've ever seen, Skipper. It could just be stray reflections from the comms mast, as it's jumping around on the same bearing, even though the software is supposed to prevent that. Even though the range is closing, now down to within 300 metres or so, it's still just an intermittent contact.'

'Is there any contact off our starboard bow at a distance?'

'Negative, sir. Clear water and sky from 0° to 90° relative.'

Paul turned to Clare, 'There's something very odd about this, XO, but I'm buggered if I can....'

That was when the ship's phone rang. It was usually such a normal, even mundane occurrence, but at this time, in this location, there was a surreal quality about it, as the young seaman talker punched a few buttons on the console in front of her.

'This is *Arafura*. To whom may I direct your call.'

A gruff laugh echoed across the bridge from the bridge speaker still selected. 'Tell the Skipper that I love his use of the turbine, and his darken ship routine is quite good, apart from the two smokers on the port aft corner of the flight deck. Good thing the only hostile intentions I have is to relieve him of some cartons of beer.'

The click of the disconnect was the loudest thing on the bridge, as Paul spat a very un-skipper-like curse and charged out onto the port bridge wing, frantically scanning the blackness astern, but he saw nothing and heard only the soft whine of the turbine at low power.

XO,' he barked, 'attend to those two smokers, if you please! Immediately!'

'Already on it, Skipper.'

Then an amplified voice came out of the darkness, shockingly close abeam the bridge.

'Good try, Paul, but no prize for you tonight, old mate. Our prize will be those couple of cartons of beer. Cold if you don't mind.'

Even closer, a set of running lights popped on, followed by a white masthead light high above the level of *Arafura's* bridge, while two glaringly bright downlights illuminated the gleaming red decks of a large catamaran under full sail, less than fifteen metres abeam their port side. Paul's stream of profanity was only matched by the laughter from *Firebird*.


## FIREBIRD


Some fifteen minutes later, as we lay stationary, bobbing gently in the low swell, one of *Arafura's* 8.5-metre RIBs swept up to the stern boarding platform, stopping expertly in position. I grinned to myself, guessing the crew were being very careful to avoid incurring any more slices of Paul's towering rage.

He was still steaming as I greeted him when he stepped aboard. 'Sorry for the stealth games, Paul, I couldn't help myself. But I didn't really know how it would work out. I thought your radar would have snagged me much earlier.'

As he took my hand in his strong grip, he shook his head ruefully, 'I should be very cranky with you, old mate, but in hindsight, it was a good wake-up call. When we have more time, you must tell me how you pulled that one off.'

'I'll be delighted, but for now, you'd better say hi to the Boss.'

Andy was standing just behind me, and chuckled as he shook hands. 'Good to see you again, Commander. I can see how Harry can be very annoying at times, but he means well and thankfully he's on our side.'

With obvious difficulty Paul restrained himself from saluting, and shook hands as he said, 'Amen to that, sir, and also very good to see you again.' We stepped aside as Terry Boone and Gillian Smith, wearing casual civvy clothes, came on with a backpack each, and since they knew Andy well from the Indonesian operation, they greeted him informally and very happily. After dumping their packs in the saloon, they helped two seamen who were heaving several heavy wooden crates from the RIB up to the cockpit.

In the dim lighting, the two seamen didn't recognise Andy and after an admiring glance around at the boat and the collection of six lightly-clad ladies, reluctantly climbed back aboard the RIB. Georgia and Beth had been hanging about in the background and were introduced to a surprised Paul, Gillian and Terry.

Obviously remembering Andy's earlier handball of responsibility to me, Paul looked at me and asked, 'I'd prefer not to lose too much time, so are there any new instructions, Harry?'

'Only to track up Bougainville via the west coast, so there's no chance of seeing, or being sighted by the mob in Kieta harbour. Other than that, just get there as soon as you can. Mathias Tari tells us there are only two negotiators in Buka Town, so he wants the support of a grey boat tied up at the main wharf. Once on shore leave, the crew should make themselves as obvious as possible around town, without causing any trouble whatsoever in the bars or with the local ladies. Absolutely best behaviour by all personnel, please. Officially, neither you nor your crew are aware of the Chinese delegation or their amphibious assault ship in Kieta Harbour, so when you grant leave, please make sure that everyone is firmly on the same page about that. You're just there on a courtesy visit which was arranged several months ago. Absolutely no mention of hasty departures from Cooktown. This was all pre-arranged!'

He grinned, 'Yes, Mum!'

'Okay. And a very big thanks for the loan of Terry and Gillian and the hardware. It'll be nice not to have to use any of it, but I can't see us being that lucky. Otherwise, I'm sure you've got it all covered. Just let us know when you arrive, and if anything else crops up, or I get any more brain-farts, I'll let you know straightaway.'

With that, he left, and even as the RIB was still being hoisted aboard *Arafura*, white-water boiled at the stern as she got underway.

By my reckoning, *Arafura* should be at Buka Town around midday tomorrow, while we should make Kieta Harbour around dawn the day after. So far, our plans were on track.


As we had plenty of time to unpack our goodies, I suggested to Terry and Gillian that they get settled in, then start relaxing into the necessary degenerate cruising yachtie mode they'd been in when last aboard the old *Firebird*. That task took all of about ten seconds.

I grinned as I said, 'I'm afraid you'll have to share a cabin... the starboard bow one. Hope that won't be a problem as we're a bit full at the moment.'

Terry chuckled as they looked lustfully at each other. 'I think we'll manage to cope with that, thanks Harry. We'll come and shift the gear once we've unpacked.'

I waved that thought away. 'No rush. There's all tomorrow to sort things out in daylight.'

He shrugged, 'Okay. We'll be back up shortly anyway. Love the new boat, by the way. Looks like there's heaps more room than the old one.'

As they disappeared down the forward, right-side companionway, Georgia asked, 'We must have missed something along the way. They seem a nice couple, but why have we picked up two Navy people in civvies, along with a pile of suspiciously heavy wooden crates from a RAN warship in the middle of the night?'

I figured they needed to know sooner or later, so I replied, 'They're the operators of the MK47, 40mm grenade launcher in that longer crate. Alex and I can drive it, but Terry and Gillian are much better with it, plus the Navy feel a bit more comfortable having their own people handling it.'

Both ladies blinked and were silent a moment, before Beth said, 'May I presume that a grenade launcher is a weapon which fires things which go bang? And if so, what do we need it for? Isn't that the job of the large warship we almost ran into?'

I smiled, 'Yes, it does fire things which go bang. Little 40mm bombs. About two per second, in fact. It's great fun firing it! We might let you have a go at it. Before we get there, that is.'

Beth's eyebrows were climbing up her forehead. 'Dare I ask why you think we might have the need to fire 40mm bombs at somebody or something?'

I contrived to look somewhat exasperated. 'Now really! How else are we going to convince that Chinese amphibious assault ship to move its fat arse out of Kieta Harbour? Asking politely won't work.'

'But it's a Chinese Navy ship with guns and stuff. You can't go shooting at a foreign warship! Won't they shoot back?'

I shrugged, 'Yeah. They probably will. Almost certainly will, in fact. But as we're the ones planning to start this little furball, we get to be more cunning than they are and get the first shots in as well. Big advantage, that. As in, they won't be expecting a bunch of pisspot, degenerate boaties to be any sort of threat. Still, the MK47 may not be necessary, although if it is needed, it'll be much too late to get it later. We'll be on our own in Kieta Harbour, *Arafura* is going to be up north at Buka Town.'

'Christ, Harry. I was only half-joking about shooting at them! You can't be serious about starting a shooting war with the Chinese?'

'Did I say we were going to start a shooting war with them, dear lady? Don't forget, we're just a bunch of degenerate yachties on a drinking, diving, sex holiday. I would, however, be happy if we helped make them uncomfortable enough to re-consider their presence in Kieta Harbour.'

Georgia gave me another suspicious look. 'Then what's in the rest of those crates?'

'Hopefully,' I said, blandly, 'a goodly supply of .50 cal. machine gun rounds. Our stock was a bit low.'

Georgia looked wildly around in shock as if a machine gun was propped up in the corner beside the snorkelling gear. 'So, you've got a .50 cal. machine gun here as well? Anything else we should know about?'

I shrugged again. 'Apart from an assortment of handguns, there's a lovely Japanese sniper rifle and the anti-shark weapons which you've already seen, along with an RPG, but there's only about twelve rounds left for it at the moment.'

She got a very odd look on her face, before asking quietly, 'Would RPG happen to stand for Rocket-Propelled Grenade launcher?'

'Yeah, that's the one,' I replied enthusiastically, 'I didn't know you were so well informed on weapons. This is great! It's a really beaut thing against armoured targets. Makes lovely big bangs that go right through the steel sides of big Chinese ships. We proved that with the Japanese whaler's ships!'

I scored one of those pitying looks which females are so good at directing at hapless males showing the early stages of dementia. They've all got the ability – I think it's in their genes. 'Someday, Harry, should we survive this encounter, I'll be fascinated to hear about how you acquired these highly illegal weapons, but for now, perhaps you should say no more.'

'Okay. No problem. There's a really interesting story attached to each one. You'll love them all. But for this encounter, I'd appreciate if you could make sure your video cameras are charged and ready. Apart from my needing an official record of almost everything said and done, your research might benefit from you seeing Jasper in a different sort of action, one which involves defending his home and humans against those who would visit harm upon us.'

On that obviously unsettling note, I left them considering the import of my words, while I went to bring Terry and Gillian up to date, and hopefully impress them with the deviousness of my cunning plans. After a quick run-through, I was gratified to find they were still bloodthirsty enough to really appreciate my plans.

Under full sail day and night, we pressed on throughout the next 30-odd hours, the trade winds helping to easily maintain, and mostly exceed our hoped-for cruising speed average of 15 knots. Terry and Gillian, who had become a unit on the Indonesian trip, definitely appreciated the chance to be openly together in the totally relaxed atmosphere of Firebird and once happily settled in, they checked the components of the MK47, although I suggested that for now, the pieces of it be distributed into various lockers around the boat where they were easily accessible, but not easily found or recognised. The same applied to the extra several hundred rounds of .50 cal, although that had to be just hidden as there was no way to make them look like anything other than what they were. Bloody big cartridges, with huge pointed bullets wedged into them!

One of my requests to Mathias was to instruct the Customs guys in Kieta to forego a search of the boat and expedite the paperwork for our arrival, so I didn't expect problems from them. It was the Chinese behaviour I wasn't so sure about and expected trouble with.

The sun was barely above the horizon when we rounded Tautsina Island, and headed for the 800-metre gap between Bakawari Island as the south headland and the mainland as the northern headland which led into Kieta Harbour. Being the crater of an extinct volcano, the surrounding hills were uniformly steep-sided and heavily clothed in green. After rounding the final point off the tiny Uruna Bay tourist dive retreat, the calm inner harbour opened up. Small clusters of houses and huts huddled together by the beaches at the base of the towering cliffs, with a larger village to our left which was near the inshore end of Bakawari Island. That island was separated from the mainland by a narrow, shallow passage, with an even shallower stretch of reef on either side. A few small wharves were straight ahead of us on the other side of the harbour, with a scattering of larger houses set back from the beach. After examining the chart, I was struck by the remarkably consistent water depth of just over 100 feet, which ran almost right up to most of the shorelines. The only shallow sections were the small strait to the southwest, and a series of shallow coral reef fingers poking a short way out from the northern shore to our right.

The otherwise tranquil, natural beauty of the port was marred by the imposing grey bulk of the 25,000-tonne amphibious assault ship, *Changbaishan*, which was a big, slab-sided vessel, albeit with a pleasant shear to her forward section.

As we crossed the final two nautical miles of the harbour, with *Queen's* rock music anthem, '*We are the Champions,*' blaring loudly from the deck-mounted speakers, it became clear that the *Changbaishan* was moored very close to shore on the north end of the main wharf area, with her stern almost against the end of the wharf, allowing her massive stern ramp to be lowered directly onto the wharf. A couple of small coastal freighters which were tied up further along the wharf, gave the appearance of huddling together, sheltering from their giant, menacing neighbour.

Consulting the depth-sounder as we crossed the bay confirmed the chart soundings, and explained why it was regarded as one of the finest anchorages. Apart from the water depth which would allow the largest ships to enter and anchor safely, a clean, sandy bottom promised good, although deep, holding. After dropping sail, I took the wheel and made radical course alterations several times, as if undecided as to where to drop anchor to await Customs. One of these erratic changes of course took us close by the Chinese ship, all the girls in their bikinis waving enthusiastically at the sailors lining the aft helicopter flight deck, as well as at many other places around the ship as word of crazy, pretty ladies spread. In turn, they stared at the ladies, but were very restrained in their response, as several officers angrily shouted and waved us clear, while they vainly tried to chase the sailors back to work.

With Bree at the controls of the mast-head camera, my clumsy-looking manoeuvrings took us close in ahead of the tall, raked bow, where I then appeared to suddenly change my mind, traversing the length of the hull close in, provoking even angrier shouts and unfriendly gestures. We couldn't round the stern because of the wharf, so I had to clumsily reverse course again, with much more arm-waving from the Chinese officers, and frustrated shouting and more arm-waving at me from Andy on the foredeck, with Alex doing the same at the stern to add to the confusion. This seemed to amuse the cluster of watchers lining the helicopter deck, and probably cemented the impression that we were just a bunch of piss-head idiots who shouldn't be in charge of a rowing boat, let alone a large catamaran. Finally, after Bree gave me a discrete thumbs-up, I appeared to give up on the wharf area, complete with appropriate hand gestures, and headed to the south of the docked freighters where we dropped anchor very close to shore in forty-odd feet of clear, green water. It wasn't long before a very large Bougainvillian man in a clean, pressed Customs uniform, puttered out in a small half-cabin launch in answer to the yellow quarantine flag we flew from the shrouds as a sign that we were healthy and wished to receive clearance to enter port.

He introduced himself as Joseph Bulli, and was a very pleasant, jovial man who spoke excellent English and happily stamped passports and issued visas on the spot.

With a broad grin, he asked, 'What is the nature of your visit to our country, Captain?'

'Just tourism,' I replied. 'We like scuba diving and heard that you have some of the best conditions in the area.'

He nodded wisely, 'Aye, Captain, that is so, and normally you would be very welcome, but this is not a good time to visit.' By way of explanation, he jerked his thumb derisively over his shoulder in the direction of the large grey ship.

Carefully, I replied, 'It must have been quite a surprise for you when they arrived?'

He gave a disgusted snort and baldly said, 'An unwelcome and uninvited bunch of arrogant pigs, they are. Ordered all the port workers to stop unloading our supply freighters and made them help unload all their own equipment.'

'Did you see if they have many men aboard?' I asked, belatedly realising that it was possibly the wrong question at this early stage of discussions, although Joseph seemed glad to continue to supply information.

'Yes, they do, and although most seem to be engineering people, there are quite a number who are armed all the time they are off the boat, and wear a different uniform. They have a great number of trucks, tractors, bulldozers, mobile cranes and other machinery and materials, which we have been told are to be used to re-build and expand the docks. This would be a wonderful thing, although they say they have come on an international aid mission, and that they have permission from our government. However, when I called my Minister, he knew nothing about any such thing. Now, while we wait for our Ministers to work out what to do about these intruders, the Chinese have already commenced to tear down many of the old buildings and are clearing land in preparation to build new and much larger buildings and wharves. I must admit that while much of this work will be very good for our port, our people are very unhappy about being treated like ignorant slaves. If the Chinese think that this is the way to help impoverished neighbours, they might get more than they expect.'

I raised my eyebrows. 'That sounds rather serious. I don't imagine this area needs any more disturbances?'

He nodded, 'Indeed not, Captain. It is even more unsettling that stories are being spread by our uninvited visitors, in which they claim they are improving the port facilities because the mine is going to be re-opened.'

Joseph was being remarkably open with a set of strangers, so I took a chance he was on the side of the angels and nodded wisely. 'We have also heard of this and it would seem to be an almost impossible project. It seems to us to be very unlikely that the Chinese would spend so much money, including the time and resources necessary to resolve all the bitter differences between your people, just to re-open the mine in order to help your country.'

'Indeed. While it is a lovely dream, very few among the locals are foolish enough to believe this could ever come to pass. We have heard empty promises like this too many times before from many sources.'

I had already revised my opinion of Joseph, from capable Customs Officer to someone who was at or very near the top of the local hierarchy, so decided to drop most of the charade.

'So, based on what you know, Joseph, what do you and your people think is the true agenda of the Chinese?' I asked directly.

Joseph looked hard at me for a few moments, before replying. 'We believe that this talk of the mine re-opening is just a bunch of pretty words meant to conceal the fact that they want to take over this port for their own use. They have made a serious mistake by commencing work on the facilities, as well as treating us like ignorant savages.'

He paused briefly to choose his words carefully. 'Please understand, Captain, that despite our history of tribal violence, we are not all stone-age savages, ignorant of world affairs, and are well aware of the expansionist ambitions of the Chinese military. We have kept careful note of the attempts they have already made to seize major harbours in other South Pacific nations, with their glib promises of lavish aid, police force protection and investment. Maybe surprisingly, we do talk to each other, and so far, little if any actual aid has been seen by those nations. Therefore, it is our belief that the presence of this mighty ship is the start of yet another such attempt to gain access to a large and superb harbour. And all for the paltry price of a lot of empty promises, and a few new port buildings and wharves.'

I nodded thoughtfully, my thoughts racing. 'Very nicely put, Joseph, and I am greatly relieved to hear that the lies of your unwelcome visitors have been so easily detected.'

He gave a sudden broad grin, showing startlingly white teeth, without the traditional, unsightly red staining caused by chewing betel-nuts, the mildly intoxicating and stimulating habit so favoured by many islanders. 'As I said, Captain, we are unfortunately all too familiar with empty promises. Now that I feel comfortable with the opinions you have expressed, I feel it is timely for me to tell you that I have been asked by my President to not only expedite your entry to our country, but to offer whatever assistance you may require to help us get rid of this potential scourge.'

I grinned and rubbed my hands together with glee. 'Excellent, Joseph. When I spoke with your President recently, this was the level of assistance I'd hoped for. May I presume that most of the locals feel the same as you?'

'That is so, Captain, or should I now call you by your proper title, Commander? Not too many years ago, we were branded as rebels, fighting against what we felt was the grossly unfair distribution of the vast wealth of the Panguna mine. Papua New Guinea and, I'm sorry to say, several Australian mining corporations, took a disproportionate share of the profits from the mine operations, leaving literally a pittance for the traditional landowners. To further compound the problem, there was no attempt to control pollution run-off from the mine, and the surrounding waterways have been left in a dangerously polluted condition. This has badly affected the living conditions of the occupants of many villages, and this alone would be a major project in itself to fully correct. However, I must say that in the years since the mine stopped working, nature has made a remarkably good start on the clean-up process, so today, this isn't quite the major problem it once was.'

He paused to collect his thoughts, then continued.

'Although I have been asked to render every possible assistance to you and your crew, my President has not explained why you are here trying to help, and how does your small group hope to convince our large, grey neighbour to leave our shores?'

'You have been very honest with us, Joseph, and I shall be the same with you, but as for our reasons, as trite as it may sound, we are here simply because we were asked by your President to assist where possible. While no one in this region wants to see the Chinese, or any other major power for that matter, establishing military bases in their country uninvited, I'm sure you can appreciate that it would be politically unwise for Australia to appear to be openly confronting the Chinese. With that in mind, although we appear to be a joke of a force compared to the might of that large warship, sometimes cunning and guile can overcome brute force and arrogance, especially when it is not expected. We would, however, require some assistance from you and your associates to achieve our goal.'

I waved around at our motley crew.

'As you can see, we are a varied group, and don't look like much of a fighting force. However, I have found that on several occasions in the past, we were able to turn that apparent problem into an advantage because we were underestimated. Because of our varied backgrounds, we are, however, well versed in some of the more unusual ways of overcoming vastly superior forces. Once again I ask, may we count on you and some others to assist with our plans?'

Joseph flashed his startling white teeth again in a huge smile before standing and holding out his hand.

'As we are under surveillance by our visitors, I must leave now, as it will look suspicious if I stay too long. But I can say that it will be a pleasure to assist you, Commander, in any way possible. When you have decided upon a plan, please let me know what you need, and what it is you want us to do. Here is my mobile phone number, but for safety, please don't discuss anything of importance on the phone. I will respond to any call from you by making a visit after dark that same day. I also suggest that you move about 500 metres further along the shoreline past the next small creek, and anchor close to shore just off the sandy beach. You and your boat will be perfectly safe from our people, although I can't guarantee the same from our visitors.'

As he puttered away with a cheery wave, everyone started talking at once, until I held my hand up.

'Okay. Cool it! Please all sit down and we'll try to make some sense of this.'

While Alex made the necessary preparations to move us further away from the dock area, I opened discussions. 'While I was fumbling my way around trying to find a place to anchor, we made a detailed video of the *Changbaishan*, and Bree is presently editing the result. We're looking for areas of vulnerability where those weapons we have might be used to best effect.'

I noticed Terry and Gillian getting excited at the prospect of action.

'Settle down, you two. From what we've already learned, you'll definitely get your chance in a starring role, but only if we can mount a covert attack on this ship relatively safely. Although it only has one 76mm rapid-firing gun mounted high on the foredeck, there are four sets of CIWS, which in this case, are 30mm, radar-controlled, six-barrelled cannons mounted on the midships upper deck. Unusually, each pair appear to be controlled by a single radar unit in a dome on each side, ahead of the forward-most gun. From what we can see so far, the best way to neutralise them would be to knock out the radar unit. It will then take some time for a crew to shift each mounting into manual control. They can, however, depress up to 12° below the horizon, which could be a bit of a problem for us if someone manages to light one off.'

By now Bree had printed out several high-resolution pictures of the ship and passed them around.

'Ahhh. Excuse me, Harry,' Beth said, 'all this talk is terribly gung-ho and positively oozes testosterone, but you can't seriously be considering attacking that ship! From what you've said, even just one of those guns could totally destroy us in seconds!'

I nodded soberly. 'Yep. That's exactly right. It could if we give them half a chance, that is. However, I believe I have a sufficiently cunning plan which hopefully will deny the Chinese that half chance, and this is what I think will do the trick. I might add that I have no intentions of putting this boat, or any of you ladies in the line of fire.'

I could see that several of the 'ladies' were ready to burr up bigtime at that statement, so I hurried on with my plan.

I explained my thoughts, and as usual, comments ranged from stupid through to utterly insane, which was about what I expected for one of my cunning plans, but that was the purpose of a brain-storming session. I'd realised early on in my former career, that when planning a complex operation with many interlocking elements, input was essential from all those about to be involved.

Finally, it was Andy who spoke out. 'Okay. We've all had our say, but as no one has come up with anything better, I say that we should get on with putting Harry's plan into action. We can always drop everything and bail out if it looks like it's not going to work or is going pear-shaped.'

With that dispute settled for the moment, I proceeded by moving my first few pieces into play. I made a quick phone call to Joseph, our newest best-mate harbourmaster, mentioning that we had found the boat's original purchase order which he had wanted to sight to establish its value.

*'No problem, Mr Stevens. I'll drop by tomorrow or the next day and take a look. No rush. Thank you.'*

The next step was to launch our dinghy, a 5-metre, side console RIB, and take a slow run along the shore past the docks and close by the *Changbaishan*. Alex and I took Sandy, Lara, Beth and Georgia with us, the ladies wearing their best – as in briefest bikinis for maximum effect. As intended, once again we drew what seemed like the entire the crew to the rails and hanging out of hatches, as well as the expected screams and yells of disapproval from officers, especially when we made it very obvious we were taking photos of the ship and the sailors. We motored slowly past the ship, then continued on into the curve of the little bay beyond the *Changbaishan's* beautifully raked bow, before making our way back home.

I took careful note that the ship was surprisingly close to shore, with her broad stern butted up to the end of the docks, but knowing that her draft was only 7-metres and the bottom fell away steeply, that made sense and also fitted in nicely with my plan.

After we returned to *Firebird* it wasn't long before a motor launch from the *Changbaishan* made its way toward us.

'Heads up, people. Game on! These guys are very touchy,' I muttered. 'This'll be fun.'

'Be nice, Harry,' Sandy cautioned.

'Yes dear. Aren't I always?'

'Not always, no,' she retorted with a grin, 'but try not to throw him overboard too quickly like that Japanese captain in Tasmania.'

The boat carried four sailors, two petty officers, a Lieutenant and a Commander, if my understanding of the Chinese naval insignia was correct, and they quickly made it clear they weren't making a convivial neighbourly visit. Without even the usual courtesy of asking if they could come aboard, the bow of their boat was pushed firmly against our left stern boarding platform and the Commander, a tall, solidly-built man with a sour expression, stepped aboard and marched up the steps.

'Who is captain,' he demanded, glaring around those of us still sitting around the cockpit, although I noticed his gaze lingering on the four ladies still in their micro bikinis.

Remaining seated, I looked around as if to see who would respond, then with a bored look, but a racing heart-rate, I lazily raised my hand. 'I guess I am. But who the hell are you and who invited you on board my boat?'

He became very red in the face. 'I Commander. You give me camera! You no take photographs of ship. Is not permitted!'

I beamed at him. 'Really? How interesting. But as you are merely a Commander, perhaps the word hasn't filtered down from the bridge yet, that your ship is in Kieta Harbour, which is in the Autonomous Region of Bougainville. Maybe to you, one Pacific Island nation looks very much the same as any other. But permit me to set you straight, my dear dick-headed Commander. Because we are all in Bougainville, that means we are all obliged to obey the laws of Bougainville, and surprisingly enough, this includes you and everyone on your ship. Now I happen to know that the taking of photographs anywhere in Bougainville, is not only a lawful activity, but is positively encouraged by the Bougainville Government in the interests of encouraging tourism. So, with the greatest possible disrespect to you and your cock-sucking mates, I must tell you to take yourself and your noisy, smelly dinghy and fuck-off away from my boat.'

He obviously understood English very well, since his face became so red, I feared he was about to suffer a coronary incident and was at a momentary loss for words. To emphasise the point, I slowly stood, stepped forward, and holding out both hands, imperiously shooed him away.

'Go on. Go, go, there's a good little Commander. Fuck-off away home now.'

I stared hard into his eyes, ignoring the seething hatred I could see my remarks had generated. 'You do understand what fuck-off means, don't you? Yes, I'm sure you do.'

I was still slowly stepping toward him, herding him back toward the stern steps, and I thought for a moment he was going to fall arse-over-tit down them, but at the last moment he turned, almost fell forwards, then marched down to the boarding platform, his back rigid with barely suppressed fury.

At the bottom, he turned and shook a finger at me, which was always a big mistake, but one that bullies everywhere never seemed to learn.

'You very rude man. You insult Chinese navy officer and not hand over camera. You leave this place now and not come back, or we make big trouble.'

Holding his gaze, I strode down the steps, stood on the tips of his immaculate white shoes, which placed my nose about one centimetre away from his, and pushed him firmly in the chest. While his upper body moved back, his feet were anchored by my weight and didn't, and it was only the quick reactions of the two seamen standing on the bow of their boat which saved him from the indignity of going swimming. As it was, he lost his gold-embroided cap, which had to be fished from the water with a boat-hook.

Again, he shook his finger. 'I not forget this insult. You take your painted whores and leave now or you suffer!'

I laughed mirthlessly. 'Stick it up your bum, chum! We aren't going anywhere until we're good and ready.' I subtly braced myself, placed my foot against the bow of their boat and shoved hard, causing the Commander to fall painfully across the cabin-top, gaining a couple of cracked ribs in the process, but was probably better for his ego than falling overboard. It did nothing for his ribs however, or to calm his temper. With perfect timing, our crew burst out laughing, clapping and cheering as the boat crew backed away, a stream of presumably vile threats in Chinese pouring from the Commander's foam-flecked lips.

While appreciating the humorous side of the confrontation, I needed to take a deep breath or two to control my rage at the arrogant fool who had so grossly insulted our ladies.

As I re-joined the others, Andy said lightly, 'That went well,' then burst out laughing, setting the rest off again. After a few moments to collect my thoughts, I grinned ruefully, 'Yeah. In hindsight, it was pretty funny, but I'm afraid that guy is going to cause trouble. I doubt he'll have the backing of his captain to do so, but I guessing he'll be looking for payback. Tonight might be interesting.'

Beth and Georgia immediately looked worried.

'What do you mean by that, Harry?' Beth asked, frown lines creasing her forehead.

Sandy spoke up. 'We had a similar situation on an operation down in Tasmania with a Japanese whaling ship captain, who was just as arrogant as this clown, and also wanted us to leave the area so he could get on with more illegal whaling in Aussie waters. They tried to make trouble, but it backfired and they didn't come out of it too well. Rather badly, in fact. I don't think this payback attempt will be as blatant as that was, but we can probably expect visitors after dark and they won't be after the recipe for our NQ tea.'

'Oh,' Beth replied, the frown lines deepening, 'but aren't we expecting Joseph to come calling tonight?'

'Yes,' I replied, smiling to lighten the mood, 'but he'll be around early in the evening. I expect that Commander Bucket-Mouth will bung on some sort of act much later when he thinks we're asleep.' I chuckled, then added, 'I did warn that you might get to see Jasper defending his home and humans.'

They both looked interested and alarmed at the same time, which was a neat trick.

'Is there anything we can do?' Georgia asked.

'Nope. Apart from keeping your pretty heads down, and getting as much as you can on videotape. If they are stupid enough to try something, it'll just be the Mouth and maybe the crew who were on that launch with him. He won't want to officially involve his captain in something as tacky as payback. Especially against a bunch of people he thinks are just degenerate civilians.'

In a straight line, we were nearly a kilometre from the *Chang-baishan* and tucked up close to shore. The occasional house was half-hidden back in the lush foliage, but in general, there was little activity by the locals that we could see. As tropical dusk always fell very quickly, we fired up the BBQ for a fish grill, where several freshly-caught reef fish wrapped in aluminium foil with lemon, butter and herbs made a very tasty treat.

With the prospect of some night action on everyone's minds, there wasn't much booze consumed for once, so with everything cleared away, we were sitting around the cockpit going over plans and playing with the pussies, when Jasper gave a soft growl. We had heard nothing as he quickly headed up to his favourite night-time lookout spot on the aft edge of the cockpit overhang, where he could make a drop-cat attack if necessary. Then came a soft call of greeting from the side of the cockpit opposite from the Chinese ship, and the bow of a long dugout canoe slid silently into the circle of soft cockpit light at the stern. These dug-out canoes are usually between forty to sixty-feet long, hollowed-out from a single huge tree, and normally equipped with a modern 40 to 60 horse-power outboard motor. As they are very slender, that sort of power can push them to surprisingly high speeds, while the flat bottom and sharp turn of bilge makes them amazingly stable. Additionally, the long overhanging bow acts like a bridge to ease the task of getting across the occasional muddy shoreline.

This one had been paddled in silence by ten well-built and handsome, grinning men and transported our new best friend Joseph, who nimbly hopped aboard, while the bowman held onto our stern.

I quickly killed all the cockpit lights, and asked Terry to take a carton of cold beer down to the canoe crew who greatly appreciated the gesture, while Joseph shook hands all around again.

'I believe you had fun with some of our visitors,' he grinned, slurping from a frosty can. 'I've already heard that the Commander is very unhappy with his disrespectful treatment and has promised to make payback.'

I nodded in the gloom. 'Well, that's what he gets for insulting our ladies, demanding our camera and telling us to leave the harbour immediately.'

Joseph looked surprised. 'Really? That's a big step, even for this arrogant man who has made himself very unpopular with all the work parties. He seems to be the one in charge of the shore-side construction effort, and might find co-operation in short supply if he's not careful.'

'Perhaps don't do anything about him just yet,' I cautioned, 'since that's one of the reasons I needed to talk to you again. In two or three days, can you arrange a big feast on the docks, supposedly to welcome the ship and invite the ship's crew, or at least all the officers and as many other crew as can be fed, telling them it's to show that the locals appreciate the generosity and assistance of their powerful neighbour?'

'Sure, Commander, no problem. But what is the real objective?'

'Okay. This is what I'd like to do, and the feast will be the start of it.'

I explained my cunning plan, adding a few refinements as I went, and my ideas made him chuckle with delight.

'We can set all that up, and the canoes and men won't be any trouble. I can promise there'll be no shortage of volunteers, provided you can supply the weapons.'

'No problem there. In fact, we even have two trained and highly-skilled operators for the grenade launcher.' I said, indicating Terry and Gillian sitting to the side,'

'Excellent. Is there anything further I can do to help?'

I thought a moment, then said, 'No. Not really. Just so long as none of your people get hurt, and make plenty of loud bangs.'

He gave an evil grin. 'There will be plenty of everything, Commander. My people will be most enthusiastic about this plan. They love devious schemes and this is one of the best I have heard for a long time! Keeping them restrained and following your plan will be the biggest problem.'

With that, he said his goodbyes and left as silently as he'd arrived.

With my master plan now out in the open for all to dissect, there was more useful discussion, which helped refine it some more. At one point, Sandy took me aside and asked, 'Are you really sure this plan to take on a fully-manned warship is going to work?'

I leant forward, kissed her gently, and said, 'Of course not. Not 100% anyway. But the way I've set it up, if everyone follows the plan, there will be great confusion which will be our greatest weapon. There also should be some serious damage to the ship, and regardless of how well it goes, everyone can blame it on someone else, except us. Although I'm sure the Chinese will be sure we are somehow involved.'

She still looked worried. 'But some Chinese sailors are going to get hurt. Aren't they?'

I shrugged, allowing my hard, military side to show once again. 'Sweetheart, nobody invited them here. They're military sailors and marines. This is what they do for a living. The Bougainvillians aren't military, just civilians, going about their daily business trying to make a living, and didn't ask the Chinese to come here to bugger-up their slice of paradise. This take-over scheme must have been cooked up at the highest levels of the Chinese Government. They'll complain bitterly about their casualties and the damage to their ship, saying that they were just on a humanitarian mission, but via video, on social media, we'll try to make sure the rest of the world knows exactly what they were trying to do, so there won't be any effective support for their complaints.'

I chuckled and added, 'In fact, if things go even half as well as

I've planned, I would think the Chinese will be too embarrassed to make any fuss at all. It's sort of like that delightful story of "The Mouse that Roared," with Peter Sellars. How are they going to explain that?'

Sandy gave me a gentle hug.

'As usual, you make the utterly ridiculous seem perfectly feasible, so I'll keep my feminine misgivings to myself and make sure the first-aid kits are fully-stocked and handy.'

'That's a very back-handed endorsement of my plan, but I'll accept it, thank you dearest. Now we'd better brief the crew on what to expect tonight.'

Her face fell. 'Oh, shit! I almost forgot about that.'

'Good thing I hadn't,' I said lightly, stroking her shapely bum as I stepped back to the cockpit discussion.

'If we only expect a small group to make a visit tonight,' Andy asked, 'what are we going to hit them with?'

'Good question, but I don't want to tip our hand as to what weapons we have aboard. In fact, it will be best if we didn't have to use any at all.'

'But we can't just let them do what they want,' Beth stated with a worried look on her face. 'I saw how angry that officer was. He isn't just going to just have a bit of a rant and rave.' She gave a decorative shudder. 'And I saw how those sailors were looking at us! For the first time, I wished we girls were wearing nun's habits.'

I grinned at her concern. 'No, you're right. He certainly won't be coming for a chat. But we've been through this sort of thing a few times before, and there's quite a few tricks we can play.'

Beth didn't look in the least bit reassured by my statement.

'Look,' I said, trying to look comforting, 'it's like this. Joseph has already told us that although the Commander has been told by his captain to cool it, he intends to go ahead with payback.'

Beth nodded, 'I remember.'

'Good. So, his visit will be un-official, under-cover, and off the books. Right?'

'Yeah... okay,' was her hesitant reply.

'I expect that he'll only bring the crew he had before, which is four seamen, two petty officers, one junior Lieutenant and himself. He won't be telling anybody else what he's up to and I'm betting they'll all be out of uniform.'

She nodded, everyone else listening carefully. 'That fits, so okay so far.'

'I can't say exactly how this will go down, because we can't strike first. We have to let the bad guys make the first play. However, I can make a fair guess on what they'll do, based on what we've experienced several times before. The main thing is that, as you've already said, it's very doubtful they're coming over here to have a drink and a chat. Of course, if they get here anytime while we're all still sitting around and the lights are on, that's a different matter and we can react reasonably normally. But! If they turn up after they think we're asleep, and try to board us quietly, then I know I'm justified in taking any and all measures to protect my boat and everyone aboard from unauthorised and unidentified intruders, who would seem to be hell bent on doing us harm. Can you accept that?'

With a pale face, she nodded grimly. 'That's reasonable. But isn't this going to involve some sort of bloodshed?'

I gave a harsh laugh, once again reverting to my other, far less savoury persona which I usually managed to keep well suppressed. 'You have yet to learn that no one is permitted to insult, or try to make attacks on those I care for and consider under my protection. Sorry if I sound melodramatic, but you've already pointed out that these guys are deadly serious. Therefore, as far as I'm concerned, if none of them make it back to their ship tonight, that's not going to disturb my sleep for one single moment.'

Beth's face showed her level of dismay and inner torment.

'But you can't just kill them!'

I shrugged, 'No? Really? If they come over here after lights out, the repeated rape of all females aboard will be the second activity on their agenda. The first priority will be to dispose of we four blokes. I'm expecting several jerry-cans of petrol splashed around would be the finale to an intimate and very prolonged get-to-know-you session with all you ladies, so what would you suggest we do to deter that? Ask them to stop perhaps? Plead even?'

In the dim lighting, Beth's face grew even more pale, and she seemed stuck for an answer.

'Excellent reply,' I said, leaning forward and patting her hands. 'I take it then, that you'll support whatever we have to do to prevent that nasty scenario being played out as I've outlined?'

Finally, she nodded silently.

'Excellent again! In that case, Alex and I will stay on watch, no lights — out of sight, while the rest of you will head for bed, appearing to do what it is you'd normally do, but please make sure all the hatches are locked from the inside. You can turn the air-con on to stay comfortable and effective. All lights will be out in the saloon and cockpit, but if you want to read in your cabin for a while, that's good as it looks normal, but don't read for too long. I want them to see a fully-dark boat before it gets too late — say by 23:00 at the latest. And for everyone not directly involved — don't come on deck unnecessarily at all or talk loudly. When the shit does hit the fan, it would be safest if everyone not given a task stays in their cabins and gets down as low as possible, in case these idiots try to shoot someone.'

Terry raised his hand. 'Ahh. Commander. Given our background, can Gillian and I help?'

'You most definitely will be, Terry. I have an essential job for both of you. Hang about and I'll get to you in a minute.'

He nodded, satisfied.

With the main problem of questions and doubts resolved and done with, and while most of the crew slowly dispersed to their cabins, I unearthed a few highly illegal weapons from their carefully constructed hiding places. I handed Terry and Gillian a PMR-30

.22 magnum pistol each, fitted with an Isis suppressor, along with a set of instructions as to their watch positions, what action to take and when.

Alex and I had a shotgun each, as well as a Ka-Bar D2 knife, as my preference was to keep any action as quiet as possible. Although we had more potent weapons, I didn't feel now was the time to reveal them, even though I was sure our opponents would be much better equipped.

Although I was relying on the perimeter defence system and Jasper to look after most of the assault, but I've learned from past experience that good planning and preparation usually provides a significant advantage against an overconfident opponent.

Despite having been through this many times before, I find that the period before action is always by far the worst. My mind refuses to relax as it endlessly rehashes plans and runs scenarios, looking for overlooked details and possible problems. I've seen troopers who could curl up and sleep until the first hint of action, and my dear friend and colleague, Corrine, was one of those. She was like a cat – deeply asleep one moment, then on her feet, fighting like a tiger the next, and I sorely missed her reassuring counsel, and competent and utterly lethal presence.

Alex knew me well and understood what I was going through so kept silent. I had considered leaving the radar on, but decided against in case our friends checked using the *Changbaishan's* detection equipment. I wanted them to think we were totally unaware of their evil intentions. I did, however, have the masthead camera up and recording in IR mode, as well as Jasper sitting on alert by my feet. I leant over to talk softly in his ear.

'Bad men coming, boy. When I tell you, you can do whatever you want with them. Just be careful as they have guns.'

He turned his head up to look at me, then gave a soft growl of agreement. I think he likes a fight a lot more than I do. The impetuous Krazy cat was already safely below out of the way in a safe locker, much to her disgust.

I'd patched the heavily-dimmed camera picture through to one of the display screens on the cockpit control station where I could listen as well as watch, but as usual, it was Jasper who gave the first warning by giving a soft growl, then flitted like a silent black shadow up onto the side deck, thence onto the cockpit roof. Moments later on the display monitor, I saw the faint image of a smallish open boat being rowed toward our bows, which were pointing roughly toward the *Changbaishan*. For some reason, there were only six men aboard, although the picture wasn't clear enough to make out more details. After telling Alex, I quickly went inside, staying low in case the Chinese had night vision goggles. Going first to the left forward cabin where Beth and Georgia camped, I warned Terry who was waiting below the open deck hatch, then went to the opposite side cabin where Gillian waited and told her. They were both nervous, but seemed steady enough.

Back at the camera control console, I re-adjusted the pan and tilt to show the approach of the boat toward our bows, where as expected, two black-clad figures slipped quietly overboard, before the boat moved down our starboard side until it rounded our stern and was silently tied to a cleat.

The remaining four figures slowly climbed out of the boat and crept up the steps toward the closed gate of the safety railing. There was a faint squishing sound as the first one trod on the wet mat I'd left in place, then came a sharp crackling sound as he grabbed for the gate latch. My perimeter defence system was based on a normal animal control electric fence, except that thanks to a skilled electronically-oriented friend, the voltage had been boosted and the current flow limited to normally deliver a non-lethal voltage and current. However, there was a second switch setting on my control panel which allowed a much larger voltage and a higher current to flow, which was almost immediately fatal. As I had little incentive to mess around with these idiots, I saw no reason to just try to deter them. Such was the case here, and the loudest sound as the first body dropped to the deck, one hand still involuntarily gripping the gate, was the clatter of his pistol as it hit the deck.

From our concealed vantage point, it would seem that the next man in line must have thought the first man had slipped, and quickly stooped to help him.

Electricity has this funny habit that it likes to follow the path of least resistance, so when presented with another human wet with salt-water and sweat, a series of shocks immediately fired through his body, producing an unfortunately similar terminal effect.

The third man, suspecting the first two must have been shot by a silenced gun, dropped flat, before bravely crawling forward. Regrettably, he tried to pull the second man back toward the stern, which caused him to suffer the same fate.

The fourth man, unable to see clearly what was happening to his shipmates, and therefore unsure of what had happened to them, decided discretion was called for and rose in a crouch, turning to retreat to their boat. At the control panel, I flicked the defensive power off, then called, 'Bad man, Jasper. Stop him!'

A black blur launched from the overhang above my head, landed with a thump on the day bed, then twisted sideways and leapt onto the back of the fourth man who'd just stepped onto the bow of their RIB.

He gave a single shriek of shock and pain, which was abruptly cut off as Jasper latched onto the back of his neck, first paralysing all movement, then ruining the very brief remainder of his life.

The man's shriek must have galvanised the other two intruders at the bows into action, as there came the unmistakable sound of the two slightly suppressed PMR-30 pistols being fired. Terry and Gillian were standing up, well-braced by the hatch surround, with their upper bodies protruding from the forward cabin hatches and must have been excellent shots, as I heard only two shots being fired.

Almost in unison, they both quietly called, 'Clear for'rard.'

At my call, Jasper reluctantly dropped the body of the unfortunate he'd caught, and trotted back up to the cockpit to receive his due measure of praise and pats.

Alex gave me an amused look. 'From start to finish, that took just less than three minutes,' he commented, 'and only two shots were fired. I don't think anyone on the ship heard them. At least, there aren't any signs of alarm from over there. A very tidy and economical operation, I reckon.'

I turned on the dim red night-lighting in the cockpit, before stepping out from my hiding place behind the driver's seat, as Terry and Gillian came aft. With a metallic clatter, they set down the two PMR-30's, magazines extracted, along with a pair of ordinary-looking pistols with long suppressors fitted to the barrels. They also placed six extra magazines beside the new pistols, along with a pair of sheathed knives.

'Well done, guys,' I said, 'one shot each. I presume they won't be causing any more trouble?'

Gillian nodded grimly, 'Both head-shots, Harry. I hope you didn't want to interrogate one of them?'

'Nope! Much easier to dispose of them this way.' By the look on her face, I wasn't sure she appreciated my dark humour, but she didn't answer.

Alex had gone to check the carnage on the starboard steps, and called quietly, 'Harry! Better have a look at this lot.'

Just beyond the gate, three bodies lay in twisted piles, looking like bundles of old rags, while a variety of nasty smells rose from them. Alex had already completed the unpleasant task of searching them, and passed up two more suppressed pistols and six extra magazines, all fully-loaded. He'd also retrieved three more long knives as well as a very interesting find in the form of a suppressed sub-machine gun and a shoulder bag full of magazines to suit.

I grinned when I saw it. 'Oh, that's lovely. These characters planned to have a real ball with all this quiet firepower. Better have a look in the boat to see what other treasures they brought.'

Alex was already searching Jasper's victim, draped over the bow of the RIB, and came up with yet another pistol, more magazines and a knife. Stepping aboard the six-metre boat with two outboard motors hung on the stern, he announced, 'You truly must be psychic, Harry. There are four cans of petrol, a bunch of large nylon cable-ties, another sub-machine gun, several boxes of ammunition, and what looks like a box of plastic explosive.'

I gave a humourless bark of a laugh. 'Sounds like your typical rape, pillage, blow and burn kit! I'm glad we took these clowns down before they did us damage. No regrets here.'

In consideration of Beth and Georgia, who wouldn't appreciate visual sighting of this level of violence, we quickly transferred the sub-machine gun, ammunition and explosives up to the cockpit and stacked them on the table, then loaded the bodies into the Chinese boat. As we did, I had an idea about how to dispose of the whole mess. While the local sharks could be counted on to take care of the bodies, they weren't too good at eating boats and I didn't want to sink the thing in the harbour as the inevitable oil slick would be a dead giveaway.

The Chinese RIB had the standard layout of a centre console with a steering wheel and a fuel tank built into the base of the console. A key was in the ignition, and when turned on, the fuel gauge showed about half-full. With Alex helping, we filled the tank with petrol from the cans, then launched our own dinghy.

All still seemed quiet on the *Changbaishan*, with just a few lights showing, so when ready, we left Terry and Gillian to let the rest of the crew know that all was well and they could come out of hiding, but not to turn on any lights, even the cabin ones. Alex and I then towed their boat with its grisly cargo a couple of kilometres further along the shore, just past the narrow, shallow gap between Bakawari Island and the mainland.

I started both engines on the Chinese boat, and let then warm-up for a minute, while I lashed the wheel tightly in the straight-ahead position, then passed Alex the bow mooring line. I then carefully attended to the buoyancy chambers with my knife. As arranged, Alex aligned the heading of both boats slightly north of due east, while I engaged forward gear and slowly advanced the throttles until the RIB was smoothly up on the plane at about half speed, then slid back over the rounded, but quickly softening sides into our dinghy which was straining at its full speed.

All that remained was to drop the Chinese boat's bow rope and let it head for the open ocean in the distance.

'Do you really think it'll miss the reefs?' Alex asked, as we turned for home.

'Yeah, I reckon so. The water here inside the outer reefs is almost dead calm, so it won't get pushed left or right until it gets past them. Then it won't matter.'

Without trying to follow it, we had no way to know if it had cleared the reef system, so had to trust to luck.

'It should work out alright.' I replied. 'At half power and a full tank, that thing should run for at least three hours, which will take it sixty or seventy miles out into open water before it runs out of fuel, which is a long way from anywhere, and in seriously deep water. Like five-figure deep!'

'But it still could be found, and two of those bodies have a bullet hole each,' he pointed out.

'True,' I said, 'but apart from poking a hole in each buoyancy bladder before I bailed out, I removed the stern drain plugs. While the motors keep running, the boat speed and the rigid lower hull will keep the thing afloat, but as soon as it runs out of fuel, it'll fill with water and sink. The lads in grey suits will do their job on the software, and the hardware will be under several thousand feet of water.'

That earned me an approving nod from my huge friend as we headed quietly back home, looking around frequently to make sure no one had decided to come out to see what the excitement was all about.

Ten minutes later we were back aboard, with our RIB hoisted and stowed, to find that the good fairies had scrubbed *Firebird's* bow and stern areas clean, and Jasper had tolerated having his face washed. In case of a rapid reaction from the Chinese, we stowed all the new weapons in the hidden lockers with our usual array of bang-bangs, and hid the ammunition and explosives in the bilges amongst the wine stocks. I complemented Terry, Gillian and Sancy for getting all that done without turning on a bunch of lights which might attract the wrong sort of attention.

At that point, we all retired to bed for the brief remainder of the night, although it was unlikely that anyone was going to get any sleep.

# CHAPTER 15

'I am sorry to disturb you at such an early hour, gentlemen, but the deliberations with my Ministers went late into last night.'

'That is not a problem, Mr Tari. We are at your service as we offered, day or night,' Dr Chen suavely announced.

'Thank you,' Mathias Tari replied, bowing his head briefly, 'however, I do not have good news for you. To avoid wasting any more of your obviously valuable time, I have to report that there was a unanimous vote to reject your offer to re-open the Panguna mine in return for Kieta Port rights and a share of the mine profits. While the Ministers appreciated the enormous economic benefits which could result for our country from the successful completion of that project, it was felt that turning over control of our only major port to such a large and powerful neighbour, would not be in our country's best interest in the longer term.'

Briefly, Dr Chen's face showed a mask of thwarted fury, before he again assumed the bland guise of the seasoned diplomat he pretended to be.

'That is most unfortunate news indeed, Mr Tari. Perhaps the details of our proposal were not sufficiently clear. In which case, may I ask that we be allowed to present our case directly to your Ministers?'

Mathias smiled a trifle grimly. 'I'm afraid that will not be possible, Dr Chen, as the decision by the Council has been made and is final. As we speak, our Ministers are making their way back to their home provinces. There will be no appeal. That was made very clear at our lengthy meeting. However, our Ministers asked me to thank you and your great nation for the very generous offer to our impoverished one, and to say that we will be continuing with the process of resolving our internal difficulties at our own pace, and expect to see a lasting peace throughout our country before very long. The Council has also made the official request that you remove your ship, the *Changbaishan*, and all personnel from our harbour and territorial waters within five days.'

Dr Chen bowed his head briefly, obviously struggling to maintain his cool, calm exterior.

'Those thoughts are greatly appreciated Mr Tari, but would you please tell me how are you are ever going to fund the enormous cost of re-opening your only real source of wealth, if you don't have outside assistance?'

Mathias smiled. 'Perhaps we will find a way to re-open our mine, or perhaps not. That is for us to investigate once we have achieved our prime objective of a peaceful, united country again. We feel that the only way forward to this goal is that our country remains 100% our own and not under any level of control or influence by another country. The terms of your proposal would make this impossible, and would become an endless source of friction and dissent.'

Dr Chen tried again. 'Perhaps I should talk to my superiors and have them come up with a revised plan which would be acceptable to you and your Ministers. I can have an answer within a week. I request that we be given this chance.'

'Of course you can talk to your people, Dr Chen. Free speech is the most basic freedom in any truly democratic country, but I have no faith that any new proposal you concoct will find a sympathetic hearing with me or our Ministers. However, in the interest of friendship between our nations, I will permit another hearing for your alternate proposal as soon as you have one. I do ask, however, that you prepare this next and final proposal without delay, or my offer will be rescinded.'

Mathias Tari stood, an unmistakable sign that the meeting was at an end, forcing Dr Chen and Mr Huang to scramble to their feet in a less than dignified manner. Mathias's towering height and silence gave no further comfort to his visitors who hastily bowed and were escorted by the secretary to the front door.

To make it easier to get the various earth-moving and supply vehicles on and off the ship, it was backed up to the end of one of the wharves, with a wide ramp lowered from the broad stern onto the land. That was also the only personnel access point and was guarded by a quartet of armed marines with sub-machine guns at the ready and a ship's Lieutenant. The marines were on high alert, and when Joseph Bulli wandered up wearing his official harbourmaster shirt, they responded with weapons at the ready.

'Halt!' barked the Lieutenant. 'You are not permitted to proceed any further!'

Joseph eyed the young man, before saying, 'Really? Even though I'm the Harbourmaster and this is my harbour you're parked in?'

'Captain's orders! No visitors!'

'Very well. How about you tell your Captain that the Harbourmaster is here to see him. I don't mind if he comes to me, or you take me to him, but I need to talk to him.'

Joseph's insistence confused the Lieutenant sufficiently to make him handball that one further up the command tree.

Finally, after hanging up the phone mounted on the bulkhead, he said gruffly, 'You lucky. Captain make inspection. He come soon. You wait.'

Joseph nodded politely and stepped aside, allowing the stream of two-way foot traffic to resume.

'Good morning, Mr Bulli. How may I be of assistance?'

The *Changbaishan's* captain was a tall, powerfully-built man, who radiated power and gave an impression of being in total control of all situations. Which was probably why he looked worried, and Joseph suspected the missing, 'training exercise' members would be responsible for his unease.

'My apologies for disturbing you at such a busy time Captain,' Joseph replied politely, 'but some of our tribal elders have suggested that they would like to stage a small feast in your honour, to welcome you to our country and show our appreciation for the work you and your men are doing to improve our port facilities.'

Obviously not being what he expected, the captain carefully considered his words for a few moments. 'That is a very kind thought, Mr Bulli and I thank you and your people for the offer. It might be just what we need to improve relations between our people. When would you like to have this feast and what are the arrangements?'

'Perhaps in three days' time, Captain. It will just be a simple offering in our local tradition, and will consist of a number of pigs roasted over beds of coals, stuffed with local vegetables and fruit wrapped in banana leaves. We will prepare all this right here on the wharf, close to your ship. Unfortunately, we do not have the resources to feed all the persons aboard your huge ship. Will that be a problem?'

The captain almost smiled, 'No, of course not. We could not expect you to feed so many. But perhaps you could manage just the ship's crew? That would be 120 persons.'

Joseph smiled broadly, 'Excellent, Captain. That number will not be a problem. It is also traditional at any feast, to have a kava ceremony to welcome visitors. I trust you will allow your crew to take part in this ancient ceremony?'

Captain Liu frowned, but then said, 'Alcoholic beverages are not permitted aboard my ship, Mr Bulli, but since this feast is to be held on the shore, and because of the occasion, I will permit my crew to indulge themselves just this once.'

Joseph let out a silent breath, before briefly bowing his head. 'I am grateful to you, Captain, and this will please our elders by demonstrating your willingness to respect our traditional customs and beliefs. You, of course will be the guest of honour.'

'I am honoured, Mr Bulli and will have my catering officer take care of the tables and seating for the crew and your elders. But you must excuse me now as I have much to do. We shall meet again in three days at 18:00 hours, if that is convenient?'

'That will be excellent, Captain. Until then.'

## FIREBIRD... THE MORNING AFTER THE RAID

As usual, I had a post-action debrief with Sandy, which took place in bed, where she insisted on sitting propped up against the pillows, with the sheet piled loosely somewhere south of her lap. I always found this to be both a great distraction and an even greater stimulation, which resulted in the debrief being rather short, and the following stress-relief session considerably longer. Therefore, I was still asleep after dawn, when I was awakened by loud voices and the sound of hard objects hammering on the hull.

I was therefore in a less than charitable mood when I stormed out into the cockpit, with Alex hard on my heels. We were greeted by the sight of yet another Chinese PLAN Commander and a Lieutenant standing at the top of the port steps, with an RIB nosed up at the stern, manned by several large sailors.

'Where is captain?' the Commander immediately demanded, eyeing off my paint-stained shorts, which was all I wore, with contempt.

With a strong sense of deja-vu hovering around like a noxious cloud, I growled angrily, 'I'm the Captain – who the hell are you, and why are you and this other clown aboard my vessel without permission?'

Just like the previous visitor, he grew red in the face, showing that he understood English much better than he spoke it.

'You no talk at Chinese naval officer this way! You very rude man!'

That remark snapped my already weakened self-control. I stalked up to him, poked him hard in the chest causing him stumble back and trip over the junior Lieutenant's feet, who promptly fell backwards down the steps.

'Rude?' I barked in my best pissed-off Major's tone. 'I'll give you fucking rude! You and your bum-boy are on my boat without permission. That counts as an act of piracy under international maritime law, which allows me to defend my vessel and crew any way I want. Now get the fuck off my boat before I throw you overboard!' I emphasised the last statement by poking him hard in the chest again. He was about to perform the loss-of-face pirouette of shame down the steps, when he froze and started past my shoulder.

'May I be of assistance, Harry?' I heard the soft voice of my darling lady ask politely.

I glanced sideways to see why the Commander, and the rest of his crew for that matter, were frozen in place and staring. As a confrontational diffuser, Sandy is supreme at any time, but when she does so without bothering to dress first, the effect is quite dramatic. I may have mentioned once or thrice, that Sandy is very well built and the net result as she stood nonchalantly beside me, was a highly discombobulated Commander and a totally gob-smacked crew.

In a mild tone, I said to Sandy, 'All under control, thank you dear. I was just showing the Commander the door. Unfortunately for him, he seems to have left his manners back aboard his ship, and was just going to pop back and see if he could find them.'

I turned back to the frozen Commander, 'Weren't you Commander? Like right now, or would you like to check out the temperature of the water this fine morning. I'm happy to assist.'

He finally found his voice, and with obvious difficulty, dragged his eyes from Sandy's abundant and very obvious assets. He seemed to be mostly a tit-man, if I judged the angle of his vision correctly.

'You very rude man and your whore is insult to naval officer!'

I gave a mirthless laugh, took a step forward and kicked him hard in the groin. He twisted as he bent forward in agony, staggered back and managed a quite graceful dive into the water, barely missing the bow of the RIB. Luckily the Lieutenant had already retired back aboard, or he would have gone with him.

As the sailors stoically hauled their sodden, crippled Commander back aboard, I added, 'Don't come back, you miserable piece of dog shit, and don't you ever call my lovely lady a whore! You're an insult to the name of your country's navy. Now fuck off and stay that way!'

As the Commander was still curled into a tight ball of gasping agony, he had no more to say, so the coxswain impassively backed the RIB away from our stern and headed for the grey bulk of the *Changbaishan*.

As they receded beyond hearing range, I started laughing and hugged my naked lady. 'My dear, you were superb! He didn't know what to say or where to look.'

Sandy was laughing too, making her lovely outstanding bits wobble delightfully. 'Two arrogant arse-holes in two days is a bit much! Are all Chinese officers the same?'

I grinned, 'I don't know, but I suspect we'll find out very soon.'

As the ruckus had woken everyone, Bree and Beth started to organise a cooked breakfast, so while Sandy dressed, I held a briefing in the saloon to update everyone on the events of the evening.

'I think that last Commander was supposed to ask us if we'd seen the raiding party, but he got side-tracked by his own rudeness and arrogance, assisted by Sandy's timely appearance. Therefore, we can expect yet another visit, hopefully from someone rather more polite.'

I looked around. 'Our story is therefore simple. Nothing happened last night as far as we're concerned! We had a confrontation with a Commander Wu yesterday morning after he boarded us without permission. He tried to confiscate our camera, then ordered us to leave the country, both of which were illegal orders, then insulted our ladies. I ordered him off the boat and he left. We didn't see him again. There is nothing to show that Wu was here last night, so we just keep denying any knowledge of his whereabouts. Is everyone happy with that?'

Beaming nods all around confirmed we were all on the same page, although Beth and Georgia had a frown each.

'What's the go from here, Harry?' asked Andy.

'We wait to see who turns up next. Then if all goes well with delegation number three, we might move across the harbour to that bay on the north-east side. It's not far away, but we'll be mostly out of sight of the *Changbaishan*. We'll try to park where we can still keep an eye on the ship with the masthead camera, but they can't properly see us. I want them to know we aren't leaving, but for us to be sufficiently out of the way when the poo finally hits the fan.'

I grinned at him. 'I think you'll find the diving over there a lot better as well.'

He grinned back and rubbed his hands enthusiastically, 'Great! Good plan.'

After a lovely breakfast, I made a call to Mathias Tari.

'*Good morning, Commander. You must be psychic. I was about to call you.*'

I chuckled, 'I'm more used to being called psycho than psychic, Mr Tari, but how are things going with you?'

'*Very nicely so far, thank you. Our Ministers totally rejected the Chinese proposal as being just a bunch of lies to keep us busy arguing amongst ourselves, while they took control of our only deep-water port. The ministers finally understood that the ridiculous offer to fund the re-opening of the Panguna mine was just a diversion for their real intentions. Yesterday, I told their negotiators that we don't want any other country becoming involved in our internal politics, particularly at this stage when we are close to achieving genuine agreement and peace between all our provinces. Unfortunately, they weren't happy with that statement.*'

I laughed. 'I bet they weren't. But surely they didn't just accept your rejection and head home?'

It was his turn to laugh. '*No, they didn't. They begged for the opportunity to talk to their government and come up with a better*' *proposal. I have given them five days to come up with one, and reserved the right to reject it immediately if I believed it still wasn't in the best interests of our country. So, whatever you have planned, you have less than one week to do something.'*

'I understand. But do you think there is any chance they'll produce a proposal which you and your ministers might find acceptable?'

'No, Commander, absolutely no chance. As I said earlier, the Council have all agreed that the Chinese proposal is false. But even if it were genuine, it would be a disaster for our country to have such a large and powerful nation so deeply involved in our affairs. As much as we need the mine to be functioning, we cannot and will not allow a foreign country to be involved. It is most unfortunate that private enterprise does not wish to take on the project, as that would be a different story. However, we have learned that the level of internal unrest which has plagued my country for so long has turned away the few acceptable applicants who may have been interested.'

I was silent for a few moments, his words causing several startling thoughts to briefly bounce around my brain. Finally, I pushed those thoughts aside for more thorough massaging at a later time, and answered Mathias.

'Thanks for your thoughts, Mr Tari, and I can say that plans are well under way to achieve our mutual objectives. I shall be in touch again soon. Good day now.'

'*Thank you, Commander and thank you for your efforts to assist. Good luck.'*

My next call was to Joseph Bulli, our helpful collaborator.

'*Good morning Captain, how may I help you today?'*

'Good morning, Joseph. I was thinking we might shift our position to the north side of the harbour, where there are some shallow areas of coral near the shore. The diving will be better than this location, but I wanted to get your approval before moving.'

'*Ahh, yes. That is a good place for your lovely crew to do some superb* coral viewing. Perhaps inside the second small bay would be the best position for your boat, I am thinking. When do you think you might make this move?'

'Later today, probably after lunch if there are no problems you are aware of.'

'No problems from me, Captain. Enjoy yourselves. Good-bye.'

'Thanks, Joseph. Bye now.'

I looked around at the circle of faces. 'Okay. I take that to mean that he's not heard of any fallout from our disposal run last night, so we'll wait a few hours to see if we get visitors before we move.'

While we waited for what I was certain would be another visit from the Chinese navy, I allowed the strange and exciting ideas which had been sparked by something Mathias had said, to develop further.

Initially, I believed I was thinking way beyond ridiculous and nearly rejected the notion, but the more I considered it from different angles, the more it made some sort of twisted sense. But as I had no knowledge or experience of international high finance, that made it hard to judge how workable my idea could be, although part of the answer could be found with one more phone call.

'Twice in one day, Commander. Your mind must be very active. How can I help?'

'Just one quick question Mr Tari. In the Chinese proposal, did it show the amount of money they had allowed for the restoration of the Panguna mine site?'

'I believe so, Commander. Just a moment and I'll look it up... ahh, yes. The basic mine restoration amount was in the range of US$800 to $900 million. That didn't include the environmental restoration works as they hadn't yet been able to make all the necessary surveys, but I believe a rough estimate of the total amount to reach full production stage again, including the environmental cleanup and fully-functional port facilities, was in the region of five to six billion US dollars.'

My heart sank to hear that, but hopefully, I concealed my

dismay and thanked him for the information, carefully dodging his question as to why I wanted that information.

Fifteen minutes later, I was sitting at the nav table, doodling random notes thoughtfully on a notepad, when Sandy came in and said, 'Harry darling, an RIB has left the *Changbaishan* and is heading this way.'

Her words took a few moments to register, then I looked up and smiled.

'Good-oh. Round three is about to begin. This one should be even more interesting.'

'You're allowed to be nice if they are,' she warned again.

'Yes, dear. I thought I was last time. After all, I only kicked him in the nuts once for calling you a whore!'

'You're 'yes dear-ing' me again, dear,' she poked her tongue out, 'but do try a bit harder this time.'

'Yes, dear. I'll play nice with the kiddies.'

The RIB only contained four men this time, two officers and two sailors. The senior officer, who was a Lieutenant Commander by his insignia, was accompanied by a junior Lieutenant, possibly the same one who was on the last bungled visit.

The Lieutenant Commander signed to the coxswain to halt the boat some five metres away, and called out in excellent English, 'Request permission to come aboard, please Captain.'

Playing nice as promised, I called back,' Permission granted, Lieutenant Commander.'

He only looked slightly surprised at the correct recognition of the single star between two thin lines on his epaulettes, then waved the boat forward. Nimbly, he and the Lieutenant stepped onto the boarding platform, and climbed to the cockpit. They both bowed slightly, before he stepped forward and held out his hand.

'Lieutenant Commander Yang, Captain.'

I shook his hand and introduced myself, then invited both officers to be seated out of the sun, offering green tea, water or iced fruit juice as refreshment.

Yang looked surprised at the cordial reception, undoubtedly having been prepared to be attacked by the crazy Australian skipper. With refreshments in hand, Yang opened the discussion.

'I present my Captain's complements, and also his apologies for the inexcusably rude behaviour of Commanders Wu and Zhao. He hopes you will accept his apologies.'

I bowed my head slightly, 'Thank you, Lieutenant Commander, please inform your captain that his gracious apologies are accepted.'

He beamed at me. 'That is excellent, Captain. However, I have another request. Yesterday evening, Commander Wu and five other men left the ship in a small boat on a routine night-training exercise. Unfortunately, they haven't returned from this exercise and we haven't received any radio contact from the team. My captain wishes to know if you heard or saw anything of these men last night?'

With a suitably expressionless face, I replied, 'I'm afraid not, Lieutenant Commander. Neither my crew nor myself heard any boats at all last night. We are not in the habit of keeping a standing night watch when in a safe and secure harbour, particularly with your large and imposing ship providing additional security. Last night, everyone retired to their cabins shortly after our evening meal. Perhaps one of the local villagers heard or saw something? We have noticed they are often moving about late into the evening. Maybe Mr Bulli can help you with that enquiry.'

He looked carefully at me, glanced around the cockpit and at the crew, then nodded. 'Yes, perhaps they have. We will continue with our enquiries, but should you receive any information about our missing team, my captain would be very grateful if you would contact us. The marine VHF radio would be best for that. Channel 16 is always monitored.'

I stood, as an indication that the meeting was over, and both officers scrambled to follow suit. 'We will be pleased to do that, Lieutenant Commander, should we hear of anything to do with this night-training exercise.'

He bowed his head briefly. 'On behalf of my Captain, we appreciate your co-operation, and I shall now leave you to enjoy your visit to Bougainville.'

I didn't reply, but followed him to the top of the stern steps, watching as he and the Lieutenant boarded the RIB and left.

'Training exercise my arse,' laughed Andy, 'what a crock of shit! But what's your take on that, Harry? Do you think they suspect we know something?'

I nodded ruefully, 'Yep... afraid so. I can't believe all the officers would be in on a pay-back raid, but there's no way the late and unlamented Commander Wu could have been able to check out those weapons, ammo and explosives without some of them knowing about it. So, barring an attack by the local villagers on the way between their ship and us, then as far as they're concerned, we must have seen them.'

'Does that mean we can expect another midnight raid?' Gillian asked, an excited look in her eye showing she was quite keen for more action, while Georgia and Beth looked pale.

'No. I don't think so, but they'll be watching us very closely and it's my opinion they won't hesitate to stage a terminal accident if they get the smallest shred of hard evidence. Good thing you guys cleaned up so well last night.'

'Did I hear you say we're going to move anchorages?' Beth asked.

'Yeah. That's one of the things I checked with Joseph. I wanted him to suggest the best place for us to be over the next few days for when we need his support, but we won't move until mid-afternoon. I don't want these turkeys to think we're running scared.'

Beth gave me one of those looks which Sandy has perfected over the years. 'Seems to me like that's exactly what we should be doing!'

I chuckled. 'No way! There's no need for that. The Chinese will behave themselves as long as they think negotiations are still in progress or until they believe they have a sufficiently secure foothold in this port. After that, it might be a different story.'

After a late, lazy lunch, it was only a short motoring run across to our new anchorage on the north side of the harbour, where several tongues of shallow coral banks extended up to 250-metres from shore, effectively forming small bays. Despite the shallow banks, the drop-off on the edge of them was very steep, going straight down to around 100 feet, so I had to anchor with care. I also wanted to make sure our hulls were out of sight of the *Changbaishan* and most of the wharf, but to leave some of our mast clearly visible, as I didn't want the Chinese to start sending patrols out to see what mischief we might be up to if they couldn't see us at all.

Naturally, Andy and Lara wanted to go diving straight away, but since it was getting late in the day, I talked them into doing some snorkel-sucking along the shallow edges of the coral bank. They came back very enthusiastic about the lovely coral, the abundant fish life and the clear water.

After they'd rinsed the salt off their gear and themselves, Andy said, 'If there's nothing planned for tomorrow, we'd like to make a couple of deep dives to get Lara some experience with those procedures. There doesn't seem to be any current flow, and we're close to the drop-off, so we can operate straight off *Firebird*.'

'Sure. Sounds good. But please take Alex along for security.'

'No problem. He's keen.'

Bree had been monitoring the *Changbaishan* with the masthead camera ever since we left our old anchorage. 'They didn't launch any boats that I saw,' she responded to my query, 'although I could see an officer tracking us with a set of those giant binoculars on a stand on the bridge wing, as we swung into this bay.'

'Good-oh. Hopefully they'll be happy they can still see where we are. I wouldn't be surprised if they send a shore party along to take a look anyway, although that won't matter since we're not going to do anything odd for a day or two.'

# CHAPTER 16

And nothing did happen. It was a peaceful couple of days with lots of laughs at Beth and Georgia's attempts to make up more meaningful tests for Jasper, and his reaction to their efforts. Now that all their serious tests were over, he seemed to think everything they did was a great excuse for a game and successfully messed around with their heads – which in turn had both of them devising a new range of tests to prove and document what they thought he was doing.

When they finally woke up to what he was doing, they suddenly became very excited all over again with the realisation that this overgrown cat was perfectly capable of outwitting them, and was jerking their collective chains just for the fun of it!

Andy, Lara and Alex made their deep dives, getting down close to the no-decompression limit of 130 feet, which was the depth limit of the immediate drop-off we were parked on the edge of anyway. Alex made sure they had near-zero bottom time, and enforced a safety stop at 15 feet anyway. On surfacing, Lara was terribly excited and wanted to do it again, but both Alex and Andy convinced her that for safety, they should all stay at snorkelling depth for 24 hours to ensure their systems were purged of any excess nitrogen.

On the first night at our new address, Beth and Sandy decided it was time to have another get-together, so I sat up with Georgia knocking back a few NQ teas for a while to let them have the run of the bed. As the teas started kicking in, Georgia became more than a little bit amorous, but in a radical change of habit for me, I thought I'd let that lovely opportunity pass for the moment, if I decently could. Luckily, the NQ teas proved the sting in their tail yet again, as Georgia developed a severe case of the sleepy wobblies, and needed to be helped to bed. Temptation almost overcame me again when I had to help her undress, but since she was really out of her tree, I left her to it and just went to my bed as usual. Well, not quite as usual and it was really good fun. Being in a secure harbour, there was no pressure to get up at sparrow's fart, so I transferred my freshly-awakened lustful attention to Beth with several delightful and predictable results.

The second night, we had visitors in the form of Joseph and his eight grinning paddlers. The now-obligatory carton of frosty cans was passed down and gratefully accepted, while their passenger quickly got on the outside of the contents of his own can.

'What's to report, Joseph?' I asked when he had demolished the first can and started on the second.

'The feast is set for the evening of the day after tomorrow,' he replied, unsuccessfully stifling a large burp. 'We're just catering for the 120 who comprise the ship's crew, not the marines and ground-engineering crew, and I've managed to convince the captain that he should allow them all to participate in our traditional kava ceremony.'

I looked puzzled, 'I didn't think you guys used kava very much?'

Joseph grinned. 'We don't – or rarely anyway. But he doesn't know that. The kava plant does grow here and we happen to have the variety which is the most potent of all. The root of our variety has a bright orange flesh, which I propose to augment with a certain variety of mushroom which also grows here.'

I looked at him with undisguised admiration.

'Oh, you cunning bugger. Well done, Mr Bulli!'

He tried to look modest, but failed, grinning widely.

'I think that by 21:00 hours, the evening after tomorrow, you'll find that 85% of the ship's company will be way off in la-la land. I predict that they'll have trouble getting aboard the ship, let alone finding or firing a gun. Herds of flying pink elephants will probably be the most aggressive things these guys will be seeing.'

'Joseph. What a superb plan! This is fucking brilliant!'

'Thank you, Commander. I thought it was rather good myself.'

'Okay. But don't forget that the marines won't be affected, unless someone sneaks some of your augmented kava aboard.'

He smiled modestly, 'I might have made arrangements to create that possibility. We certainly won't get all of them, as they tend to be a very task-focussed bunch, but even some incapacitation among the marines will be a help.'

'It's an absolute pleasure to work with you, Mr Bulli,' I said sincerely, 'but how are plans going with organising the 'enemy forces'?'

'All good there. They have their instructions and plenty of their own weapons. Your signal to act will be when you hear shouts, explosions and guns firing ashore.'

'That sounds great, Joseph. This seems to be coming together nicely.'

'Indeed, it is, Commander. Apart from being the most pleasure my people and I have had for years, getting rid of these arrogant arse-holes will be a huge step forward for our country.'

I looked at him more carefully, sensing a new dimension to the perpetually smiling Joseph.

'Do I detect a political side to you, my dear sir?'

He gave a tight smile. 'You never know, Commander. As a great man once sang, 'the times they are a'changin'.'

'Nicely put, Joseph. Now, back to business. Should we set up the mount for the weapons tomorrow night?'

'Let's do it by daylight, Commander. Much easier. The Chinese have already sent a shore party to have a look at you and have retreated back to the ship. You are now fully protected by the locals from surveillance, day and night, so we can fit your mounting tomorrow morning. If you are still concerned about being spotted, we could hide both canoes between your hulls where they will be almost invisible, and can stay there until needed.'

After an uneventful evening, we had just finished breakfast next morning, when two long canoes with new-looking 60-hp outboards bolted to their sterns motored quietly up to our stern. The incongruity of seeing a vessel carved from a single giant tree trunk in a style which was centuries old, but with a modern outboard motor bolted to its stern never failed to amaze me. These two canoes had three men in each, dressed in the local fashion of ragged shorts and gaudy T-shirts advertising beer. Despite their scruffy appearance, they were clean and healthy.

'Morning Boss,' the main man called to me. 'Mr Joseph sent us to get fittings attached to our boats.'

'Good morning,' I replied, 'please come aboard.'

'Thank you sir,' the leader said. 'My name is Alfred and my brother who owns the other boat is Martin.'

We weren't introduced to the other four men who were content to remain with the boats after they had tied them up, chattering quietly with each other. Bree passed several cartons of chilled fruit juice to the men who grinned their appreciation and thanked her in Tok Pisin, the pidgin English which is the only common language throughout the country, where more than 40 different languages and dialects prevail.

Meanwhile, Alfred and Martin, who also had a reasonable command of English, were introduced to all our crew and supplied with food and drink.

'What has Joseph told you of what we intend doing?' I asked Alfred cautiously.

'Mr Joseph, him say you and we make attack on big ship with your powerful guns.'

'Okay. But do you understand that the ship has many sailors and much bigger guns than our guns, and they will probably be shooting back? Therefore, there is a chance we might all be killed?'

He grinned again, seeming to find delight in everything. 'Yes, Boss. Mr Joseph say this. But he also say you do this to help our country and to be friend. Therefore, we do what you need to get rid of bad men. They no friend to our country.'

'Thank you, Alfred. Did Joseph say that we might need three more canoes running around tonight just to make some confusion?'

'Yes Boss. We can do that if you want. You say – they come. All our people want to do hurt to these bad men.'

'Okay. That's very good. Now before we start work, how about you move your boats under our boat into the shade. Much better for working.'

That suggestion was received with great enthusiasm, as the air temperature was in the high thirties Celsius, and the humidity above ninety-percent as usual. Within minutes, both canoes were tucked under *Firebird's* wide bridge deck in the shade, with just the bows poking out beside the stern boarding platforms.

After talking further with Alfred and Martin, we decided to mount both guns just forward of midships and as the canoes were all wood, with sides and bottom about 70mm thick, it was easy to just screw the mounts for the MK47 and the Browning M2 .50 cal. machine gun directly into the wood. The narrow hulls caused a slight restriction to the operator, which only allowed each weapon to be fired in a narrow arc to the front and not much to the side. I wasn't too worried about this limitation, compared to the huge advantage of having the Chinese only seeing locally-built dugout canoes scooting around in the dark, instead of our distinctive RIB. Having them assume that it was just the islanders who didn't want them, was the main purpose of that part of the deception.

Securing the mounts to the satisfaction of Terry and Gillian only took a couple of hours, so we went ahead with a trial fitting of the guns as well to make sure everything would work properly.

They did and the canoe crews were fascinated with the MK47, which was visually smaller and much more compact overall than the long-barrelled M2 Browning, but which packed a much more devastating punch. I took the opportunity to make the point to both drivers that the guns needed a stable platform to be able to score hits in exactly the right places. They assured us they understood and explained that the mass of the canoes, which weighed several tonnes each, would keep them steady even when moving.

I didn't bother trying to explain that simply spraying the bulk of the *Changbaishan* with 40mm grenades and .50 cal. machine gun bullets was akin to throwing rocks at a charging rhino. Based on the photos and video we'd shot when we first arrived, had allowed me to decide exactly where the rounds needed to be placed for maximum effect, and I went over the targets again with Terry and Gillian.

'What rounds have you got for the MK47?' I asked.

'High explosive, of course,' Gillian replied, 'but we also decided to throw in some incendiary and a few of the new semi-armour-piercing.'

'Oh, that's excellent. How about you make you make up your belts with two HE, one incendiary, and one armour-piercing, rinse and repeat?'

They looked at each other and shrugged.

'Sure. We can do that. It's a bit of shagging around to reload the belts, but you're right, it should have a bigger impact.'

'Good. I think it'll help a lot.'

'You said you had specific targets, Harry?' Gillian reminded me, so I grabbed a print-out of several of the photos we'd taken.

'Yeah, I did. Sorry about that. Remember, don't get too close in case there are some troops who are quick to react with their rifles, but your first target will be the boat storage deck which is through that large square opening in the side. Really spray that area with rounds. We need to start and spread some internal fires as quickly as possible. Your next target will be the helicopter hanger, which should be the three large windows in the hull forward of the flight deck. I'll try to bust the windows first with the .50 cal. There are two helicopters in there, which means plenty of fuel and oil to burn. Get a heap of rounds in there as well. Then, if all has gone well to that point, I'd like you to target the smaller opening just below the mid-point of the flight deck. That should be where they keep the hovercraft. They're nasty buggers – heavily-armed and capable of 80 knots. That should be worth a few more fires, as well as eliminating more opposition.'

They nodded agreeance. 'How long do we stay on site?' was Terry's question.

I grinned. 'Only until they start seriously shooting back. We aren't here to be too heroic! I'm counting on most of the crew being stoned, along with the element of surprise to let us get some good solid licks in first, but if they get their shit together quickly and look like getting the CIWS or the main cannon working, we'll have to bail immediately. If they only use small arms, we'll stay a bit longer but pull further back. I don't want anybody getting shot. Copy?'

They nodded. 'Yep. No problem with that, Harry.'

'Good. I plan on taking out the gun radars, radio aerials, the searchlight and the big-eye binoculars first up, then the hangar windows, then just keeping heads down on the open deck. If you do get a chance, have a crack at the bridge as well. If we can knock out a bunch of electronics, that'll help, although we won't be able to hit the Combat Operations Centre, unless fire does that for us. Once again, don't be too heroic. We're just trying to make their life very uncomfortable.

When we bail out, head straight back across the harbour to the far shore, then head north along the shoreline at slow speed to avoid leaving a wake. They'll be chasing us fairly quickly, so don't mess about once you run. The boys will drop you back at *Firebird*, before they head for a hide-out'

'We want to hurt them, and cause as much chaos as possible, but we honestly can't expect too much more. By that, I mean there's no way we're going to sink the thing. I'm hoping that just the fact they are being attacked by what they should think are local rebels, should make them think twice about having further ambitions in this region. I'll also be having Bree record the whole episode with the masthead camera, so we have to dress rough and dark, wrap our heads and our faces with a scarf or something, and cover all remaining exposed skin with dark make-up. The attack has to look like an all-local affair.'

Terry looked at me with a sly grin. 'I don't suppose you still have that Russian RPG-7 we liberated from the Indonesian pirate's den?'

I returned his grin. 'As a matter of a fact... yeah we do, and it's going with us as well. There's only ten HEAT rounds left, so in between changing the .50 cal. ammo belts, Alex is going to lay a couple of rounds into the bridge, the forward cannon and the CIWS, then the rest through the hull into the engine room. But I'd still like you to try to puncture the water-line with the MK47 if there's time. You've got a lot more rounds than Alex has.'

With that settled, we decided to leave the armed canoes where they were, then ferried the crews ashore in our RIB.

## KIETA WHARF

Starting early next morning, several firepits had been dug in the soft ground just beside the end wharf, not far from where the massive steel wall which was *Changbaishan's* stern reared high above. Several local women fed a steady supply of wood into the flames, where over several hours, it burned down to a thick bed of glowing coals, leaving the women gleaming with sweat from the heat. They solved that problem by periodically diving off the wharf to cool off in the water. Then the chefs took over as ten freshly-butchered pigs, their belly cavities stuffed with a variety of vegetables and fruit wrapped in banana leaves and roughly sewn up again, were mounted on steel poles and set on stands over the coals. It wasn't long before the appetite-enhancing smell of roasting pork began wafting around the dock area and drifting aboard the ship where it was distributed by the air-conditioning system.

Any crew who perhaps had considered not attending the feast, were soon inclined to change their minds. The ever-smiling locals who tended the cooking and stoked the fires, were also careful to mention to the sailors setting up the trestle tables, that a kava ceremony had been approved by the captain.

In a dry ship, that news spread even faster than the tantalising smells of the roasting pork.

At around the same time as the feast was cooking, in a small house close to the dock area, large containers of kava had been in preparation for several days. Beside the back door, a growing mound of the husks of the crushed and filtered orange root, and the numb lips of the tasters, testified to the potency of the brew. In another room, a man and a woman, both wearing gloves and close-fitting masks, were feeding small mushrooms into an electric blender. A per-head dosage had been worked out and the fact that it would be added to a mildly intoxicating beverage taken into account. The resulting fine mush had some freshly-crushed ginger added before the combination was added to the raw, unfiltered kava brew and allowed to sit for a few hours.

In the late afternoon, the kava was strained through filters, in deference to the uneducated palates of the Chinese sailors.

As 18:00 hours rolled around, sailors began to gather around the tables, now covered in plates of steaming vegetables. They were still wrapped in their cooking blanket of banana leaves, and had spent the last hour on the coals under the dripping juices of the succulent meat above. There were jugs of fruit juice, although prime space was left for the giant wooden bowls of kava.

With everything in readiness, Senior Captain Liu, was asked to present himself at the feast in order to be welcomed by the local chief and the tribal elders. By the time that was organised, the time had marched around to 18:30 and the crew were getting both hungry and thirsty.

Under the guidance of Joseph Bulli dressed in his official uniform, festivities opened with the dramatic sound of drummers hidden back in the trees, announcing the chief and his tribal elders, in full dress regalia, who marched solemnly down to the feast site. In turn, they were followed by a line of decorated warriors carrying large wooden bowls of kava. The captain was seated at the head of the first table in a throne-style, hand-crafted chair, with his senior officers all seated at the same table. A huge wooden bowl of kava was placed in the centre of the captain's table, before many other bowls of similar size were placed on the other tables.

The chief launched into a speech of welcome but unfortunately, it was in the local dialect and was wasted on 98% of those present. Finally, Joseph managed to encourage the chief to move along, and dipped a coconut shell cup into the kava, took a sip, then presented it to the captain. As he had already been told it was a mortal insult to refuse the kava when presented this way, the captain bravely drank the rest of the cup. A round of applause signalled the feast had begun and both the food and the kava were attacked by the voracious sailors, keen to relax away from rigid shipboard discipline and routine, if only briefly.

As the noise level rose from 120 appreciative throats, and the captain's attention was briefly diverted, two large buckets of kava were surreptitiously passed to the gangway guards, who didn't need to be told twice what to do with them. Joseph, smiling broadly as usual, was pleased to see that the supplies of kava were being depleted at a steady rate. Visitors rarely appreciated the earthy taste of the traditional drink, although in this case, the addition of the special mushrooms and ginger made it far more palatable. The way the alcohol-starved sailors were tossing it down was testament to the improved taste and the servers made sure supplies didn't run dry.

It was well after dark, and closer to 20:00 hours before the first effects of the enhanced brew started to show. Under normal circumstances, open displays of hilarity were rare in front of the ship's officers, and non-existent when the captain was present. It was very odd therefore, when several sailors began laughing so hard that they fell backwards off their chairs.

That caused the hilarity to spread, until the captain took notice and told his Executive Officer to pass the word that further unseemly displays would not be tolerated. Unfortunately, the ship's XO had been quietly knocking back a few extra cups of kava whenever his captain wasn't looking and regarded the order as a great joke when it was issued by what he now saw was a pink bear with four stars on its shoulders.

This enraged the captain who smashed his fist on the table and demanded the XO settle the crew down or the feast would be terminated immediately and all crew sent back aboard.

Joseph grinned to himself and whispered some instructions to one of the kava servers, who grinned and hurried off.

## FIREBIRD

We were a nervous crew who didn't much feel like an evening meal and although I tried hard to relax and appear normal, I felt the tension even more than the others. It was, after all, my crazy idea which was about to put my friends and many of the locals directly in harm's way. Sandy was well aware of my feelings, but substituted our usual stress-relief session for a more decorous neck and shoulder massage.

'Just tell me again what you hope to achieve out of this insanity, please Harry?' Beth asked yet again as I smeared on the last bit of dark tan make-up, so I drew a deep breath and patiently told her.

'I've set things up with Joseph, so that his mates on-shore will fire guns, let off firecrackers, and scream and yell a lot, making it sound like they're attacking the feast and the ship. With nearly all the crew ashore, there'll be a mad scramble to get back aboard, which seeing as nearly all of them are totally wacked-out and can hardly walk, is bound to cause a heap of confusion. That should give us plenty of time to fire a bunch of those lovely 40mm grenades into that huge opening in the ship's side where they launch their small boats, as well as lob a few into the helicopter hanger through the side windows. I expect casualties on the ship to be minimal.'

'But why risk anyone's life, Harry?' she almost cried.

'The objective is to cause enough damage so the ship has to go back to base for repairs, and in turn, that will give everybody time to make sure the Chinese don't come back. By making it look as though all the trouble is caused by the locals, removes any suggestion that Australia or Papua New Guinea is involved. The world can be told that the locals took unilateral action to get rid of the ship which had imposed itself, completely uninvited, on Bougainville. Australia had nothing to do with it, as our only warship is way up north visiting Buka Town on a pre-arranged visit.'

'But they've got fucking big guns all over that thing! I saw them! You'll all get shot, for sure!'

'Well. I'm hoping that the kava brew, heavily laced with a puree of magic mushrooms, which Joseph and his team are feeding to the crew right now, might slow most of them down enough that they couldn't hit the side of the ship from ten paces with a shotgun. That's if they can even find a gun! From what Joseph has told me, the most they'll be able to see will be pink dragons!'

'Oh,' she said, more calmly, 'that might help a little bit.'

'I hope it'll help a lot!' I retorted. 'I don't actually fancy being in the sights of any of those 30mm cannons.'

Alfred and Martin had come aboard at 17:00, and they made sure everything was in order on their canoes, including warming up the outboards. Alex was coming with me in Martin's boat to help load the Browning and play with the RPG-7, while Alfred took Terry and Gillian and the MK47. We had checked the weapons twice and without actually pulling a trigger, could do no more to prepare. Three more canoes had turned up, a driver and a crew-man armed with AK47s in each, ready to provide an extra level of confusion and firepower. Their grim, excited expressions really brought it home to me that the locals had been fairly busting to lash out at these arrogant intruders, and that this was their first real chance.

The plan was for us to wait until Joseph's colleagues started the mock attack on the feast and the ship from the land-side, before we raced in. On the heels of my previous thought, it occurred to me that it mightn't take long for the mock land attack to turn real and deadly.

My biggest concerns were the AK-630, 6-barrel 30mm CIWS mountings, of which the *Changbaishan* had four, two on each side of the upper centre deck.

Each pair was directed by a single radar unit which automatically tracked and fired at any moving target. They could even be targeted against objects as small as floating mines. If the radar was knocked out, as I intended, the system could still be operated in manual mode, but I was hoping the operators would be too busy dodging pink dragons to worry about taking control of their guns. One of my main jobs with the M2 Browning machine gun, was to knock out the CIWS radar unit which sat at the forward end of the upper deck, under a weather-proof cover which ironically made it look a bit like a large, grey mushroom. Once this unit was hopefully crippled by the .50 cal. bullets, the cannons should be rendered relatively impotent.

The other worry was the 76mm, rapid-fire main gun mounted on the foredeck. This was also radar-guided, although I felt that fast-moving wood canoes would be very difficult targets to lock onto. However, just to be sure, I was going to use the .50 cal. to chew-up every radar dome in sight.

# CHAPTER 17

Despite my confident explanation to Beth, I still had a lot of concern that we could take on this huge warship with what amounted to a trio of pop-guns, although the RPG-7 could be a formidable weapon if used carefully. So, it was with a rare feeling of dread tingling my spine, that we mounted up and waited for the start of the simulated land attack. Waiting has never been my strong point, so when my watch showed the time was close to 20:00, I announced we were going to head slowly around the point so we could see better.

Everyone was as nervous as me, so that move suited our crews, and as we rounded the point, we could hear the surprisingly loud sounds of revelry from the docks. I checked the ship through my binoculars and couldn't see any undue movement, or any crew on deck for that matter, although I knew that at least a skeleton crew would be on duty on the bridge.

It was good to be at least moving and I immediately felt better. I could see the others were too, as we slowly closed the distance to our target. Our call to action came suddenly, consisting of a series of loud bangs and volleys of gunshots from the other side of the ship, accompanied by a lot of yelling and blood-thirsty screams.

'Okay,' I announced, waving the other canoes forward, 'that's it. Let's go light things up!'

We were already within a few hundred metres of the ship by then, which was almost point-blank range for both weapons. The three drivers in the canoes charged with providing distraction and confusion took to that task with enthusiasm, by cranking their motors up to full-power, and making what looked like attack runs at the ship, that put our two gun-canoes in the middle of a confusing melee of canoes charging about in all directions, the crews whooping, yelling and firing their AK-47s. Our drivers kept our speed low for stability, as Terry and I opened fire almost at the same time. My first target was the radar dome controlling the CIWS cannons and it was gratifying to see pieces of housing and the radar dish itself flying into the air under the impact of the heavy slugs. When I judged the radar unit to be well out of action, I turned my aim toward the CIWS cannon mountings, although I wasn't sure if they'd be in an armoured mounting. They might have been, but there still seemed to be pieces flying off the barrel assembly itself, which might stuff it up a bit, so I hosed down the second gun mount as well. Then it was the turn of the other radar units, starting with the big one at the aft end of the upper deck, then the smaller one above the bridge. Neither of the domes appeared to be armoured, as the coverings just flew apart as the contents were equally trashed by the relentless hammering of the big slugs. I had to duck down briefly as Alex fired the RPG-7, the smoke of the launching charge blasting out over my head. I looked up in time to see his first shot impact the aft CIWS mounting, with a lot more success than I'd had with the .50 cal. It definitely wasn't going to be firing anytime soon. Based on that, I quickly revised the plan and told Alex to keep firing at the targets we'd selected and I'd help reload.

The forward CIWS mount was similarly wrecked, then the main gun on the foredeck took a couple of rounds which behaved as advertised and blasted through the armoured turret without problem. We could only presume the internal damage was sufficient to cripple it. I hoped the bridge watch had taken cover, as the next two rounds flew through the closest bridge windows and exploded inside. It can't have been too healthy inside for either humans or electronics.

I'd been too busy to see what Terry and Gillian were up to, but a whoop of joy from Alex drew my attention to the gaping boat launching port in the ship's side, where a broad tongue of yellow flame was already licking up the outside of the hull. It quickly increased in intensity, punctuated by a series of small explosions inside, as fuel, oil and maybe munitions cooked off. I quickly scanned along the ship's decks to see if any defence was being mounted, but since there was still no visible reaction, I hosed the bridge windows for a few seconds, then took out the searchlight and the giant binoculars on the bridge wing, which Bree had spotted earlier.

While Alex fed in another fresh ammo belt, I took a moment to watch Terry's action. He was still pouring grenades into the boat storage area, the MK47 chugging away steadily, while the flames and explosions increased by the second.

'Shift target, Terry,' I muttered to myself, and he must have heard me, as the stream of grenades momentarily stopped, then resumed as rounds started exploding against the hull in the vicinity of the hanger deck windows.

He quickly found his target and most of the grenades flew inside, gouts of yellow flame showing through the now glass-less openings. Moments later, there was a soft explosion followed by three mighty sheets of flame which belched out of the hull openings as fuel tanks lit off.

Alex picked up the RPG-7, which I'd already re-loaded for him, and took aim at the water-line below the raging inferno which was the hanger deck. There was a brief flash of flame as the shaped-charge hit the hull, but no further visible reaction.

'I've got three left,' he said, 'do you want them in the same area?'

'Yes, please. They must be penetrating, so we're still doing damage.'

His aim was true and the final three impacted close to the first, although the lack of results was the same. He laid the launcher down and I took up my task of pounding whatever I could with the 12.7mm slugs.

Several yellow blinking lights on the flight deck drew my attention, especially when a series of hammer blows jarred the boat, and something slammed into my shoulder, stinging like buggery for a few moments, and briefly throwing my aim off from the impact. My arm felt a bit numb, but as it sort-of still seemed to work, I made a quick sweep with the Browning's muzzle which soon wiped those shooters off the deck, until two more appeared on the upper deck, followed by a small group who started firing from the foredeck. I hosed them down, but decided it was time to bail out before someone on our side got hurt.

I signalled to Alfred to steer close past Martin's canoe, and signalled to him to head back to base. As both canoes turned away, all our guns fell silent as both skippers opened up the throttles, and chased by a veritable forest of small water spouts from the small arms fire still chasing us, we headed straight across the harbour toward the far shore, the other three canoes in trail.

I hoped this ruse would be sufficient to send the Chinese searching the wrong area first, giving us time to remove all evidence from our improvised gunboats. At full speed, we went most of the way to the far shore, before slowing and curving around in a wide arc until we were heading for *Firebird*. Alex and I used the time to dump all empty shell casings overboard, and remove the Browning .50 cal. from its mounting.

Alfred and Martin nosed the canoes up to *Firebird's* stern platforms, where willing hands took the weapons from us, and with a power screwdriver, I quickly removed the mounting frame from the canoe hull, while Alfred ruefully fingered the line of gouges along the outside of the hull.

'Can you fill those with mud or something?' I asked, working quickly.

'No problem, boss,' Alfred answered with his now-trademark broad grin, 'we go around north headland to other side. Many hiding places. Bad men never find us.' I shook his hand, and that of Martin, as Terry had finished unscrewing the MK47 mount, and the others were busy breaking the guns down to small parts and hiding them throughout *Firebird*.

'Thank you both for your work,' I said sincerely, 'you are truly brave men.'

They grinned and bobbed their heads, before pushing off and melting into the darkness.

I expected it was now quite late, but was shocked to see that less than twenty minutes had elapsed since we left. The shooting part must have lasted less than ten minutes. I was equally surprised to see the cockpit table covered in empty beer bottles, wine coolers and glasses, but then realised that the stage had been set for the expected visit from the Chinese.

'Good thinking,' I said to the group in general.

'Someone has to do that when you're not here, Harry,' Andy smiled, 'but you both might like to go and change your clothes and wipe the make-up off. You reek of gun smoke, and there seems to be a fair bit of claret leaking from your shoulder.'

Bree hustled Alex down below, while Sandy, with a disgusted look on her face, hauled me under a light to inspect my shoulder, which was starting to hurt, now that I'd slowed down and adrenaline stopped pumping through my system.

'Fuckin' hell, Harry. You've gone and done it again by getting shot! What is it with you, being a white-knight and playing with guns?'

I twisted around, trying to see what she was on about. 'Nah. Can't have. It's only a wood splinter or something. I hardly felt a thing.'

She glared at me. 'Of course you didn't feel it at the time. That's what adrenaline does, you silly goose. Come on down below, let me have those smelly clothes, and a better look at that teeny weeny scratch.'

In a mirror, I could see that a bullet had actually grazed the top of my left shoulder, leaving a shallow groove, but luckily without removing too much flesh. Still, it stung like buggery with the hot water pouring over it. I didn't have the time to waste relaxing under the cleansing stream, and once the make-up was off, was soon towelling down while Sandy dusted the wound and taped a dressing in place.

'Okay. Get dressed, then you need to tip a couple of beers down your throat. For medicinal and camouflage purposes only,' she finished with a grin.

Alex and I were back in the cockpit at about the same time, grabbed beers and set to telling our avid listeners what had happened.

Part way through the tale, I remembered something and asked Bree, 'How did the recording session go?'

She beamed, 'Really good, Harry. It's still recording, and zoomed in on the *Changbaishan*, so there's nothing to show where it was taken from.'

'Great. Thanks for that. But don't forget to stop it and retract the camera when our friends arrive.'

Beth, the perpetual worrier, asked, 'How sure are you that they'll come here?'

I gave a bark of a laugh. 'I reckon this boat will be their first call. And they won't be happy campers, either.'

'That's for sure,' Bree chipped in, 'the last I saw on the video, the ship was still burning in several places.'

Beth hadn't finished. 'That's even more reason for us to get out of here now. Why wait?'

Alex spoke up to give me a rest. 'Because they still have plenty of small boats, troops and small arms. What's worse, if we didn't get them all, they can off-load up to four large hover-craft through the stern bay. Those things are armed with heavy machine-guns, can carry 60 to 70 troops and travel at up to 80 knots. There's no way we could outrun them. Plus, of course, trying to run would be taken to be an admission of involvement in the attack. Our best chance is to stay put, act innocent and deny all knowledge.'

She looked a bit crestfallen as those obvious facts were pointed out. 'Oh. Yeah, sorry Alex. I didn't think it through.'

She looked at me with a pleading look in her eyes. 'But what will be our story, Harry? As you just said, they won't be happy campers. I'm happy to admit I'm more than a little bit scared.'

I nodded seriously. 'I understand, Beth. It's the old story about pulling the tiger's tail.'

I looked around the crew, not doubting that they all realised the precarious situation we were in.

'Look. Our story is simple. We came here to see a different part of the world, and to sample the superb diving. We didn't even know the Chinese were here before we arrived, and with one exception, we've been treated very badly by the Chinese officers, without any reason. We can also claim to be unaware of the attack. We can't see the ship from here and thought the bangs were just fireworks which we know the Chinese invented and love.'

I paused and looked around again. 'That's the story. Nothing more and nothing less. It's mostly the truth, except the bit about prior knowledge. That's all we have to keep repeating, but if any of you want to get upset and have a bit of a rant about our rights and how we were abused, then go right ahead. But don't forget that with Joseph's help, we've done all we can to deflect the blame onto the local rebels. The whole world knows this region is politically unstable, so the fact that sooner or later, the rebels were going to be attacking the Chinese ship, is almost a given.

You can be assured that Mathias will publicly wash his hands of having any knowledge or involvement in this, and I'm told there will be plenty of evidence left around to show that the attackers were the local rebels.'

There was general agreement with my words, and a noticeable easing of tension. Then Andy spoke up. 'I presume that I'll remain anonymous?'

'Yeah. For now anyway, thanks Andy. But I'll keep you in reserve in case our friends try to play a bit too rough. You can be one of our surprises.'

He grinned and raised his eyebrows. 'Just one of your surprises, Harry?'

My prediction that we would soon have the Chinese banging on our door, turned out to be overly pessimistic. We put up with the heat, and sat around the cockpit, kicking around all I'd said and the operation in general. By intent, I made no phone calls, although I did send a very brief email, with innocuous wording, to a good friend.

There was a lot of activity on the harbour, with RIBs zipping around. One made a pass a few hundred metres away, but didn't stop. We had the cockpit lights on low, which was enough to show that we were sitting around drinking, as was to be expected.

When, despite the general tension everyone felt, yawns started to appear, I suggested we should all head for bed, and let the game play out in its own timeline.

Oddly, there was no objection to that suggestion, and there was almost a traffic jam in the doorway to the saloon. I checked the camera and saw that the fires on the ship seemed to be out, with just smoke still rising slowly from several openings. I stopped the recording, stowed the camera and saved the data. Editing the recording would be a task for tomorrow.

By then, I really felt tired, had a very sore shoulder and arm, and as the bed had rarely felt so comfortable, I was asleep seconds after my head hit the pillow.

# CHAPTER 18

There must be a section in the Chinese PLAN Operations Manual which is headed, 'Boarding, Inspecting and Intimidating Procedure for dealing with Foreign Civilian Vessels', as we were yet again rudely awoken just before dawn by loud hammering on the hull and imperious shouts.

I headed topside rather more slowly than previously, clad in my usual paint-stained shorts, but with a T-shirt covering the dressing on my shoulder. I didn't rush as I was 100% certain who the noise-makers were. Naturally, I wasn't disappointed, being greeted by Lieutenant Commander Yang, the polite one from our last visit. He wasn't being quite so polite this time, although at least, he hadn't boarded us yet.

With the massive bulk of Alex behind me, I walked to the top of the stern steps to be faced with two RIBs full of armed troops. The one which was nosed up against our stern had Lieutenant Commander Yang aboard, and I noted with rising anger that the banging was caused by a soldier using the butt of his carbine against the boarding platform. The other RIB with six armed troops, was slowly circling us.

'Permission to come aboard, Captain,' Yang asked, although this time he wasn't smiling.

'Not until you tell me why you've woken me and my crew in this incredibly rude and arrogant manner! In addition, if that ignorant thug pretending to be a soldier has caused any damage to my boat, I'll be sending an invoice for the damage repair to your government.'

He looked surprised at my outburst, apparently expecting I was going to be intimidated by his show of force, then doubt flicked across his otherwise bland face, and his eyes dropped for a moment as he barked an order at the soldier.

'Very well. I have been sent by my captain to ask if you have any knowledge of who was responsible for the cowardly attack upon our ship last night.'

'Attack? What attack? What the hell are you talking about? We heard you having a noisy party last night. It must have been your New Year or something? I must say that you people do love your fireworks, I'll give you that. It was a shame we didn't see any of those beaut starbursts. I really like them. But what's this crap about an attack?'

I saw that flicker of doubt again, before anger took over and he spat his words out. 'They weren't fireworks, you fool! Our ship was attacked from the land and the water, by several boats armed with automatic weapons and rocket-propelled grenades. The ship has suffered damage and many crew have been killed and injured!'

Sometimes I think I should have taken up an acting career, as I immediately let concern and sympathy take over from my angry expression.

'Oh, bloody hell. I'm so sorry. Please come aboard, Lieutenant Commander, and tell us all about it.'

He bobbed his head in acknowledgement of my attitude change, and stepped aboard, accompanied by one soldier who I stopped at the foot of the steps by holding up my hand. 'You stay right there mister, unless you want to hand your gun to me first. Your officer is perfectly safe with us.'

The soldier looked at Yang for permission, who reluctantly nodded agreement.

Yang gratefully accepted a tall glass of chilled fruit juice, before starting on his tale.

'Thank you, Captain. This is greatly appreciated. Last night, our whole crew were sitting down to a native feast, put on by the local chiefs, when apparently rebels attacked the party and the ship from the land.'

Those of us in the cockpit with him, made suitable noises of amazement and sympathy.

'Yes, indeed. But then there was an attack from the harbour, by several dugout canoes armed with automatic weapons and a heavy machine gun. At least one of the guns fired rocket-propelled grenades, and another fired small bombs of some description. These caused great damage to the ship, started many fires and killed four sailors and injured seventeen more. Fortunately, we are well-equipped to fight fires and treat the wounded, but this unprovoked attack on a peaceful Chinese ship cannot be tolerated. We have already notified the Bougainville President of this shameful matter, and this is why we must ask if you have any knowledge which might help us find those responsible.'

I sat back, letting a range of emotions flick across my face, while internally, I tried to judge the import of his words. Like, did they seriously suspect we were involved or was this, most likely, just a fishing visit?

Measuring my words carefully, I replied, 'This is a terrible thing for you, Lieutenant Commander, but I cannot supply any information which might help your investigation. We were here all night, of course, as you know, and the sounds of your joyous celebrations travelled well across the water. We also heard explosions, but truly thought they were fireworks being let off as part of the celebration. That's why I was surprised not to see any star-bursts.'

I looked around at the crew, who shrugged or nodded solemn agreement.

'We did hear some boats running around the harbour just before and after we went to bed, but as none came close to us, I wasn't concerned. We don't keep a harbour watch in such a safe, protected place, as I mentioned at your last visit, so we heard nothing after that.'

I shrugged helplessly, glanced around again, then added, choosing my words carefully. 'We are very sad to hear of the loss of life and injuries to your crew, but cannot add anything which could help you find the perpetrators. The only thing I can suggest is that before we came here, we were warned not to stray ashore without a police escort, as the local people are still very suspicious of outsiders. We were also told they may react violently if they thought visitors were spying on them or trying to meddle in the local politics. Something to do with a mine of some sort. For that reason, you may have noticed that we haven't been ashore and don't plan to.'

He nodded, considering my words.

'Very well, Captain. I will convey those thoughts to my captain, but I must warn you that he is, as you would say, in a towering rage and looking for blood! Privately, I might add that you should expect further visits from more senior officers than me.'

I shrugged again. 'That is your captain's prerogative, Lieutenant Commander, and he may send more officers if it makes him feel better. But you can pass on to your captain that as private Australian citizens, here with the permission of the Bougainvillian Government, we will not tolerate unwarranted harassment by persons who are themselves visitors to this country! We have told you all we can, and if you care to spell it out in simple words for your captain, it is my opinion that the rebels made the attack because they strongly object to your presence. The solution would appear to be simple.'

Yang seemed to be struggling to maintain composure.

'These are dangerous words, Captain. I could not say them to my captain without fear of strong retribution myself, and I strongly suggest you refrain from saying them to any who may follow me.'

I stood in tacit dismissal, and bowed my head in acknowledgement.

'Point taken, Lieutenant Commander Yang. You have been a very reasonable representative, and I thank you for your advice.'

'Thank you, Captain. Good day to you and your crew.'


'Well,' Andy cheerfully said as Yang and his two boats motored away, 'that went better than I expected.'

I shook my head. 'Apart from the fact that he didn't mention that most of the crew was stoned out of their minds, I'm afraid not, old mate.'

'What? What'd I miss?'

Charlie, reverting instantly to the politically-savvy PPS, was nodding in agreement.

'Harry's right, boss,' she said grimly, 'Yang just gave us a clear warning that someone a lot harder than he is, is about to come and sort us out.'

Andy looked at me for confirmation, which I delivered with both barrels. 'Yep. That's exactly the case, Andy. But if I can steer things in the right direction, we should end up in a stronger position.'

He looked puzzled. 'How's that going to happen? We seem to be waiting for a large Chinese boot to fall on us!'

I smiled gently, 'Let's wait to see what the Chinese do. This is another situation where we have to let them make the next play.'

He wanted to know more, of course, but I refused to be drawn. 'We really do have to wait and see, old mate. Making the wrong move now could be dangerous.'

He reluctantly settled for that, so we sat around discussing Yang's visit and watching assorted RIBs criss-crossing the harbour as each village and settlement was searched, including the ones close to us.

Gillian made the most insightful statement of the day when she said, 'With all this running around, how the hell are the Chinese going to know if they do find someone involved in the raid? It's not as though the bad guys are going to be wearing uniforms, or have the word 'rebel' tattooed on their foreheads.'

That was worth a round of laughter.

We had just finished up a late breakfast or early lunch – brunch... or whatever it was called... it was bloody good, when our next visitor arrived. I could have made a bet as to who it would be – and would have won, when Commander Zhao in a two-boat deployment of RIBs full of armed troops, roared around the point of land between us and the *Changbaishan* and aggressively maintained that speed until almost on top of us. The lead boat with Zhao aboard, slowed just in time, swamping the sterns with its wash, while the other RIB circled us at speed.

Without asking, or waiting to be invited, Zhao stepped neatly from the bow of the RIB onto the freshly-wetted stern platform, then marched sternly up the steps to the cockpit. In contrast to the last time he arrived like this, I took a different tack and totally ignored him. There were six of us in the cockpit; myself, Sandy, Alex, Andy, Lara and Bree, with late morning teas and coffees in hand. Lara was in the middle of telling a funny story about doing her scuba course on the south coast, and I indicated that she should continue. Which she did in superb fashion, while the red-faced Commander stood bleating for attention behind us.

I waited until she'd finished, then looked over my shoulder.

'Oh, dear me. You've gone and done it again, Commander. You've come aboard illegally, as no permission was requested, nor given. Don't you people ever learn! Perhaps you should take some lessons from that nice, polite Lieutenant Commander Yang. He knows how to behave. But now that you are here, however unwelcome you are, you might as well say what's on your tiny mind.'

Zhao looked like he was going to explode. 'You insult Chinese officer again! You ignorant, rude man! You now listen to me!'

I turned away from him, and drawled, 'Oh, really! Do we have to? You really are dreadfully boring and tedious, do you know? Always saying the same thing. But get on with it if you must.'

His next words confirmed my worst fears, so I stood to face him.

'By my captain's orders, you and crew are under boat arrest! You stay on this boat until my captain has time to conduct investigation into attack on ship. Armed troops will guard and make sure you no leave harbour.'

He smirked annoyingly, 'Now who smart man?'

I stepped up close to him and glared. 'You have no right to arrest anybody outside of your own country, arsehole! In particular, you have no right to detain foreign civilians who are legally in another country, you pathetic dickhead! I therefore refuse to accept your order.'

He smirked again. 'Who you complain to? Bougainville have no military. If you want make complaint to my superiors, I have telephone number. They make big laugh to hear your complaint.'

His expression hardened. 'I repeat. You all under arrest. You cannot leave until my captain give permission. Try to leave – marines shoot. One boat of marines here all day, all night.'

I looked at him for a few moments, then shrugged and said quietly, 'Okay. If that's what you really want to do, so be it. But in front of witnesses, I formally warn you that you are making a huge mistake. A mistake which will cost you your career in the PLAN and maybe your life.'

'What stupid talk is this! You not in position to complain. We make complaint against those who attack us!'

I shrugged again, 'Very well. So why aren't you doing just that? Why are you standing here bleating pathetically at us? You know we had nothing to do with the attack that Lieutenant Commander Yang told us about. Go chase the rebels who actually made the attack on a foreign warship which has parked itself illegally and uninvited in their harbour! You're wasting valuable time annoying innocent foreign civilians and in doing so, just creating a lot more trouble for you, your captain and your government. But if you really feel you must persist with this stupidity, I need to see your captain as soon as possible. Send him here, please.'

He barked a mirthless laugh. 'My captain very busy – very important man. He no visit prisoners in jail!'

'Yeah, whatever. But however important he thinks he is, you tell him I need to see him.'

'You arrogant man. Forget you prisoner! You wait for Captain to make investigation.'

With that, he spun around and departed, leaving the other RIB loaded with six very alert, armed marines slowly circling us about twenty metres out.

Andy looked at me with a thoughtful expression. 'You were right, again, O Wise One. But I wasn't expecting to be placed under arrest.'

I laughed. 'No. I didn't dare hope he'd go that far, but that's what arrogance does. Muddles the thinking.'

'You mean that you were hoping he'd arrest us? What's the point of that?'

'Well... I didn't know he'd stoop to arrest, but I was hoping he'd overstep logical bounds. Because it's such an outrageously illegal order, the Chinese government won't dare try to back it up. Although we actually do need to obey it for now, since I'm sure those marines have strict orders to shoot if we start raising the anchor. Still, this is a nice place to stay for now while we wait for others to make their moves.'

Even Sandy gave me one of those looks. 'You're being way too cryptic, my dear man. What are you cooking up now?'

I tried to look innocent. 'Just letting the last few pawns move into place, my dear. But we do need to see how my last message is received by our cranky Chinese captain.'

While we waited, I took Sandy and Alex aside and gave them a set of instructions just in case things went in the wrong direction.

It was just as well I'd made preparations, as ninety minutes later, Commander Zhao returned with another showy flourish of speed, a huge foaming wake and a shit-eating grin. Without any formalities, he marched up the stern steps, this time accompanied by two marines holding their carbines in the ready position.

Pointing at me he barked, 'My captain sends you his reply! You come with me!'

He looked around, then pointed at Andy. 'You come too!'

I jumped up and started to protest, but he made a gesture, and the two marines quickly cocked their guns, raised them to their shoulders, and pointed one at me and the other at Andy.

'No more stupid words! No more delay. You come now or marines shoot!'

I could only hope that Beth was getting all this on video, as she and Georgia were sitting in the shadows of the saloon, playing with Krazy cat, with Jasper remaining out of sight.

Letting my shoulders slump in my best theatrical style, I looked at Andy. 'Sorry about this, mate. We'd better go along with this idiot for now. Play it cool and no one will get hurt. For now.' I managed to get a wink in when Zhao couldn't see, before I shuffled dejectedly down to the RIB, where I was roughly grabbed by two marines and forced down into a seat. Andy received similar treatment, and I was glad to see that he'd taken my hint and kept his mouth shut. There was no disguising the revulsion and anger blazing in his eyes however, and I hoped he'd remain quiet for now.

Zhao wasted no time getting us back to the ship, where the scene resembled an ant's nest, stirred violently by a kid with a stick. Sailors and marines scurried about, and a ring of armed marines closed off the portion of the wharf where the *Changbaishan* tiredly rested its broad rump, thin tendrils of smoke still leaking upwards from shattered windows and various other blackened openings in the side of its hull. Several RIBs full of armed marines patrolled the water at some distance from the ship, obviously making sure a long canoe armed with a harpoon guided missile didn't sneak up for another shot at the big 'C'.

With zero ceremony and considerable haste, we were hustled aboard the ship and along what seemed like miles of narrow passageways lined with masses of pipes and cabling. Gratifyingly, many of the passageways were smoke-stained and had puddles of water, the whole overlaid with the eye-watering stench of deep-fried wiring and crispy-skin paint. We then descended a series of ladders until we were roughly pushed into a large room with five cells along one wall. Bars made up the front of each, along with two bunks, a washbasin and a toilet to complete the facilities. It definitely wasn't the Carlton-Ritz. We were both shoved into one, the barred door clanging shut behind us with what sounded like awful finality.

Andy looked at me, and totally deadpan said, 'Well. This is a fine pickle you've got us into this time, Ollie.'

I couldn't help grinning, and replied, 'Sorry Stanley. I'm sure we can resolve this minor misunderstanding before long, although tossing innocent civilians into the brig while in a foreign country without permission, is normally cause for an international incident of the highest order.' I also stepped up close beside him, and with my head bowed, breathed, 'Probably audio and video surveillance. Stay anonymous for now.' before stepping away.

Andy casually looked around, then said, 'Yes. Not the best accommodation, but at least it's pleasantly cool.'

We chatted about nonsense for a while, then as Andy sat on his bunk, I stretched out on the other one and closed my eyes.

The afternoon stretched into evening, and at 19:00, a sailor entered the outer room and slid two bowls of rice and some sort of stew to us under the lower edge of the door. Chopsticks were supplied, and I found the food was quite tasty. Andy said he wasn't hungry, but I suggested that the soldier's adage of eating and sleeping anytime one got the opportunity, was a good one.

One hour later, the door to the brig opened again to admit two burly sailors ahead of an officer with four stars on his shoulder boards. This I took to be the much-discussed, rage-afflicted captain of the *Changbaishan*.

He stepped up to the bars and with a look of disdain, inspected us.

'What are your names, please gentlemen?' he asked in an accent-free, well-modulated voice.

'Harry Stevens, Australian citizen,' I said, 'and this is Andrew Friar, also an Australian citizen. Who are you?'

'I am Senior Captain Liu, the captain of this vessel. What is the business of your yacht in this place?'

I shrugged, 'We're on holiday and like diving in different places. We were last at Vanuatu doing the same as it has a similar and well-deserved reputation. The island of Bokissa is a prime example if you are ever in the area yourself and have some spare time. This harbour has a world-wide reputation for unpolluted water of the finest quality for diving. How about you tell us why we have been kidnapped and illegally detained in this manner?'

In an instant, his polite, easy manner changed to that of blazing fury, as he grasped the bars with white-knuckled hands, his face turning red as he screamed at me.

'You have no rights here! You have been assisting the cowardly rebels who have attacked my beautiful ship and killed my men! Firstly, you somehow disposed of a boat load of men on a night-training exercise, and now you assist others to attack my ship.'

Equally abruptly, his rage vanished, he drew a deep breath, then spoke in his former reasonable tone.

'I regret to inform you that I intend to make charges against you for aiding unknown persons to attack my ship and kill my men. I wait for orders from my superior officers as to what they want me to do with you.'

Unfortunately, I couldn't help myself and laughed in his face. 'You must be kidding! You have no proof whatsoever that we were involved in anything to do with the attack on your ship, or the disappearance of the men on your training exercise. How could untrained civilians mount any sort of attack against a warship of the mighty PLAN! This is rubbish and you know it. I must warn you that you are digging a very deep hole for yourself and Commander Zhao. I doubt your career will survive the fallout from this preposterous episode, as you'll find that your superiors will not support your actions.'

He started to get red in the face again.

'How dare you speak to a Senior Captain like that! You are rubbish! Worthless lay-abouts!'

I looked him in the eye. 'Make up your mind, Liu. Either we're worthless layabouts, or we're trained mercenaries assisting the local rebels trying to destroy your ship! We can't be both, and since there isn't a shred of proof that we had anything to do with the attack on your boat, we must be innocent. I know an International Court will decide that! To you and your country's detriment. I also demand to know what you are doing to my boat and crew?'

'I await instructions as to what to do about them as well,' he replied, obviously struggling to regain control of his emotions.

I surreptitiously looked at my watch.

'Very well, Captain. If it is your intention to proceed along this ill-advised path toward your personal disgrace and destruction, we shall wait to see what surprises the next few hours shall bring.'

He glared at me through the bars.

'What is this nonsense you speak? Zhao said you were very smooth with your words, but I do not think words will allow you to avoid answering for your crimes against the Chinese nation.'

I smiled gently and sat back down on the bunk. 'As you wish, Captain. We shall see who will have to answer for his crimes! Very soon you will find out that it won't be me!'

Furious at my insults, he turned and followed by his guards, stomped out of the compartment.

As the door slammed closed behind them, Andy looked at me, deadpan. 'Once again, that went well.'

I chuckled. 'Well said, Andy. But I fear the good captain's blood pressure will bring him undone if he keeps getting upset like that.'

We said no more, mindful of microphones and video cameras. Two more hours passed, making the time 21:30, before the captain returned in person, a triumphant grin on his face. Andy remained seated while I compounded the insult by remaining lying down as he halted close to the cell bars, where he launched into his little speech without preamble.

'I wish to personally inform you that I have received instructions to hold you both in custody, until such time as my investigations reveal the identity of all the other perpetrators involved in the disappearance of my night-exercise crew, as well as the direct attack upon my ship.'

I sighed heavily, 'Oh my dear, foolish captain. You have no rights under international law to arrest and detain civilians while you are in a foreign country, and you and your supposed superiors know it! These are totally false and fabricated charges with no evidence to support them. I give you one last chance to unconditionally release us, my boat and crew.'

He got a dangerous glint in his eyes again. 'You continue to protest your innocence. You are a fool. I shall have all the proof I require very shortly, and then we shall see what you have to say.'

I glanced at my watch again, then decided I'd pushed this farce as far as it could reasonably go.

'Captain,' I said, 'I wish to inform you, in front of these witnesses, that not only have you kidnapped and illegally detained the owner and master of the Australian-registered, civilian vessel *Firebird*, but you have also kidnapped and illegally detained the Prime Minister of Australia, the Right Honourable Andrew Friar.'

Liu's face went red again. 'What is this nonsense! More lies from a guilty man trying to delay the inevitable?'

'Moreover,' I continued, as though he hadn't spoken, 'the Australian government have already been informed of your crimes against two of its citizens, and are taking active measures to bring you to justice as we speak.'

Liu continued to bluster, until I cut him off in mid-rant again.

'Don't stand there flapping your gums like the fool you obviously are! Go to the nearest computer with an internet connection and bring up a photograph of the current Australian Prime Minister. Come on, chop, chop. Surely you have the skills to do that simple task? If not, perhaps one of your junior seamen can do it for you.'

Captain Liu was now white-faced with rage and without turning his eyes away from mine, barked an order. Instantly, the three guards raised their sub-machine guns, and cocked them with a discordant rattle of charging handles.

'Gee, that's a really clever move,' I sneered, 'now you add the crime of threatening to kill an innocent Australian citizen and the Prime Minister of Australia to the other list of crimes against you! No wonder you got sent on this job. Your bosses needed a stupid, first-class bully-boy to kick the innocent locals into submission, and that's all you're good for.'

From the demented look in his eyes, I thought I might have pushed him too far, but the repetition of the words, Prime Minister, was just enough to make him pause giving the fire order. Which was just as well for all of us in the cell block since the ricochets would have hit everyone, including El Capitano, or whatever he was called in Chinese.

After several moments of glaring silence, he spat several words which were probably something foul and disgusting in Chinese, then turned and stormed out, roughly pushing through the guards. They looked confused — not sure whether to shoot someone, stay or go, but belatedly decided to follow their captain. Hopefully, they would forget to make their weapons safe and might even shoot the captain.

Andy gave me a feeble grin. 'You pushed that one a bit close, Harry.'

'Yeah. Sorry about blowing your cover, Andy. But the timing of the rest of my plan seems to have gone astray, so I needed to put the brakes on and keep El Furioso Capitano tied up with us as long as possible.'

'Oh', he said, with a wry grin, 'of course. How silly of me – it was an excellent delaying tactic. So long as some fool didn't pull a trigger!'

I laughed rather weakly as well... the tension slow to drain away. 'Yeah. I must admit, that was a bit tense for a minute or two. He doesn't seem to be the sort of bloke who puts up with any backchat, so we'll see what he does with this new info. I figured we couldn't be any worse off.'

Our wait was much shorter than before until the brig door banged open and Captain Liu stalked in again, a piece of paper fluttering in his hand. It was a full-colour head and shoulders photo of Andy, dressed more like a Prime Minister and less like a boatie bum, which he held up against the cell bars and compared it to the real Andy.

'Do you claim to be the Prime Minister of Australia?' he asked almost politely, having morphed back into his more reasonable persona.

Andy nodded. 'Yes, I am. If you care to send the polite Lieutenant Commander Yang over to *Firebird*, tell him to ask my personal private secretary Charlie, to show him my diplomatic passport. He won't be allowed to take it away, but maybe that will convince you as to my identity.'

He grunted, and thought a moment before replying.

'Why are you travelling with these persons on this small boat if you are such an important person? And without security guards?'

'I travel with these people because they are my very good friends and I enjoy their company as much as I enjoy the sailing. I'm on holiday and as there normally isn't any threat to my life, I don't need security. In Australia, we are allowed to do almost anything we like. Given the authoritarian regime you choose to live under, where everyone is under threat of being imprisoned or executed for voicing their own opinion, you may find that hard to believe. However, that's what life is like in a democracy. You should try it sometime. It's very liberating for the spirit and adds years to your life expectancy! It's a shame you won't be allowed to experience true freedom.'

Liu considered Andy's words. 'Perhaps. We will see. But if you are lying, it will be much worse for both of you.'

I started to get a bit tired of this goose with his bullying rhetoric.

'Oh, for Christ's sake, Liu! Pull your head out of your arse and take a look at what's really going on. This shit-fight all happened because you weren't invited to come here in the first place, but you and your misguided leaders think that might is right, so you decide to push your way in regardless. Then when you find out that the locals don't fall for your bullshit, obviously don't want you, and decide to push back at your invasion, you chuck a hissy fit! Take the hint and fuck off out of here before it happens again! If most of your officers are arrogant shit-heads like yourself and Commanders Wu and Zhao, it's no wonder you're all hated. Then to top it all off, when you can't find the guys who gave you a bloody nose, you chuck another hissy fit and grab two of the most inoffensive and accessible blokes you can, just because we happened to be close-by, minding our own business. Except that you had the exceptionally bad judgment to kidnap and lockup the Australian Prime Minister.' I laughed and shook my head. 'What a total fuckwit you are!'

His face darkened again. 'Do not insult me again, Mr Stevens, or you will feel my wrath for real! However, I will make further enquiries into your most unlikely claims. Do not go away. Ha, ha.'

'Nice work, Harry,' Andy said admiringly, 'he actually seems to be listening this time, despite you winding him up yet again.'

'Yeah. Sometimes I can't help myself. He really is such an arrogant goose! Their whole arrogant leadership is the same! They come here to make a harbour grab and expect everyone to fall over themselves in gratitude. Helping our impoverished neighbours! What a load of crap! When are these idiots going to learn that most of the lesser-developed nations just want to be left alone to live as they always have – to sort out their own problems in their own way and at their own pace?'

Andy nodded sagely. 'Well said. I wish my diplomatic team were able to think as clearly as that.'

We sat in silence for what seemed a long time, but was actually only forty-five minutes, when an alarm sounded loudly, followed by the thunder of many running footsteps on the deck overhead.

'Hullo,' said Andy, 'what's this lot then? More trouble?'

I checked my watch. 'Hopefully, it's more trouble for the Chinese, but we'd better keep our heads down in case something goes bang.'

They were prophetic words, as ten minutes later, there were two very loud explosions close-by. They didn't seem to be actually on the ship, but were close enough to make it shudder violently and shower us with dust and paint flakes from the overhead.

'What the hell was that?' Andy asked in alarm.

I grinned, relief surging through my system. 'I think we'll find that it was a couple of shells going off in the water, just ahead of the bow. From the distance we walked when we came aboard, I reckon this brig is right up in the bow, probably below the waterline, so those things weren't far away.'

'Who the hell would be firing shells like that at this thing?' he asked again, 'Surely not the rebels?'

'No. They've got nothing like that. But I strongly suspect it's our relief package in the form of the Royal Australian Navy if my messages got through.'

Andy gave me one of those looks which the ladies usually fire in my direction when they think I'm being more than usually mysterious and devious. "And you didn't think this was something you should share with me?'

I tried to look contrite.

'Yeah, sorry about that Andy. Especially since it landed us in here, but I'd made some calls a day ago, and we should have had support long before this. I couldn't say anything when we were first shoved in here, in case Liu was alerted and did something to bugger up my plan.'

Andy finally nodded acceptance of my apology, so we settled back to endure another anxious wait, while my over-active imagination generated doubts about whether my plan was actually going to work, or be a fizzer. Finally, a junior lieutenant rushed into the brig with two marines in tow and unlocked our cell door.

'You follow,' he said in his fractured English, but if it meant getting out of jail, he was forgiven. We repeated the long trek through the ship at a much faster pace than earlier, but it seemed we climbed more ladders this time, and bashed our shins on the high sills of more step-through water-tight doors than on our first trip.

'This isn't the way we came in,' I muttered to Andy, as we hurdled yet another shin-cracker.

My arms and legs were starting to burn with the unaccustomed exercise, when we stumbled over a final door sill to find ourselves on the expanse of the stern flight deck, which was bathed in harsh, white blinding light. Shading my eyes with my hands didn't help much, as the light was coming from two different sources on the water, a couple of hundred metres away. We remained there with our escort of the Lieutenant and the two armed marines, with nothing seeming to happen for a few minutes, then Lieutenant

Commander Yang walked up with Captain Liu, who wasn't in a very happy mood. So what else was new?

Liu nodded to Andy and myself, then said, 'It would appear Mr Friar, that you are who you say you are. This point has been forcibly reinforced by the untimely arrival of two of your country's warships, who, it would seem, just happened to be in the vicinity. This would seem to be a very inconvenient co-incidence which bears further investigation, however, I find that following advice from my superiors, I am obliged to release you from my custody.'

He looked at me, a mirthless smile on his face.

'It would also seem, Mr Stevens, that the thoughts you expressed earlier this evening were quite prophetic, and showed a deeper understanding of the situation than I would have expected from an innocent civilian boat-owner on a pleasure cruise. In which case, you will have to forgive me if I believe that you had considerable prior knowledge of this enterprise. Although, despite your explanations, I cannot understand the timely presence of your Prime Minister aboard your boat.'

He shook his head in what seemed like genuine puzzlement.

'However, now that you both have been sighted as unharmed by your warships, I am here to inform you that you are free to return to your vessel. My only comment is that you would be wise to avoid ever making a visit to my country. We have very long memories.'

I wasn't going to let this arrogant prick have the last word, and stepped closer to Liu, prompting the two guards to raise their carbines. With my face close to his, I said softly, 'So do we, Captain Liu, so do we! So stay the fuck away from Australia and all our friends.'

Wordlessly, he stepped back, allowing the polite Lieutenant Commander Yang to step forward and say, 'Please follow me, gentlemen.'

There was nothing more to say, so we followed Yang to an outside stairway down off the flight deck, crossed the ship to the shore side via a long corridor, then down more flights of stairs to the floor of the hovercraft deck where the broad vehicle ramp still stretched across to the wharf. I was gratified to see a huge pile of still-smouldering remains loosely piled up toward the front of the vast space, and guessed that the PLAN was down a few hovercraft as well.

As we stepped onto the wharf, Lieutenant Commander Yang stopped and spoke from the end of the ramp. 'This is where I leave you, gentlemen. May I say that personally, I regret all which has happened and know it could have been avoided. I wish you good sailing and calm seas.'

He saluted briefly, then spun around to march back aboard.

'Mr Friar? Commander Stevens?' A quiet, yet familiar female voice sounded out of the darkness. Moments later, Clare Stahall, the Executive Officer of the *Arafura* appeared, flanked by two very alert sailors armed with EF88 Austeyr carbines held in the ready position.

'Clare! What a lovely surprise,' I exclaimed, 'and a very welcome sight under any circumstances, but especially this one.'

Even in the gloom, I could see her wide grin. 'Good one, Harry. Very smooth. However, may I say that even by your standards, this is one giant clusterfuck you've created! And I'm not sure this counts as looking after our Prime Minister in the style to which he's become accustomed.' She smiled at Andy. 'Good to see you in one piece, sir. Consorting with Harry isn't always good for one's health.'

Andy grinned back. 'No, it isn't, Lieutenant Commander, but I'm happy to say that it's never boring and usually extremely interesting.'

She laughed. 'Well said, sir. Anyway, if you'd care to come this way, Commander Davy and Commander Sanders need to have a bit of a chat. They aren't used to being called to bail up a major Chinese warship in a foreign port, so now that we have done so, we're not quite sure what to do with it.'

Ten minutes later, we were comfortably seated in the more spacious wardroom aboard the *Ballarat*, an ANZAC-class frigate with Commander Jim Sanders in charge. He was a little older than Paul Davy, as well as shorter and more heavily built, but there was no mistaking the gleam of intelligence in his piercing blue eyes. Both boats were lying bows-on to the *Changbaishan*, holding position using manoeuvring thrusters, their searchlights still illuminating the much bigger ship. At the same time, their quick-firing main armament bow guns held steady aim on the bridge, while the secondary armament of various .50cal machine guns on each boat lazily roamed the length of the big ship, ready to discourage any attempt to thwart the rescue. Much of the open display of firepower was superfluous, as the various armaments scattered around the *Changbaishan* were decidedly second-hand and didn't pose any sort of threat.

Andy took control of the briefing. 'Thank you, gentlemen, for your timely arrival. Things were getting rather tense between us and Captain Liu. He was getting set to ship us back to China under lock and key.'

'What!' Jim Sanders exclaimed. 'He couldn't have done that!'

Andy chuckled, 'Correct. Harry tried to tell him that, but Liu was set to do it anyway. Then, after Harry pointed out several of his personal shortcomings, he was about to shoot us. I'm happy to say that Harry managed to talk him out of that one, but it was rather close! However, what I'd really like to know is how you both came to be here?'

After he and Jim finished looking amazed at Andy's brief recital of our incarceration, Paul picked up the story.

'Two days ago, I received a coded message from Harry which said I should be ready to head south at top speed if he called, so I cancelled leave and made ready. President Tari seemed to know what was going on, but wouldn't say much. Then I get a call from Admiral Stallman telling me that Jim had been taken off patrol and told to go straight to Kieta Harbour at maximum speed. I was to co-ordinate with him to ensure we arrived at the same time. Being closer, and knowing a problem was brewing, I headed down early and hung around just outside the off-shore islands until Jim arrived. Then just before we entered harbour together, we both got another call from the Admiral to say that he'd been advised by Harry's crew, that he and Mr Friar had been arrested by the captain of the *Changbaishan* and were being held in custody aboard the ship. We'd also been told about the raid on the ship, and that apparently her radars and guns had been knocked out.'

Jim took over the story. 'We approached the *Changbaishan* slowly, making repeated radio calls on all known frequencies, but there was no response we could detect, nor was there any radar emissions detected, so I finally called on VHF marine band channel 16. They only had a hand-held radio still in working order, but we managed to work out what they said. They were very surprised to hear from us and when I told them they had to release the two of you immediately, they got a bit aggro. That was when I tossed a couple of 127mm shells into the water off her bow, and suggested that if we didn't see the pair of you on deck, on your feet within fifteen minutes, the next two rounds would be through the bridge.'

I interrupted his tale by chuckling. 'That would have stirred the pot. They'd already had a bunch of high explosives delivered there! No wonder they only had a hand-held VHF working.'

Jim paused to give me an old-fashioned look before carrying on. 'My threat worked, and you were brought to the flight deck within the designated time. Naturally, we were extremely glad to see you both were alright. I told the captain that you were to be escorted off the ship immediately, and that under the orders of the Bougainville government, he was to haul his anchor and leave Bougainville waters. We were under additional instructions to provide an escort to the National thirty-mile limit, in case he had any navigational or ship-handling difficulties. The captain said that he couldn't leave immediately, as he had to recover all his earthmoving equipment, cranes and trucks before he could do anything else, so I informed him that once again by the direction of the Bougainville Government, he had the choice of being underway within thirty minutes under his own power, or he could have a series of 127mm rounds through the bridge and engine room, before getting towed out of harbour and abandoned outside the thirty-mile limit. He took a few minutes to get back to me, but we now see they have started engines, raised the stern ramp, dropped the stern mooring lines, and are presently pulling in the anchor. We'll have to get going ourselves if we're going to do the escort bit, so what would you like to do?'

Andy grandly gestured for me to pick up the decision-making ball from there.

'Great work both of you, and thanks very much for getting us out of there so effectively. We know that Captain Liu has been in almost constant contact with his superiors over the last few hours, and from what we know of his temper and attitude, to give in so easily, he must have been told in no uncertain terms to fold his tent and bail out. We'll let you go and do the escort, but let's resume this discussion as soon as you come back. Tie up at the wharf when you return – it'll be totally safe once the Chinese have gone.'

Jim frowned. 'Are you sure about that? As this is Ground Zero of the rebel stronghold, we've been warned by Foreign Affairs not to tie-up at any wharf, or for any personnel to go ashore under any circumstances. Not only that, but aren't these the guys who caused all that damage to the *Changbaishan?*'

I grinned, 'Of course they are. But you'll find that we have friends in high places, so we're the good guys in this. Trust me. All is well.'

He still looked dubious, but a brief nod from Andy stopped further argument, so he picked up a phone, and told the bridge to get underway.


Paul, Clare, Andy and I were picked up minutes later by one of *Arafura's* RIBs which had been hovering nearby, and taken aboard, where I asked for a phone to call *Firebird*, assuring Sandy and Lara that we were both okay, and to ask Alex to bring *Firebird* into the wharf.

Done with that, I suggested to Paul that he also might like to head for the wharf and tie up. As soon as *Firebird* was berthed, Andy and I hopped aboard, to a joyful reunion with our ladies and the whole crew including the cats. Sandy checked me over, and was surprised, but relieved that I hadn't been shot or otherwise punctured during our incarceration. Before we exchanged stories, I had a couple more urgent phone calls to make. The first was to Mathias Tari, who picked up immediately, despite the late hour.

'*Good evening Commander*', he replied to my greeting, '*I despaired of ever hearing from you again.*'

I laughed, 'Admittedly, it was a close thing at one point when things became a bit heated while we were behind bars, and on the wrong side of three cocked sub-machine guns. However, I'm happy to report that the *Changbaishan* is presently just getting underway, under close escort by the frigate, HMAS *Ballarat* to beyond your thirty-mile boundary.'

'*That's wonderful news, Commander. I wonder if events down there had anything to do with the sudden departure of our two diplomats this evening.*'

'Really?' I asked in surprise. 'They've gone already?'

'*Yes, indeed. We were having a late discussion, when they received a phone call. They abruptly broke off the meeting and left the building without further words. Then my Police Chief reported they had checked out of their hotel, and their jet had departed on a flight plan direct to Beijing.*'

'That's even better news,' I replied, 'to know they've officially given up on this attempt.'

'*Yes, I agree it seems to be over for now, but I get a strong feeling that we haven't heard the last of this.*'

'Yeah. I agree with you, Mr Tari. Bully boys never like being beaten.'

'*Which means we can expect a repeat performance before long, but I would imagine the next one will be much more forceful. I don't suppose you have any more of your clever ideas about preventing that?*'

Those shadowy thoughts which had been lurking on the back-burner of my warped brain, suddenly clamoured for attention.

'Quite possibly, sir. I need to think about the situation some more, and talk to a few people I've met down here. And thanks for your introduction to Joseph Bulli. He was an invaluable help and deserves a lot of the credit for the successful outcome.'

Mathias chuckled. *'Yes. I have come to know that he's a very good man. Perhaps he can assist you with your new thoughts?'*

Pennies started to drop for me, so I just said, 'I'll take you up on that suggestion, Mr Tari, but for now, I'll let you get some well-earned rest and we'll talk again soon. Good night, sir.'

*'Good night to you, Commander, and thank you for your remarkable efforts to help our country.'*

I terminated the call, but then made another one to Joseph.

*'Excellent work, Commander,'* he complimented, with a chuckle in his voice. *'Although I was surprised they went so easily.'*

I chuckled, 'Thanks to our Navy, we managed to put them between the proverbial rock and a hard place Joseph, but after just speaking with Mathias, we believe that this is probably only round one, so the fight isn't over yet.'

*'I agree with those thoughts,'* he rumbled in his rich, deep voice. *'The return visit will probably be sooner rather than later.'*

'I'm afraid you're right. Perhaps we could discuss this further tomorrow. I have a very wild idea which might work, but I need and would appreciate your input.'

*'No problem, Commander and before you ask, there is no ship traffic expected for the next week or two, so you and our new friends are welcome to use the wharf.'*

'Thanks, Joseph. We'll catch up tomorrow.'

While Jim Sanders was away playing nursemaid to the wounded *Changbaishan*, we took the opportunity to return a reluctant Terry and Gillian to the disciplined world of the *Arafura*, along with the MK47 grenade launcher and the few remaining unused rounds. I was very glad to be able to deliver them unscathed, with myself as the only minor casualty of the operation. For now, I thought it best to avoid having to explain to Jim Sanders the true extent of our very active part in the attack on the Chinese, but I well knew that comfortable state of affairs wouldn't last long, once he saw the damage to the *Changbaishan* in daylight and realised that it hadn't been caused by angry Bougainvillians armed with machetes and shotguns.

Andy and I spent the next couple of hours swapping stories with our crew, and thanked Charlie for organising the naval support which almost certainly saved our necks, or at least a long sea-trip eating rice with chopsticks. That is, Andy said 'thanks', while I gave her a long, hard hug and kiss. I mean, he does have to maintain a sense of proprietary, doesn't he? Happily, I don't!

'Thank Admiral Stallman for having the foresight to keep *Ballarat* heading this way at max speed,' Charlie replied, looking slightly flushed. 'Then it was just a matter of co-ordinating arrival times with *Arafura,* so they confronted *Changbaishan* as a combined force.'

'Well, it certainly worked perfectly, although a little later than was comfortable. We'd got to the stage of having loaded guns with safeties off, pointed at us through the cell bars. That Captain Liu has fearsome trouble controlling his temper. He really needs anger-management classes.'

With a chuckle, Andy tossed in, 'Yeah. Especially when Harry kept winding him up. You'd better stay with your Defence Advisor position, sport, and keep away from diplomacy. You suck at that.'

I tried to look indignant, but with the whole crew laughing, I gave in and joined them, putting further discussion on hold until tomorrow, as the hour was late and it had been a long day fraught with high tension. I also had a bloody sore shoulder and arm.

## CHANGBAISHAN

As the damaged amphibious assault ship limped away from Bougainville, Senior Captain Liu was in a towering rage. Not only had he suffered huge personal loss of face, but had to endure the embarrassment of having his beloved ship savaged by what he classed as a bunch of ignorant, illiterate natives. None aboard were spared his wrath, and many officers carried the fresh, physical scars of his rages. That some interfering, degenerate Australians on a private sailing boat, who had no right being in the area in the first place were somehow involved, was a puzzlement he reserved for later dissection.

After making his report to his superiors and receiving the expected rebukes and promises of severe discipline, he was ordered to take his ship to the South Sea Fleet naval base at Zhanjiang, which was not far north of Hong Kong, then to stand-down pending further investigation of his actions and behaviour. In the strict, unforgiving world of the PLAN, that was tantamount to a death sentence.

He was also informed that a Type 055 heavy destroyer, the *Dalian*, would take up patrol duties close to the island nation. To know that what he considered to be a vital mission for his country was to be taken over by what he believed to be an inferior ship, commanded by a junior captain, added considerable insult to injury.

## DALIAN

Captain Guo, in command of the 13,000 tonne, heavy destroyer *Dalian*, read his orders with great satisfaction. There was no love lost between himself and Senior Captain Liu, stemming from the many unpleasant experiences he'd personally suffered under the harsh discipline of Liu when he had served as his Executive Officer. Now he had his own ship, which he regarded as being a much more exciting and prestigious command than the lumbering barge which was Liu's assault ship. It also allowed him to occasionally indulge his own brand of independent behaviour, while staying as much as possible within the strict guidelines issued by the Party leadership.

Addressed for his eyes only, the new orders were carefully worded so as to suggest, at least to Captain Guo's independent spirit, that he was to keep a close eye upon the nation of Bougainville, and to *'do what he could, short of physical encounters or use of weapons, to maintain pressure upon the Bougainville government and if possible, without the use of force, to prevent any other nation's warships from entering Kieta Harbour or docking at Buka Town.'*

It was no coincidence that he wasn't too far away when the unfortunate incident involving the *Changbaishan* occurred, so he ordered his navigator to plot the shortest course for Bougainville at best cruising speed. With that taken care of, he consulted the charts of the area and started planning how to make the most of what he interpreted was an opportunity to intimidate the hell out of the Bougainville locals and impress his superiors with his cunning and expertise. It didn't take his fertile mind long to come up with some strategies which might help accomplish that mission.

After a lovely breakfast next morning, the discussion session kicked off with all of us in the saloon.

'What are your plans?' Andy asked me. 'Bearing in mind we three need to get back to the pickle factory before too much longer.'

I nodded understanding. 'I was talking to Mathias and Joseph last night, and they both believe this isn't the end of the Chinese ambitions toward this area and its beautiful harbour. There might be some international diplomatic push and shove with the Chinese for a while, but unless something significant is done to change the balance of power in the right direction, this will happen again and Mathias and his Council of Ministers aren't equipped to be able to push back hard enough.'

Andy frowned, 'Yeah I know what you mean, but unfortunately Australia can't just step in and say bugger off to the Chinese. We certainly can't establish a permanent military presence on the island, even though that's what is required to keep the Chinese out, and Papua New Guinea hasn't the troops, ships or firepower to do the job either. The United Nations could do so if they got off their arse, but they've got a lot of commitments in the Middle East and elsewhere, and it'd take them months to decide anyway. Everyone's pussy-footing around the Chinese because no one, including the mighty USA, wants a direct confrontation. Particularly the way things are at the moment over Taiwan.'

'Yeah. I understand Australia can't get involved directly, but I do have the makings of a wild plan based on something Mathias said the other day.'

Sandy rolled her eyes and gave a mock groan, while Andy just grinned and invited, 'Good boy. Tell me more.'

I shook my head. 'Nope! Can't just yet. It's way too sketchy at the moment, since I haven't worked out the details, but it has to do with trying to get private enterprise involved in the mine re-opening project. If that carrot got pushed off the table, to muddle a couple of metaphors, it might remove the only faintly legitimate excuse the Chinese would have for trying to move in once again.'

That raised his eyebrows. 'Back up the bus! I thought that was permanently off the table! You're talking about a massive investment in a project with a very high-risk to return factor. No individual or organisation would be prepared to take on something of that magnitude, especially in a country so riddled with internal strife. As in, there's next to zero political stability for starters. I mean, they're even having arguments about the main airport at Buka Town where the veggie farmers on the north side want the right to be able to walk across the main runway to get to town instead of having to go the long way around! Footpath land rights across an airport for Christ's sake! At times I think the whole country is totally nutso! Anyway, there are precious few organisations big enough to be able to fund something like this, and I can't think of any of those silly enough to take on that insane level of risk!'

I nodded, 'Couldn't agree more, old mate. But there's one very left-field possibility I want to explore. The only problem for you is that it might take a few days to get an answer to my suggestion, and I still need to chat further to Mathias and the local chiefs. So, the long answer to your question is, to see the job completed, we might need to stay here a while longer.'

Andy looked at Charlie, who nodded, 'Yeah, sorry Boss. That'd make it at least another week, and we do need to get back sooner than that. I'd better call in the Falcon jet for a pickup tomorrow, if we can get up to Buka Town.'

I nodded, 'Yeah, fair enough. Maybe Paul can run you up there. It should only take him three hours or so.'

Alex spoke up in his deep, accented voice I always found so appealing. 'Why don't you ask Jim to fire up that lovely Sea-Hawk helicopter he's got sitting in his hanger gathering dust? He's been bragging about it often enough. Much faster, and a lot cheaper than using Paul's flash boat!'

Charlie looked seriously annoyed with herself. 'Good thinking, Alex, thanks. I've been living this life of decadent, laid-back luxury for way too long. I'm losing my edge. Anyway Boss, are you happy with that plan?'

Andy thought a few moments, then nodded, 'Yeah. As much as I'd like to stay and see this through, we can't afford the time right now. But I'd appreciate a daily report through Charlie, please Harry. Especially if you get your mysterious plan worked out.'

'No problem with that, Andy. But I'd like to ask a big favour.'

He raised his eyebrows in reply.

'Would you mind leaving one of these grey boats here for a little while longer? I can get Mathias to make the request if you like, which should make it more official. One will be enough.'

'I don't think that should be a problem, given the situation. I suppose you want Paul with *Arafura*?'

I chuckled, 'I'd like to keep Paul, since he's learned to fit in with how I operate, but in this case, I'd prefer Jim, as I might need access to his Sea-Hawk. There shouldn't be the need for any weird stuff which might get Jim's sensibility knickers in a twist. Plus, *Ballarat* looks even more imposing than *Arafura*, so I reckon she'd be a better choice. Provided, of course, Jim doesn't mind fitting in with my developing plans?'

'No problem organising that,' Andy replied. 'I'll make sure he does what you need, short of endangering his boat or crew. The usual deal. Charlie will clear it with Alan Stallman first, and Paul and *Arafura* can head back to Darwin to take their delayed leave.'

'That'll be great, thanks Andy. And as for danger to *Ballarat*, I don't expect any action will be required during this next phase of the operation. Just his boat's presence, his helicopter, and his co-operation should take care of my needs.'

'Good to hear you aren't planning to blow up anything this time around, Harry.'

Within the hour, Charlie reported back to Andy and me.

'Our pick-up is organised for today, Boss. The aircraft and crew are available, so the dispatcher says that if it suits, the aircraft can be at Buka Town by mid-afternoon. That would get us back in town by early evening. Will that suit?'

Andy considered for a moment. 'Yeah, Charlie. We might as well. There's no point in delaying our departure now we know Harry is staying, and I'm sure there's plenty of crap to sort out back home. Plus, we can let Harry get on with his devious plan in peace.'

Charlie nodded. 'Okay. It's all arranged, then. We just need to be at Buka Town by 14:30, so we'd better ask Commander Sanders for a helicopter ride.'

She paused to think a moment, then looked at me. 'Do Beth and Georgia need a ride back to Oz? We've got plenty of room.'

I found them in the cockpit, playing with the kitties as usual, and announced, 'There's a bunch of stuff still to work out in connection with this local rattle, so we'll be hanging around for a while longer, possibly another week or two. However, Andy, Lara and Charlie have called for a lift home this afternoon so they can keep Australia running – which means there's a free ride back to Canberra if you ladies would like to bail out.'

Beth looked at Georgia, who promptly said, 'Not unless you want us to, Harry. We'd be delighted to stay and get more research data. We've already told the Uni that the work is going extremely well on our animal project – ground-breaking stuff and all that crap, so there's no rush from our side.'

I got a little warm feeling to hear that. I'd become very fond of both ladies, especially now that Beth had learned how to play nice.

'No problem then. You're welcome to stay.'

'It's a shame Andy, Lara and Charlie are leaving,' Georgia said. 'They're really nice people. We've had fun.'

I passed that message back to Charlie, then suggested that perhaps she and I should visit Jim Sanders on *Ballarat*, to ask for his helicopter. I also had a little test in mind to see how he reacted to unusual situations.

Five minutes later, with Charlie in shorts and one of her psychedelic Vanuatu flowered shirts, and myself a picture of sartorial elegance in my usual paint-stained shorts and a faded AC/DC, *Back in Black* T-shirt, we slip-slapped along the wharf in our thongs, past *Arafura*, to where the *Ballarat's* gang-way rested on the wharf. Jasper was with us to give him a bit of a walk and meet some new people, and the few locals we passed kept their distance as I hadn't bothered with a leash. I chuckled to myself, that we must make the ultimate weird trio – a short, pretty and pleasantly-rounded woman, a tall, lean and scruffy man, and a large, black, green-eyed cat, whose back was above the level of my knees.

I could almost read the panicked thoughts of the young seaman who stood guard at the top of the gang-way as we strolled toward him.

'May I help you, sir?' He politely asked, eyeing Jasper nervously now that his true size was apparent.

'Indeed you can, Leading-Seaman,' I said. 'Miss Langley, Commander Stevens and companion cat to see the Skipper, if you please.'

'Ah, one moment, if you would, sir,' he stammered, groping for the phone on the bulkhead beside him. He muttered into it, then hung up and turned to me with a look of relief.

'The officer of the watch is coming down, sir. He'll sort this out for you.'

I frowned. 'I don't see that there's anything to actually sort out, Leading-Seaman,' I said sternly. 'We just need to see the captain on a matter of some urgency, but if this is the way you blokes insist on doing business, we'll wait.'

The seaman guard blushed, while Charlie and I traded silent

looks for the next five minutes or so, until an officer ambled toward us from the main cross-passage. Up close, I saw he was a Lieutenant Commander, short and somewhat over-weight, with thinning sandy hair and a sour expression permanently fixed in place. On a ship where the captain held the rank of Commander, his rank probably made him the ship's Executive Officer or XO. I also noted his eyes scanning Charlie and me, before a heavy frown appeared when he spotted Jasper.

'Help you folks?' he asked in a flat tone, the sour expression deepening.

'You can, Lieutenant Commander. We'd like to see the Skipper, please.'

He promptly shook his head. 'No can do, I'm afraid. He's in a meeting and can't be disturbed.'

I fixed him with a hard gaze, a faint red mist starting to form, even as Charlie laid her hand gently on my arm and kept it there. 'Harry!' was all she said.

'I find it hard to believe he's in a meeting at a time like this without the ship's XO being present. Perhaps you'd like to actually tell him we're here.'

He met my gaze. 'Perhaps you'd like to tell me what this is about, although I can tell you now that you aren't bringing that animal aboard.'

I tried hard to suppress the now-seething rage I felt toward this arrogant fool.

'I believe the chain-of-command, Lieutenant Commander, requires the captain to be the judge of that. Please let him know we're here to see him, and don't waste any more of our time.'

He drew a deep breath. 'Look... Mate! Just because you like living on this crappy island, doesn't give you or your wife any right to expect to be allowed aboard an Australian Navy ship. Especially with that animal, whatever it is!'

I thought I heard Charlie suppress a giggle at the 'wife' bit.

'For the very last time, Lieutenant Commander, the captain

should be allowed to make that judgement call. Please call him. Immediately!'

He shook his head again. 'Nope. Not happening. Now move off the gang-way before I call an armed security detail and have you removed.'

I sighed and shook my head. 'Oh dear. I really dislike having to come the heavies, Lieutenant Commander, but please remember that we asked repeatedly and politely, to see the captain, and that you have refused.'

As a look of confusion temporarily replaced the sour, arrogant one on the XO's face, I turned my gaze on the young seaman who looked fascinated by this dick-sizing match. 'Like it or not, young man, you're a witness to what's been said,' I stated, pulling a small UHF transceiver from my back pocket.

The XO now demonstrated his very negative attitude by folding his arms and standing across the width of the gang-way, his feet well apart, although a look of uncertainty crossed his face as his eyes followed my hand.

'*Firebird*, this is Harry,' I announced.

'*Go ahead*,' came Sandy's voice almost immediately.

'Bit of a roadblock at the gang-way, unfortunately,' I stated, my words causing a frown to re-appear on the XO's forehead, 'Please call the Admiral and ask him to call Captain Sanders direct. Tell the Admiral that we've been stopped at the gang-way by the XO who refuses to tell the Skipper we're here. Also tell him it's bloody hot as we've been kept waiting in the sun for over fifteen minutes already.'

'*Copy that*,' was the crisp reply, '*calling now. Standby.*'

The XO was starting to look almost as nervous as the leading-seaman, and seemed about to speak, when his expression hardened again, and he smirked as if to say, '*Bullshit!*'

Two minutes later, the little radio gave a squawk. '*Message passed. Action imminent.*'

'Thanks Sandy.'

It actually took nearly five more minutes, before there was the sound of hurried footsteps approaching along the cross-passage, then Commander Jim Sanders stormed into the boarding space, red in the face.

'What the hell's going on here, XO?' he demanded. 'I've just got off the phone from Admiral Stallman himself, asking why these people are being detained here, in the sun, instead of being immediately escorted to my quarters. I'll talk to you later, in private,' he added ominously, 'now get back to whatever it was you thought you were doing!'

The XO was as white as a sheet and tripping over his words, heedless of the presence of the leading-seaman. 'But sir. They're just local civilians and have an animal with them!'

'You are such a total bloody fool, XO. They are not local civilians! This is Commander Stevens, the officer in charge of the local situation in which we've just been involved, and Miss Langley, who is the Australian Prime Minister's Personal and Private Secretary. I've been asked by both the Prime Minister and the Admiral to extend all possible courtesies and assistance to the Commander and Miss Langley, and I've gladly given that assurance. Dare I remind you that my word means that all officers and ratings aboard my ship also have to comply?'

'Ah... yessir, that is, no sir. You don't have to remind me. My apologies, sir.'

'Don't apologise to me, you bloody fool! Apologise to the Commander and Miss Langley! They're the ones you've kept waiting! And as a by-the-way, the Commander is entitled to append the letters VC after his name, if that means anything to you!'

The Lieutenant-Commander stared in disbelief at me, taking in the stained shorts and faded T-shirt ensemble, before stammering, 'Ah... yes sir. Miss Langley and Commander Stevens, please accept my most sincere apologies for my inexcusable behaviour.'

Charlie and I nodded acceptance of the forced apology, which unfortunately seemed to convince the XO that all was forgiven.

'But sir. What about the animal?'

The Skipper rounded on him again. 'You still don't seem to get it, XO. The Commander can bring a troupe of dancing monkeys aboard if he thinks it's necessary. And if he did, I'd expect you to clean up their shit! That's what the term 'total co-operation' means when we are asked by the Admiral to oblige the Prime Minister and the Commander. Get it now?'

'Yessir. Again my apologies, Commander and Miss Langley.'

With that, the humiliated, hapless officer turned and marched away, his back stiff with outrage at being roundly chewed out in front of a rating, while Jim Sanders thanked the leading-seaman, then apologised to us, before leading the way to his quarters, Jasper padding happily behind, a big catty grin on his face, much to the amazement of the few crewmembers we passed on the way to the Skipper's cabin just below the bridge.

With the door closed and safely away from the crew's hearing, he chuckled. 'Sorry about the reaming and boring act, but I've been stuck with that moronic excuse for an XO all cruise. My regular XO developed appendicitis just before we were about to leave on patrol, and Teller was the only frigate-qualified officer available at such short notice. My apologies again, but now we are here, I'm fascinated by your cat. Paul told me about him, but to see him for real is something else.'

I smiled, then said to Jasper. 'Jasper, this is Captain Sanders. He's a friend who is going to help us.'

My beautiful big cat looked at me, huffed gently, then stepped forward and held out his right paw to Jim, who paused before gingerly grasping it and giving it a gentle shake. I could see by his expression that he'd felt the sharpness of those sheathed claws.

Jim looked up in amazement. 'How did you train him to do that? I thought it was impossible to train a cat to do anything.'

'Actually Jim, I haven't trained him to do any of the many unusual things he does. He just does that one with people he likes, and won't do it with those he doesn't take to.'

He shook his head in wonder. 'Fascinating!' He gave a chuckle and asked facetiously, 'What does he do with people he really doesn't like?'

I gave him a flat look. 'He usually bites them first, then kills them if I ask.'

Jim started to chuckle again, then noticed that neither Charlie nor I were laughing.

'You can't be serious... are you? I mean – I wouldn't like to be clawed or bitten by him, but kill! That's a bit much.'

Aware that I was making myself appear even more eccentric than I'd prefer, I said, 'It's quite true, I'm afraid. It's to do with Jasper developing the idea that he must defend those who he believes he needs to protect. He'll do exactly the same for you, now that you've been nominated as a friend who is helping us. For instance, if he were to witness someone threatening or trying to attack you, he'd respond with matching violence, up to and including killing the offender.'

'But how can he work that out? I mean, he can't understand what you say to him... can he? Like, that's not possible.'

I smiled gently, 'Short version – yes he can. But if you really are interested, why don't you come over this evening for dinner and meet our crew, which currently includes two ladies who have been making a study of Jasper's habits and abilities. They're both associate professors at Melbourne Uni, on a study break for their veterinarian PhDs. They'll tell you about Jasper in much better detail than I can. I've only been living with and feeding him for the last five years or so. Come over around 17:00 for happy hour, and we'll eat after that. Super casual dress, please.'

'Thank you. I'd love to do that. Eating by myself gets a bit lonely at times, and I refuse to socialise with my XO. But enough of that nonsense. What did you want to see me about?'

'Firstly, to confirm that you have received orders from Admiral Stallman regarding your next deployment, although it sounds like that has happened.'

'Yes. We're to stay here, and short of directly endangering the boat or crew, I'm to do whatever you require. I must say that I've never received such open-ended and non-specific orders ever before and my curiosity is seriously aroused.'

'We'll discuss that in detail later, if you don't mind. But in the short term, there's a need to get the PM, his lady and Miss Langley to Buka Town airport by about 14:30 today, so they can fly back to Canberra. Can your helicopter make that run?'

He shrugged, 'Sure. No problem at all. It'll take about thirty minutes for the ground crew to wheel it out, rig and pre-flight it, but that's easy. The flight crew desperately need something to do instead of sitting around all day feeding their faces and watching videos.'

He looked at Charlie. 'If you can be here by 13:30, Miss Langley, that will allow for briefing and loading time.'

'Thank you Commander,' Charlie said with a lovely smile, 'the Boss will be very pleased.'

'Good-oh. Now, what else can I do?'

I grinned. 'We might leave it there for now, thanks Jim, but we'll talk more tonight. The only thing I can say is that I hope and expect there will be some rather unusual aspects to what we'll be doing over the next few weeks, so apart from the helicopter trip, I guess I just wanted to ask, now that you've received such non-specific orders, what you thought about being involved in things a bit out of the ordinary.'

He nodded, and indicated Charlie, myself and Jasper, who was stretched out, sphinx-fashion, on the thick scatter-rug on the deck, his head raised watching Jim carefully. 'A case in point and an interesting question, Commander,' he said thoughtfully. 'As you are aware, service life can be quite controlling in many respects, but the general brief of a patrolling frigate requires us to expect and cope with the unexpected. For that reason, I think you'll find that despite that fool of an XO, my crew and I are quite good at thinking outside the box and responding to strange situations.'

I stood. 'Nicely put and thanks Jim. Please call me Harry, and I hope we'll see you on *Firebird* at 17:00. Charlie will make sure she and the other two are here by 13:30 and I'll clear your flight with the airport authorities in Buka Town.'

He shook hands with us, including Jasper who solemnly lined up again, paw raised, then escorted us to the gang-way. It could have been my imagination, but there seemed to be many more sailors of both sexes hanging around than when we'd arrived.

As we strolled back to *Firebird*, and after sharing a chuckle at the stir we'd caused, Charlie asked seriously, 'Do you think Jim will work out?'

'Yes. Now I've met him and chatted, I think so. He might baulk at a few things at first, but we'll break him in gently. Paul has had a lot more time to come around to the unconventional way we do things, but hopefully Jim won't take that long to get used to us.'

Back aboard, we found Paul waiting to say his goodbyes.

'I've received our new orders to head direct for Darwin and our delayed crew change-over,' he said, 'so we'll get going. We're overdue for leave, so I just wanted to say thanks for the interesting diversion and excitement, and we'll see you next time you get your tits caught in the wringer and need the Navy's help to get free.'

'Cheeky bugger,' I said affectionately, as I gave him a man-hug and hand-shake. We'd been through a lot together over several operations, and he and his crew had been dependable friends.

We all trooped onto the wharf to wave goodbye as the *Arafura* quietly burbled away on her diesels.

Back aboard again, I gave Charlie a flash-drive copy of the un-edited video record of the attack on *Changbaishan* as taken by *Firebird's* masthead camera. 'Just in case you need to prove to the right people, that unidentified locals made that attack because to them, the Chinese weren't welcome.'

She nodded appreciation.

Early afternoon, we said a sad farewell to three more of our dear friends, then watched as the grey Sea-Hawk fired up, before smoothly lifting off *Ballarat's* flight deck and accelerating into a climbing turn out across the sparkling, nearly-deserted and once-again peaceful harbour.

# CHAPTER 21

It wasn't long after the helicopter departure, when Joseph strolled along the wharf wearing his harbourmaster uniform, and was invited to join us in the cockpit. With a cool one in hand, he said, 'You've had a rough time of it, Harry, but that was a good job, very well done. There are a lot of people around here who are very grateful for your efforts on their behalf.'

I nodded appreciation. 'Thanks Joseph... it did get a bit rough at times, but it worked out nicely in the end. However, as I said earlier, having talked to Mr Tari, we agree that this push to gain control of your port probably isn't over yet. They'll try again and soon.'

'Yes. I agree. But what can we do about it? They won't fall for the same tricks next time.'

'That's right. I expect they'll be much better prepared and that will translate to almost unstoppable. At least given the scale of resistance we can muster here and now, that is.'

He had an amused glint in his eye when he replied, 'Are you suggesting you have another plan?'

I looked hard at him for a moment, remembering that I'd already seen him in a different light. 'I might have. Rather than brute force, which we only have in limited quantities, it's a different and very weird approach, and is based on something Mr Tari said a few days ago. If it were to work, then it might render another Chinese attempt at a port take-over impossible, or at least not worth their efforts.'

His eyebrows raised, showing his interest.

'That sounds a lot better than getting into another bunfight we'd probably lose. Go on.'

'The plan depends on my discussions with two separate groups of people who need to go along with the idea.'

He returned my look, but the spark of interest was still there. 'Okay, I'll bite. Who might those groups be?'

I leant forward to emphasise my words. 'The first group would be the leaders of the local rebel group who shut the mine down in the first place, and who apparently helped with the attack on the ship. I need to have a talk with them and perhaps you could help me with that. I've heard they are very suspicious of all outsiders, and tend to shoot first and ask questions later.'

Joseph got a wary look in his eye, and said gravely, 'Yes. You're right there. Even after so much time has passed, suspicions of outsiders, particularly if they're associated with a government, any government, are just as strong. There have been too many government persons who have come here with marvellous-sounding promises to get the mine going, but when all the cards were on the table, they all wanted the same thing. To look after themselves first by taking most of the pie, only leaving crumbs for the country and the local landowners. Which of course, was why the rebellion and fighting started in the first place. I'm sure you are aware that Australian companies, along with Papua New Guinea, were at the centre of the last lot of troubles.'

Once again, I started to get the feeling that Joseph was much more than he appeared, and my mind back-pedalled to a few things he'd said the last time we spoke. I nodded. 'Yes. We're fully aware of the situation. But I think you know by now, that even though we turned up here with our Prime Minister as part of the crew, we did not and do not claim to represent the Australian government nor any commercial interest. We truly were on a genuine holiday cruise and happened to be diving at an atoll not far away at the south end of the Solomon Sea when the Chinese arrived here. It was in response to the request for assistance Mr Tari made to PNG, who then asked Australia for temporary assistance. Having my good friend, the Prime Minister aboard, was a genuine coincidence, but one which helped speed the limited action we were able to take.

Joseph smiled. 'Point noted and accepted Commander, and our people are extremely grateful as your actions have proved that you and your crew took great personal risks, for no gain other than to assist us. For this reason, suspicions in your case have been suspended, and I will gladly arrange a meeting with the local leaders to discuss your ideas. I would also like to assure you, that you and your crew will be perfectly safe for however long you remain in our country. However, I must ask for the reason why one Australian Navy ship is remaining here?'

My good suspicions about Joseph just solidified, but I replied evenly. 'That is purely at my request, Joseph, not by Australian Government choice. My reasoning is to maintain a short-term military presence as a temporary deterrence to the Chinese in case they decide to make some sort of move in the very near future. It has been done with Mr Tari's knowledge and agreement. It may also be useful to have the frigate close-by for other reasons, should my ideas pan out. The captain's orders are to take no action of any sort, unless directly requested by myself and approved by Mathias Tari. Apart from the skipper's visits to this boat for briefing purposes, none of his crew are being allowed ashore. His boat's main task is simply to sit there and be seen by whoever cares to look, as I'm certain the Chinese have this area under constant surveillance, both satellite, aerial and ground-based.'

Joseph nodded. 'I understand and that's good reasoning. Is there anything more you care to tell me at this point?'

I shook my head. 'I'd rather discuss my ideas with all the leaders together, thanks Joseph. No offence, but second and third-hand briefings tend to create too many opportunities for mis-interpretation. This wild idea, and it really is just that, needs to be presented with the utmost clarity.'

He grinned approval, taking no offence.

'Very well then, Harry. When would you like to have this meeting?'

'As soon as possible, please Joseph. Perhaps tomorrow morning, as I have Commander Sanders from the *Ballarat* visiting this evening for both business and social purposes.'

He thought a moment. 'That's no problem. Would it be convenient if I collect you at 10:00 tomorrow?'

'That would be excellent, Joseph. Is that sufficient time for the leaders to get here?'

He laughed and waved a large hand casually at the surrounding lush, green slopes. 'They already are here, Harry. This is where their homes and families are. They're within a five-minute walk of this boat, and have walked past you many times.'

I felt slightly foolish not to have realised that. 'Yes, of course. My apologies. In that case, I will be ready at 10:00 tomorrow, thanks Joseph.'

At that, the big man smiled and stood, shook hands with everyone present, then departed.

'You're back to playing with the big boys, dearest,' Sandy said thoughtfully. 'I'm glad Joseph said we were safe.'

'Yeah, I know what you mean. But I do trust him and obviously the rebel leaders do as well.' I thought it best not to spell out my thoughts about Joseph's actual position in the rebel hierarchy at this stage.

By 17:00 that evening, our cockpit happy hour had only been going for 30-minutes, and the crew were nicely settled, drinks in hand, when Jim arrived. He was as prompt as expected, and as he wandered up, I noticed that he'd taken the hint about casual dress, wearing shorts, sandals and a loose, lightweight shirt.

'Come aboard, Jim,' I called as he stopped on the wharf, looking down on our happy, slightly-rowdy group. As the tide was low, our deck was below wharf level, so he went forward and swung easily down using one of the woven carbon-fibre shrouds as a handhold, before coming aft.

'Lovely boat, Harry. I've not had the chance to sail on a big catamaran before. It looks like it should be quite fast in a good breeze.'

I grinned modestly, 'We've seen over 30 knots in flat water, with just a 5° heel, and the ladies serving tea and coffee in the cockpit. Before he had his turbine fitted, Paul Davy was quite jealous as we passed him like he was in idle-mode. I'll give you a tour after you've had a thirst quencher.'

'Yes please.'

I introduced him to everyone, and smiled to see him take a particular interest in Beth and Georgia. When he was seated with a frosty beer in hand, Jasper wandered out with Krazy cat perched on his shoulders, and gave Jim's leg a brief nuzzle.

'Oh good,' Sandy said happily, 'he approves of you.'

'After seeing the size of his teeth and claws, I'm very glad about that,' Jim said sincerely.

To which Jasper gave a loud huff, causing Jim to look concerned.

'Did I say or do something wrong?' he asked nervously.

Sandy laughed. 'No, not at all. That's just his way of agreeing with you. He can't quite speak English, of course.'

'Oh dear. Harry told me about this. Do you really mean Jasper understands what I say as well?'

Sandy grinned, 'Unfortunately for us sometimes, he understands everybody, although Beth and Georgia have become the official experts on Jasper's talents.'

Jim looked at Beth and Georgia.

'Harry told me you were doing Jasper research for your PhDs. How is that going?'

'Brilliantly!' Georgia enthused. 'We've shown that he understands normal proper English almost perfectly, can carry out complex instructions and has a high level of intelligence. We've been discussing a way to rate his IQ, but that needs a bit more work. He's also demonstrated an uncanny and unprecedented ability to interact with other species.'

As this point hadn't come up before in our limited discussions, Jim looked very interested in that aspect of the big cat's behaviour.

'I'd like to hear more about that if you don't mind sparing the time. According to Harry, we won't have much to do over the next few days or weeks.'

Both girls looked delighted to be asked.

'We'd be happy to,' Georgia answered, 'and we can also show you some absolutely amazing video of Jasper's various encounters with wildlife. The giant croc videos are by far the best!'

Jim looked suitably impressed. 'Giant croc? As in big crocodile? That would be something to see!'

They both grinned at his interest, but Georgia answered. 'How about six to seven metres big. Two of the videos are real piss-whizzers with Harry in a much-too-close and personal starring role both times.'

Jim gave me a calculating look up and down. 'That sounds even more intriguing. Particularly as you don't seem to be missing any obviously vital bits.'

I waved my hands, waggling all fingers and thumbs. 'No problem. As you'll see, after Jasper introduced me to his newest best friend, the croc and I were sweet. Like best buds!'

Jim sat back in his chair, looking a bit stunned. 'Even before I see the videos, I'm blown away by what you're suggesting. And you reckon these encounters have been all due to Jasper making some sort of mental contact with different wild species?'

Beth nodded, 'Absolutely. But there's even more than just mental contact – there's sometimes a verbal element as well. But best if you see for yourself. It'll save a lot of questions.'

She looked over at me. 'Can we show Jim one of the videos, Harry? Unless you need to talk business.'

'No business tonight. We can save that for tomorrow. You go ahead and bend his mind all you want.'

While Beth went to get her laptop, Jim said, 'I saw the harbourmaster wander past a bit earlier. What's happening tomorrow, if I may ask that much?'

'When Joseph Bulli dropped in, I asked for a meeting with the local tribal chiefs, who are also the former rebel leaders, to discuss a bit of a wild idea I've come up with. If it pans out, there might be a chance of preventing the Chinese from ever trying to make another attempt to grab the port, and possibly settle the mine dispute as well.'

He looked suitably stunned, 'Wow! You don't do things by halves, Harry. Gutsy move!'

Sandy leant over and patted my leg. 'That's our Harry. All or nothing! But he won't even tell us what this cunning plan is. Yet!'

I felt uncomfortable because I don't like holding back information from those who may be closely involved in a developing operation.

'Sorry everyone, but it really is a very flaky idea, even for me and I need to float it past the local chiefs as a first step.'

Jim said with a wry look, 'I hope you'll keep me updated as soon as you can. Seeing as we seem to be involved in some strange way.'

I addressed Jim. 'Yeah, sorry for the mystery. But in the morning, how about I ask Joseph if he's willing to have you join us at the meeting? That'll save me from explaining it to you afterwards.'

Jim happily agreed, so that was business concluded, as Beth and Georgia came out with the laptop set-up with the video of the croc joining our beach BBQ up at Cape York.

Fortunately, Bree had planned one of her finger-food dinners, where she keeps a steady supply of very tasty little snack foods coming to the table, so Jim was able to feed himself, while watching the shorter of the two croc encounters with rapt attention.

He watched the episode in silence, before sitting back, a look of amazement on his face. He looked at Jasper, Krazy cat and me, before saying, 'That is the most amazing thing I've ever seen! And you say that was the second time you've come across this croc?'

I nodded. 'Yep. The first time was purely accidental, as the big fella must have been just checking out who'd sailed into his creek. Jasper spotted him, called him over, and the rest is recorded on video. It runs quite a bit longer than the one you just looked at, but you're welcome to have a copy if you're interested.'

'Interested? Hell yeah!' he exclaimed enthusiastically, becoming quite animated. 'That's totally incredible stuff. Both my Gunnery and Nav officers are like me, in that we take a strong interest in wildlife, and they'll be fascinated to see it as well. They'd like to meet Jasper, too. I'm sure by now everyone has heard about him from your visit this morning.'

'No problem, Jim. I'm sure the girls can whip up a copy of the videos for you.'

Bree nodded. 'Sure. No problem. I'll put them on a flash-drive in MP4 format.'

'Thanks Bree,' he said, 'and thanks for the tucker. It makes a nice change from mess food. Our cooks are good at the basic stuff which suits the crew, but nothing like this.'

Thereafter, the evening was relaxing and fairly boozy, although Jim took it easy. I guessed having such a moron for an XO didn't allow the Skipper the liberty to kick back too much.

Next morning, Joseph's large form strolled along the wharf, his trade-mark easy-going grin firmly in place.

'Good morning, Harry,' he greeted, 'how are things with you this fine day?'

With the temperature already in the mid-thirties, and the humidity around 80% and climbing rapidly, I guessed that for him, it was a fine day. However, with towering storm clouds already building over the mountain peaks just inland from the coast, I'd learned that while the usual daily downpour wouldn't do anything to lower either figure to more comfortable levels, it did keep the boat well-washed.

'All well, thank you Joseph.' We exchanged further pleasantries for a few moments, before I said, 'As Commander Sanders and his boat are involved in my plan to an extent, would you and your colleagues allow him to join us at this morning's discussion?'

The big man thought carefully for a few moments, before saying, 'I don't see any problem with that. Especially as he was involved in the expulsion of the *Changbaishan* from our waters. However, it would be best if he didn't wear his uniform. My associates still don't take kindly to uniforms of any type, even when they are on our side.'

I smiled. 'Excellent, thank you Joseph. I took the precaution of suggesting that very thing to him last night.'

With a cheery wave to my very apprehensive crew, who looked as though I was headed for my own personal beheading ceremony, we set off along the wharf, collecting Jim as we passed by *Ballarat*. As suggested, he was dressed much as he had last night, and greeted Joseph warmly, thanking him for his inclusion in the discussion.

With a tight grin, he rumbled, 'Don't thank me yet! If we think the Harry's plan is yet another a pile of dogshit, that'll be the end of discussions. The chiefs have had too many clever, self-serving plans tossed at them over the years to have much hope left that a genuinely equitable solution is possible. As I've told them before, the best we can hope for at the moment is peace between the provinces, and the Council of Ministers is bringing that along slowly, but quite nicely. The dream of a united country is still a possibility, but that of a prosperous united one has pretty much faded.'

After a pause I said, 'Fair enough, Joseph, and I understand your feelings of despair, but all I ask is that my thoughts be heard with truly open minds and given careful consideration.'

'I have told the chiefs this, Commander and your assistance so far has earned you the right to a fair hearing. That's the best I can promise.'

'Good-oh,' I said lightly, 'that'll do very nicely.'

# CHAPTER 22

We followed the road which ran along the back of the wharves for a few hundred metres, returning the many cheerful greetings from locals going about their business at a typically gentle island pace. I was impressed that despite their low standard of living, everyone was still cheerful, clean and tidy. Not quite my expectation, which shows the danger of all preconceived notions. Leaving the open area near the wharves, we then turned right down a wide track through the forest which roughly followed the north shore of the harbour. The cacophonous chorus of millions of insects and screeching flocks of brightly-coloured birds were non-stop, as was the fluttering parade of beautiful butterflies, also in a rainbow of colours. I was particularly fascinated by the incredible assortment of different-coloured dragonflies zipping about, their bright body colour replicated by a small, but neat rectangular patch on each wing-root. I would have loved to stop to inspect them more closely, but more pressing matters demanded my full attention.

We soon stopped at a well-built and neatly-kept timber house with its ubiquitous corrugated-iron roof extended out to cover a wide shady veranda on three sides. A group of children were playing happily near the front steps and laughingly scattered to let us through. With Joseph leading the way, we turned left at the top of the steps, to where a rugged, hand-made table was surrounded by comfortable-looking cane chairs. Three burly men sat at the table, their white hair denoting their age, and according them an air of calm dignity. They regarded Jim and me impassively as Joseph introduced us. They introduced themselves as John Noki, Thomas Arva and Moses Kami and politely invited us to sit. As we did, a smiling young girl served coffee in large, mis-matched mugs.

After we had taken our first sips of the fragrant brew, I commented on the excellent taste. John Noki said in a deep, gravelly voice, 'Coffee is one of our few worthwhile products, Commander and I'm pleased you appreciate it. But Joseph has brought you here to discuss more serious matters. Would you care to explain to us just what is this very important idea you have come up with, which might have such a powerful effect upon our nation?'

After taking another appreciative sip of coffee, I carefully set my mug down, sat back and started.

'Firstly, I thank you all for agreeing to hear from me today, gentlemen, and I wish to add that I haven't mentioned this idea to Mr Tari, Commander Sanders, or anybody else for that matter. You are the first, as I consider your opinion to be the most important. I do not say this as false praise, but because I appreciate that the overtures which have been made to you in the recent past, did not offer any worthwhile gain over that to which you objected all those years ago.'

My words raised a fleeting grin from the four men, and my suspicions were confirmed that Joseph was a full-blown member of this Council and not just a trusted messenger.

'However, something which Mathias Tari said to me recently, started the train of thought which has brought me here today. His exact words don't matter, but the gist was that all the proposals you have received to try to re-open the Panguna mine, have been from organisations with strong ties to, or even representing the government of a country. This latest abortive effort by the Chinese held out a similar promise, although as we strongly suspect, they really only wanted the harbour and had no intention of developing the mine.'

I was grateful they were following my story with careful attention, although the lack of feedback from their stern, expressionless faces made it hard going, so I fortified myself with another sip of the truly excellent coffee.

'Mr Tari went on to suggest that it was a great shame that some truly independent private enterprise couldn't become interested in the project, as at least they would not be acting in any national interest which could prove to be a long-term threat to the true independence of your country. However, he was sufficiently realistic to acknowledge that he wasn't aware of any non-aligned, private organisation with sufficient resources to tackle such a project. At least, not one which would be interested, given the relatively unstable nature of the political situation on Bougainville. No offence intended.'

'No offence taken Commander,' John Noki stated, 'since you have quite accurately stated the problem. We freely admit that our provinces are still uneasy with each other, although the excellent work Mathias Tari has been doing to bring everyone together, does appear to be slowly working. We remain hopeful that before long we can truly say our impoverished nation is at least at peace with itself.'

I nodded agreement. 'Indeed, Mr Noki. However, it was these words from Mr Tari which caused me to consider a possible solution, although it is one which will require both you, and shall we call them, your potential investors, to reach agreement. It is for this reason, that I am presenting this idea to you first.'

A nod from John Noki was apparently all the encouragement I was going to get, and a gentle reminder that I was waffling. I was because they made me bloody nervous!

Therefore, I rapidly collected my thoughts and got on with it.


'As Mr Tari said, finding a non-aligned private organisation with sufficient resources to make this project, with such a high-risk to reward factor, become a reality, appears to be impossible. However, not long ago, I had an occasion to be briefly associated with, and to perform a valuable service for what I believe could be just such an organisation.'

That, at least, raised a few eyebrows, which I took to denote a heightened level of interest, so I drew a deep breath before making my best and only move.

'This organisation of which I speak, is the largest clan of the Japanese Yakuza, the Yamaguchi-gumi clan.'

I paused deliberately, as five faces showed shock, although I noted with concealed interest, that it was only Thomas Arva and Moses Kami who growled almost in unison, 'What is this nonsense? You cannot seriously propose we become associated with a major criminal organisation? Impossible!'

I leant forward to lend intensity to my words, and said sharply, 'No! Not impossible! Listen to my words before you pass judgement!' My sharp rebuke raised eyebrows around the table, but no further censure was made for my unseemly outburst, so I went on in a much more reasonable tone.

'It is true that the Yakuza are indeed one of the world's major criminal organisations, engaging in a wide variety of illegal activities, but intriguingly, they are also openly and officially recognised as a legitimate business organisation by the Japanese government. In more recent times, they have increasingly diversified their activities into wholly legitimate, and highly successful enterprises. While primarily a Japanese organisation, they are definitely not connected with, nor controlled in any way by the Japanese government or any other nation for that matter. I have also learned from personal experience that they conduct all their legitimate business dealings with a very high degree of honour, to a degree which far surpasses that of any other business or legitimate government! Mine included! From discussions I have had with some of the clan leaders, I learned that they are actively looking for additional lucrative, and legal enterprises with which to become involved. Whether this project qualifies as one which might be of interest to them, I cannot say until I present my idea. However, I must have your preliminary approval to at least present this idea to them, before I dare make contact and commence that depth of dialogue.'

Jim was staring at me as though I'd lost my mind, while John and Thomas were shaking heads and muttering dark thoughts in their snowy beards. Only Moses and Joseph looked interested, although they didn't say anything. I knew that John and Thomas were undecided and thinking hard, so casting caution to the non-existent wind, I pushed my point a bit further.

'If you set aside for the moment the fact that this organisation is based at least partly on criminal activity, remember that it is given a high degree of legitimacy by being recognised by the Japanese government for its legal business activities. That very same government is constantly trying to shut down the Yakuza's criminal enterprises, but they totally support their involvement in the legitimate ones. The situation is absolutely bizarre, but if you understand Japanese culture, it is one which is very Japanese. In other words – condemn the bad, while applauding the good! I wish to emphasise at this point, that this is entirely my own thinking based on what I have learned of this organisation. In my own very limited dealings with them, I found them to be men of the very highest honour and integrity who do exactly what they say they will do, and expect their business partners to do the same.

Today, at this first airing of my wild plan, I merely ask for your objective thoughts on the concept of this proposal. If you agree in principle, that will be sufficient for a start, allowing me to make an approach to the senior persons I know in the organisation.'

After a thoughtful pause, John Noki spoke. 'While at first glance, the idea appears to have considerably more merit than any we have heard in the past years, I still have difficulty becoming enthusiastic about being associated with a major criminal organisation. How could we possibly remain distanced from their illegal activities?'

I was reassured by the practical nature of his question, which showed that he was taking the proposal seriously.

'Your assurance that the two types of enterprise would be kept separate, is virtually guaranteed by the way the organisation has to operate. They keep the two sides of their business well apart because of the way the Japanese government treats the organisation.

As I have already said, the government recognises the organisation as a whole and embraces their legitimate enterprises, while working relentlessly to shut down the illegal ones. Perhaps it might be easier to look upon it as two totally separate organisations – one legal, one not so, sharing a common name. This, of course, is the way the Yakuza themselves view their activities. Your dealings, at all stages, would be with totally professional persons of the highest ethical standards. Their code of honour is incredibly strict, and as I said earlier, what they say will happen – does happen. Additionally, in dealing with them, there is the comforting benefit that they would not have any aspirations toward taking over or subverting your country in any way, unlike our recently-departed Chinese friends. If the Yakusa also see merit in my proposal and agree to enter discussions, they will be seeking to run a wholly legitimate business, and it will be up to you and their negotiators to reach an agreement acceptable to both sides. There will be never be any shady politics or under-the-table deals with these people!

However, I must warn you that in return, they will demand and expect total honesty from you at all times, and unwavering adherence to the terms of the agreement you all sign, so you must be prepared for that. Despite seeming to be at odds with their core enterprises, they take a very harsh view of any form of dishonesty in business dealings.'

Grudging nods of agreement came from the four leaders, until John Noki said, 'You have made a good case, Commander, for approval to present this project to our potential investors. However, we need to discuss your idea further between ourselves. May we ask that you not mention this to any other, outside of your crew, until we deliver our answer?'

I bowed my head in agreement. 'Of course, gentlemen. Discretion is essential at this early stage. I await your decision.'

They all stood, as John Noki spoke again. 'We thank you Commander, for this intriguing idea. However, I must ask one important question. Why are you going to such extraordinary lengths to assist our country, with no apparent gain to yourself or your country?'

I thought a moment, as I didn't have an immediate answer.

'Truly, I do not have a ready answer to that question, Mr Noki. I can certainly confirm there is no gain for myself or my country, apart from having peaceful and friendly close neighbours. As for motivation, I can only say that it's an Australian viewpoint where we hate to see a bully getting the best of someone who can't readily fight back. Aussies always have and always will stand up for the perceived underdog. The concept of getting the Yakuza to invest in the Panguna mine project is, as I see it, just an extension of that national feeling, because if you both reach agreement, neither the Chinese nor any other nation will dare to interfere ever again, since the eyes of the world will be upon you and you'll have their support.'

'That's a very interesting sentiment, Commander, and we are inclined to accept your motives as refreshingly genuine. Thank you. We will speak again soon.'

Joseph walked us to the front gate, the same bunch of happy kids and dogs darting away like scattering chooks from around our feet. 'Thank you, Commanders. I'll stay to discuss this with my associates, as you've given us a great deal to consider. Just follow the track until you reach the road, then turn left. I expect to speak with you tomorrow.'

We shook hands, and with a great feeling of relief at having survived a meeting with the fearsome leaders of the rebellion, headed back to our boats.

We had reached the wharf before Jim said, 'I find it hard to believe you came up with, and presented that incredible plan. It all hinges on getting the Yakuza to co-operate. What the hell were you thinking? Even I know you don't fuck with them. They're the baddest of the very bad boys!'

'Yep. I know all that. But it truly was like I said, in my limited dealings with them, I learnt about their strong sense of honour and that they really are looking for legitimate business opportunities. To me, this would seem to be one such opportunity, provided they don't find the asking price too much.'

Jim was obviously having a lot of trouble getting his head around the idea of anyone actually wanting to work with the Yakuza! And even worse, being allowed to!

'But what makes you think you are able to even get the chance to start a dialogue with their senior leaders? And why on earth would they listen to a foreigner? A *Gaigin!*'

I smiled. 'Perhaps Jim, it's because quite recently, I was fortunate enough to be in a position to save the life of the granddaughter of the second-in-command of the Yamaguchi-gumi clan, and that of her best friend. The girls were very grateful, and their grandfather and the other girl's very influential parents even more so! Granddad seems to think he owes me one!'

I chuckled as a stray thought crossed my mind. 'Although if this turns out the way I think it could, I'll end up doing him an even bigger favour. But as something to ponder, if they decide to proceed further, you might get the chance to sit in on the talks with the Chief Underboss.'

He looked slightly horrified, 'Shit, Harry! That'd be like sitting down to dinner with Hannibal Lecter!'

I laughed at his concern. 'No, no, no, Jim. You misunderstand. They're really very nice people once you get to know them. They just have a commendably low tolerance to bullshit! Bit like myself, I guess.' Feeling slightly euphoric now the endgame had been entered, I laughed again and said, 'this is all becoming quite good fun, don't you think?'

He shook his head. 'What I really think, Harry, with all due respect, is that you're totally, fucking nuts! A top bloke, and all that, but batshit crazy!'

I was still laughing as we reached *Ballarat's* gangway. 'Good assessment, Jim. I know my crew will wholeheartedly agree with you. Now, how about you come with me and we'll have some lunch while we bring the crew up to date. I haven't told them my crazy idea yet and I won't get any peace until I do.'

'Bloody hell! This really will be fun!' He muttered, waving 'stand-down' to the *Ballarat's* alert and curious gangway watch as we continued past.

Over lunch, it didn't take very long to present my idea to the crew, who initially laughed incredulously, then grew thoughtful as they thought things through a bit more. At least my permanent crew had the first-hand experience of meeting Hiroto Sakamoto, the Chief Underboss's right-hand man, when he came to collect the rescued girls. However, Beth and Georgia gave me some very wary looks.

'Dare we ask how come you know some top-level Yakuza persons well enough to lay a ratbag plan like this on them?' Georgia disrespectfully asked, so I explained the circumstances surrounding our last operation. I didn't bother mentioning the operation before that one where we first had contact with the bad side of the Yakuza down in Tasmania.

She nodded, 'Yeah. I can see that they would think they owe you one, but if this idiot plan actually works, you'll be doing them another favour. Possibly a very big one!'

I laughed at how closely she'd echoed my words to Jim. 'Yeah. It's a bummer having the top Yakuza clan owing us favours.'

'You're unbelievable Harry,' she added, shaking her head. 'Talk about falling into the sewerage pond and come up smelling like roses!'

Discussion raged back and forth over lunch and beyond, until Jim excused himself to go see what fresh fuck-ups his inept XO had created in his absence.

'Come back for happy hour and dinner if you'd like,' I invited, and there was such a chorus of assent from the others, he gratefully accepted.

It was another happy, relaxed night among friends, although I personally felt a slight level of tension, wondering how the rebel leaders would vote. Although, when I thought about it, if they said 'No', we could just pack up our bat and ball and head home, leaving them to deal with the Chinese assault, round #2, whenever the next takeover bid for Kieta Harbour was launched. Still, it would go against my instincts to be forced to step aside and let such an arrogant, bullying nation push their territorial expansions onto a much smaller one unable to stand up to such a vastly bigger aggressor.

It was nearly midday the next day, before Joseph wandered down the wharf again, the usual cheerful grin on his face not revealing what was on his mind.

Sitting down with a cool drink in hand, he said without preamble, 'We have agreed that you should go ahead and make contact with your dangerous friends, and present the plan to them. If they wish to proceed further, we will agree to a meeting with them and with Mathias Tari. Should the meeting go ahead, we would like you and Commander Sanders to act as mediators and neutral witnesses.'

I mentally breathed a big sigh of relief as I nodded, 'That's excellent news Joseph. I shall make contact as soon as I can and call you when I have information.'

He stood and grinned. 'Thank you, Harry. Personally, I have high hopes that this insanely, loopy scheme of yours could actually work.'

# CHAPTER 23

With that back-handed encouragement lifting both my spirits and heartrate, I checked the time difference between Japan and Bougainville and after deciding they were about three hours behind, decided to wait a couple of hours before heading for the SatPhone.

When I thought the time was appropriate, I consulted the card I'd been left by Hiroto Sakamoto, the envoy who had represented Raijin Tanaka when he came to collect Raijin's granddaughter and her friend after we had rescued them from sex-slavers.

'Moshi, moshi.'

'Good morning. This is Harry Stevens. I was hoping to speak with Tanaka-san, please?'

'Ah... Commander Stevens. So very good to hear from you. This is Hiroto Sakamoto. We met when I collected Daku, Chiaki and Fumiko. I hope you are keeping well.'

'Of course I remember you Hiroto, and I am very well, thank you. However, if you will excuse my impolite haste, I have business which I wish to discuss with Tanaka-san, if I may be so bold as to intrude upon his time.'

'Of course, Commander. Tanaka-san will be delighted to hear from you. Chiaki never tires of telling tales of your extraordinary courage and resourcefulness in rescuing her and Fumiko. You will always have a special place in their affections. But to this very important business of yours. As I am Tanaka-san's personal secretary, may I ask if this is a personal concern or a business matter? The reason I ask, is that if it is personal, I shall ensure the conversation is totally private, but if it is business, then I am required to listen in, so as to be fully informed as to what is discussed.'

I chuckled, mentally adjusting again to the very polite and formal manner of Japanese discussion. Even to my *gaijin* way of thinking, I found it refreshingly respectful and productive, although it often took time to get to the point.

'In this instance, Hiroto, it is very much a business matter and I would greatly welcome your involvement and wise counsel. To briefly summarise, I have accidently become involved in an international situation which has escalated to the stage where I am presented with two paths which I might follow. To the right, I take no action, and let a major international power bully a much smaller country into submission. However, if I should choose to take the left path, I reach out to powerful friends with the offer of what could develop into a highly lucrative and legitimate business opportunity for them, while at the same time, possibly prevent the major power from proceeding with its unwelcome and invasive plans.'

*'Goodness me, Commander. You have certainly grasped the tiger by the tail this time! International intrigue at the very highest levels indeed! I can hardly wait to hear the full story of how you came to place yourself in this position. However, I shall not delay your discussion with Tanaka-san any longer. He will be with you momentarily.'*

'I am greatly obliged, Hiroto.'

There was a short pause, then the gravelly voice of the senior under-boss of the Yamaguchi-gumi clan of the feared Yakuza spoke.

*'Good morning, Commander Stevens. It gives me very great pleasure to hear from you again. I fear it has been too long since we last spoke.'*

'Good morning to you too, Tanaka-san, and it is entirely my shame for not speaking with you sooner. I beg your forgiveness, and hope I find you in good health this day?'

*'Indeed, you do Commander. But I see by my secretary's excited gestures, that there is something of importance you wish to discuss with me?'*

'Indeed there is, sir, and thank you for allowing me the opportunity to mention it. Briefly, I have found myself in a situation, not of my making nor choosing I hasten to add, where I have come up with a strange idea which could assist a small, struggling country avoid being overtaken by a major world power, which has the most unfortunate expansionist ambitions. At the same time, there could be a very lucrative and totally legal business opportunity available to an organisation willing and able to take on a large and initially very expensive project.'

His rich chuckle echoed down the clear line. '*Very well, Commander. You have piqued my interest sufficiently that I am seated in a comfortable chair with a fresh pot of green tea and prepared to hear more of your strange idea.*'

He gave another chuckle at his choice of words, so I started.

'Tanaka-san, what do you think about the idea of investing in a copper and gold mine?'

Over the course of the next half-hour or so, I carefully explained the situation, starting with the Chinese moving into Kieta Harbour and commencing refurbishment operations, all without permission. This I followed with our co-ordinated attacks upon the crew and the ship, which drew a delighted chuckle from both audience members. I then detailed the ultimately successful efforts to oust the *Changbaishan*, preceded by the kidnapping of myself and Australia's PM.

'Please excuse my excessively lengthy explanation of events to date,' I apologised, 'but I wished to explain as clearly as possible how we have arrived at this current situation.'

'*No apology is necessary, Commander. This has been a most entertaining story, and one which I would greatly enjoy hearing in even greater detail at a later time. Neither our nation, nor our organisation has any love of the arrogant Chinese and their expansionist policies, which they stupidly pretend are humanitarian aid missions. However, now you have so entertainingly explained the situation, what is the strange idea you have by which we may assist this struggling country of Bougainville?*'

'Along with the large warship, the Chinese sent a small, two-person diplomatic delegation to conduct talks with the Bougainville

President, Mathias Tari and to make a business presentation. Basically, their offer was that China would be willing to wholly underwrite the immense cost of re-opening the Panguna copper and gold mine, if Bougainville would concede the Chinese full usage rights to Kieta Harbour. In addition to those harbour rights, China would also take a majority share of the mine's output, leaving the remainder to be divided between the government and the mine landowners. It only took a couple of days of discussion for the Council of Ministers to reject this proposal as being completely without merit. Their reasoning was that in reality, the Chinese only wanted the harbour rights, and had no intention of actually spending the huge amount of money necessary to re-open the mine. It was believed that once the Chinese were suitably entrenched in Kieta harbour, it would be impossible for Bougainville, with no military assets, to evict them. I might add that within a day of the *Changbaishan* arriving in Kieta Harbour, her civil engineers had commenced the destruction of the existing port buildings.

When this rejection was presented to the delegation, they begged for more time to come up with an alternate plan which perhaps would be more acceptable.

As we believed that this was yet another delaying tactic, it was then that my crew and I, with the help of many of the local people, created the situation where the damaged *Changbaishan* was forced to leave the harbour under escort by a Royal Australian Navy warship, and return to China.'

Although I still had not mentioned my wild idea, I felt I needed to establish more background, and apologised for taking so long to get to the point.

'*I understand, Commander, but please continue. You still hold my interest.*'

'Thank you, sir. With the immediate problem temporarily resolved, I was talking with President Tari, when he lamented that previous commercial proposals to re-open the mine have always involved other countries who wanted to take control of the whole operation along with nearly all the profits. Therefore, they vowed to never again allow a foreign country to become even indirectly involved in operating any enterprise, especially the mine. They would prefer to let the mine sit idle, rather than risk repeating the mistakes of the past.

Mr Tari went on to say it was a shame there wasn't a non-aligned, private organisation which would be interested in taking on the project. He felt that a straightforward commercial agreement would be much more acceptable to being tied up in the tangled web of politics which an offer by a foreign country would bring to the bargaining table.

My strange idea, therefore, is that perhaps your organisation might be the one interested in opening negotiations with both the local provincial land-owners and the Bougainville government, with the objective of re-opening the Panguna copper and gold mine?'

There was a prolonged silence on the line, but I held my breath anyway and waited nervously, until Tanaka-san gave a lengthy chuckle.

'*You surprise me yet again, Commander. This is a most thought-provoking proposal which will require careful consideration.*'

'I appreciate your hesitancy, Tanaka-san and deeply apologise if I have wasted your valuable time, as I believe the amount of money required to bring the mine back into production would be quite – prodigious, if I may use such a term.'

He laughed, dryly, '*Do you have any idea of what the Chinese were planning to spend if they had proceeded with the operation?*'

I swallowed, convinced this was the final deal-breaker, but was determined to honestly lay all my cards on the table. 'President Tari mentioned the ultimate figure of around US$6 billion to get the mine back up to full capacity again, including the upgrade to the port facilities and the environmental clean-up. Although I must add that the latest independent estimates I obtained, put the value of the copper and gold reserves at greater than US$60 billion. Despite the potential excellent return and allowing for the share the Bougainville government and landowners will demand, I realise this is a totally outrageous sum and apologise again for wasting your time.'

Surprisingly, he remained in a good mood and chuckled again. *'Nonsense, my dear friend. In wanting to consider your idea more carefully, I am not dissuaded in the slightest by the amount of money. I do not wish to suggest that it is an insignificant amount, and our clan may well be forced to affiliate with others to raise even the initial capital. But in broad terms, when the outlay is offset against the returns, it becomes a very sound financial investment and could become an excellent vehicle through which we may wish to move large amounts of cash, although that last observation was strictly for your ears only! Therefore, the money is not a problem. The biggest problem I see, and which I believe will be well-nigh insurmountable, would be convincing the local rebel leaders to sit down at the negotiating table with the dreaded Yakuza! We do not delude ourselves that despite our highly successful efforts to branch out into legitimate business enterprises, we are after all, a major criminal organisation at heart. It is therefore difficult to imagine any group or organisation who would welcome us into a partnership, let alone a nation!*

*Please understand, Commander, that at the urging of our government, we have made great advances into legitimate business, and a project like this, as large as it would be, is precisely what we look for to further those objectives. I can say with conviction, that even our government would be delighted with the motives behind this scheme and the expected outcome. I know they would be very interested in purchasing much of the mine's output to boost our nation's resources. So, while we can talk on about the multitude of benefits which may arise from this proposal, the end result will be almost a foregone conclusion. A polite refusal from the other party once they learn who their potential new friends and investors really are.'*

I took a deep breath, feeling slightly dizzy from trying to steady my racing heart, and hardly able to believe the incredible turn the discussion had just taken.

'I thank you, Tanaka-san, for your honest reply and initial assessment of my suggestion. While I will naturally accept any decision you make without question, I beg forgiveness to disagree with you on one quite important point. That point is – what if I were to inform you that just four hours ago, I received approval from the four leaders of the provincial rebel group who represent the mine landowners, to present this proposal to you? They stated that should you be interested in proceeding further, they desire a meeting as soon as convenient with you and your advisors, such meeting to include President Tari of the Bougainville Council and myself.'

There was another pregnant pause, before Tanaka-san spoke again in a slightly bemused tone.

'*Once again, Commander, you astound me. Should you ever tire of living on your marvellous catamaran, I would be honoured to have you working with me. However, enough of that daydream. You have performed a near impossible act by convincing these gentlemen to even consider your strange idea. This does indeed change the complexion of the whole plan and based upon that, I will give you a very definite yes to the offer of a preliminary meeting. Naturally, I will still discuss the basic proposal with my Kumicho and our Council, and will have Hiroto contact you soon. I presume the rebel leaders would prefer to hold the meeting in Kieta?*'

'I would say so, Tanaka-san, as it would make them more comfortable to be on home ground, so to speak, providing that is agreeable to you?'

'*Of course. I will be happy, even delighted, to make the journey, as it will be advantageous to see the local land for myself. May I presume there is a suitable airstrip we can fly into?*'

'Only in Buka Town, the national capital to the north, is there one suitable to take a small business jet. A Falcon 9X used it recently. The other two airstrips which are much closer to here, are in varying states of disrepair due to the troubles. Hiroto can find all the details in official aeronautical publications.'

'*That will not be a problem, Commander. We have a range of suitable aircraft available. Is there transport from Buka Town to Kieta?*'

'A road journey is possible, but lengthy and uncomfortable. However, I can arrange to have you, your staff and Mr Tari transported by a Royal Australian Navy helicopter, if that will be acceptable?'

He laughed delightedly. '*I am further impressed, Commander! You seem to have all the answers to my questions, but I will not presume to push the boundaries of our friendship any further for now. I will say however, that you have done outstanding work in making this project appear to be a strong possibility. It will be up to my team and the local landowners to see if it can be turned into viable reality. Unless you hear differently, my highly-efficient secretary informs me that we can be with you in two days. Hiroto will call with the arrival times. For now, I again thank you for your remarkable efforts and look forward to meeting you in person.*'

'Thank you, Tanaka-san, for your time and patience. Ja ne.'

I sagged back in my comfortable chair, tension and sweat draining in equal measures from every pore, followed by a euphoric feeling of relief that we'd done all that was possible to give this impossibly immense project the best chance to succeed. Most of the crew had been listening in to at least my side of the conversation, and I momentarily basked in their approval of my efforts, as my lovely lady awarded me a cold, long-neck beer.

# CHAPTER 24

I made an immediate phone call to Joseph, letting him know the outcome of my contact with the Yakuza.

'*That is excellent news, Harry. I will pass it on to the chiefs. Additionally, have you given thoughts as to where we should hold this meeting?*'

'I have, and thought that while you and the chiefs should be given all due consideration, Raijin Tanaka is also a very powerful man who is travelling a great distance. For that reason, I believe it appropriate that you and your associates make a gesture of respect as well. To that end, I suggest a neutral setting such as the wardroom aboard the *Ballarat* frigate?'

Joseph chuckled in his rich, deep voice, '*Are you sure you aren't a politician, Commander? I think that will be sufficiently neutral, especially as Australia is not involved to this project.*'

I laughed. 'Excellent, Joseph. I shall make it so. I'll let you know as soon as I receive confirmation of the date and time from Hiroto.'

My next call was to Mathias Tari, who was amazed to hear not only of my wild scheme, but was delighted at the progress made.

'*Appropriate words fail me, Commander. That is marvellous news, and even though I've not had time to consider all ramifications of your plan, the ready acceptance by the landowners and the investors of the scheme concept, suggests that it is feasible. I do not know how you have achieved such an arrangement so quickly, but I will be praying that all goes well.*'

'Don't forget that you'll be front and centre as well, Mr Tari,' I reminded him, 'and you'll need to be able to speak with one voice for your Council of Ministers. We can't have a multitude of Provincial Ministers and their differing opinions at this meeting!

I have used the very small amount of influence I have to bring the only acceptably possible investor in your country's future to the negotiating table. It is up to you and the landowners to actually work out an equitable arrangement with your potential investor. I'm sure I don't have to remind you that any agreement reached will be regarded by your new investors as set in stone. Regardless of their somewhat unsavoury background, these people have great honour and integrity in business dealings, and expect no less in return. Overlooking this fact could provoke severe consequences. I hasten to add, that the last statement was a guideline or at most, a gentle warning – not in any way a threat.'

*'I understand and appreciate your words, Commander. I also must add that I and my Ministers are very grateful to you for your efforts to not only remove the initial Chinese threat, but to open the door to our possible economic independence and ultimate prosperity. We all thank you.'*

'Early days yet Mr Tari, but I appreciate your thoughts. I'll call when I get travel details, but please be prepared for things to happen in two days from now.'

With my mind buzzing with a million thoughts, I took a deep breath, and decided to take Alex along to have a chat with Jim on *Ballarat*, especially as we needed to borrow his wardroom and Seahawk helicopter again.

'This should be fun,' Alex commented cheerfully, as we wandered along the wharf toward the grey ship's gangway. 'Jim seems to be getting with the plan rather well, I think.'

'Yeah, he is,' I replied, as we turned to climb up to the deck. 'He was a bit strait-laced at first, but I think that by being tossed in the deep end by this crazy plan, he's almost getting used to the weird way we do business.'

'Good afternoon, Commander,' we were greeted by a seaman with a junior Lieutenant hovering in the background.

'Good afternoon, Leading-Seaman. Permission to come aboard to visit the captain?'

'Permission granted, Commander, but who is your guest? Just for the record, sir,' she hastened to add with a nervous smile.

I grinned, 'No problem, Leading Seaman. This is Alex Chetty and he's known to the captain.'

She fired off a sharp salute, 'Very good, sir. Lieutenant Hill will show you the way.'

Jim was in his cabin, dressed in working uniform and wearily ploughing through the usual stack of paperwork. He flapped his hand in greeting, and smiled when he saw Alex's huge form following me into his small cabin. 'Good afternoon Alex, and to you too Harry. I was going to drop by later and catch up.'

We parked ourselves in chairs and I gave him a grin. 'Well. We certainly hope that you'll drop by anyway, as usual, but I thought we'd come and bring you up to date, now that we've finished most of our part in sorting out Bougainville's internal affairs.'

That earned me an inquisitive look.

'Okay. That sounds positive. What's the story?'

'We have an agreement-in-principal between both parties, to have a sit-down in two day's time, to see if they can agree to terms for the project.'

'Wow!' Jim leant back in his chair, 'that's huge! You actually convinced the deputy head of the major Yakuza clan to come here to meet with Mathias, Joseph and his mates?'

I nodded, 'Yep. That pretty well sums it up. There's just a couple of things. We need to borrow your helicopter again, if you don't mind, and your wardroom for a day or two.'

'No problem with the helicopter,' he exclaimed, looking quite excited, 'where do you want to go?'

'Not us – it'll just be a pickup from Buka Town then back here for Raijin Tanaka, his secretary and probably a couple of heavies, as well as Mathias Tari and a secretary representing the Bougainville government.'

He shook his head, grinning like a schoolboy. 'Outstanding! As for the wardroom, I can have the officers fed in the crew's mess for the duration, so that won't be a problem.'

He paused and thought a moment, 'Just one random thought… may I presume that Papua New Guinea is being left out of discussions?'

I replied, 'Yeah. Getting them involved up front is the last thing Mathias would want to do. I reckon he'll have a quiet chat with Jimmy Mori after they've done the deal. Presuming they do, that is. Last time the mine worked, PNG's involvement with that Aussie company, Bougainville Copper and their major grab of the loot, was the main cause of the whole bust-up. Bougainville can't afford to let that happen again if they really do want to boost their economy and become fully self-supporting and independent.'

We kicked a few more details around before heading back, with Jim saying that he'd be along for an early happy hour when he'd knocked over some more paperwork.

With more cause to celebrate, it was a happy evening, and even Jim had the wobbly boot on as he finally meandered back to his ship.

Next day, while the crew lazed around and Beth and Georgia alternated playing with the kitties, still trying to find a way to measure Jasper's IQ, and writing up more notes, I sat myself at the chart table and jotted down a few ideas to do with the coming meeting. While I was there, Hiroto called to say that everything was organised at their end, and that he, Raijin and two security guards would fly into Buka Town tomorrow afternoon.

'*By the time we arrive, it will be too late in the day to have our meeting,*' he said, '*so I have made accommodation arrangements in Buka Town for the evening, if you could arrange the helicopter flight for the next morning.*'

'No problem, Hiroto. I will have the helicopter at the airport at 09:00.'

'*Excellent, Commander. Until then. Ja ne.*'

I called Joseph and Jim to pass on the information, then called

Mathias Tari to update him. Jim promised to have the Seahawk ready, and Mathias said he would meet Raijin when he arrived tomorrow and look after him.

By the time I'd filled a couple of pages with notes and was as ready as I could be for the morrow, the crew had decided happy hour was already underway somewhere in the world, and had opened the bar.

The next day I devoted to leisure – playing with Sandy, Jasper and Krazy and poking around the boat looking for maintenance stuff to do. Trouble with that idea was that Alex had beaten me to it. Although we opened the bar early, I still planned a reasonably quiet night. Jim came down again for a feed and few cool ones, and we briefly discussed next day's arrangements.

Next morning, I was on the *Ballarat's* flight deck at 08:15, receiving a detailed safety briefing from the Seahawk's pilot, Lieutenant Graham. An air warfare officer and a systems operator, who doubled as the crew chief, rounded out the standard three-person crew and made sure I was strapped in securely. I experienced the usual spine-tingling thrill of the rising whine as the first of the two GE T-700 turbines spooled up, and a few minutes later, with all checks complete, the pilot lifted us smoothly off the deck, eased sideways out over the water, then dipped the nose sharply to accelerate out over the harbour before easing into a climbing turn to the north. Even with the best helmets and hearing protection available, the internal noise was intense, making normal speech difficult. I learned later that the crew enjoyed the luxury of a noise-cancelling system. On the way north, I was treated to a breathtaking, low-level scenic flight to Buka Town, the capital, located on the separate island of Buka, which in turn formed the northern, and most populated section of Bougainville.

The southern part of the island nation was dominated by the remains of a massive volcanic cone, with a base more than 50 kilometres across. The central spine of the island held at least one active and several barely-dormant volcanic peaks. These had produced a landscape which was both ruggedly spectacular and brilliantly green, with the mostly narrow coastal plain rising steeply to the jagged peaks. In most areas, the jungle came right down to the narrow beaches, with small villages scattered at regular intervals along the coast. From what I could see, there were far fewer villages in the highlands, although the dense jungle may have hidden many more. This eastern coastal plain also had the only north-south road linking the more-populated north of the country to the less-settled southern districts. Just before reaching the narrow Buka Strait separating the mainland from Buka Island, the island narrowed to form a stubby peninsula just under four kilometres wide. The strait itself was barely 300 metres wide, with Buka Town on the northern, or Buka Island side. The water-way was constantly criss-crossed by the white wakes of a steady stream of boats ferrying back and forth. If ever a place needed a high-level bridge, this was it! Maybe if the mine did fire-up as hoped, they could afford to build one.

From the air, the town looked reasonably neat and modern, being comprised of low-set buildings sprawling along the shore-line, with the contentious airstrip close beside it on the north side. I was amused to note that in common with home-owners everywhere, there were a lot of homes built on the north-side of the airstrip. That sight reminded me that the current airport problems came about because the north-side residents wanted to be able walk directly across the airstrip to access the town, without having to make the lengthy trek around the end due to the necessary security fences. As there were several scheduled flights per day into the strip and no air traffic control, pilots needed to be very careful when trying to land. At least with a helicopter, the human traffic hazard was not so much of a problem.

Despite our aircraft type, our pilot made a very cautious approach, coming in more like a slow-moving fixed-wing aeroplane, and parked not far from a new-looking business jet. The crew-chief turned out to be a dedicated plane-spotter, and informed me that it was one of the new Embraer Praetor 600 jets.

I was kept in my seat until the pilot idled the engines for cooling, then shut them down. The rotor brake quickly slowed the four overhead blades to a groaning stop and I was free to head for the terminal and our passengers, while behind me, the crew walked around, poking and prodding their beloved helicopter, making sure that everything that was supposed to be attached, still was.

Typically, the terminal wasn't air-conditioned although there were many overhead fans, so our passengers met me just outside under a wide awning which provided shade, assisted by the cooling effect of a gentle sea-breeze.

There was a group of six persons who filed away from the building with the tall, solidly-built figure of Mathias Tari standing out. A shorter, nervous-looking man hovered around him, who I presumed to be his secretary. Gleaming white teeth shone in a welcoming smile against Mathias's dark skin as he politely stepped aside for a short, stocky Asian man with a carefully brushed-back mane of white hair and a very impressive pair of white, bushy eyebrows. He was flanked by two tall, well-muscled younger men with an astonishing array of tattoos covering every square centimetre of visible skin. As I stepped up to him, he made a deep bow, which I countered with a shallower one, not being very well versed in the more subtle nuances of Japanese greeting etiquette.

Tanaka-san held his bow for a heartbeat longer, then stepped forward to vigorously shake my hand, a beaming smile on his face.

'Commander Stevens! What a delight to finally meet you in person and under such interesting circumstances.'

I smiled broadly, 'Tanaka-san. It is also my very great pleasure to greet you in person. I trust your flight was uneventful?'

'It was, my young friend. For an old man, the excitement which the prospect of a new enterprise brings, makes me feel youthful again. And of course with the opportunity to visit a new part of our fascinating world.'

'Good to hear, sir. I must thank you once again for making this journey, and agreeing to discuss the dubious merits of my wild plan.'

He chuckled and patted my arm in an unexpected, but pleasing grand-fatherly gesture.

'Nonsense, young man. It is I who am once again in debt to you for creating this opportunity. I have great hopes that we all may benefit from this enterprise, should we reach agreement.'

'Thank you, Tanaka-san. You are most kind with your words.'

Tanaka-san graciously stepped aside so I could say hello to Mathias, who so far, I had only spoken to on the phone. I then spotted a familiar figure who'd been lurking in the background. Seeing Hiroto Sakamoto, Tanaka's private secretary, gave me a momentary flash-back to when I last met him in the bar of a restaurant in Port Bundaberg, escorted by two burly outlaw motorcycle gang bikies. He had been tasked with collecting Tanaka-san's grandson, a bad dude called Daku, his charming grand-daughter Chiaki, and her friend Fumiko.

Excusing myself from Mathias, I shook Hiroto's hand warmly.

'Very good to see you again, Hiroto. I hope you have also been keeping well?'

'Thank you Commander. I am well and looking forward to what this day may bring.'

'As we all are, my friend,' I laughed, noting that the quizzical look on Mathias's face indicated that he hadn't been told of the circumstances by which I'd first come to know Tanaka-san and Hiroto.

The heat and humidity didn't encourage hanging about indulging in too much idle chit-chat, so I suggested we get moving.

As we walked out to the Seahawk, I hung back slightly to have a few words with Mathias.

'I just wanted to say Mr Tari, that in today's discussions, my role is that of mediator only. This is your country and you, Joseph

Bulli and the chiefs, are the ones who are trying to reach a fair and equitable agreement with Tanaka-san.'

'I understand, Commander. It will be as you say.'

I added, 'And as I advised, the conference will take place aboard the frigate *Ballarat*, which as well as being neutral and totally secure, has plenty of space and facilities including all necessary communications. Purely as a courtesy, and as he was included in the preliminary discussion with the chiefs, her captain, Commander Sanders, will be invited to sit in, but will not take active part in discussions.'

He nodded. 'That is perfectly acceptable.'

The flight crew were to be commended for not blinking an eye, as they smoothly briefed and loaded our high-powered and diverse group, so that we were seated, fired up and on our way south within ten minutes. Once again, the noise levels precluded any sensible speech, so most just played tourist by looking out the windows. All except Tanaka-san's silent, menacing bodyguards that was, who watched everyone, including the flight crew, with endlessly suspicious eyes.

Twenty minutes later, we were on approach to *Ballarat's* flight deck, with groups of curious sailors sheltering from the rotor blast around both sides of the hangar. Once the engines shut down and the rotor stopped, the disembarking protocol was neatly decided by Mathias Tari, who politely ushered Tanaka-san and Hiroto off the aircraft first. His bodyguards forcibly insisted on following closely, then Mathias and his secretary, while I trailed behind. By the time I climbed down to the deck, Jim Sanders had welcomed Tanaka-san and Mathias Tari, then led the way below decks to the wardroom.

Jim's stewards had set the long table in conference mode, with writing tablets and pens at each of the ten places, all grouped around one end. Jugs of iced water and fruit juice were within easy reach of every seat. Joseph Bulli and his three associates, John Noki, Thomas Arva and Moses Kami were already in the wardroom, waiting to greet Tanaka-san, who bowed deeply to each man, before enthusiastically shaking their hands. His two bodyguards stepped back against the wall behind their boss, delivering a fierce look at each person as we filed in. Two stewards were standing ready to take any food or drink orders and once all were seated, the passageway door was closed, with two burly seamen wearing sidearms, posted outside. The large portholes let in plenty of sunlight, while the efficient air-conditioning kept the heat and crushing humidity banished outside where they belonged.

I found myself parked at the head of the table with Jim on my left. Tanaka-san and his secretary Hiroto, were beyond Jim, with Mathias Tari and his secretary beside them. To my right were Joseph, John, Thomas and Moses.

Once food and drink orders had been delivered, the stewards retired and closed their door and serving hatch.

I opened the discussion by saying, 'Gentlemen. We all know why we're here so I'm not going to waste anyone's time by making a speech. I shall, however, point out that Commander Sanders and myself are here purely in the role of mediators. Despite our nationality and that of this warship, we do not represent our country or any other interest in this matter. While we may at times, offer suggestions, it is entirely up to you gentlemen to try to reach an equitable agreement which will enable this highly desirable project to proceed. To speed up the production of an accurate record of this meeting, Commander Sanders has made a digital recording device available, provided you all agree to its use, otherwise you may simply rely upon the notes you are taking. Is there any objection to having the recording device in operation?'

I looked around and saw no objections. 'Very well. To the best of my knowledge, this is the only recorder in the room. A transcript and a verbatim copy of the original recording will be made for each of you at the completion of discussions each day, and no additional copies of the transcript will be made unless you request it. Now, who would like to start proceedings?'

Not surprisingly, Joseph briefly flapped one huge hand.

'On behalf of my colleagues, I would like to welcome Tanaka-san to our country and thank him for taking the time to travel here for these discussions. I would also like it noted, that without the incredible efforts of Commander Stevens and his crew, we would still have a Chinese warship parked in this very position. If that was the case, we would not be having these discussions which have the potential to re-vitalise our country and raise us to a level of growth and prosperity unimaginable just a week ago. I would also like to thank President Tari for his unceasing efforts to promote unification throughout the many regions which make up our sadly-divided country. If not for the great strides made toward unification, these talks also would not be possible. We thank you, sir.'

I let my vivid imagination supply the applause this rousing speech deserved, while both Tanaka-san and President Tari silently bowed their heads in appreciation.

Joseph held the floor and continued. 'All here know of the terrible events before and after the closure of the Panguna mine which resulted such horrific loss of life and, equally bad, the decay of living standards here in the southern districts to basic subsistence levels. Therefore, I will not recount nor dwell on all that has passed, but will simply say that my colleagues and I desperately want to forge a way forward. Since the time when the Commander proposed his daring plan, we have been in contact with the most influential tribal members of our area, in an effort, shall we say, to test the water. I am delighted to report that nearly all are firmly in favour of the concept plan as proposed by the Commander. We believe that the recent encounter with the Chinese and the exposure of their blatant lies, may have helped to unite the local people like nothing else before. They have placed their trust in us to negotiate on their behalf and have promised that if we reach a fair and equitable agreement, the men and women who have the skills to work the mine, will return to their former jobs without reservation or complaint.'

He paused to take a sip of water.

'I say this to point out that from our side, the way is clear for those at this table to agree to a fair return of profits to the landowners as well as to our country. Therefore, as we see it, there should be only three entities involved in these discussions. The Panguna Landowners Association, the Bougainville government, and whichever entity Tanaka-san designates will be the operating company investing in the mine.

No other nation is to be involved, nor does any other entity have any claim on the return from this project. We appreciate that the investment required to re-activate the mine will be substantial, and deeply regret and are embarrassed that none of that investment can be provided from sources in-country, except, perhaps for the unreserved enthusiasm of our people to see the mine brought back to life. Naturally, the necessary level of investment is worthy of an appropriate return, otherwise, why do it at all? We expect nothing less. Therefore, I now defer to the honourable Tanaka-san to present his assessment.'

Tanaka-san briefly bowed his head, and with a broad smile said, 'Most eloquently put Mr Bulli, and I heartily agree with all the points you have made. I too, have no wish to be verbose, and prefer, as our American friends would say, 'to cut to the chase'. The most recent estimates of the Panguna reserves show that the mine still holds approximately 5.3 million tonnes of copper, and 19.3 million ounces of gold. The sum worth of those reserves, is estimated at US$69 billion, FOB at current prices.

Broadly speaking, the costs to rehabilitate the area, reactivate the mine and commence ore extraction, are in the region of six to seven billion US dollars, for which we will be completely responsible. That amount should see copper and gold ore being delivered to the docks, and takes into account the necessary upgrades to the harbour storage, fuelling, loading facilities and wharves. It also allows for an unknown amount of rehabilitation work to restore the local waterways as close as possible to their former condition and the implementation of on-going pollution prevention strategies. There may have to be a sum set aside for marketing the material, although I don't expect that to be a problem, as the Japanese government has already indicated a strong interest in taking most of the mine's output. All sales prices are based on the ore being FOB Kieta harbour.

Once the mine has reached the stage where it is functioning smoothly and efficiently, producing and selling ore, we will consider our financial input obligations to be complete and expect the project to support itself on income alone from that time onwards. Provision will be made to handle the inevitable unforeseen contingencies during the transition period.

Based on our financial and logistical investigations, once ore is being produced and sold, and with income being received, the mine should be capable of making the expected substantial profit. Provided it continues to be operated correctly, with no labour disruptions, there is no reason why this profit should not be realised and distributed as per our agreement.

As there are a number of other advantages to this scheme which my organisation can utilise, we have decided that a return of 45% of the FOB price of the mine's output will be sufficient to justify our investment. We further expect the on-going operating cost of the mine to be covered within the remaining 55%, which should still see a very healthy residual to be divided between the Panguna Landowners Association and the Bougainville government in whatever proportion you agree upon between yourselves. This split will not form part of our negotiations.

Although we cannot accurately estimate the operating costs of the mining operation, due to the many unknown factors, we suggest there should be approximately 40% or greater of the FOB price remaining to be divided between the two remaining partners. This would be a significant increase on the paltry 1.25% which was the amount received by the Landowners Association the last time the mine was functioning, as well as a huge increase in the nation's income. I appreciate that there are many finer details which need to be worked out, but at this point in time, I believe we should be talking in the broadest of terms. I remind you again that we expect the mine to be operationally self-funding from the time that payments for ore exports start to be received from the customer or customers.'

He paused to take a small sip of the iced water and made eye contact with each man opposite.

'I'm sure you have looked at the same reserve figures I have just quoted and worked out the earning potential as I have. Based on those figures, I can say that the stated necessary return to my clan is considered to be a very generous offer simply because we do not wish to be greedy. Greed caused most of your country's problems before, so I urge you not to let it influence your decisions this time. I also wish to add that along with the eventual income stream and side benefits, it will be considered useful to both our organisation and our country, to have the thrust of Chinese expansionism blocked, at least in this area. I therefore invite your thoughts on my proposal.'

I seized the pause to stand and suggest, 'Gentlemen, perhaps this would be a good time to take a break and have some refreshments, while you consider Tanaka-san's proposal. Shall we say a break of thirty minutes? Should anyone wish to have a private space for discussions, the captain's steward will be happy to assist.'

That suggestion was received with looks of relief from everyone and there was a semi-dignified rush to the heads. Joseph, John, Thomas and Moses were happy to simply move to the far end of the spacious wardroom to have their private discussion, graciously including Mathias Tari and his secretary. The stewards quietly placed plates of finger-food and jugs of fruit juice handy to them, before discretely retiring out of hearing range again.

When the discussion re-started, I was pleased to note there was no argument about the basic percentage carve-up offered by Tanaka-san. Instead, the talk was all about the finer details of how the work would be scheduled, who would do it, and when work could start. It was heartening to hear Tanaka-san suggest that locals should fill most of the labouring and machinery operator jobs as much as possible, with specialist engineering and mine management teams from Tanaka's clan, or contractors if necessary, to attend to the huge task of overseeing and guiding the whole project, working closely with the four local leaders and a permanent, on-site government representative.

At one point, Tanaka-san commented, 'Gentlemen. I would like to take this opportunity to make it very clear that although this is a joint project, my clan and our associates have neither the desire nor the intention to impose our will upon your people in any way, except as is considered necessary to make sure the project proceeds as smoothly and efficiently as possible. I particularly emphasise efficiency, as this is, of course, the key to making the project viable, to safeguard the huge investment we are making and to ensure we all gain maximum benefits in the future. It is true that while we are making a business investment, you and your country are also investing in a dependable economic future. We will therefore be relying upon you to maintain the focus of your workers and prevent any discord which may harm or slow progress. May I have that assurance?'

The Bougainville team unreservedly hastened to assure him that was how it would be, that the locals had finally realised the scope of the incredible opportunity presented to them, and were truly grateful. It was also appreciated that there would never be another chance for economic recovery, should this opportunity be wasted through argument or misguided egos.

As the discussions drew to a close and final details were being thrashed out, I called another break to allow Jim's admin team to convert all the words into a relatively simple agreement. The guys and girls must have already made a start, since it was only another twenty minutes before the first document was ready for reading in digital form. Jim supplied iPads for each participant, which made the task of making amendments much faster. The first round of revision produced quite a number of changes, but these and subsequent ones were minor and quickly dealt with.

With 17:00 approaching, I called a halt to proceedings for the day.

'Gentlemen. You have made amazing progress in just one day. I therefore suggest that each of you take the latest iteration of the agreement back to your lodgings and review it overnight. I set the time for re-convening the meeting to be 10:00 tomorrow.'

At that, the meeting broke up with cautious smiles and sincere handshakes. I chose not to accompany Tanaka-san and Mathias back to Buka Town in the helicopter, figuring they had plenty to discuss in private. Joseph and the chiefs gravely thanked Jim and me for our efforts, then left the ship to walk home.

After the helicopter departed, I waited while Jim changed into civvies, then we strolled back to *Firebird*, to be greeted by our crew who had started happy hour long ago by the cheery look of their faces and the occasional tangled tongues. They were naturally eager to hear of the outcome, which I kept short and slightly vague, as the fat lady hadn't had a chance to even clear her throat yet. I also felt a great sense of mental weariness, being quite unused to making sense of day-long verbal barrages.

Next morning, Jim and I were waiting near the *Ballarat's* flight deck for the incoming flight. Tanaka-san, Hiroto and Mathias plus his secretary looked rested and had smiles and handshakes for everyone, although the two impassive bodyguards had the same scowling look for everyone. We were soon joined by Joseph and the chiefs and by 10:15, discussions had resumed. As expected, there were some more revisions to the agreement, but as all were minor, and none even slightly controversial, they were quickly agreed to.

Finally, we reached the stage where I was able to ask our scribes to convert the digital words to print on paper, with a copy for each person present. With a distinct lack of drama, the main signatories duly signed and amid a flurry of handshakes, one of the most amazing and unlikely partnerships, had kick-started an almost impossible project on the rocky road to reality.

When all the appropriate farewells had been said, and Joseph and the chiefs had departed, I was surprised and delighted when Tanaka-san asked if he might have a look over *Firebird*.

'My granddaughter has talked much about your marvellous catamaran, Commander,' he enthused as we walked along the wharf, 'I am so glad you are able to indulge me this way. I would feel ashamed to return to her without seeing it for myself.'

'It is my pleasure and honour to show it to you, Tanaka-san. My crew were greatly taken with the young ladies' beauty and the dignity displayed by both Chiaki and Fumiko under conditions of very great hardship. We felt they will both grow up to be formidable ladies who will bring great credit to your families.'

Sometimes, I amaze myself with my slick speech, and it was just as well Sandy and the crew hadn't heard that little lot! However, Tanaka-san hadn't come down in last night's downpour either, and replied with a gentle smile, 'Ah, Commander. For a *Gaigin*, you truly do have the gift of the gab!'

That shut me up until we reached *Firebird*, where luckily, the tide was high, making boarding a simple and safe step across. To the consternation of his brawny bodyguards, Tanaka-san fairly leapt across onto the deck, where he almost ran into Sandy who clutched his arm to steady him. Recovering his balance, his eyes widened in recognition.

'Ah... what a delightful surprise to meet the lovely Sandy. I have been told much about your kindness to my two young ladies and for that, I am indebted to you.' He stepped back slightly and bowed, as his bodyguards pushed aboard ahead of me, poised to repel attackers. I'm not sure if the looks of shock and surprise on the faces of my crew were caused more by the sudden appearance of the suave and powerful Yakuza under-boss, or his two tattooed warriors.

Nevertheless, it was my lovely Sandy who made an immediate recovery and welcomed Tanaka-san most effusively and literally with open arms before she introduced him to the rest of the crew. The bodyguards were almost in a panic as Tanaka-san mingled among the ladies, charming them instantly with his courtly manner, but as Alex unfolded his tall, muscular form from a chair, they saw that he towered over them, and was broader across the shoulders.

'Ah, the mighty Alex. You also I have been told about and have longed to meet. Your brave deeds to assist the recovery of my girls will never be forgotten. But who are these two lovely ladies, Commander? They were not part of your rescue crew I believe?'

That simple enquiry led to an explanation of the how and why of the presence of Beth and Georgia, and there was no way I was allowed to shorten the story. Naturally, Tanaka-san demanded that Jasper be allowed to join the dog and pony show, an event which caused the old man to cry out with pleasure when without his usual carry-on, Jasper offered his paw to be shaken, and his bodyguards to have another security scare to see their VVIP kneeling on the deck nuzzling my big cat, who responded with an air of affectionate dignity he'd never shown anyone else before, and probably wouldn't again.

Finally, Tanaka-san looked up at me, beaming with delight. 'Ah, Commander. What a treat this is to meet such a wonderful animal. I too have certain abilities, gained from years of training, and sense an air of mystery about him which I have never felt about an animal before. With your permission, I would like to know more about his origins.'

'Of course, Tanaka-san,' I replied smoothly, 'perhaps the best way would be to get Beth and Georgia to forward a copy of their notes when they are completed. They have made by far the most thorough investigation into Jasper's origin and abilities.'

The ladies managed to look suitably modest and promised to forward their notes and all the Jasper encounter videos to Hiroto, as soon as they could.

With Jasper in close attendance, we finally set off on the tour of inspection of *Firebird*, after he had firmly told the bodyguards to remain in the cockpit. The old man seemed genuinely interested and wanted to be told many of the finer details of design and construction. He was particularly fascinated by the electric drive and the under-sail recharging system. As we returned to the cockpit, he insisted on shaking hands all around, and was delighted when Jasper lined up to hold his paw out.

'Now I must leave you, Commander, but not before I thank you and your crew once again for what you have done for my organisation and my family. I fear we are more indebted to you than before, and I urge you to remember that all our resources are available to you and any of your crew – anywhere and at any time, should you ever need them. Now, unfortunately, I must not keep our excellent helicopter pilot waiting any longer, but hope to greet you all again soon. Ja ne.'

With that, the energetic old man bustled off the boat, closely followed by his pair of relieved bodyguards and Hiroto, who whispered, 'You have made a yet another lasting and highly favourable impression on Tanaka-san, Commander. You have only to call my number at any time for any level of assistance.'

We were a slightly bemused group who watched the small group stride down the wharf and turn up the Ballarat's gang-way. Minutes later, the Seahawk lifted off and departed north.

# CHAPTER 26

Following the two stress-filled negotiation sessions, I was happy to stay tied up to the wharf in Kieta harbour, together with *Ballarat*. There was a noticeable lifting of tension now that the project had been signed off on, even though the timetable for action depended on the Yakusa clans getting organised, along with the first few truck-loads of cash. Being no longer directly involved in the project, we only had Joseph to provide us with information, something he cheerfully did each day around smoko time, when he strolled by to say 'hi'.

The Yakusa must have believed in moving quickly, as Joseph soon told us that a working company, the newly-created Bougainville Investment Group, had already made initial funding to the tune of one billion US dollars available through the Central Bank of Bougainville. The first item on the work schedule was to utilise the abandoned Chinese earth-moving equipment, cranes and trucks, to continue the task of upgrading the port warehouse and storage facilities. Local men set to with a will, happy to have work to do on a project which had such immediate local benefits. And they were being well-paid! Joseph reported that within days of work commencing, much of the air of despondency afflicting everyone within the local community had lifted dramatically.

When we learned that small teams of Japanese engineers had started flying in to Buka Town, I suspected that Tanaka-san must have made a lot of arrangements in advance, on the presumption he would be able to make the landowners and the government an offer they couldn't refuse.

Joseph said the engineers were tasked with surveying the Panguna mine site, as well as the former capital and bustling town of Arawa, just eight kilometres north of Kieta harbour. It had been severely damaged in the riots and unrest following the mine closure and was a shadow of its former glory, but was the closest town to the mine, although repairing the damage there wasn't part of the mine upgrade package. That was a Bougainville problem to be undertaken when funds were available.

Also in for an upgrade was the Aropa regional airport, fifteen kilometres down the coast to the south-east from Kieta. It had been allowed to become totally overgrown through the years of the civil war, before being partially refurbished by the PNG government in 2014. Although long enough to handle small jets, it had been restricted to turbo-prop airliners, but would now be upgraded further as it was much closer to the mine than Buka Town. This had been included in the mine project funding, as it wasn't going to take much to upgrade it fully, and was very necessary to the main project to have such close aerial access to the mine.

Now we were no longer involved, all this activity quickly became of passing interest only, although we didn't dare say so to Joseph, who seemed to regard us as heroes who had made miracles happen.

Regardless of this, we began making plans to head home, including the *Ballarat*, who had a patrol schedule to resume. That was until Mathias called, in a slight panic, to say that he had just received a series of official Chinese protests, concerning the damage to the *Changbaishan* and the loss of many items of machinery and trucks.

Therefore, they were sending another of their warships to make sure there were no more expressions of unrest from the southern rebels, while discussions concerning the level of reparations to the PLAN for damage to the *Changbaishan* were in progress.

In a conference call to both Andy and myself, he said, '*I have already sent a sternly worded reply to their diplomatic people saying that 'the independent nation of Bougainville has no need of any such support, and they would be well advised to find employment for their ships closer to home where they wouldn't get damaged by becoming illegally involved in other nation's affairs.' So far, they haven't replied.*'

'That's a beautifully worded reply, Mr Tari,' I replied, 'and most interesting. It would seem, as we suspected, they haven't given up yet.'

'Indeed not, Commander. That is how I take it as well. Andy, may I presume upon our friendship a little further, and ask that you leave one of your warships in our vicinity for just a little while longer? Further deterrence would seem to be needed.'

*'Just arranging that now, Mathias,'* Andy smoothly replied. *'I should have an answer for you shortly.'*

After consultation with all concerned, Andy asked Alan Stallman to keep one Australian Navy warship of some description, either at Buka Town or more usefully down at Kieta Harbour for the duration of the project. After complaining about how his... that is, Hilary's carefully worked out patrol schedules would be messed up, he agreed to keep one there on a rotating basis of three weeks at a time per boat. He added that it would usually be one of the patrol boats, including the *Arafura*, but sometimes a frigate or even a destroyer would score the duty if they weren't swanning around further from home.

Based on the report of the incoming Chinese ship and after talking things over with Jim Sanders and my crew, we decided to stay in Kieta for a little while longer as well. I got the feeling that Jim was happier to have someone else who was dialled-in to the situation to bounce ideas off, as the politics of the operation seemed to be taking a turn for the worse again. Based on one of those itchy feelings I sometimes get when things start changing in an unexpected manner, I decided to make a phone call to a number I'd kept in reserve for difficult situations just like this. After explaining the entire situation to the great delight of my listener, I was assured that supportive action would be swift as an appropriate asset was conveniently not too far away. I took the opportunity to call Charlie so she could fill Andy in on the latest happenings, and she approved my action. Feeling much happier with those arrangements in place, I joined the crew, relaxing in the cockpit.

## ABOARD THE CHINESE HEAVY DESTROYER, *DALIAN*

Captain Guo, tall, fit and just 38 years of age, was considered young to be the captain of his country's newest heavy destroyer. Widely acknowledged as a superb seaman and ship-handler, he nevertheless possessed a serious character flaw which hadn't yet been detected by those tasked with determining his fitness for command. He was a closet and severely-frustrated show-off, and would have been better suited to the relative freedom of manoeuvring a harbour tug, than the constraints of warship command. Nevertheless, he loved the feeling of power as he stood on the bridge of his wonderful ship, knowing he had a 180-metre-long warship under him and 347 sailors anxious to do his every bidding. He reviewed his latest orders again, choosing with a thrill of excitement, to interpret them as almost complete freedom of action, short of firing a gun, which was quite a long way off what the planning staff back at his Zhanjiang base intended.

On this bright, sunny morning, with his ship an hour or two north of the northern tip of Buka Island, he was bent over the chart table, deep in discussion with his Executive Officer.

'Because our orders are to create the maximum amount of trouble for the Bougainville inhabitants, without firing a gun at the arrogant fools, it is my intention to use my ship as a weapon. Therefore, we will make one or two high-speed passes through the Buka Strait. Since it is so narrow, our wash will create problems on both shores and to the myriad of craft crossing to and from the main island. I intend to show the locals that they cannot create trouble for the PLAN and not be punished!'

The XO, who had also read the orders and come up with the correct interpretation, tried hard to conceal his feeling of dismay and dread. He had already noted the frequent signs of a frustrated cowboy in his young captain, and after a quick scan of the chart spread out in front of them, started to doubt his sanity as well. Before he had time to express those doubts in a suitably diplomatic way, his captain went on with his insane briefing.

'To achieve maximum effect, we will pass down the eastern side of Buka Island, so as to be able to enter Buka Strait from the north-east end.'

He pointed to the narrow passage of water.

'Without slowing from maximum cruise speed, we will make our transit staying in the centre of the channel where there is, on average, 45 to 65 feet depth of water.'

He moved his finger down the strait.

'It would appear that this Sohano Island is where the more prestigious residences are located and as the channels around it are very narrow and shallow, they will not expect such a large ship to circle the island at speed. But if we are careful, we will be safe, while making our presence felt to the maximum extent possible. We will turn in this open area to the south of Sohano Island and re-enter the Buka Strait via the deeper channel up the east side of it.'

His Executive Officer peered more closely and swallowed hard before cautiously saying, 'The strait is quite good water, my captain, although the small boat traffic will be heavy, but these channels down to the south-west are very shallow and narrow for the speed you propose. We should negotiate them at less than 10 knots to avoid a grounding.'

'Nonsense, my dear XO. The tide will be near peak high, and if we have our best helmsman on duty, we can maintain a speed which will make a dramatic impact on the town and the fancy homes on Sohano Island. Our run down the strait at top speed will make a very strong statement to those in the town itself. We'll teach them that the Chinese Navy will not tolerate being attacked by savages under any circumstances.'

The XO nodded nervously, 'I heartily approve of your excellent plan, my captain, but I still urge caution with the circuit of Sohano Island.'

Guo stubbornly shook his head. 'No XO. You miss the point of the statement I wish to make. Therefore, this is how it will be. We will make a continuous high-speed pass down the strait, through the narrow channels where they will not expect such a large ship to be able to navigate, circle around in deeper water, then re-enter the strait via the east side of Sohano Island. That channel is deeper although slightly narrower than the one on the west side. This will be an excellent opportunity to show the pathetic, barbaric locals the power of a well-handled modern PLAN warship!'

In his heart, the XO knew when his protests would be falling on deaf ears, so bowed his head and said, 'It shall be as you have planned, my captain. I will have our best man on the wheel, and I shall stand by him for safety.'

Captain Guo beamed at the younger officer, and clapped him on the back. 'Excellent, XO. That is the spirit we must show to all who would attempt to prevent the Chinese nation from achieving its manifest destiny.'

Privately shaking his head at the useless spouting of Communist Party rhetoric, the XO called for the best helmsman, a petty officer second class, to report to the bridge. Privately, he considered the captain's plan to be an insanely stupid, reckless show-off stunt, and one which would endanger the whole ship. He had done his best to change the captain's mind, and had covered himself to an extent by speaking more loudly than was necessary, so that at least all other members of the bridge watch should hear his words of caution. He was grateful his captain, in his excited state, had not noticed the raised level of his speech.

One hour later, the *Dalian* was on the run-in to Buka Strait, tracking between Cape Kori on the left and the mass of Buka Island on the right. Water depths had been well over one thousand feet, and didn't shoal appreciably until the last mile to the start of the strait. At maximum sustainable cruising speed, the *Dalian* was at 28 knots, and a massive, white-foaming wake was thrown up behind her stern, with the usual powerful displacement waves angling back from each quarter.

# BUKA TOWN – BOUGAINVILLE HOUSE OF REPRESENTATIVES

Situated on the shores of the strait, right at the north end, in what was effectively Government House, was Mathias Tari's rather plain office. He was working through some papers, when he was distracted by the excited babble of voices from his staff in the open-plan main office just outside his door. Suddenly, his usually unflappable secretary, a matronly woman, burst in un-ceremoniously in a state of high agitation, her hands actually flapping.

'Sir! Quickly, sir. You must come and see! This is unbelievable!'

Mathias lumbered to his feet and followed her out into the main office area, where a group of his staff were clustered in front of the large glass sliding doors opening out onto a shady balcony. As the scatter of single-story buildings were situated on a low bluff, there was usually the most marvellous view across the mouth of the strait to the land mass of the main island to the south. At the moment however, that view was totally dominated by a very long and sleek, pale-grey warship, surging past at what seemed like enormous speed, its huge bow-wave arcing up to near deck level The boiling mass of white-water at the stern created huge waves which thundered on the shore just below them, washing up way beyond the high tide mark.

After taking in the mini-tsunami rolling along the shoreline, and washing high above the highest tideline, Mathias's attention was drawn back to the ship and to the huge red flag streaming stiffly back from the main mast, barely flapping in the powerful wind of the ship's passage.

'Those insolent mongrels!' he said, shocking his staff with a highly un-presidential outburst. 'It's more of those bloody Chinese navy people again! Why don't they go and annoy someone else!'

In a mixture of shock and awe at the display of marine might, they all watched helplessly as the massive ship thundered on down the narrowing waterway, scattering, running over and sinking many of the small boats which made the strait crossing many times every day. Although Mathias couldn't see much of the low-lying town itself, he could imagine the chaos and damage being created along the wharves by the insanely fast passage of this large warship.

Quelling the babble around him by waving both arms, he instructed staff to contact the police to mobilise all officers to commence flood rescue operations on both sides of the strait, and in the middle.

'Where is that idiot going to go at that speed?' he rhetorically asked the open air. 'He can't exit the lower end of the strait at that speed, and turning around in the narrow main channel will be impossible for such a large ship.'

## DALIAN

Standing out on the starboard bridge wing, Captain Guo looked as delighted as a small boy splashing through puddles, with a delighted grin stitched on his face as he viewed the destruction being wrought by the huge wash from his ship. To his XO, he appeared to totally disregard the many small boats which were swamped or simply run over by the speeding ship, instead gloating over the sight of waves more than two-metres high, washing up into the low-lying town streets. Stepping back inside the bridge, he cried out, 'Isn't this marvellous, XO? Just look at the damage our wash is causing! What a wonderful idea I had to make this speed run!'

The XO bowed his head in agreement, trying to hide his apprehension as the shallow end of the strait was fast approaching.

'Undeniably, it is an amazing sight, my captain, but we are almost to the shallow channels. May I reduce speed just a little while we perform the turning manoeuvre?'

'No. You may not,' Guo snapped, momentarily losing his air of glee. 'Maintain maximum cruise speed, but steer very, very carefully, Petty Officer.'

The last was directed directly at man with his hand on the tiny wheel, hardy more than an over-sized knob, which steered the ship. This hapless individual was sweating profusely, despite the chilly air-conditioning.

With close to 150,000 shaft-horse-power being fed to the two huge propellors, the demented captain totally ignored the fact that the stern of the *Dalian* was sucked down well below her normal draft by the incredible suction effect created by those propellors, and as the water began to shallow even more, that proximity drew it down still further. This caused ominous clouds of mud and sand to be flung up in her wake, and those sailors stationed externally where they could view the now multi-coloured wake, looked first to their officers in alarm, and where possible, moved to where they had a firm hand-hold or could wedge themselves in place. Several deck officers urgently rang through to the bridge, passing on frantic messages that the ship was running too fast into shallowing water, with the shoreline of Sohano Island barely thirty-five metres away. Their concerns were heightened when the warnings were rebuffed by the bridge and they were told to stay off the telephone circuit, and hold their stations. However, it was hard to ignore the occasional hard jolt which ran through the ship, as well as the increasingly frantic calls from the engine room where they were closest to impending disaster each time the keel briefly touched sand or mud.

On the bridge, the sweating petty officer on the wheel alternated his flick glances between the view out through the bridge windows and the repeater screen of the chart plotter in front of him. Mindful of the hovering presence of the XO at his elbow, he made a careful adjustment to their course and felt a surge of relief as the bumps of the keel dragging ceased. The XO whispered that their propellor-wash was still sand-coloured, but it seemed the worst was over for the moment, as the speeding ship entered a more open expanse of slightly deeper water just south of the tip of Sohano Island. The helmsman had no time to relax, as the more open area was still studded with shoals which must be avoided and at the speed they were travelling, there was little time to plot a safe, weaving course between them.

With his concentration blocking out all the alarms and buzzing phones around him, the helmsman used his consummate skill to coax the ship into a tight turn around a sandbar so shallow, he could see small waves breaking over it, before lining up with the narrow, but deeper channel leading back up toward Buka Strait. The term deeper was only relative in this case, as there was barely three-metres of water under the bow and much less at the stern where the thrust of the screws still pulled the keel lower. Faintly, he heard the XO begging the captain yet again to slow down, but that just caused Guo to flash into another rage. Therefore, with a silent bridge bristling with tension, the *Dalian* rushed onwards towards the entrance back into the strait, where the channel narrowed further to just 100-metres wide. That they made the transition safely, was solely due to the skill of the helmsman, who was a nervous wreck after tossing the 13,000 tonnes of speeding warship around like an oversize ski-boat. In hindsight, it was her speed which actually saved her by making the rudders much more effective. Slower speeds would have slowed their response and parked them on the first sandbar they tried to avoid.

To the relief of the entire ship's company, they made the insanely dangerous transition back into the Buka Strait without further incident, although the previously clear-green waters behind them were now heavily stained with suspended mud and sand, and the damage ashore from the huge wake was considerable. The bridge crew felt slightly relieved when the captain's mood improved dramatically as his ship bullied her way back up the middle of the strait, swamping yet more small craft, including several rescue boats whose crews were frantically trying to save those already dumped in the water, or injured from the first pass.

With more than a hint of madness in his eyes, Guo exclaimed to all who could hear, 'This is wonderful! We have shown the ignorant savages the might and skill of the glorious Chinese Navy.'

The XO stepped away from the helmsman and timidly asked, 'What shall be our course, Captain? Should we head for Kieta Harbour?'

Guo turned away from the scenes of destruction, both ashore and in their wake, to casually say, 'I think we have proved our point here for now, but we might add some more confusion to what we already have created, by contriving to disappear for one or two days.'

The XO looked puzzled, 'Disappear? What do you mean?'

Guo smiled, and pointed to the Bougainville chart. 'We shall pretend to leave the area to the north, but instead, we hide for a few days, then re-appear when we are not expected and the fools have relaxed. Look here. Down at the southern end of the country, this area has few villages and the islands close offshore are actually part of the Solomon Islands nation. If we turn left out of the Buka Strait as though we are returning to base, then stay well-offshore, we can circle around Bougainville on the western side, then tonight we make landfall here at Moila Point, closest to Shortland Island. There is good water on the east side of the point, very close in to the beach, with no villages close-by. If we are sighted by anybody on Shortland Island, the government of Bougainville will not be informed as it is Solomon Island territory. These fools will think we have left, but then after a few days, we will appear in Kieta Harbour where all this trouble started and we will have the chance to create some more retribution trouble of our own.'

The XO was seriously bothered by the look of wild anticipation on Guo's face, but knew better than to show any trace of concern. 'That sounds like a very good plan, my captain. I will consult with the navigation officer to plot a safe course.'

'Do that, XO, do that,' Guo murmured absently, flapping his hand in dismissal, his warped mind already working on what mischief he could cause in Kieta.

# CHAPTER 27

Several hours after the Chinese heavy destroyer departed Buka Strait, Mathias was on the phone, so angry I feared for his health.

*'Five persons killed by being run over by that madman's ship,' he ranted, after telling the story of the high-speed pass by the Chinese warship, 'and another forty-four injured. Seven boats were sunk and twenty-five severely damaged. Even some shops close to the waterfront suffered serious flood damage! That captain is completely insane! I have reports from people on Sohano Island who saw the ship bouncing off the bottom in the shallows because the fool didn't slow down. He was obviously trying to cause as much damage as he could with the wash from his ship, without actually firing his guns or missiles. And he succeeded, although the risk to his own ship was immense. He truly is crazy!'*

'I'm very sorry to hear that,' I replied. 'Is there any assistance we can provide? The *Ballarat's* helicopter, for instance?'

He sighed deeply, while in the background, I could hear a babble of voices and constant ringing of telephones. *'Not at this time, thank you Commander. We have sufficient boats and rescue persons on the job now the madman has gone and our hospital is able to cope with the injuries. I think it will be best if your warship stays in place. Kieta Harbour and your two vessels are likely to be the next targets.'*

That quickened my interest.

'Do you know which way he went or where he is?'

*Mathias gave a dry chuckle. 'This mad captain thinks he is clever and can easily fool we ignorant savages, but this is not quite the case. We know he turned left out of Buka Strait, then stayed very close to the coast all the way to Cape Hanpan on the northern tip of Buka Island, where he continued due north for a time, appearing to be heading out* of the area. But it was reported to me that he turned west when he was out of sight of land, then tracked south down the western side of our island, staying well out to sea to avoid being sighted.'

I was silent for a few moments as I sifted through the information.

'You must have some good information sources Mr Tari, to know so much about his movements.'

*Despite the chaos around him, he chuckled again. 'A brief history lesson, Commander. At the end of the nineteenth century, the first of several nations moved to take control of our homeland. The Germans were the first, and the Japanese were the last to do so. Therefore, we have become used to living under the control of another nation. However, it wasn't until the most recent Japanese war-time occupation and the availability of some modern technology, that we developed a simple, covert system to observe and report the activities of our oppressors. Are you familiar with the name, Coastwatchers?'*

'Yes, of course. But it was set up and used back in WWII. Are you suggesting the system is still functional?'

*'But of course, Commander. The habits we ignorant savages learned while suffering having other nations occupying our country and controlling our lives, have never been forgotten. The reporting network, particularly those stations high in the mountains, are equipped with modern, powerful telescopes, radios and mobile phones, and have kept sight of our unwelcome visitor. I will report when I receive the next update.'*

'I'm most impressed Mr Tari, and appreciate the information. I look forward to hearing from you.'

I passed the information onto my crew, then walked along the wharf to do the same with Jim.

'So, Mathias reckons this clown is likely to come here? From his description, it sounds like a bloody big ship.'

'Yeah. I should have asked if anyone took a photo. In fact, I might just do that now.'

I dug out my mobile, marvelling again that this strife-torn

nation managed to support mobile communications technology. I connected with his harried secretary who said Mathias was in yet another meeting.

'That's okay – don't disturb him. I just wanted to ask if anyone took a photo of the ship?'

'*Oh, my goodness, yes, Commander. Many photos were taken. Would you like me to send you one?*'

'Yes please, Mary. I'll text the URL to send it to, thanks very much.'

I got the *Ballarat's* address from Jim and sent it. A few minutes later, an email appeared with an excellent hi-resolution photo of a large, grey warship, steaming at high-speed through the narrow strait, with a huge red Chinese battle ensign streaming from the masthead, and an equally huge boiling white wake spewing from its stern.

'Wow!' was Jim's first response, as he dived onto the internet searching for the list of current Chinese warships. 'That's a bloody big ship. It looks like a cruiser. Beautiful lines to the hull. I thought only the Russians designed beautiful-looking ships these days.'

Moments later, he reported. 'Here 'tis. It's actually listed as a heavy destroyer but NATO classify it as a light cruiser based on length, tonnage and firepower. According to the bow number, it's the *Dalian*, one of their newest boats. That skipper's a certified lunatic for running that thing through the strait like a speedboat! Their top Navy brass will have his nuts, or more probably his head if he knocks a prop off, or runs it aground playing silly buggers like that!'

I had to agree with his concise analysis, but was more concerned by the firepower aboard the ship, particularly given the lack of mental stability the captain had already displayed. Although smaller than the *Changbaishan*, it was a far more powerful adversary. I chatted with Jim a while longer, then wandered back home, after inviting him to come along as usual anytime during the afternoon for happy hour. Since the excitement of the *Changbaishan* eviction had settled, he'd been a daily attendee and we were amused that he was becoming very friendly with both our visiting professors, but with Georgia in particular.

Three hours later, Mathias called again to report that the Chinese ship had been sighted dropping anchor just to the east of Moila Point at the southernmost point of the country.

*'Unless they're damaged,' he said, 'I'm guessing they think they can remain unobserved for a day or so, to give the impression they've left the country. However, my best guess is that the skipper intends playing games in Kieta Harbour. May I leave it to you to warn our local friends?'*

'Excellent thinking, Mr Tari,' I replied, 'that sounds just like what he'd do. However, given the distance they've covered since your last report, they must have travelled at close to full speed, so unfortunately there can't be any damage.'

*'Good point, Commander. Anyway, my hidden army of eyes are on them and as soon as they move, I'll call.'*

With that tactical information, I consulted a piece of paper on which I'd written a lengthy SatPhone number.

*'Good evening,' replied a polite voice in excellent English, with just a slight accent, 'how may I help you?'*

'Good evening,' I replied, 'this is Commander Stevens, and I have a message for Commander Sasaki.'

*'Certainly sir. One moment please....'*

*'Good evening, Commander Stevens, this is Commander Sasaki.'*

I mentally sighed. 'Good evening Commander. I trust you have recently received a change of orders from your superiors?'

*'That is correct, Commander. I have been instructed to terminate our courtesy visit, head south to your location as soon as possible, and place my ship and crew under your command. As we were already scheduled to depart tomorrow, this earlier start is not an inconvenience and we will be underway within the hour.'*

'That's marvellous, Commander. I have just received fresh news of our target, who, incidentally, has been identified as the Chinese heavy destroyer, *Dalian*. He has been making an anti-clockwise circuit of Bougainville, unsuccessfully trying to remain beyond visual range of the shore and is presently anchored very close inshore, on the east side of Moila Point, the southernmost point of the island. Our best guess is that he'll remain there for a day or two, hoping to take advantage of what he hopes is our relaxed security before continuing on to Kieta Harbour.'

'*Ah. That is good information, Commander. If he delays more than 45 hours, we will arrive first. Presuming we do achieve this, I will remain west of Kieta Harbour entrance, where the risk of detection would be minimal, yet I will be only minutes away from the action station you have designated for us.*'

'I concur Commander and thank you. I will call again when our target departs his present position.'

'*Excellent. Thank you for the information, Commander. Ja ne.*'

'Ja ne, Commander.'

By the time I'd finished with my phone calls, happy hour had morphed into feed time, and our lovely cooks had prepared the evening meal. Jim had been aboard for some time and had a happy, rosy glow about him. The close presence of Georgia, looking very desirable in short shorts and a tight tank top might have also helped him relax. As the meal was served, I brought the crew up-to-date with the latest movements of the *Dalian*.

'That's a good coast watch network Mathias has working for him,' Jim observed, before adding with a touch of sarcasm, 'and even better to have a good idea of when that Chinese cruiser, which I might point out, is three times the displacement of *Ballarat*, is due to lob on our doorstep and kick our collective arses out of the area!'

I grinned at him. 'All is not lost yet, my friend. I've ah... arranged a little back-up.'

That distracted Jim from perving yet again on Georgia's delightfully displayed chest, and parroted almost comically, 'Back-up? What back-up? What are you waffling on about? The

Admiral doesn't have any spare ships he could send in time, which is why I'm here. So who's your mystery guest?'

'It's a Japanese heavy destroyer, the *Maya*. She's almost the same size and displacement as the *Dalian* and has similar armament, although I don't envisage this confrontation turning into a shooting match.'

Jim looked as bewildered as the others. 'Now I really don't understand! How the hell can you call up a Japanese heavy destroyer? Even Andy and the Admiral would be pushing shit uphill trying to organise that! And you reckon you've done it in a couple of days! C'mon Harry. In the words of our favourite red-haired Queenslander – please explain?'

I shrugged modestly. 'Fairly simple, really. Following that run-in with the whalers in Tasmania, the Japanese government reckoned they owed me a favour or two, so I decided to call a friend. Namely, their PM, Shinzo Ito. Andy and the Admiral know about it on the quiet, but I didn't bother going through normal official channels. Takes way too much time and we don't seem to have too much of that, if we're to keep this project on track. I figured if we can bloody the Chinese noses again, they might back off long enough for the project to get sufficiently well established that any further interference by them will be seen by the rest of the world for what it would be – an invasion. Anyhow, that's my take on the situation and it seems the Japanese government agrees with me. Shinzo was delighted the Yakuza are financing the mining project and even happier to have the chance to quietly put the Chinese Navy in check yet again.'

Jim and the crew were silent, with Jim shaking his head, and Alex and Sandy grinning with delight.

'You might have just done it again,' Alex rumbled. 'Although, if this works out, we'll definitely be off the PLAN's Christmas card list. Permanently.'

I chuckled. 'Yeah. I suppose a holiday cruise to Shanghai will be out of the question!'

I could see Jim's mind churning over the ramifications of this latest bit of intel.

'Okay, Harry. You've had a little chat with the Japanese Prime Minister – he's tossed a Japanese heavy destroyer into your lap – but where is it? Is there any chance of it getting here in time to help face down this maniac and his cruiser?'

Unable to resist the chance to be a smart-arse yet again, I looked at my watch. 'According to the Skipper, who I just spoke to, I reckon right about now, she's departing Guam, where she was making a courtesy visit, and as they have full fuel bunkers, after about 44 hours of full-speed cruising, they should be passing between those two headlands over there. We have to keep our fingers crossed that the *Dalian* hangs about Moila Point for the next two days, so the *Maya* can get here first.

When she does, she's going to anchor up the western side of the Kieta Peninsula until we know the *Dalian* is close. Which reminds me, I forgot to have Mathias put in another back-dated request for a courtesy visit by the Japanese Navy.'

Jim shook his head again. At this rate, he was going to get a serious headache, but at least he would have a lovely nurse to take care of him.

'I hope you have a plan for how we're going to use our two ships to handle this character.'

As I stood to go call Mathias, I waved a hand nonchalantly. 'Yeah – sort of... maybe. Work in progress. You know how it is!'

Jim let some frustration show. 'Actually, no Harry – I don't know how it is! The Navy is more used to having at least a rudimentary plan in hand prior to confronting an enemy. Obviously the Army does things differently.'

I tried to look hurt. 'Very unkind, Jim, after I've gone to all this trouble to arrange for you to have a Japanese heavy destroyer to play war-games with, using an antagonistic Chinese heavy destroyer as a real, live adversary. After-all, you're the resident naval expert. It's forty-four hours to game-on, sport, so get with the strength and kick your tactical brain into gear!'

I left him trying to work out a clever come-back, while I went to call Mathias.

'*No, it's never too late, Commander. What can I do for you?*'

'In light of the impending arrival of that Chinese ratbag and his overgrown destroyer, I took the liberty of inviting the Japanese government to send one of their heavy destroyers on a courtesy visit to the nation of Bougainville. I do apologise for not telling you sooner, but I didn't have confirmation of its availability until less than an hour ago.'

To my relief, he chuckled delightedly. '*I won't waste time now by asking how you managed to get yet another foreign government to supply one of their warships to aid a third-world nation, but I do want to hear the story later. In the meantime, I suppose you need me to send another one of those carefully-worded, back-dated invitations to the Japanese government suggesting that a courtesy visit by one of their warships was well overdue, and would be welcomed in the very near future?*'

'Perfect, Mr President. Couldn't have worded it better myself. The destroyer *Maya* is leaving the island of Guam as we speak, and will be here in about 44 hours, which will hopefully precede the arrival of our Chinese maniac. The *Maya's* captain will be messaging that for maintenance reasons, he needs to call at Kieta Harbour for a few days before arriving at Buka Town to commence the official courtesy visit. Once again, my apologies for making such high-level arrangements on your behalf, but time was tight.'

Mathias laughed again. '*No apologies necessary, Commander. I have found that your actions are impeccably timed and very much in the best interests of my country. We owe you a great deal already, although I fear that is a debt we may never be able to repay.*'

'Very kind of you to say so, Mr Tari, but there is no debt if we can keep your project on track without the triple-cursed Chinese Navy sticking their sweet and sour noses into your affairs every week or so. I also must call Joseph and the chiefs to let them know what's happening.'

'*Very well, Commander. I shall do my belated diplomatic duty and wish you well. I will call when our friend moves in your direction. Good night.*'

'Good night, sir.'


I spoke with Joseph to let him know that there might be another two grey ships visiting his harbour, one friendly, the other very much not so. I took the opportunity to warn him of the tsunami-style tactics used in the Buka Strait, prompting him to say that he'd already heard of the havoc caused in the Buka Strait, and that he'd warn all villagers living close to the water to move to higher ground. He also took that to mean there was a good chance of another marine fur-ball of some sort developing on his doorstep in the next few days, and said he might make a few arrangements of his own to interfere with the expected style of enemy behaviour.

Unused as I was to all this international intrigue, I again found it was mentally exhausting and was content to plant myself at the cockpit table, where the crew were into post-dinner drinks, switch my mind into neutral and have my mug of spiced tea replenished as required by lovely ladies.

As the evening progressed, sensible talk rapidly degenerated into braille, before people started drifting off to bed. I must have been a bit wasted, as I didn't notice Sandy and Beth leaving, although Jim and Georgia were still sitting across the table from me, apparently attached at knee, hip and shoulder, and murmuring intimate nothings to each other. I took that to be a good hint to bugger-off, so lurched down to the stern to dump some liquid ballast back from whence it came, before heading for bed. Down below, the ladies had obviously been having one of their sessions, with Sandy on her usual side of the bed, their heads together on the pillow and Beth angled across the rest of the bed. They were chatting quietly and made several rude comments about me not having my stabilisers turned on, as I finally found the bathroom and cleaned my teeth.

With that important job done, I took only moments to shed clothes and head for the security of a stationary bed, except that my side was mostly occupied by a naked female. Beth broke off what she was saying to Sandy and said, 'Sorry Harry. I'll just move over a bit.' Her re-arrangement of body and limbs was sufficiently erotic to grab my attention, so sleep was postponed for the moment as I prepared to behave like the perfect gentleman I was supposed to be.

'What are you doing back there, Harry. Can't you see I'm having a serious discussion with Sandy?'

'Of course, I can,' I replied, 'I can hear it as well, since I'm only half-blind at the moment, and the last thing I'd want to do would be to interrupt your fascinating discussion, so please carry on. Maybe just pretend I'm not here?' I added helpfully. 'That could work.'

'Nice thought, dear man, but it's rather.... oh dear... nice... difficult to concentrate when... you're... you're doing things like that!' she finally got out.

'Nonsense,' I replied cheerfully, feeling better by the moment, the more I felt of Beth. I was thoroughly enjoying playing at being a gentleman, and said, 'I'm sure an Associate Professor knows how to do several things at once. Multi-tasking it's called and is supposed to be a female thing. All you have to do now is continue to solve the mysteries of the universe with Sandy, while I just...'

'Yeah... oh my golly goodness!... It's the 'just' bit that... Oh bugger! I can't even speak properly when you... oh, that is good! Please stop giggling Sandy! I'm trying to have a serious discussion with Harry, but it... doesn't ... working... I seem to be...'

It was just as well there was no need to get up in the early in the morning, although when I did, it was to find breakfast cooking and Jim sitting at the cockpit table with a mug of coffee, a slightly smug look on his face.

'All well?' I asked.

'Absolutely!' he replied. 'A good night's sleep and a hot breakfast served by a lovely lady – what more could a lonely sailor want?'

I noticed Georgia was also having trouble keeping a straight face, but when you're among good friends, does it really matter?

# CHAPTER 28

The day passed in the same laid-back vein, although late in the morning, a young leading-seaman did venture down the wharf with a sheaf of messages in her hand for her errant captain. I officially invited her aboard, then Jim asked her to take a seat while he sorted through the messages, initialling and/or scribbling an action note on several. The attractive young lady was very interested in her surroundings, but was especially delighted when Jasper became sufficiently curious to wander out with Krazy perched on his shoulders. She looked a little concerned when he carefully sniffed her, but then relaxed when he offered his paw to be shaken.

'Steady there, Evans,' Jim growled, looking up from his reading, 'the big pussy might like you, but you can't take him with you. The Commander might have something to say about that.'

'Yessir, I mean, no sir. But the rest of the crew would really love to meet him. We've all heard so much about him.'

I thought a moment, then said to Jim. 'It's your call, Skipper, but I've got no problem if Leading-Seaman Evans wants to come back here when she's off-watch to take Jasper to meet the crew. He does seem to quite like her.'

Jim considered my suggestion and I could see he was grateful that I left the ball in his court. 'Hmmm. Very well then Evans. Report back here to the Commander when you come off-watch for a briefing on handling Jasper. But you're to keep the visit reasonably short and not disrupt the boat's routine too much, is that clear?'

Her pretty face broke into a beautiful, radiant smile. 'Aye sir, and thank you.'

Jim gave her a grin. 'Don't thank me. Thank the Commander – Jasper's his cat.'

Evans turned her smile to me. 'Thank you too, sir. I'll be off-watch at 12:00. May I return at 13:00?'

I returned her smile. 'That'll be fine, Leading-Seaman. I'm sure he'll be ready for you.'

'Aye sir, and thanks again.'

Jim handed her the stack of messages and said, 'Tell the Watch Officer that I'll be back before 13:00, please Evans.'

'Aye, sir,' she replied, before saluting, then marched briskly away.

I admired her departing stern view for a few moments, before sighing and saying to Jim, 'Some days, I think I'm just becoming an old fart.'

Jim chuckled. 'Me too, but at least you're allowed to look.'

We indulged in a pre-lunch beer or two, then enjoyed a pile of Bree's gourmet sandwiches. I don't know how she manages to create such tasty fillings with the rather basic stock of supplies we carried. Maybe she had her own stash of special spices and sauces. When only a few crumbs were left, Jim left to go make sure his boat wasn't in danger of sinking, while I scratched through the chart-table drawers and found the silver-plated chain collar Sandy had had made for Jasper. It was attached to a length of red, laid rope with spliced ends, which was strong enough to have done duty as one of *Ballarat's* mooring lines. The rope was Bree's idea of a joke, but it did tend to reassure little old ladies that the vicious, wild beast attached to the other end was properly restrained. Jasper also thought it funny when he had to wear it.

Promptly at 13:00, Leading-Seaman Evans returned, having changed into the casual dress of shorts and a tight T-shirt, which left no doubt she was female.

'Permission to come aboard, Commander?' she asked politely.

'Please do, Leading-Seaman, but as I'm not part of your chain of command, and if you're taking my cat on a social meet and greet, I need to know your first name. I can't keep calling you Leading-Seaman all the time. Dreadfully formal, don't you think?'

She grinned and said, 'No sir, I guess not. It's Alice... my name that is.'

'Got it, Alice. Now – the cat. He's suitably restrained by this bloody great hawser instead of a normal lead, which is my crew's weird idea of a joke, as he doesn't need to be restrained at all. I'll tell him not to leave your side at any time until you return here. I presume you just want to show him around the crew's quarters?'

'Yes, sir. I'll keep him away from the bridge, the engine room and other manned watch areas. Although everyone wants to see him.'

'That's fine. And try to avoid the galley if you can, although you might find that rather difficult. He's a proper pig around food.'

She nodded, her gaze alternating between myself and the object of these curious instructions, who was stretched out on the deck, doing his Sphinx impression and totally ignoring me.

'I know you'll take care of him, but keep in mind that he's more than capable of looking after himself and you as well. Just as a side-note, he has killed quite a few bad persons who have tried to harm us.'

She looked slightly shocked at that bit of news, while Jasper's response was to give a bored yawn. As a reassuring gesture, it usually failed since it also showed his large, sharp set of fangs in graphic detail.

I squatted down and addressed him. 'Listen up, fur-ball. Alice is our friend and is going to take you to her ship to show you off to her shipmates, who are also our friends. Please try to be on your best behaviour, don't leave her side until you come back here with her, and don't bite anyone. If you meet someone you don't like, a loud growl is the limit in that company, and please try not to bite the XO.'

Alice tried to look suitably shocked at the last bit, but couldn't help giving a quick giggle.

'Sorry, Alice,' I grinned, 'that just slipped out. Better keep that between ourselves.'

'Aye, sir. Potentially embarrassing remarks will be kept suitably private.'

As usual in these situations, my smart-arse cat gave a loud huff, climbed to his feet, picked up the free end of his lead in his mouth and stepped over to sit beside Alice.

Alice was torn between laughing at his antics, and curiosity. 'Why did he make that huffing noise, Commander?'

'He's just being a smart-arse. Again. It's his way of telling me that he understands, knows what's going on and will go along with what I said.'

She looked astonished. 'You mean he understood what you told him?'

I smiled, 'Yep. He can't talk, but he sure understands what people say.'

'No way! You mean he can understand me as well?'

I shrugged. 'Of course. Just talk to him normally and see what happens.'

Looking dumfounded, Alice squatted down beside Jasper and spoke slowly and clearly, 'Jasper, I'm going to take you to my ship to meet my messmates. Do you want to do that?'

Pussy gave a loud huff, then firmly nudged her with his head toward the cockpit side closest the wharf, almost knocking her off her feet.

She looked at me. 'He really did understand me?'

'Yep. You don't have to talk slowly, but talking clearly like that is good. And if you use his name as a prefix each time, he'll know for certain that you're talking to him. If something is going wrong around him, he'll growl, but it won't be directed at you, and he won't harm you in any way, so don't be afraid. It's just his way of telling you that something, or someone is wrong! He only growls at people he really doesn't like or who he senses are planning to harm you. I should add on a more pleasant note, that he really likes to be scratched and patted in all the usual places – just like a normal cat.'

That comment earned me another loud huff, while Alice just shook her head in bemusement. Jasper obviously wasn't satisfied with progress toward the *Ballarat*, as he leapt up onto the wharf, the lead still in his mouth, and huffed at Alice.

I chuckled. 'That means he's really keen to go meet your messmates, so you'd better head off or he'll go there without you. He already knows the way.'

She looked alarmed and with her chest bouncing nicely, scrambled up to the wharf. She tried and failed several times to take hold of Jasper's lead, as the rotten cat kept twisting away from her grasping hands, then trotting off, lead in mouth, just staying out of reach. She gave me one more puzzled look, shrugged, then raced after Jasper who led her, head held proudly high, back to the ship, his tail curled up in full-on happy mode as he played a new game with a new human.

I didn't hear any screams, so Alice returned un-bloodied several hours later, Jasper leading the way again, and she happily accepted my invitation to have a seat. While I removed his collar, she was bubbling over with excitement about her show-and-tell.

'He was brilliant, sir. Everyone loved him and he was very well behaved. The cooks wanted to see him and naturally spoiled him a bit, or maybe a lot, but other than that, he was no problem at all. I have to pass on a big 'thank you' from the crew and to say that they'd love to see him again if that can be arranged.'

I nodded. 'I'm glad it worked out well, Alice. Another visit isn't a problem, but we'll have to see what happens in the next few days. Tomorrow might be the last chance we have for some quiet time for a while, so you can come over and collect him again anytime you're ready. We're expecting to have a bit of a problem here with another unwelcome Chinese warship in a day or so. I can't say any more for the moment, as that situation is highly dynamic. Your Skipper will let you know as soon as we find out more.'

She stood, 'Aye, sir. In that case, I'll keep that piece of intel to myself until the Skipper lets us know officially.'

'That might be best. So unless the situation changes in the morning, you can come over whenever suits your watch schedule and collect the big pussy. If there's a problem, you'll know about it anyway, but in the meantime, thanks for looking after Jasper. He does love to meet new humans.'

'Thank you again, sir. It's been great, so I really hope we can do it again tomorrow.'

'Now that he's had so much fun, I'll probably have Fur-Ball making sure you do.'

She giggled, patted and hugged Jasper , then had a quick cuddle with Krazy. With pussy duties complete, she barely avoided saluting me, before trotting off along the wharf to her ship.

Jasper nuzzled me and purred loudly, which I took to mean that he really had enjoyed himself, and wanted to do it again.

'If things are quiet tomorrow, you can go play with Alice and your new friends again, fella. But after that, we might have more work to do, getting rid of more bad men.'

He huffed softly, then hopped up on the stern daybed, where he lay down, head on his forepaws, gazing wistfully at the broad grey stern of *Ballarat*, parked just metres ahead of our bows.

## ABOARD *DALIAN*

At 15:00, Captain Guo took a walk around the decks, enjoying the fresh sea air on his face and the feel of his beautiful ship under his feet. He also liked to inspect some of the more unusual places around the ship, where a careless crewmember might have let some dirt accumulate, or for traces of the endless enemy of all steel ships – rust. He was in a good mood, as so far, he'd found no evidence of either to complain about. His favourite place was on the foredeck, which was where his XO found him.

'You wanted to see me, sir?'

'Yes. Have you plotted our course to Kieta Harbour?'

'Yes, my captain. Staying outside the coastal islands, it is just sixty-eight miles. At an economical cruising speed of 22 knots, the journey will take two hours and fifty minutes. There are, however, many navigational hazards on the way which we need to be wary of.'

'How so, First Lieutenant?'

'Despite the very deep water in many places around this island, the area of our intended passage contains a great number of very shallow seamounts and shoals. Additionally, some of the inshore areas are listed as not having been fully surveyed, which means there may be additional unknown hazards.'

'I see. And your recommendations?'

'That we depart this position no earlier than 10:00, to ensure we have the best visibility for navigation. In addition, I recommend that our course north should be outside the outer reefs, until we reach the deep pass between Moto and Banaru reefs, which is directly opposite the entrance to Kieta Harbour.'

'Very well, Hiro. While I would like to show the natives what form of retribution is heading their way, I appreciate the problem posed by uncharted shoals and reefs, therefore, in this case we shall take the safer course. You will deliver us safely to Kieta Harbour, while I will plan how we will inflict the maximum disruption upon the unsuspecting fools who have dared to make an attack upon our comrades on the *Changbaishan*.'

Hiro quietly breathed a sigh of relief as he bowed his head. 'I shall make it so, my captain.'


## FIREBIRD


That evening, I had a brief call from Mathias, who reported there was nothing to report. The *Dalian* was still peacefully at anchor just east of Moila Point and not showing any signs of imminent departure.

'Thank you, Mr Tari. I appreciate the update and the delay. It gives our new friends a better chance of being here in time to join the party.'

'*You're welcome, Commander. I shall report tomorrow evening, or earlier if there is movement.'*

I placed another call to our new friends on the *Maya*.

'No movement as yet by the *Dalian*, Commander,' I reported, 'and I doubt they'll try a night-time run, although from where they are, it's only two to three hours to Kieta harbour.'

*'That is good news, thank you,'* Commander Sasaki replied, *'our ETA is 11:00 local time tomorrow. We must hope we are in time to be of assistance.'*

'I'm sure you will be, thanks Commander. I'll call as soon as I hear more. Ja ne.'

*'Ja ne, Commander.'*

We had a quiet night, and once again, Jim and Georgia were deep in conversation or planning something on the cockpit lounge when I went to bed.

The morning dawned with a cloudy sky, which kept the heat down slightly, but increased the humidity to somewhere north of the stifling stage. As the phone stayed quiet, we settled in for a leisurely breakfast, but the expectation of impending action kept everyone on edge, and no one could really relax. It was a little after 10:00 when the phone rang with Mathias reporting the *Dalian* had just hauled her anchor and was moving in our direction.

'Thanks, Mr Tari. Based on that, we estimate that he should be here around 12:30 or 13:00. Our back-up should be here at 11:00 so that's worked out well. We'll just have to see what the captain plans to do. We won't react in any way unless he does something stupid, so hopefully, just the presence of two warships will be sufficient to make him behave.'

*'My thoughts and prayers are with you and your crew, Commander. Until later.'*

My call to the *Maya* was equally brief.

*'We are still on schedule, Commander, and should be in position by 11:00.'*

'Thank you, Commander. I hope to be able to update you shortly.'

As I found Joseph's number, I mentally kicked myself for forgetting one of the most important items of planning for a coming conflict – to use all resources available. Holding off on Joseph's call for a moment, I asked Bree and Sandy to prep our in-house, surveillance UAV, the *Dragonfly*.

'I'm kicking myself for not thinking of it earlier. We could have had eyes on the *Dalian* while it was at anchor, but if you can get it airborne fairly soon, we can at least find out exactly where the fool thing is.'

The ladies assured me they'd have it flying in fifteen minutes, so I called Joseph with a heads-up.

'*We'll be ready, thanks Commander. Our men have come up with a little surprise of their own, if he tries to pull that tsunami wake-wash stunt again!*'

'That does seem to be his preferred style, which is far better than using guns, but please keep your people safe Joseph, this captain seems to be a real nut-case.'

Jim was still with us and had heard all the messages. He was torn between wanting to wait to see the *Dragonfly* launch, and the safety of his ship, but of course, that was an easy decision.

'I'm going to get away from this wharf,' he said as we left the saloon. 'I'll stay in the harbour, but being able to manoeuvre freely will make me feel a lot safer.'

After a quick chat with Alex, I decided we also should get away from the wharf, and maybe take up a holding position close to the edge of the narrow, shallow strait between the mainland and Bakawari Island. That would leave us ready for our version of quick manoeuvring and with our shallow draft with dagger-boards raised, we could retreat into the shallow water where even the demented captain of the *Dalian* couldn't venture. Although if he was going to play tsunami games again, I'd rather be in deep water, so maybe venturing over the reef wouldn't be such a good idea.

Before we left, Joseph turned up in his official workboat, with one of the powered long canoes in close attendance. As they came alongside, I saw the canoe had a long length of well-worn, heavy mooring hawser, carefully laid out in S-shapes, back and forth on the floor of the canoe between the bow and stern, with the grinning crew perched up on the stack of ratty-looking old rope. What looked like empty plastic soft-drink bottles with their lids screwed on, were tied to the hawser at intervals with long lengths of cord. Even more strange, the crew were wetting the hawser down with buckets of seawater as I told Joseph of our intended movements.

'Good idea, Commander. Being mobile is safest for you. You'd be in a bad position to handle a big wash still tied up to the wharf, as I think he will try to swamp the wharf and storage sheds with his wake, whether you and Commander Sanders are here or not. We would like him to try to do that, however, because then we can spring our surprise.'

He chose not to elaborate, so we continued to make ready to move away from the wharf. Even though we still had the Browning .50cal and plenty of ammunition aboard, it would be pointlessly stupid to escalate the encounter until we saw what the Chinese planned to do. If necessary, we still had hand guns, shotguns, a box of hand-grenades, a carton of the Chinese version of Semtex, and one rifle left to defend ourselves against a heavy destroyer. By comparison, we made David look positively over-equipped against his particular Goliath.

As we motored slowly away, the girls launched the *Dragonfly* off the foredeck, and I asked them to send it south down the channels between the off-shore reefs and the mainland, looking for the *Dalian*. From the vantage point of 2,500 feet above the gently heaving ocean, no ship was sighted inshore of the reefs, but after a turn to seaward, a now-familiar, menacing, long grey shape was sighted outside the reefs, at the head of a long line of boiling white wake.

'What's the distance?' I asked Sandy.

'Ten nautical miles direct,' she replied, 'which would mean he's got about fourteen or fifteen track miles to run if he does the logical thing and takes the deep passage opposite the port entrance.' The girls directed the UAV closer to the ship to allow us a good view using the zoom function, and to do a speed check.

'Looks to be about 22 knots,' Bree reported, 'which would put her off the harbour entrance in about forty minutes.'

'Well found, ladies. Now can you send our eyes north-west to the other side of the Kieta Peninsula? I'd like to check on our new friends.'

'No problem, boss.'

Twelve minutes later, our high-res display showed another long grey ship anchored close to shore, just south of Kapo Point, on the other side of the peninsula, where it would be well out of sight of any ship approaching from seaward. As the girls allowed *Dragonfly* to slowly lose height over the *Maya*, I called her number.

'*Good morning, Commander Stevens. I trust your plans are proceeding smoothly?*'

'Indeed they are, Commander Sasaki. We have sighted the *Dalian* some fourteen miles to the south-east, cruising at twenty-two knots and staying seaward of the outer reefs. We estimate his ETA off the harbour to be 12:00, forty minutes from now. His present course suggests he will enter through the deep pass opposite Kieta Harbour mouth, and will be unable to sight you in your current position south of Kapo Point. You have a very handsome ship, Commander. You must be very proud of it.'

My attempt at being a show-off raised a chuckle.

'*I am intrigued to know how you have such excellent intel, Commander. Although I have a helicopter aboard, I didn't wish to risk radar detection by launching it and cannot imagine you have such an aircraft.*'

'That's correct, Commander. My boat is much too small for a helicopter and we didn't wish to use the *Ballarat's* helicopter for the same reason. However, we do have an excellent and quite stealthy, small UAV, fitted with an advanced camera system. Our operators can demonstrate that stealth feature if you'd care to tell your gunners not to shoot if they do happen to detect it.'

Sasaki chuckled again. *'I'm glad you told me. I have my men at action stations already, and our CIWS will certainly detect your unit.'*

'Very good. Commander. It is approaching your bridge now, on the right-hand side.'

Our view of the long warship was growing rapidly, as Bree expertly guided the *Dragonfly* down on top of the *Maya*, in a tight spiral, transitioning into low-speed semi-hover mode at the same time. She made a close-in approach to the right-side bridge wing, then a slow pass along the curved array of bridge windows. The looks of astonishment on the faces of the crew were comical.

*'That was a most dramatic demonstration Commander, and compliments to your operators. I'm very glad you cannot carry any munitions aboard, as I must confess that none of our sensors, nor the excellent eyes of our lookouts, detected your UAV until it appeared beside the bridge wing.'*

'Thank you, Commander. I'll pass that on to the ladies. But to return to the business at hand, the *Ballarat* is presently underway from the wharf area, although she will remain within the confines of the harbour, probably close to the village on the harbour-side of Bakawari Island. Likewise, I have also moved my catamaran away from the wharf area and intend to maintain a position near the narrow and shallow strait between Bakawari Island and the mainland. If you are able to move in behind the *Dalian* after she has entered the harbour, to assume a blocking position in the harbour mouth, it is my hope that the presence of two warships of different nations will allow for a degree of pressure to be directed at getting the Chinese to abandon their disruptive plans and leave the area without further unpleasantness.'

*'Excellent, Commander. That is roughly the plan I had envisaged, and I will do my best to make it happen. May I ask that you advise me when the* Dalian *is entering the harbour?'*

'No problem. I can see that the *Dalian* is presently about halfway along the Moto Reef, but I'll call when she enters the harbour.'

# CHAPTER 29

Once underway, however, rather than move all the way along to the narrow strait, I decided to hold position close to the shore only about 500 metres from the wharves, so as to remain in deep water and better see what the *Dalian* did.

As usual when a combat situation is imminent, and various scenarios have been hopefully allowed for, I felt the tension knotting my digestive system, mostly because of not knowing what the Chinese would do next. Unlike our last encounter with them, where we had the advantage of being able to plan the attack in advance, now we were hoping to avoid a confrontation altogether, although based on what we already knew about this ratbag captain, I had little hope that peace and harmony would prevail. However, I consoled myself by recalling the saying attributed to Field Marshall von Moltke, that 'no plan survives the first contact with the enemy'. I guess they weren't his exact words, but that was the gist of it and I hoped we could take advantage of the well-proven concept.

I asked Bree to take the UAV up to 1,500 feet over the harbour entrance, so we could watch the *Dalian* as it passed at un-diminished speed between the two outer reef systems and headed straight for the harbour, and also to keep the camera rolling to record whatever might happen. I asked Sandy to do the same with the masthead camera. After I passed the information to the *Maya's* skipper, we looked out the saloon windows, where we saw the decidedly chilling sight of a slender grey hull heading straight for us, two high, curling bow waves framing the grey sliver of her slender hull. Just then, the marine VHF radio, channel 16 crackled into life.

*'Warship entering Kieta Harbour. This is the Kieta Harbourmaster advising that the harbour is closed to incoming ships until further notice.*

*Please make a 180° turn and leave Bougainville territorial waters on the most direct course without delay.'*

Our overhead view showed that for the moment, the *Dalian's* captain couldn't see the *Ballarat*, which Jim had tucked in close to the Bakawari Island shore and his answer was predictable. Even as the bow waves grew larger and diesel smoke streamed from the exhaust stacks, the radio came to life again.

*'The Chinese navy does not recognise the authority of a Bougainville Harbourmaster! You will have to try a lot harder than that to prevent me doing my duty to revenge your cowardly attack upon our peaceful ship, the* Changbaishan, *which was delivering aid to our impoverished neighbours.'*

It was about then I saw the massive boil of white water from the stern of *Ballarat* as the throttles were opened probably a lot more quickly than they should, allowing more than 47,000 horsepower to shift her 3,600 tonnes remarkably quickly.

The *Dalian's* response was immediate.

*'Ah. Now I understand your defiant attitude! You think your puny little frigate is a match for my mighty ship? You are such fools! But never fear, you will not provoke me into an attack, nor will I destroy you, little one, as I so easily could. That is not my intention. I merely wish to demonstrate to the cowardly natives, that they cannot make war upon the Chinese Navy without incurring repercussions. So stay out of my way or risk being run over like all those fools in the Buka Strait!'*

I wasn't sure what Jim's plan was to thwart the actions of the *Dalian* and could only watch helplessly as the long, grey ship altered course slightly away from *Ballarat* to aim for the south-west corner of the harbour adjacent the wharves. Her captain's intentions were all too clear, however, as while closing the shore at an alarming rate, the cruiser-size ship began a sharp heeling turn to the left, its huge, boiling wake already swamping boats and washing far enough up the northern shoreline to flood any low-set houses.

At least Joseph's early warning had allowed the locals to evacuate the most vulnerable homes.

From our position several hundred metres past the wharves and tucked in close to shore, we had severe doubts that the crazy captain's ship was going to make the tight turn necessary to avoid sliding broadside into the wharves, but he did so with just metres to spare and only by reducing power momentarily on the inside engine. As the ship straightened to run parallel with the wharves and diesel smoke again vomited from the exhaust stacks, Joseph made what at first looked like a suicide run.

His official boat had been parked behind the end of the wharves, and charged directly out from where he and the long canoe had been hiding. At full speed, it raced to cut close across in front of the bow of the *Dalian*, but from where we stood, it looked like he was going to be neatly T-boned and dissected by the destroyer's sharp bow. However, Joseph's judgement was far superior to ours and he cut across the speeding bow with what looked like barely a metre to spare. What we did see, and the Chinese crew apparently didn't, was the long length of ratty mooring hawser being dragged out from the long-canoe by Joseph's speeding boat. I now saw the purpose of wetting the line first, and of the empty plastic floats, which allowed the hawser to sink deep enough to pass under the bow bulb of the destroyer, but kept it shallow enough to scrape along the bottom of the hull.

It was what was waiting at the far end of the hull which was now the best chance of bringing the crazy captain's plan undone. Two massive, six-bladed propellors, spinning at high speed, were terribly efficient at gathering in water to be accelerated rearwards. Unfortunately for the Chinese, they were equally efficient at gathering in any stray, solid submerged objects.

Which meant that this particular submerged object was quickly drawn in and wrapped in an iron-hard bundle of coils around the left-hand propellor and shaft, which seized solid within a couple of seconds. Due to the sheer mass of the propellor and the waist-thick shaft, rotating at close to three hundred revolutions per minute, all that dynamic energy had to go somewhere. For the unfortunate *Dalian*, that somewhere was back up the propellor shaft which promptly twisted like a plastic drinking straw, tearing the stern shaft bearing right out of the hull. The initial howl of metal, as the remains of the tortured shaft and bearing thrashed around tearing additional holes in the stern of the ship, was overlaid by a rising scream which abruptly cut-off as gearboxes and motors self-destructed with the abrupt removal of the load, and the forceful re-alignment of their mountings.

An ominous cloud of black smoke vomited from the aft exhaust stack, followed by more from several open hatches at the rear of the superstructure. This was followed by the once mighty ship, slowing dramatically, although still under the drive of one engine and functioning propellor.

Spontaneous cheering broke out on *Firebird*, and was echoed along the shoreline. Although we didn't know the full extent of damage to the *Dalian*, it quickly became apparent that she was taking water at a huge rate into the largest compartment on the ship, the engine room. Her stern slowly began to settle and her bow visibly rose, exposing the swollen mass of the bow-bulb, as streams of water suddenly vomited from her normal bilge-pump ports, but it was only a fraction of the amount still pouring in through the huge hole torn in her stern where the driveshaft bearing had been torn loose.

We were in the box seats to view this developing disaster, as the dying *Dalian* was barely thirty metres off our bow, although still under power and apparently on course for the narrow and shallow strait between the mainland and Bakawari Island.

There were two passages across the shallows which would have been just deep enough for the *Dalian* to safely use, the island-side one deeper and wider than the mainland-side one. The passages were, however, divided by a broad, flat coral reef which was much shallower than the ship's draft.

Normally, the helmsman and bridge crew would have seen this hazard on the chart plotter and avoided it, but with the pandemonium apparently rampant on the bridge, we watched, dumfounded, as the huge ship, its bow now just clear of the water and stern almost submerged, ran straight up on the reef in the middle of the strait with the sickening sound of tearing, grinding, buckling steel.

As she was still under power by one engine, the combination of thrust and momentum was sufficient to carry slightly more than half the ship's length up onto the shoal, where she came to rest, on the level, but lifted bodily part-way out of the water. As bizarre sights go, this one was right up there with the best of them! Fortunately, someone in engineering had the sense to cut power to the right-side engine, as the thrashing prop was only converting water and pulverised coral into dirty foam, and the ship wasn't going anywhere – not anytime soon, that is.

I looked around at the stunned faces of my crew. 'Well. That worked! At least she isn't going to sink.'

I turned to Bree and Sandy, still at the control console of the *Dragonfly*.

'I hope we caught all that on video?'

Bree flashed a broad grin. 'On the UAV's camera and our masthead camera. The YouTube version of this will go viral in minutes. What a brilliant way to lose face!'

'Great work, ladies,' I replied, 'but keep the cameras rolling and bring *Dragonfly* down lower. Just make sure it doesn't get picked up on our masthead camera, though.'

'No problem, Boss.'

I looked at Alex. 'While we go and look like we're doing the rescuer bit, how about you break out a couple of shotguns in case one of those clowns tries to blame us for this clusterfuck.'

He grinned and went to dig out weapons as we headed toward

the incredible sight of a warship, almost the length of two football fields, sitting level with a large amount of red anti-fouling paint showing all around. As we closed on her position, we could see water pouring out of a large, jagged hole on the left side of her stern, while on the right, an intact shaft and propellor were partly exposed to open air.

Alex doesn't often crack jokes, but as we came past her largely exposed stern, he drawled. 'I guess she makes a very expensive channel marker!'

With our dagger-boards raised, we could motor right over the shallow reef, even at low tide without risk of grounding. Therefore, I had no concerns about motoring all around the ship taking a good look at the damage, which was substantial, our masthead video still recording. One ship's boat with what appeared to be engineering types aboard had just been lowered, and started doing the same thing, it's crew peering anxiously around the stern area, and studiously ignoring us. The main problem as I saw it, was the way the ship was stranded high and half-dry, on a rock-hard coral reef. Even when the holes in the hull were sealed, high tide might not be enough float her off, and an attempt to pull her off as she was, could tear the bottom out completely. While the right-side propellor appeared undamaged, the left-side one, with several bent blades, hung at a crazy angle, still attached to a twisted length of shaft, with the whole mess poking out to one side. The old mooring hawser which had caused the problem, was twisted around the shaft and prop-hub in a tight brown ball.

As I saw it, there were only two possible ways to free the stricken vessel. The first was going to be to dig and blast the coral out from under the hull until it floated by itself and the cost of that option would be eye-watering!

The second way would be to lighten the ship by removing everything which could be unbolted or pumped overboard, in the hope that a high tide and a lot of tug-power could get it off. Failing those options, I had the feeling that Kieta Harbour might have just gained itself a permanent memorial to the stupidity of a rogue captain, and the misguided dreams of a bullying major power.

However, very much mindful how close Andy and I had come to being shot at the whim of *Changbaishan's* megalomaniacal captain, I was concerned about the mental stability of *Dalian's*, who I reckoned would try to lash out and blame everyone within range. For this reason, I was very glad to have the presence of *Ballarat* which was already carefully positioning herself in the centre of the deeper channel on the Bakawari Island side of the *Dalian*.

Now we'd had a close look at the damage, and in case of further unpleasantness, I decided to move away from the stranded destroyer and let Joseph, as the local Bougainvillian representative, and Jim Sanders as the military guy with some serious firepower under his control, take charge of the situation. Then to add to the maritime scrum, the *Maya* thundered through the heads at near full-speed, to have a look at what was going on. Suddenly, the marine VHF radio erupted.

*'What you do to my ship! You commit act of war on Chinese warship! You make war on Chinese nation! You all in big trouble!'*

A very Aussie voice drawled sardonically, *'Oh, stop bleating, you pathetic excuse for a ship's captain. If you hadn't tried to be a smartarse by doing that high-speed run past the wharves, you might not have picked up that old mooring line in your props. At least your dingbat mate on the* Changbaishan *managed to limp home with his rusting bucket of bolts under its own power, but it looks like you're stuck on that reef permanently. Somehow, I don't think your Admirals or your Glorious Leader will be very happy. I heard they still shoot incompetent PLAN arseholes in China!'*

There was radio silence for a while, so I placed a SatPhone call to Jim on *Ballarat*, who was still maintaining position in the narrow channel using engines and bow thruster. Two hundred metres astern of the *Dalian*, the *Maya* had come to rest and was doing the same, both ships with their main bow guns very obviously trained on the immobile *Dalian*, ready to either move or shoot instantly should the Chinese captain attempt to do something else equally stupid.

'I don't trust this clown, Jim. He could start shooting or even decide to blow the whole thing up!'

'*I agree, Harry. I wouldn't like to see him try a 'Graf Spee' blow-up. That would cause a real mess.*'

'Agreed my friend. How about trying to talk him into getting all the crew off the ship?

Jim laughed. '*After that last rant, I don't think there's any chance of that. And unfortunately, as we're all visitors to this country, we don't have any rights to enforce Bougainville laws.*'

'True. But I can soon fix that. I'll call back in a few minutes.'

I called Commander Sasaki on the *Maya* to give him an update, only to find he was way ahead of me.

'*I find this is a curious situation, Commander. We are invited guests to this country, but until we receive direct orders from our respective National commands, we cannot take any action, except to save lives, and that doesn't appear to be a problem at the moment.*'

'That is correct, Commander. However, I propose to discuss the matter with President Tari and get back to you shortly. May I ask if you are prepared to remain on station in a potential life-saving mode?'

'*Under those conditions, I regard it as my duty to do so.*'

I waved for Joseph to come aboard, since he was hovering nearby.

Once we were seated with icy fruit juices in hand, I said, 'We have a bit of a standoff, I'm afraid. Whilst my crew and I are regarded as visiting civilians, the Australian and Japanese warships are invited representatives of their respective countries. Your stranded, uninvited and unwelcome visitor represents yet another, much more powerful foreign power. Officially, none of the three friendly vessels are able to take any action on their own, apart from the saving of lives. We cannot even board the *Dalian*, although I have some doubts it will ever leave that reef again.'

Joseph regarded me gravely. 'It is an interesting situation, Commander, and I agree with your reasoning. I must confess that it is also way above my humble position as Harbourmaster to direct any action against that ship, so what do you suggest?'

I nodded. 'Stay with me. I just needed to lay out the situation to you as the local government representative. Now we call Mathias.'

*'He's done what? Oh, dear Lord! What a dreadful mess this has become! Commander, I'm afraid I'm in urgent need of advice. Please – what are your thoughts and suggestions?'*

'Very well, Mr Tari, since you ask, here are some suggestions. My first is that you place phone calls to both the Australian and Japanese governments advising them of the situation. Given the belligerent and unstable attitude already displayed by the *Dalian's* captain, request them, as a matter of urgency, to authorise their captains to provide whatever assistance is necessary to peacefully resolve the confrontation. This is to be done with the intent of preserving the safety of both the local Bougainvillian people, and the crew aboard the *Dalian* who have been so badly led by what seems to be a rogue, deranged captain. Secondly, I suggest you draft up a strongly-worded protest, detailing the actions of their warship in both the Buka Strait and Kieta Harbour, culminating in its possibly permanent stranding. Mention that through the International Court in the Hague, you intend to sue the Chinese government for loss of life and the property damages caused. This will include the ecological damage already done to the reef, and the potential pollution damage to this pristine area which will be caused if the ship leaks oil, or cannot be removed and breaks up over the next few years.

It would be best if you were to direct this protest to the Chinese government via their Ambassador at their Embassy in Port Moresby. I'm sure by now that the captain of the *Dalian* has advised his superiors that there has been a slight upset to their intimidation plans and can he please have another ship, as he seems to have broken this one.'

There was a pause, before Mathias replied, '*That is excellent advice Commander, and I shall act immediately. However, while we wait for decisions to be made and replies to be received, how can I maintain the status quo?*'

'This is the situation as I see it. The two friendly warships cannot take any form of action, short of life-saving duties, without direction from their superiors, which as you say, will take some time to receive. However, you should immediately appoint Joseph Bulli as your Senior Military Commander in the area, at whichever rank you choose. Colonel would be the preferred rank, so he would have the authority to directly request support and assistance from the two officially-invited warships present to contain the situation and maintain peace against a proven aggressor, should the situation deteriorate sufficiently to require such action.'

'*That is another excellent suggestion, Commander. While I would prefer to appoint you to that position, I realise I cannot appoint a foreign national that quickly. May I ask however, that you work closely with Joseph in a liaison role until we get some answers from Australia and Japan?*'

'No problem at all with that, Mr Tari. I'll leave you to put your diplomat's hat on and try to sort out this problem with the other three governments involved, while we work to contain the situation locally.'

Having heard most of the conversation, Joseph looked at me with a questioning gaze.

'Do you really think this will help the situation?'

I shrugged. 'Maybe, maybe not. But at least we might be able to stabilise things until the four governments involved get their act together. Look at it this way – the Chinese will be highly embarrassed to have their ship parked high on a reef in the harbour of a country where she had no right to be in the first place. They'll blame it all on their crazy captain, but the world will be laughing at them when the videos are shown. And be assured, we will make sure the videos are shown! An unidentified voice-over commentary can explain that the Australian and Japanese ships were officially invited here by the Bougainville government, while the Chinese ship was not only not invited, but took what can clearly be seen as unprovoked, dangerous manoeuvres which resulted in loss of life, property damage and ultimately, the stranding of the Chinese ship.

While there may be some who might wonder out loud why the Australian and Japanese ships were both invited at the same time, the fact remains that they had been. However, they cannot take any military action, except only in a defensive capacity if the crew of the *Dalian* act against them first. But the real elephant in the room is the Chinese destroyer. As in – can it be removed from the reef? That's the problem mainly for the Chinese, but also for your people. As it is in your waters illegally, you could well be entitled to seize the vessel, although the Chinese will be a little bit upset if you do.'

Joseph had a brief chuckle at the thought of telling the Chinese government that their once-lovely, very expensive ship had been seized by the Bougainville government. 'Okay, Commander. What do you suggest we do?'

I grinned at him. 'Now that we've got the legal stuff sorted out, let's go visit them and have a chat. This'll be fun!'

After Joseph had finished rolling his eyes at me, I called Jim to tell him what we planned to do and he said I was crazy.

'Aww... c'mon, Jim. Tell me something original. I get that every second day from Sandy as you well know!'

'*Nope. Crazy will do nicely. Anyway, what are you going to talk to them about?*'

'I thought we might inform the captain, that as his ship is not going anywhere and he and his crew are classified as illegal immigrants, he, his crew and the ship are all under arrest. Joseph has just been appointed Senior Military Commander in this region. That should make him at least a Colonel, although as he's the only Bougainville military person they have, it wouldn't matter what rank he's given. But on second thoughts, and if I remember correctly, a Colonel is equivalent to a four-stripe Navy captain. That's not good enough for what we're doing – it'll be better if he outranks the *Dalian's*' captain. A Brigadier has a nice ring to it and should do nicely. When we finish, I'll tell Mathias for his official records.'

'*Bloody hell, Harry! You can't do that! And that ratbag captain won't submit to arrest! He'll throw you over the side for even suggesting it!*'

'He might try. But sooner or later, he's going to have to accept it. The ship can't be recovered without a hugely expensive operation. Maybe the Chinese will be prepared to pay the cost to repair and re-float the thing, but the Bougainville government are going to have to agree first. And after the dramas the Chinese have caused in the last few weeks, they aren't obliged to co-operate in the slightest. However, if permission were to be granted to remove it, I'll get Mathias to ask Australia and Japan to have their respective Commanders officially supervise the crew's removal, and to supervise the Chinese entering their waters with any recovery vessels. Therefore we would have, I reckon, at least a 'check', if not, 'checkmate!'

*'Bloody hell, Harry. You sound like you've got it all worked out! But even though your cock-eyed explanation makes it sound half-way feasible, I still think you're crazy!'*

'Maybe,' I replied airily, 'but to spread this fun stuff around a bit more, how about you and Commander Sasaki join us?'

There was a pregnant pause, before he gave a deep sigh. *'Oh, hell! Why not! Nothing else about this ridiculous situation is normal. But you'd better check with Commander Sasaki first. He seems the most rational of the three of us, and might just talk you out of it.'*

Commander Sasaki, however, was strongly in favour of the boarding party once I told him that Brigadier Joseph Bulli, as Bougainville's Senior Military Commander, was going to arrest the *Dalian's* captain for crimes committed against the Bougainvillian people and property.

*'Arresting this highly unstable captain and removing him from his ship, might be the best way to defuse the situation, Commander,'* he replied to my suggestion, *'before he incites his crew to do something even more stupid.'*

Fifteen minutes later, I made a VHF radio call to the *Dalian*, announcing that a delegation comprised of Bougainville's Senior Military Commander, the two captains of the warships legally in Bougainville waters, and a government-appointed civilian negotiator, was about to visit the ship,.

*'You not welcome on my ship! No visitors!'* was the initial, and not unexpected response.

'Listen up, captain,' I tried sounding more forceful, 'and I'll remind you yet again that you, your crew and ship are illegally in Bougainville waters. You have already ignored a legal request from the local Harbourmaster, who is also Bougainville's Senior Military Commander by the way, not to enter the harbour and to leave these waters immediately. Therefore, he is fully entitled under international maritime law to board your vessel. He has requested the presence of the captains of the officially-invited warships from two friendly nations and included myself as a Government-appointed civilian advisor to act as observer and negotiator.'

'*No person visit my ship! Not permitted!*'

'Once again, you are not in any position to refuse, Captain,' I replied, 'we will be approaching your ship in the next few minutes and ask that a gangway be lowered for our arrival. We are unarmed and are acting under the combined authority of the Bougainville and Papua-New Guinea governments.'

The last was a slight stretch of the truth, but it sounded suitably authentic and would do for now.

There was no reply to my latest statement, so leaving Alex in charge of maintaining position, Joseph and I were shortly collected by *Ballarat's* motor launch with Jim aboard in his normal working camo uniform, accompanied by two very solid Petty Officers. The cox'n headed for the *Maya* where we picked up Commander Sasaki, who turned out to be a tall, cheerful man, also wearing similar working uniform.

As Joseph was in his harbourmaster's uniform and I had nothing official-looking, Sandy had made me change into smart casual clothes.

Sasaki seemed to view the proceedings as highly amusing, but I had no doubts as to his competence. Command of one of Japan's major warships isn't turned over to fools, unlike the Chinese example before us.

As we approached the side of the *Dalian*, wonder of wonders, a proper gangway had been lowered. I'd half-expected a scrambling net or knotted rope at best! Disconcertingly, my fellow captains shuffled about until I was pushed to the front of the queue and despite my earlier bluster, felt a chill tickle the hairs on the back of my neck as I stepped onto the deck above, where just two officers waited. One was a Lieutenant Commander and probably the First Officer, while the other, wearing the three stars of a junior captain on his epaulettes, was a short, squat man, younger than I expected, given the class of ship he commanded. With a fearsome scowl twisting his features, his face strongly resembled that of a rabid cane-toad. Neither officer made any move forward to welcome our party, so I stepped closer and introduced each person in ours as they appeared.

Having apparently been elected spokesman, I started.

'Good afternoon, Captain. May I ask your name?'

'Guo!' was the barked reply.

'Thank you, Captain Guo. As I stated on the radio, we are here at the request of the Bougainville and Papua-New Guinea governments who control this territory you have chosen to invade. Please note, I use the word 'invade' deliberately. Additionally, both the Royal Australian Navy frigate *Ballarat* and the Japanese Maritime Self-Defence Force heavy destroyer *Maya,* have been officially invited by the Bougainville government to pay courtesy visits to their country, and are here legitimately. Regrettably, the same cannot be said for you and your ship. Not only were you not invited, but due to an incredibly stupid display of reckless and incompetent ship-handling, you caused considerable damage to boats and waterfront properties in the Buka Strait, including the deaths of several people you deliberately ran down in the strait. In addition to those crimes, you clearly demonstrated your intentions to cause the same or similar trouble in Kieta Harbour. I might add that your actions here in Kieta harbour have been recorded on high-definition video.

For all these acts of criminal violence and murder, you will be held personally accountable. It is indeed ironic that your reckless and incompetent behaviour has led to the destruction of your very handsome ship.'

Jim eased up beside me and murmured, 'Good motivational speech, Harry. Love it! Gets straight to the point! I can see it's doing a heap of good!'

Captain toad-face ratcheted his glare up a notch or two and

spat out, 'Ship not destroyed! You speak nonsense!' He flapped one hand disparagingly at Joseph, 'These ignorant people make cowardly attack on mighty *Changbaishan* and now on *Dalian*. Must be punished.'

I shook my head and smiled gently, 'Not so, my dear, deluded captain. There is no evidence that anybody ese was involved in the stranding of your vessel, other than your incompetent self.

But speaking of being punished, Captain Guo, perhaps if you hadn't been so foolish as to drive your ship at such a dangerous and reckless speed so close to shore, you might not have picked up that old mooring hawser in your propellor.'

Guo's face turned a deeper shade of beetroot and he had just opened his mouth to spew some more abuse, when Joseph stepped forward. Clearly, he'd had enough bluster from this pompous little toad and cut him short as he towered over the vertically-challenged captain.

'Enough crap, Captain! Under the authority of my government, I hereby arrest you, your crew and your ship for the crimes as stated by Commander Stevens. I have also been instructed by my government to detain you personally, pending a trial where you will answer all charges. You will come with us now, but your crew shall remain aboard under ship-arrest until further notice.'

Before Guo had a chance to respond to what was a clearly unexpected turn of events, the two Australian Navy Petty Officers, well used to dealing with unruly, drunken seaman ashore, stepped smartly forward and seized Guo's arms. In a move which even Clint Eastwood would have admired, one deftly flicked a pair of handcuffs around the struggling officer's wrists, then they marched him down the gangway to the launch. His last words echoed pathetically up the ship side.

'You not do this. I Captain! My crew cause you much trouble!'

Ignoring the bluster behind me, I stepped forward to stand nose-to-nose with the First Officer, alone, isolated and looking decidedly nervous with the disappearance of his captain. There were no crew in sight to act a moral backup, although I'd no doubt many were lurking within hearing range.

'Your name, please?' I asked pleasantly.

'Commander Wang, First Officer.'

'Did you understand all that was said to Captain Guo?'

His head bobbed – his eyes fearful. 'Yes, sir. I understood.'

I smiled. 'Excellent. Here's the go.' Seeing his look of confusion, I guessed that Aussie slang wasn't high on the list of things which were taught in the glorious PLAN officer's college.

'My apologies. I meant to say that this is what will happen now. With the arrest and removal of Captain Guo to detention, you are now appointed the Acting Captain of the *Dalian*. You and your crew are under arrest and your ship is impounded by the authority of the Bougainville Government.' I nodded to Joseph, standing beside me, looking quite menacing. 'It is the orders of Brigadier Bulli here, that you and your men remain aboard the ship until further notice. Understand?'

He nodded again, slightly less frantically.

'Yes, I understand.'

'Good. Are your generators able to provide power – that is, do your seawater pickups still function and do you have plenty of food?'

He looked briefly confused, caught by my change of subject.

'Yes to all three questions, Commander Stevens.'

'Good. Because the ship is legally impounded, it is under the total control of the Bougainville military Commander, who has requested the assistance of the Australian frigate and the Japanese destroyer to enforce those orders by all necessary means. Therefore, there must not be any attempt to man or display any weapons, including small firearms, and no crewmember is permitted to leave the ship for any reason. Do you understand these orders?'

'Yes Commander. But what if our engineers need to make further checks of the condition of the hull, particularly the stern fittings which suffered the most damage?'

'You will make any inspection request on VHF channel 16, and wait for an escort from one of the three ships, which will remain in close company at all times. Any breach of this rule will be regarded as a hostile act, and will attract immediate gunfire from one or both guard-ships. Given that this ship remains with live ammunition aboard, their crews have orders to shoot to kill in this instance. Is that clear?'

'Understood, sir.'

'Very good. The situation is admittedly rather unusual, but I can tell you that Captain Guo is going to remain in a jail cell until such time as the Bougainville Government or an international court convenes a trial. I have no doubt that your superiors are already extremely annoyed with the actions taken by Captain Guo, and I hope for your sake, that it can be shown you had no part in the extraordinary and reckless actions which took place over the last few days.'

He thought a few moments, before replying. 'I can only say that Captain Guo is a very headstrong person, with a strong sense of vengeance, and I fear it was this which led to his unfortunate actions, regardless of how hard I tried to dissuade him.'

I stared long and hard into his eyes, until he looked away. 'Very well, Commander. I shall take you at your word for now, but remember that from this time on, your actions speak very much louder than any words, so please try very hard to convince me you intend to co-operate fully. You should inform your men that the news of the deaths and destruction which this ship has caused in the Buka Strait, has been passed all around the island. This means that according to local payback tradition, the locals will be very keen to take their own revenge for the loss of friends and loved ones. Should any crew be so misguided as to try to escape ashore, either to the mainland or the island, I can guarantee they will die a horrible and painful death. Cannibalism is an honoured ritual in this country and has not been outlawed.'

There was a noticeable tremor in the Commander's voice when

he replied, 'But Commander, we simply performed our duties as directed by our captain. We cannot be held responsible for the deaths of those people!'

I gave my best, evil laugh. 'Oh, my dear simple-minded Commander. That old excuse was tried by the Nazis at the Nuremburg Trials, and I'm sure you know how that worked out for them! Therefore, by mere association, you are held responsible! Be assured that if the locals get their hands on any of you first, protests about responsibility will not be considered, and a trial will no longer be a concern. As I just said, in this country, as in Papua-New Guinea, it is called payback. The old biblical, 'eye for and eye, and tooth for a tooth' idea, if you understand that reference, but taken to the extreme!'

Wang nodded to indicate understanding, but I felt the urge to reinforce the point even further.

'It is most unfortunate that your fool of a captain has stranded you so effectively within such easy reach of the relatives of those you have killed! Your ship's bow and propellors carved up many innocent Bougainville people in Buka Strait, so can you imagine what the locals will do to your bodies in retaliation? Those machetes they all carry are literally razor-sharp. It is said that you don't even feel the first caress of the blade as part of an arm or leg is removed, but it sure hurts moments later. And what's worse, they usually let you watch as they cook the first few portions and eat them in front of you. I've heard that sometimes, they even make the victim eat some! The buttocks are a particular favourite, and I find it most interesting that they insist on cooking their meat first. Quite civilised!'

He would have been a bad poker player, as I could almost read his thoughts as those dreadful verbal pictures swirled through his head. Wang swayed on his feet in front of me and I thought for a moment I might have overdone the graphic verbal descriptions, but if it stopped his men trying to jump ship and kept them under control, it was a job well done.

In an effort to reclaim his attention, I said, 'We're going to leave you now, Commander Wang, but heed my words well. Your ship is stranded in a zone where there is a lot of small boat traffic to and from Bakawari Island at all hours, day and night. I strongly suggest you advise your crew to do nothing to even attract the attention of the locals any more than you have already, until we can arrange alternate, secure accommodation ashore.'

'You have my word, Commander, that the crew will be model prisoners and we will do nothing to provoke any retaliation from the local population.'

I nodded grimly as I passed him a card. 'Very well, Commander. We will see. You may call that number at any time you think you have a problem. I must warn you, however, that the crews of the two warships will be ready at all times to respond with all the weapons they possess, should so much as a single pistol be sighted or discharged aboard this ship! I shall return tomorrow to have further discussions. After we leave, you should hoist the gangway, to make it more difficult for uninvited visitors to access your crew, but be prepared to lower it immediately if we need to come aboard.'

Wang delivered a short bow. 'It shall be as you have ordered, Commander. There will not be any trouble from this crew.'

I fixed him with my Major glare. 'I'm going to hold you to that, Commander.'

With that, we made our way down to the launch, where Guo sat glowering in the bow and as we pulled away, I asked Jim, 'Can you put that miserable excuse for a sea captain in your brig for the time being?'

'It'll be a pleasure, if that's okay with you, Joseph. He is officially your prisoner after all.'

The big man chuckled, his whole frame shaking, 'Whatever you do will be fine with me, Commander. That was the most fun I've had since we blew the crap out of the *Changbaishan*!' He gave me an amused look. 'All that cannibal stuff you laid on that poor officer!

Almost makes me afraid to walk home alone this afternoon. Wait until I tell the chiefs. They'll love it.'

By common consent, we convened a brief meeting on the flight deck of the *Ballarat*, after a sullen and surprisingly silent Guo was taken below to be searched, stripped of his uniform, then locked in the brig.

'Thank you for your support, Commander Sasaki, it is greatly appreciated and helpful. May I ask that you position your ship where you can maintain watch on the starboard side of the *Dalian* and perhaps light her up with your searchlights through the night?'

He smiled and bowed his head. 'That will not be a problem, Commander. This has been a most entertaining afternoon, but I must express some concerns as to the exact legal position we all find ourselves in.'

I nodded. 'A good question and I admit that it might appear that I have acted with unseemly haste. However, I can justify my actions by saying I felt that given Guo's obvious unstable state of mind, if he'd been allowed time to get over the initial shock of the grounding and to consider his options more carefully, he would have been a far more stubborn opponent. Also, as his ship remains fully armed, he might have caused all of us a lot of trouble and damage. By moving quickly to arrest and remove him from contact with his crew, I hoped to avoid most of that unpleasantness. The plan only has to work until either we get the crew off the ship, or the Chinese send a ship to do that for us. As to the legal issues of his arrest and the ship seizure, we're going to have to handball that one uphill to the politicians, and my first calls will be to Mathias Tari and Andy Friar, our Prime Minister. I'll have Mathias talk to your Prime Minister to define your position.'

I paused to marshal my thoughts, as I was sorting all this out on the fly, but tried to look as though it was all pre-planned.

'Since all actions which took place today were officially taken or at least approved by Joseph, the appointed government representative in this region, I'm confident that those decisions will stand up in court should it comes to that. To get international opinion stirred up even further against the Chinese, it is also my intention to make public the events of today, by using the power of social media. Once one of my crew puts together all the camera video we have on these episodes and uploads it to YouTube for the world to see, with suitable commentary, I hope China will want to distance itself as much as possible by blaming all the problems on the actions of a rogue captain or two. They won't want to be accused of committing an undeclared act of war upon a nation totally unable to defend itself, for no reason. At best, they would look like fools to the rest of the world.'

My words brought relieved nods of agreement, so I continued.

'However, getting the politicians working on this, and maybe transferring Guo to Buka Town jail ASAP, will tidy up some of the loose legal threads.'

Commander Sasaki agreed, happy with the thought that his on-going presence was covered by an official request from the local Bougainville government.

Jim had a final thought. 'When you talk to Mathias, how about you suggest that he requests Guo be flown to Buka Town tomorrow morning in my helicopter? That gets him off my ship soonest and into the hands of the people he has acted against. That would surely make his continued incarceration more legal.'

'Good thinking. Plan on it, and I'll tell Mathias what he's going to do.'

Commander Sasaki thought that was even funnier, so with his hearty laughter ringing in our ears, we broke up the meeting, Jim's launch running Commander Sasaki, Joseph and me back to our boats.

*'Ah, Commander Stevens. Good to hear from you. How are things in Kieta Harbour?'*

I chuckled, as so much had happened in a short space of time,

I'd almost lost track of it. 'My apologies for not getting back to you sooner Mr Tari, but we've been rather busy the last few hours.'

He laughed in return. '*No problem. But please tell me what has happened.*'

'With Joseph and the other two captains, we visited the *Dalian* where Joseph arrested Captain Guo and his crew, and impounded the PLAN heavy destroyer *Dalian*, all in the name of the Autonomous Region of Bougainville. You will have to forgive me acting so freely in your name, but we had to act smartly to take best advantage of the state of shock and confusion which we found aboard the *Dalian*. As a sidebar, I must ask you to note that officially, you have appointed Joseph as Brigadier of the newly-created Bougainville Defence Force.

Under Joseph's authority, we have also removed Captain Guo from his ship in handcuffs, and confined him temporarily in the brig aboard the *Ballarat*. Upon receipt of a formal request from yourself to Commander Saunders of the *HMAS Ballarat*, asking for him to be transferred to Buka Town jail at the earliest opportunity, we plan to fly him to Buka Town tomorrow morning so he can be confined to your jail under your control. At your convenience, he can then stand trial for his numerous crimes against your people and property under your established justice system.

On a lighter note, you could say that at least for the moment, your nation has gained possession of a 13,000-tonne heavy destroyer, although keeping it long-term might be somewhat problematic.'

That flippant comment at least drew a chuckle from Mathias.

'For now, we have left the crew aboard the ship, under the leadership of the First Lieutenant, Commander Wang, who has so far been compliant with our orders. After making a bunch of dire threats concerning what would happen if he or his crew made any sort of trouble, or tried to leave the ship, we are confident the crew will behave, but as that situation is very volatile, we don't expect the good behaviour to last long. Two days at best, I'd say.'

'*You have excelled yourself yet again, Commander. But where do we go from here? I must confess it is a very new and rather frightening situation this madman has created for us. I have the feeling of holding a very large and angry tiger by the tail!'*

'As it is for us as well, I can assure you. However, these are my suggestions for moving forward. Following this conversation, I will update both the Australian and Japanese Prime Ministers as to what has happened, and I propose we let them make their own appropriate protests to the Chinese and the United Nations. You should draft another strong note of protest to the Chinese government, again via their ambassador in Port Moresby. That note should declare that you have impounded their ship, placed the crew under ship-arrest, and arrested and locked up their captain ashore, pending trial for numerous crimes, including murder, against the people of Bougainville. Add that you demand suitable reparations from the Chinese government for the loss of lives, boats and damages caused to shore installations. Also, you might like to demand that they remove the stranded ship as soon as possible and where possible, make good any damage caused to the pristine environment.'

There was a pause, before Mathias spoke. *'It is just as well I decided to record this conversation. Much easier for my secretary to sort things out! Do go on, please, you're doing very well!'*

'Thank you. Locally, don't forget to send a formal request to Commander Sanders of the *Ballarat*, asking him to fly Captain Guo to Buka Town for confinement in your jail. Also, send an official message to Commander Sasaki on the *Maya*, thanking him for his efforts so far and requesting his continued presence to maintain safety and security in the vicinity of the *Dalian* while the crew are still aboard.'

*'I shall do all of those things. Is there more?'*

'I'm afraid so. I suggest that the crew, who number more than 300, be left on the ship for now, as they have shelter, power, food and facilities. However, the longer they stay there, the more chance there is that they will find many ways to create mischief. The ship remains fully armed, and apart from being unable to move, is fully-functional.'

*'That sounds like a major problem waiting to erupt.'*

I thought a moment, before replying. 'I agree sir, but it just occurred to me that in your protest note to the Chinese ambassador, you might like to demand the Chinese send a ship immediately to collect the crew, although a skeleton crew will have to be left aboard to maintain security and functionality. I see no advantage in holding the crew aboard any longer than necessary – just 300-plus disadvantages.'

*'No problem with that, Commander. I shall attend to these matters immediately and let you know when we receive results.'*

'Thank you, Mr Tari. I'll report any further developments, but you can expect your prisoner to be delivered to the airport tomorrow morning.'

*'We'll be waiting for him and thank you again for your outstanding efforts, Commander.'*

# CHAPTER 31

Back aboard *Firebird*, Joseph left in his official launch to go tell the three regional chiefs what was still going on in their beautiful, peaceful bay, while I brought my crew up to date. Predictably, Sandy said, 'Just what is it with you and playing with warships, dear heart? A few years back, you started with a small patrol boat, then graduated to a bigger one, then escalated to a frigate, a heavy destroyer, a light cruiser and a bloody big, heavily-armed, transport ship! Please don't go looking for an aircraft carrier to seize or play with, even though the Chinese PLAN have got one.'

I smiled sweetly, choosing at this time to ignore her sarcasm, and as much as the crew found it highly amusing, I got on with fielding the expected barrage of questions. Once that had died down and before total mental exhaustion floored me, I placed a call to Charlie and explained the latest situation.

*'Fuckin' hell, Harry. We leave you alone for five minutes and you go and nick a Chinese heavy destroyer. Complete with crew! Beijing will be going absolutely berko! However, back to being serious, I think that legally, you'll be okay with the arrest of the ship and the captain, since Mathias and Joseph made it official. I agree with getting rid of the crew as soon as possible. They could turn into a serious problem given the weapons load still aboard. I'll tell the Boss and suggest that seeing as how Australian citizens and an Aussie Navy ship are involved in this latest furball, we're entitled to come down a lot heavier, and call the Chinese Ambassador over for a chat. That should swing a bit of weight in the right direction. Nice move getting that Japanese heavy destroyer. I guess you'll be calling Shinzo next. Can we help?'*

'Yeah, thanks Charlie, anything would help. Even though I'll be calling Shinzo's secretary, maybe just a few unofficial words to him or even better his ambassador cousin, would help a lot.

Despite what Sandy keeps on telling me, I don't actually feel very comfortable messing about with another country's warships.'

Charlie laughed. '*I wouldn't think that would make you uneasy, as you manage to do it so well and often. I also don't think the Japanese would have sent the Maya in the first place if they had any doubts about the legitimacy of the operation. I can tell you on the quiet, that Shinzo and his government have been wanting to stick something up the Chinese for ages. They'll be loving this!*'

'Thanks Charlie. I'll leave all that heavy political shit to you and Andy. Now I'd better call Japan.'

'*A good job, well done again, Harry. Stay frosty.*'

I then had to explain the situation to Shinzo Ito's secretary, who was equally delighted with the outcome and assured me that I was welcome to hang onto their destroyer for a while longer yet – provided I didn't break it! I briefly wondered why everybody who owns one of the ships I borrow, trots out the same concerns about me breaking stuff!

His secretary also said that Shinzo would be very pleased with the outcome of the operation, and would use the information and the video which I promised to send ASAP, to make the maximum amount of face-losing fuss for the Chinese.

At that point, I think I'd called everyone who needed calling and went to get myself on the outside of a few frosty beers, followed by one of Bree's lovely roast lamb dinners.

Two relatively uneventful days later, fully restored in spirit and determination, we same fearless four made another foray to the *Dalian*. With Kenji Sasaki, Jim, Joseph and myself aboard *Ballarat's* launch again, the mood was considerably different to the last time.

'I did say,' I muttered as we made the climb up the destroyer's side, 'I mean, how much warning do they need? It was only the cannibal bit where I stretched the truth a little.'

'Look on the bright side, Harry,' Jim replied, being disgustingly cheerful under the circumstances, 'it's bound to cut down the desertion rate.'

We were met on deck by Commander Wang and two Petty Officers. Wang appeared calm and in control, but had a new and very disturbing air of arrogance about him when he spoke.

'Good morning, gentlemen. To what do we owe the dubious honour of this visit?'

Deciding that a bullish approach was always best at defusing arrogance, I stepped forward, studied him for a long moment in silence, then replied.

'Do you remember my words of two days ago when I said you should tell your crew to keep a low profile and not try to leave the ship?'

He nodded smugly. 'I heard your words, but Chinese seamen not like being kept as prisoners!'

I nodded thoughtfully. 'A most unfortunate sentiment, Commander, although not entirely unexpected, given the behaviour of your former captain and this crew. However, when rules are broken, penalties must be paid.'

'What you say? We Chinese sailors – this Chinese ship – Chinese property. You no make rules!'

I noted that under pressure, his English had deteriorated, and smiled grimly, thoroughly enjoying the take-down fast approaching.

'I had hopes you would be sensible, Wang, but now I see that you are as bad as your former captain. Last night, four of your men left the ship and swam ashore. I warned you against this foolhardy course of action, but you chose to disregard the warning. The result was horribly predictable as I said! As well as being predictably horrible!'

I half-turned to Joseph, who dug into the end pocket of the large, lumpy duffle bag he was carrying. He fished out four ball-link chains with glittering silver and red metal strips dangling off them. With Wang and his men looking on curiously, I distastefully lined the chains up along one finger on my left hand, and held them out to Wang.

'Here you are, Commander. This should help with the paperwork you're going to have to generate for the families and your superiors.'

Worry started to replace curiosity on his otherwise unlined face. 'What this?'

Further questions were cut short as two glittering red drops fell from the metal strips, to splatter on the deck below my outstretched hand.

'This, you stupid, arrogant dickhead, are what we call dog-tags, although you might know them as identification tags. They belonged to the four seamen who defied the shore leave restrictions. Had you paid more attention to my words two days ago, they might still be around the necks of those men.'

As Wang seemed reluctant to take the tags, I let them slide off my finger to clatter to the steel deck at his feet, splattering blood onto his white shoes.

I gave him another nasty smile.

'And just in case that's not sufficient for identification, we decided to help you and brought more evidence.'

I stepped aside to let a broadly grinning Joseph hump the heavy duffle bag forward, where he dropped it on top of the dog-tags, thumping down with a heavy, soggy thud. The immaculate Commander Wang with his freshly-splattered shoes, took a hasty pace back, before waving one of the Petty Officers to come forward and open the duffle.

The red, well-lubricated zip slid easily, allowing the sides to peel wide apart, revealing the gut-wrenching contents. At least, that was what the sight did to the unfortunate seaman, as he took in the sight of four heads, all with short, black hair and neatly severed at the neck. Their eyes were open, with the mouths distorted in a deathly grimace, hinting at the degree of terror the men had experienced in their final moments.

Whatever the Petty Officer had eaten for breakfast, was

promptly sprayed over Wang's feet and lower legs before the man could recoil from the horrible sight, falling over his feet in his haste to backpedal away from the bag full of hideous, violent death.

I tut-tutted. 'Oh dear. I thought you chappies in the PLAN were made of much sterner stuff than that. I mean, I did tell you what the locals would do if they got their hands on anyone from this ship.'

I waved at the mess at the Commander's feet. 'Hopefully, this delivery service won't have to happen again. You'll find out about the next lot by seeing who is missing from tomorrow's roll-call. However, I do have some wonderful news! The locals have asked me to pass on their sincere thanks for sending such tasty men in good condition. They love a bit of long-pork to vary their diet! They actually asked for more, but I had to say that depended on you.'

I had to pause briefly as the other Petty Officer, his eyes like saucers, added the contents of his stomach to the mess already on the deck. 'Anyway, that's about all we have to say for now, except that we have asked your country to send a ship to collect you. I don't know when, or even if that will happen, but in the meantime, all our boats will retire to the main wharf where we can tie-up in comfort. Now that they've had a taste, and approve the flavour, the local villagers have told us they will be very happy to take over the guard duties. There's no need for two naval ships to sit here watching you all night, when the locals can do a much better job, in return for a few good feeds. We're sure your crew will oblige and I'm sure you'll agree?'

Wang had gone quite pasty-looking in the face, but must have been listening, as he replied in much better English, 'Perhaps I was too hasty with my earlier remarks, Commander. Could you maybe keep at least one ship close by? If we are your prisoners, you really should be looking after us.'

I laughed. 'Oh, no, dear foolish Commander. You told us that as you are Chinese on a Chinese ship, even immovably stuck on a Bougainville reef, you don't like anyone else making rules for you to follow. Don't you fellows have a saying, 'Be careful what you wish for'? Terribly apt saying, isn't it. I think so, anyway. But getting back to your question, I think we're being extremely co-operative. We're going to let the locals look after you! I'm sure you'll all get along very well once you get to know them. I mean, look at Mr Bulli here. Lovely big fella, and the blokes ashore are just as nice as he is!'

I waved dismissively at the horrific mess on the deck at his feet.

'Anyway, it would seem you have a bit of cleaning up to do before you start the paperwork, so we'll just trot off and leave you to it.'

I turned toward the gangway, but then suddenly turned back. 'I nearly forgot. There's just one more thing to remind you about, Wang. Should there be the slightest hint of any of the ship's weapons being readied for use, day or night, both of our ships will open fire immediately with every weapon they have, including missiles, and will not cease firing until every crew-member is killed and this ship is so utterly destroyed, there will not be any need for your foolish, misguided country to send a rescue vessel! Goodbye for now, Commander. Pleasant dreams.'

With no further discussion, we about-turned and trotted down the gang-way, Joseph breaking into rumbling chuckles long before we reached the launch.

'Oh dear, Harry,' he said, 'that was even more fun than our last visit. You do have such a wonderful way with words. Those three will have nightmares for years!'

'Do you really think so?' I asked happily. 'It would be even better if they can scare the shit out of the rest of the crew as well!'

We stuck to our word and all three boats retired to tie-up at the wharves, leaving the Chinese destroyer perched in terrified isolation on the shallow reef. The usual shuttle of powered long-canoes and smaller boats between the mainland and Bakawari Island quickly resumed, except that following a few cunning suggestions to the locals from Joseph, each slowed as it passed close by the *Dalian*, the occupants making threatening gestures with their machetes.

Using my excellent stabilised binoculars which my darling Sandy had bought me, I couldn't see anyone brave enough to even venture on deck, and all doors which opened onto the upper deck remained firmly closed. The only sign of life was just the occasional pale face showing at the bridge windows.

'Well,' I remarked to our crew, including Jim and Kenji Sasaki who was pleased to be invited for happy hour, and proved to be an excellent guest, 'that might keep them quiet for a few more days. Or hopefully until the Chinese send a ship for them and work out what to do about the *Dalian*.'

'I've already been instructed to hang around for the duration,' Jim stated, 'but Kenji and I would like to get back to our patrol duties as soon as we have some sort of resolution to this mess.'

'Yeah. I understand. But I do expect we'll get things sorted very soon. The Chinese won't let their latest destroyer full of secrets sit on a reef for too long without doing something.'

That hoped-for action did happen, but not for another three days. In the meantime, following assurances from Joseph that the Japanese crew of the *Maya* would not be held accountable for the sins of their grandfathers, Kenji allowed his crew leave to stretch their legs ashore. Jim did the same with his mob and the village was soon overrun with masses of young men and women in civvies, with short haircuts. True to Joseph's word, all the sailors were made welcome by the locals, who ironically, went ahead and put on a feast for them, using the same cooking pits they'd used to feed the *Changbaishan* crew. It was a great party, and half the village joined in, although strangely, no kava was served!

It was Jasper who roused me early on the morning of the fourth day, dragging me up on deck in time to see a large, high-sided cargo ship, painted all-over grey, slowly steaming in through the harbour entrance, a red flag streaming from her mast.

Joseph was already on his way out to meet it, as it dropped

anchor about half-way between the wharf and the stranded *Dalian*. It looked like a normal, mixed-cargo ship, with the derricks of four especially large cranes poking high above several low stacks of containers sitting where two of the large hatch covers would normally be. A quick check with Wikipedia revealed nothing in the PLAN collection of ships which matched what we were looking at, so I activated the masthead camera to gather what images we could of what must be the rescue ship for the *Dalian* crew.

I saw Joseph board the ship via a gangway lowered down one side and have a brief discussion with two officers on deck. He then left and headed our way.

'They are here to rescue the bulk of the *Dalian's* crew,' Joseph confirmed. 'They also have a number of salvage experts aboard to inspect the damage and work out the best way to extract *Dalian* from the reef.'

I grinned. 'I wish them good luck with that.'

Joseph agreed, but still looked concerned. 'I didn't think this through, but it is logical that the Chinese will have to leave a security crew aboard the *Dalian*. None of us can afford to have a fully-armed warship sitting unattended in a foreign harbour, especially where the locals are still a bit hot-headed at times. I took the precaution of warning the captain that his crew will not be welcomed ashore and mentioned that there already had been some unfortunate incidents with *Dalian's* crew who broke the rules. Anyway, the captain has requested a meeting with 'the delegation who met with Captain Guo' as soon as possible. Can we arrange that, Harry?'

'Sure thing,' I replied cheerfully, sensing an end to this messy affair fast approaching. 'I'll call Jim and Kenji. When they're ready, we'll just head on over to whatever that ship is. Does it have a name?'

He shook his head. 'Not that I could discover in the short time I was there. Just the pennant number painted on the bow – *107.*'

As we approached the *107* in *Ballarat's* launch, a gangway was lowered down its side. On deck, two officers waited to meet us, one of them asking in halting English if we would please follow them to meet Captain Zhou. They lead the way to a spacious cabin where a tall, thin, sour-faced officer waited. He wore the epaulettes of a full PLAN captain, and unlike our escorts, spoke excellent English.

With no formalities, he started right in. 'I have been sent here to collect most of the crew of the stranded *Dalian*. For security, twenty men will remain aboard, including Commander Wang as acting-captain, until such time as we secure the release of Captain Guo presently being detained illegally by the corrupt government of Bougainville in Buka Town. This meeting is to inform you of my work here and to demand that my engineers be allowed to make all necessary inspections of the *Dalian* without fear of attack by the local population.'

As our crew remained silent, he paused to direct an arrogant glare at both Jim and Kenji, before continuing.

'In addition, I have been instructed to protest the unnecessary presence of two foreign warships who are threatening the stranded *Dalian*, and have directed fatal attacks to be made upon her peaceful crew. My country is informing the Bougainville government that these two ships must be instructed to leave these waters immediately or suffer repercussions.'

In the face of this aggression, I could see Joseph was out of his depth, and Jim and Kenji looked unsure of how to respond, so I got my feet ready and opened my big mouth as usual.

'Just back up the bus, captain. Firstly, Brigadier Bulli is the senior military commander and government representative in Kieta, so any complaints should be directed to him. Secondly, Commanders Sanders and Sasaki are here by invitation of the Bougainville government. You have no authority to demand anything, let alone their removal! I am a private Australian citizen, here with my crew on a diving holiday, although I have been requested by the President of the Autonomous Region of Bougainville, to act as spokesperson and independent observer in this matter, since that fool of a captain of the *Changbaishan* chose to imprison me without proof of misdoing. The *Dalian* is the uninvited ship who invaded Bougainville territorial waters. As for Captain Guo's incarceration, it is well justified by his murderous and destructive rampage through the Buka Strait, plus his display of appalling seamanship by attempting to swamp the harbour facilities here in Kieta Harbour, which caused the stranding of his ship. Because of all this gratuitous carnage, I have been instructed to say that neither the ship nor her crew are welcome in this country. And you're only here under sufferance, so be very careful what you say!'

His dark eyes flashed dangerously as he took a step toward me.

'I have heard of you,' he hissed venomously. 'The loud-mouth Australian with an answer for everything! This meeting is finished! I have declared my intentions, and you are not to return to my ship!'

Joseph finally spoke up. 'Just a minute, captain. As well as being the ranking military presence in this region, I'm also the harbourmaster and as such, I have the final say as to who does what in this harbour, not you! On instructions from my government, I have already given permission for you to transfer as many crew members from the *Dalian* as is necessary, and for your engineers and salvage experts to examine the ship. However, neither you nor your crew have permission to go ashore for any reason. Should you defy my order, I will not be held responsible for the outcome. Armed men are watching both Chinese ships as we speak, since many of the local people had relatives who were killed or injured by the insanely murderous ship-handling by Captain Guo in the Buka Strait. These people are actively seeking revenge for his actions, and I must advise you that I have no control over this traditional practice.'

Zhou made a dismissive motion with his hands. 'Your words do not frighten me, Harbourmaster. I will stay here as long as it takes for my engineers to make their assessments. Any attempt to interfere with either ship or their crews will be met with powerful retaliation. This is my warning to you! Now leave my ship!'

Jim had raised eyebrows, obviously expecting my usual terse reaction, but I just shook my head and let them precede me out of the cabin, where a Lieutenant waited to escort us to the gangway.

'What now, Master Planner?' Jim asked with a grin, as we chugged back to the wharf.

'Let's have a round-table with tea and coffee to discuss this,' was my reply.

Back aboard *Firebird,* our lovely ladies supplied the beverages and a late breakfast, which gave me time to think about the situation.

'As things are at the moment, Captain Zhou is doing exactly what we wanted the Chinese Navy to do, although his attitude will probably cause some problems if he keeps the aggro going. We needed to get most of the crew off the *Dalian* before they got up to too much mischief and the Chinese salvage experts and engineers do need to check the ship so they can work out how to re-float the fool thing. However, despite what Zhou said, he or his engineers are going to have to talk to us about that before long.'

Joseph agreed. 'Correct. Whatever plan they come up with to shift it, we have to approve it first. We don't want the reef destroyed or the port flooded with fuel oil from ruptured tanks.'

# CHAPTER 32

For the next two days, we watched as a near-constant stream of salvage experts were shuttled to and from the stricken vessel, until surprisingly, Captain Zhou called us for another meeting. We were further surprised to find the captain in a surprisingly pleasant mood.

'My salvage crew and engineers have made their initial assessment and I wished to discuss the results with you.'

I let Joseph take the lead for that one.

'Thank you, Captain,' he replied, 'that is appreciated.'

'Yes. Well, the report indicates that the ship appears to be in better condition than expected, as it impacted an area of reef covered with mostly soft corals which cushioned the impact, and reduced potential damage to a small degree. There is relatively minor damage to the hull bottom, which is already receiving temporary repairs from the inside, and there has not been any leakage of fuel oil as the ship has a double hull on the bottom. This report does not cover the damage to the left shaft and propellor, although the ship's engineers have managed to seal the shaft tunnel on the inside, preventing further water ingress. It has been assessed that at high water, the ship is only 0.8-metre away from floating, and for that reason, the salvage crew have recommended that it should be possible to re-float the ship if it can be sufficiently lightened.'

I took over and responded. 'That's good news, Captain. Are we to presume that you have a tanker coming to drain fuel oil, and that you will be taking everything else moveable onto your ship?'

He inclined his head. 'That is so. My ship is designed to carry either cargo or troops, or a mix of the two. I have ample capacity for the *Dalian's* crew and all her removable items. I have been instructed to inform you that a tanker vessel is en-route and expected within two days. However, now that a decision has been reached to lighten the *Dalian*, I will have our combined crews commence removing all materials possible from the ship immediately.'

He looked at Joseph, and said with a strong flavour of sarcasm, 'I hope this plan meets with your approval, Harbourmaster or Brigadier, whatever you are.'

Joseph didn't rise to the challenge; merely nodding and blandly replying, 'I am both, Captain and that action will be acceptable. I might add, that I'm glad your crews have taken my advice and refrained from venturing ashore. It does save a lot of needless bloodshed and report writing.'

Zhou's dark eyes flashed dangerously at the challenge and unsubtle reminder of who was really in charge of the situation

'That remains to be seen, Harbourmaster,' he replied cryptically, standing to indicate that both the meeting and the limits of his cordiality were concluded. No further words were exchanged as the same Lieutenant escorted our small group back topsides.

'Well done, Joseph,' Jim complimented as we headed back to the wharf, 'although I didn't like his parting comment. Sounds like he intends to test your warning.'

Joseph ruefully replied, 'Indeed it does. Oh, well. I'm sure if that does happen, we'll be making another visit with a soggy duffle-bag.'

Zhou must have been under extreme pressure from the upper echelons of the PLAN staff, as within the hour, he carefully, and very competently, moved his ship so that it was lying at right-angles to the stranded destroyer, with his midships area almost touching the stern of the *Dalian*, which in turn was protruding clear of the reef.

This risky manoeuvring was only possible because of the deep water close beside the reef, and the lack of any strong winds. Carefully placed sets of bow and stern anchors made sure the *107* wouldn't accidently join the *Dalian*. It also allowed two of the *107's* huge cranes to easily reach across to the stern deck of the *Dalian*.

The heaviest item aboard was the belly full of fuel-oil, but that would have to wait until the tanker arrived, however, the combined force of both crews soon had a stream of missiles, gun ammunition and a plethora of other stuff lining up to be hoisted aboard the *107*. Even the two massive anchors and the chains were dragged up on deck and made ready for removal. Naturally, it was a huge task, especially the missiles as they needed special handling and stowage.

The work proceeded non-stop all that night and all the next day, although naturally, the *Dalian* showed no change of level. The same couldn't be said for the *107*, since her waterline slowly lowered as the seemingly endless stream of items were swung aboard and stowed.

When Jim and Kenji came down for the now regular happy-hour and a feed, I asked Kenji about the likely fuel capacity of the *Dalian*, as his ship was of similar displacement.

'We have 1,850 tonnes total capacity,' he said, 'so I expect he might have a 2,000-tonne capacity with perhaps 1,300-tonnes or so left. With that removed, along with all the other items being taken off, there is an excellent chance she will float on the next peak high tide.'

I'd already checked the tide-tables for the area and worked out that the next full-moon high tide would be in just five days, so there was still a lot of work to be done for the Chinese to meet that schedule.

It was another quiet night, with our crew, plus Jim getting quietly shit-faced, mainly on the deadly NQ teas. Being alongside the wharf was convenient for access ashore, but not so good for privacy as even in the wee-small hours, there were always a few locals wandering along the waterfront. That made it a little more difficult for Jim and Georgia to indulge in the more physical aspects of their new romance. I had made things a little easier for them by mooring 'Mediterranean-style' or stern-to the wharf, which left just the foredeck netting as the only semi-private area for their romps which had become quite regular to the amusement of all our crew. Judging by her muffled noises, Georgia was as keen as Jim to make up for previously lost opportunities.

Next morning, the day we expected the Chinese tanker to arrive, Joseph turned up for breakfast in his official launch. He was in a very jovial mood and after disposing of an alarming amount of Bree's cooking, he patted his bulging stomach, then announced that apparently several seamen from the *107* had braved a trip ashore during the night.

'I didn't hear anything,' I said with a grin.

He chuckled, 'No, you wouldn't have. It was kept very quiet with no firearms involved. Unfortunately for them, the result was the same as last time.'

'How many?'

'Five!' was his chilling reply.

The girls looked a bit green at the words, especially as I asked, 'Another soggy sack?'

'Yes. The bodies are long gone and I won't be asking any questions. They were warned.'

'Shall I come with you to make a house-call?'

'I would appreciate that, Harry,' he rumbled. 'We might as well get it over with now if you're ready?'

Ten minutes later, we were approaching the side of the *107*, where the gangway remained hoisted, although a Lieutenant did lean over the rail to enquire the nature of our business.

'We need to have a brief talk with Captain Zhou,' I said.

'Captain very busy. Not available for talk,' was the surly response. We couldn't argue with that, as the ship's decks were swarming with sailors and piles of stuff off the *Dalian*.

'I can appreciate that,' I replied politely, 'however, this is a particular something the captain needs to deal with in person.'

Again, the Lieutenant shook his head. 'No talk, too busy.'

As a silent answer to his continued refusal, Joseph reached into the hessian bag at his feet and tossed a small, wet bundle up at the officer, where it landed with a soggy splat at his feet. We couldn't see his immediate reaction as he had smartly stepped back when it arced across the railing. When he re-appeared, however, a line of red spots stitched a curving line down across his face and the front of his immaculate white shirt. Without further protest, the gangway slowly lowered.

'You come aboard. I fetch Captain.'

Grimly, Joseph and I marched up the narrow steps, to be halted at the top by two burly, stone-faced seamen armed with sub-machine guns held at the ready.

'This isn't very hospitable,' I commented, grinning at them, but not getting any response. Joseph's little bundle lay on the deck between us, surrounded by a red splatter of blood.

I looked at our two guards. 'I hope none of your mates went ashore last night?'

Unlike the incarcerated ex-captain Guo, they would have made brilliant poker players, as their expressions remained utterly devoid of emotion and their eyes didn't leave us.

A commotion further aft, revealed the cadaverous Captain Zhou stomping up the deck, ploughing his way through the clusters of sailors, his hapless Lieutenant trailing behind. While he was still several paces away, Zhou started yelling.

'What is this nonsense you bring to my ship? We are very busy and I have no time for more of your foolishness!'

Joseph and I remained silent, as he panted to a stop in front of us, finally looking down at the small tangled ball of red-stained metal chains and tags at his feet.

Zhou glared at us and barked. 'What is this? What you trying to do?'

I gestured to the bundle of identity disks. 'Commander Wang of the *Dalian* asked the same question, and I give you the same reply. Take a look. They speak for themselves.'

Impatiently, Zhou waved his Lieutenant forward to pick up the bundle, something he was very hesitant to do, although defying his captain was obviously not an option. He picked them up, and with a grimace of distaste, held them out to his captain who merely peered at them from a safe distance. Zhou's face promptly turned almost as red as the puddle of blood on his deck plates.

'How you get these tags,' he barked in rather more fractured English than he normally used. 'These belong to Chinese seamen.'

I smiled gently. 'They did, my dear, stubborn Captain – until last night that is! They were around the necks of the five seamen who went ashore last night, in defiance of the instructions Brigadier Bulli issued. Despite your callous disregard of our warning, we thought we'd do the right thing and let you have them back. In order to assist official identification and family notifications, Brigadier Bulli has additional identification for you, but you needn't worry about planning discipline for them. We reckon they've already paid a sufficiently steep price for their disobedience.'

I could see Joseph was trying very hard to suppress a grin as he stepped forward and silently dumped the very heavy sack on the deck at Zhou's feet, before stepping back.

Tentatively, Zhou poked the sack with the toe of his deck shoe, then lifted his furious gaze.

'What this?'

Once again, I waved at the sack. 'Take a look. Not a pretty sight, but you were warned.'

Naturally, it was the Lieutenant who got to untwist the top of the sack and spread the top open, letting loose a swarm of blue-green flies. His reaction was remarkably similar to the petty officer aboard *Dalian* who had the misfortune to open their bag of heads, although in this case, he fortunately managed to avoid splattering Zhou's shoes.

Nevertheless, the sight was enough to cause Zhou's face to change from red to white.

'What have you done?' he asked in a deathly whisper.

I dropped my smart-arse, bantering tone and reverted to being a pissed-off Major.

'WE didn't do anything, Captain Zhou. Either your men chose not to heed our warning, or you were stupid enough to send them ashore to test the truth of it. Either way, you and you alone are responsible. I think we've given you enough to consider for now, so we'll be on our way. Good luck with the rest of your unloading.'

As we turned to leave, I swung back abruptly, happy to use the chance to stir this arrogant captain a bit more. 'By the way, don't bother asking for the rest of the bodies. They seem to have mysteriously disappeared, although I noticed there are a lot more cooking fires blazing along the beachfront this morning. Yum, yum. Don't you just love the smell of barbequed long pig in the morning?'

Zhou was sufficiently affected by my remarks to refrain from any further comment as we left, Joseph predictably breaking into gut-shaking chuckles before we were even half-way down the gangway.

'Thank you, Commander,' he rumbled when had recovered sufficiently, 'another excellent story to amuse the Elders over morning coffee. They loved the first one!'

It was around midday when a mid-sized, grey-painted tanker made her way cautiously into the harbour, escorted by a pair of large ocean-going tugs which looked like small ships themselves. In what became an obviously pre-arranged manoeuvre, the tugs nudged the tanker against the hull of the *107*, where several large hoses were already laid across her decks, completing the connection between the *Dalian* and the tanker. As a display of rapid positioning and seamanship, it was most impressive.

For the next couple of days, work continued as before – day and night, as both the tanker and the *107* settled lower into the water under their loads, until the time came when the cranes regular movement slowed, then finally stopped.

I commented to Jim about the streams of water suddenly jetting from several places low down on the hull of the *Dalian*.

'I don't think they're emergency pumps,' he responded, 'it's more likely that now all the hardware which can be moved, has been, and they're getting ready for tonight's high tide by pumping ballast. They wouldn't have wanted the ship getting a bit light prematurely and starting to bounce around on the reef, so they would have ballasted her down to keep her in place until the right time.

His appraisal seemed correct as firstly the tanker was moved away from the side of the *107* to anchor well out of the way over near Bakawari Island. Then *107* moved herself away from the stern of the *Dalian* and anchored near the tanker, as if pointedly remaining clear of the mainland. Little did they know, that most of the locals who had shortened both the length and the life of the wandering Chinese seamen, lived on the island.

With ballast water still being discharged in foaming, brown torrents, the two tugs backed up to the destroyer's stern and attached heavy towing hawsers. Naturally, all this took much longer to execute than to describe, but as the tropical dusk settled with typical swiftness over the peaceful harbour, the two tugs moved away from the stern of the *Dalian*, the towing hawsers paying out until the skippers were satisfied with their positions, which they maintained as they waited for the tide peak, due around 21:00 hours.

The scene was quite surreal as the darkness was firmly pushed back by the searchlights of the four Chinese rescue ships which lit up the *Dalian* as bright as day.

At 20:30, the discharge of ballast water from the *Dalian* eased to a trickle, before stopping a few minutes later. As the tugs were almost abeam our position, we could hear the moment when both skippers throttled up, the twin engines on each rising from a muted grumble to a spine-tingling, full-throated bellow which echoed across the harbour, as a combined 13,000 horsepower created a furious white boil of wash from their sterns. Most eyes, however, were firmly fixed on the *Dalian* as she seemed to effortlessly resist the mighty power of the straining tugs.

But then, after several minutes of thundering effort, the *Dalian* seemed to shiver as the reef slowly, reluctantly surrendered its grip of the long, sleek hull, and with a grumbling, grinding roar of metal across coral, slid meekly back off the reef which had held her captive.

As *Dalian* had no anchors left aboard, the tugs reversed back toward the freed ship, quickly winching in their towing hawsers. One tug remained attached to the stern, while his mate went to the bow and re-attached his tow line there.

'They aren't going to head out tonight, are they?' I asked Jim, who had become our resident salvage expert.

'No. I suspect they'll move her close to shore in the shallows in case the patches leak too much. They'll keep an eye on water ingress overnight and see what else got torn up as she left the reef. If all is well, they'll re-ballast her for the trip home and head out. If there aren't any problems, they could be gone tomorrow.'

I gave a heartfelt sigh. 'That'd be really good. I'm a wee bit over all this.'

'Amen to that, brother,' was Jim's reply.


Apparently, additional damage was judged superficial, or was repaired overnight, as at dawn, a small convoy formed up with the tug-assisted *Dalian* ahead of the tanker, with the freighter, *107*, bringing up the tail as they made a cautious exit through the heads and out of sight. Overnight, the tide had cleared the cloudy remains of the ground-up reef, caused by the removal of the destroyer, and visually, the harbour looked almost exactly the same as it had before the series of unwanted intrusions by the dreaded Red Dragon.

# EPILOGUE

The departure of the Chinese led to a flurry of phone calls, and after discussion with Jim and Kenji, an arrangement was reached between their respective naval chiefs, whereby *Ballarat* was released from guard duty and sent back to finish her patrol. *Maya* assumed Kieta Harbour guard duties in the short term, pending an arrangement being hacked out between the Australian and Japanese governments to share the security of the port in the immediate future.

*Ballarat* departed that same day, with a round of heartfelt farewells from both crews and the locals.

I received a message from Hiroto Sakamoto which indicated that now the port was clear of interference, a convoy of merchant ships would be arriving in Kieta harbour within 24 hours, one of which was a fuel tanker to replenish the bunkers ashore and provide fuel for the mine and construction machinery. There was also a container ship which was carrying office and accommodation modules for housing the construction engineers, construction supplies and other small supplies and equipment, while a large freighter was carrying additional supplies and more heavy construction machines to supplement the ones left behind by the Chinese.

With all that happening, I consulted my crew and we decided this would be a good time to bail and head home. Accordingly, we said our goodbyes, which surprisingly included a simple, but emotional ceremonial one from Joseph and the three chiefs in their traditional dress. It was therefore with mixed emotions that we motored across the harbour next morning, passing through the vibrant green-clothed headlands and turned our slim bows south.

We had no plans to stop and visit anywhere on the way, and once clear of the Solomon Sea, there weren't any places to stop anyway. Bree had made sure we had plenty of supplies, so there was no need to ration anything. The trip length was around 1330 nautical miles and should take about 4 days. For the first time since leaving Vanuatu, we all felt we could truly relax, although the SatPhone kept ringing as various people either updated us on the Bougainville situation, or wanted to find out more about what had really happened.

Amongst ourselves, we'd agreed that we'd keep our stories simple, as, apart from the Bougainville mob, only Jim and the *Ballarat* crew, Kenji and the *Maya* crew, Andy, Charlie and Lara, knew what had really happened in Kieta Harbour. I figured that keeping the true stories away from the media would be wise.

Nevertheless, some very nice words were sent our way by Mathias Tari and Joseph and the chiefs.

The day after leaving Kieta, I received a call from Raijin Tanaka, the senior boss of the Yamaguchi-gumi Yakuza clan.

*'Once again, Commander, you have managed to win an amazing victory. Your story has spread throughout our clan, generating much respect, and I despair of ever being able to repay our debt to you and your crew.'*

I laughed, simply pleased that we had been able to get the mine revival operation back on track. 'It was a pleasure to be in a position to be able to assist, Tanaka-san. The Chinese proved very difficult to deflect from their objectives, but hopefully they will now turn their attentions elsewhere.'

*'Indeed, Commander. We can but hope, and trust that we will be ready if they do try again. I thank you again, and remind you that should you need any level of assistance in any endeavour in the future, you only have to call. Ja ne, Commander.'*

'Ja ne, Tanaka-san.'

On the afternoon of the fourth day after leaving Kieta, the familiar hills behind the Gold Coast reared above the horizon. Most obvious was the long, blue-tinged one which looked like a south-facing, crouching lion, with the point'ed finger-tip of Mt Warning showing behind its shoulder. These two landmarks had been a guide to sailors returning from the north for generations. Soon after, the cluster of glittering towers marking the CBD lifted into view.

It really felt like coming home when we slipped between the welcoming rocky arms of the Seaway and travelled the last couple of miles to our mooring in smooth water. There was a joyful reunion with our very dear friends, Dave and Corrine and the story-telling went on far into the night.

Three days later, the day before our resident professors were due to return to the halls of academia with a treasure trove of data, videos and memories of my magical cat, Jasper, I received a phone call from a local number. With Sandy safely at work, I made a quick trip across to the Southport Mall, where I visited a neat, upmarket shop to collect a small package.

That afternoon, with Dave and Corrine aboard *Firebird* we waited for Sandy to arrive from work. I let her change from uniform to boat clothes, before parking a large serve of her favourite Lillypilly Sav-Blanc wine in her hand. Then, with everyone watching, I passed her the parcel, wrapped in anonymous brown paper.

She was immediately suspicious. 'What's this Harry? I know it's not a present, because you don't do that crap! Is it going to explode and spray me with pink dye? You tried that once before, remember, and all it did was stain your shorts and the deck.'

I just nodded. 'For fuck's sake woman, just open it!'

'Gee. It must be a present after all. You've gone all romantic!'

She must have been at least interested, since she stopped with the questions and ripped the paper off, exposing a flat, rectangular box, the surfaces covered in fine leather, and with a gold latch on one side. A discrete embossed symbol indicated which was the right way up. Lifting the lid showed that it held a necklace with a wide band in rose gold, made up of thousands of tiny links. From its widest part in front, the necklace tapered toward the clasp, while a large, 15-carat pear-shaped diamond, in a deep shade of blue-green, hung from its centre. Either side of the magnificent main stone, four smaller, rectangular-cut 5-carat teal-coloured diamonds were mounted on the band.

In the dying rays of the setting sun, the cut of the stones grabbed every ray of light, magnifying them and bouncing them around the cockpit and across the stunned faces of our friends.

'Oh, Harry!' was all my lovely lady could say.

'Well,' I demanded, less than impressed by her lack of response. 'Do you like it? I left the design up to Mr Jacobs, and of course the stones were cut to whatever Teresa Rubens could make of the rough, but if you don't really like it, we can always try to sell it. It's not as though it cost us anything.'

I was prevented for saying more as Sandy was suddenly plastered against me, and it was some time before I could prise myself free.

'Like it?' she suddenly found her voice. 'I love it, you dopey man! I've never seen anything like it. Not even in the pirate treasure! It's magnificent!'

'Oh. Well, that's good then. Are you going to try it on?'

She did, with trembling fingers, and even with boat gear on, and mussed up hair, she looked like a true princess.

Georgia and Beth, not as used as the rest of the crew to seeing fabulous gems, gold and jewellery, were stunned. 'What stones are those, Harry? They're an unusual colour. It's a very deep shade for Aquamarine.' Georgia asked.

'Not Aquamarine, I'm afraid, they're diamonds.' I looked at Bree, our business manager. 'That reminds me, we'd better insure it. Mr Jacobs reckons that if we were to put it in the next auction, it'd probably pull at least $25 mil. Apart from his design, the stones are flawless, and their deep, even colour is really rare. So maybe don't drop it overboard, or anything like that.'

Both Georgia and Beth recoiled as if it had just turned into a live taipan.

'Ahhh... how much did you say, Harry?'

'About $25 mil or so, Mr Jacobs reckoned. He's very pleased with himself and delighted with the way it's turned out. He's already sent photos to all the gemstone and jewellery publications around the world. Not naming the owner of course, but he feels that it's both the best and probably the last piece he'll ever design and manufacture, and wants to go out on a high note.'

Beth obviously had trouble adjusting to what she was seeing, and like at a tennis match, was glancing from necklace, to me, to Sandy and back to the necklace.

'So this beautiful necklace is worth $25 million dollars?'

'Yep. That's a rough estimate, and is in US dollars, of course.'

'Oh, yes. Of course,' she said faintly.

Two weeks later, I received a brief message from Mathias Tari's office, to say that Captain Guo had been tried before a court in Buka Town, found guilty of murder, along with a slew of lesser charges, and despite the near-continuous howls of protests from the Chinese government, had been executed by firing squad.

Personally, I felt more emotionally drained by this latest operation than even the previous one. Maybe because I was just getting older, but obviously not wiser, or maybe because playing for such high stakes on the international stage was way above my pay-grade.

## THE END
### (Until the next time)

# ALSO BY THE AUTHOR
# BOOK ONE IN THE FIREBIRD SERIES

Harry Stevens, a Middle Eastern war hero, thought that recovering in Eden with his huge and mystical cat, Jasper, after his catamaran is bashed around by a storm, would be a delightful break from his sailing voyage around Australia. However, the finger of fate in the very pleasant form of an abused, runaway wife and her two lively, wilful and beautiful teenage daughters lands Harry in more trouble than he could ever imagine.

Harry's hopes for a quiet time in this beautiful and peaceful town are shattered as he learns that the psychotic, vengeful husband is pulling out all stops in an effort to locate, not just his wife, but even more so the girls for his own, much darker purposes. Suddenly on the run, Harry is forced to fall back on his natural inventiveness and SAS training to combat an increasingly resourceful foe who shows that there is truly no limit to human lust, greed, depravity and treachery.

Barely staying one step ahead of his pursuers, Harry forms some most unlikely alliances to try to defeat his many opponents with their limitless resources.

---

"It is always a pleasure to read a new and entertaining series from a first-time Australian author. This novel will take you on one hell of a ride where the goodies are okay and the baddies are really BAD."
—John Morrow's *Pick of the Week*

"The hero, Harry, when asked what he has been doing lately, answers "Boats, bad guys, bullets and old friends." What he fails to add is — beautiful women, sex, a bad-ass black cat, and Bond type cunning to overcome the bad guys. Piqued your interest? This is a great fast paced read and I am looking forward to the next phase of Harry's life as promised by the author.
—Judith Flitcroft, Author of *Walk Back in Time*.

# ALSO BY THE AUTHOR
# BOOK TWO IN THE FIREBIRD SERIES

Harry Stevens, the Middle-Eastern war hero from Hitch-Hikers, the first book in the *Firebird* series, thought that having dinner at the pub and chatting up the waitress was a safe and pleasant way to pass an evening, but circumstances conspire to dump the delivery of a new super-drug as well as a large bag of bikie gang cash in his lap. Assumptions are made, confusions are leapt to, shots are fired, people are dead and Harry finds himself in the middle of a bikie gang war with both sides looking to take him out. And that's not to dinner!

Being on the hit lists of all the Outlaw Motorcycle Clubs in SE Queensland, Harry is

forced to run for his life, but not before stocking up on lovely girls, rum and a few select close friends. Harry's mystical giant cat, Jasper once again proves that he's more than worth any two humans in a fight.

Harry, the floating trouble magnet, discovers that being shot in Afghanistan was nothing like being the focus of attention of all the OMC's in South East Queensland. His inventiveness gets the workout of a lifetime as he tries to stay one jump ahead of the bad guys as they form strange alliances to find him.

---

"This is Book 2 in the Firebird Series, and *Backpackers* leads us on another adventure with a maritime background. All the drama and action we have come to expect from Ian, we are left with just one question... when can we expect book three?"
—Alison Lewis, author of "Missing"

**Praise for *Hitchhikers* (Book 1 of the Firebird Series)**

"The hero, Harry, when asked what he has been doing lately, answers "Boats, bad guys, bullets and old friends." What he fails to add is — beautiful women, sex, a bad-ass black cat, and Bond type cunning to overcome the bad guys. Piqued your interest? This is a great fast paced read and I am looking forward to the next phase of Harry's life as promised by the author.
—Judith Flitcroft, Author of *Walk Back in Time*.

EARTH CARE
A TALE OF BOATS, GIRLS AND A BIZARRELY PERVERSE GROUP OF INDIVIDUALS
IAN DOLBY

# ALSO BY THE AUTHOR
# BOOK SIX IN THE FIREBIRD SERIES

After a huge and unexpected windfall from a previous operation, Harry Stevens, ex-Australian SAS Major and undercover Commonwealth Police operative, has ordered a new and bigger catamaran to be built in South Africa. When it's ready, together with a diverse and changing crew, he leaves the violence and horror of the Lord Howe Island operation far behind as they first visit peaceful Vanuatu. Then it's off on the long voyage to South Africa to pick-up the new boat. Along the way, the perennial trouble-magnet survives encounters with an old friend, a giant crocodile, as well as sundry storms.

Harry's South African introduction includes a close encounter with thieves, then a deadly boat hi-jacking operation, where violence strikes a bit too close for comfort.

With the new boat finally underfoot, Harry surprises the crew by making a slight detour to the south on the trip back to Oz. On an icy, remote southern island, Harry and crew have the first of several nasty encounters with a flotilla of Japanese whalers plying their foul and illegal trade in Australian waters.

But annoyance turns to puzzlement as the intensity of the encounters escalates to relentless and lethal violence. Why are the whalers so upset with Harry and crew? Could there be a hidden agenda behind their naked aggression? As the body count grows, natural and other forces are brought into play, leading one of the crew to comment, 'Next time you go on holiday, Harry, we'll stay behind.'

## ALSO BY THE AUTHOR
## BOOK SEVEN IN THE FIREBIRD SERIES

A woman's head is found in mangroves on a tidal riverbank, but the rest of the body is found on an ocean beach nearby.

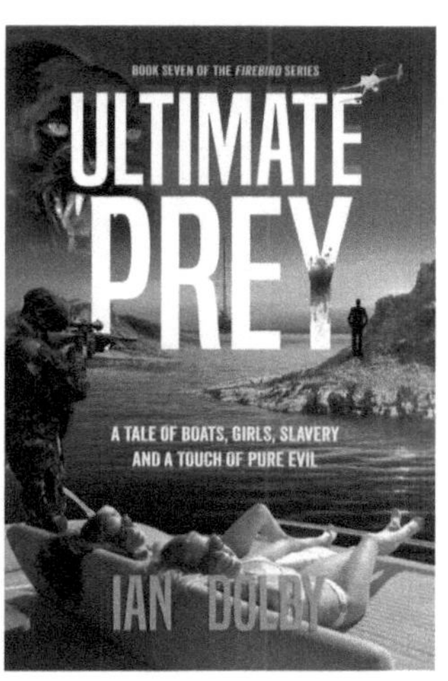


The coroner is baffled by the strange method of separation of the head and some missing bits.

Harry and crew receive an odd phone call, resulting in the retrieval of a beautiful, bikini-clad girl with a sickening, spine-chilling tale to tell.

Jolted into White Knight mode, Harry pursues, then infiltrates a sex-slavery ring, which in turn leads to the horrifying discovery of what the evillest of minds consider to be the 'ultimate prey.'

With a multitude of nubile young ladies providing the usual distractions, Jasper gets plenty of chances to play tough cat, and Corrine gets to do what she does best – blow things up and burn things down!

Harry faces his most evil challenge yet, with way too many young lives at stake.

As Corrine observed, 'If we pull this off, it'll be the best thing we've ever done!'